The PRIDE

The PRIDE

WALLACE FORD

Dafina
Books

KENSINGTON PUBLISHING CORP.
http://www.kensingtonbooks.com

Dedicated to my father,

Wallace Ford,

1922-1995

ACKNOWLEDGMENTS

I wanted to avoid clichés in writing every aspect of this book, including the acknowledgments. But some things simply cannot be avoided. I really do want to thank my friends, family and colleagues for their support and inspiration.

Special thanks goes to four charter members of The Pride for providing you, the reader, with some assurance that the fictional world described in this book bears some resemblance to the real world in which they work and have succeeded—Bernard Beal, Chief Executive Officer of M.R. Beal & Company; Cathy Bell, Managing Director of Loop Capital Markets; J. Donald Rice, Chief Executive Officer of Rice Financial Products Company; and Christopher Williams, President and Chief Executive Officer of Williams Capital Group.

I really must thank and acknowledge my literary agent, Marie Brown, who was the first person to encourage me to write a novel and without whom there would only be some unconnected meanderings unworthy of any reader this side of solitary confinement. My sincere gratitude is also extended to Karen Thomas, my editor at Kensington, who has gently introduced me into the not so gentle world of publishing and has helped this rookie writer stay on his feet. Also, special thanks to Walter Moseley, who will not remember his words of encouragement to an aspiring novelist that were taken to heart and helped to inspire the completion of this book; and to Patricia Means, the publisher of *Turning Point Magazine* who was an early believer.

Finally, I have to acknowledge the past, the present, and the future. My friend Herschel Johnson, who died earlier this year, was the person who first inspired me to write during our early days at Dartmouth. Johnnie L. Cochran Jr., who also died earlier this year, was a friend who taught me that graciousness and excellence when combined create greatness. My wife, Connie, is a source of motivation for this book. And my son, Wallace III, teaches me every day that tomorrows have the promise of great wonder and infinite possibility.

TRUE LOVE

The romance of dreams
Is the ecstasy of anticipation
Never really knowing
Even after waking
Never really knowing
What is a dream?
And what is real
And what happens
When dreams
Really do come true?

—WF

If I were to wish for anything, I should not wish
For wealth and power, but for the passionate
Sense of potential, for which, ever young and
Ardent, sees the possible. What wine is so
Sparkling, so fragrant, so intoxicating, as
Possibility?

—Soren Kierkegaard

CHAPTER I

Sture

My name is not Ishmael

Every story has to start somewhere, and mine starts the first time that I saw New York City. My name is Sture (pronounced "Stude" as in "Studebaker") Jorgenson, and I am from Bergen, Norway, a small town not too far from Oslo. Until I came to New York City, Oslo was the biggest city that I had ever seen.

There is only one serious high-rise in Oslo, and from the observation deck of this hotel/office building you can see the harbor, you can see the Eggar Bryge, which is the Norwegian version of the South Street Seaport. You can see the incredible Viegeland Park statuary garden that, if not one of the seven wonders, is certainly one of the seventy wonders of the world. At night there is a small coverlet of lights that modestly covers Oslo from the hills to the sea. And then there is New York City.

The first time that I saw New York at night, it seemed as if the sky and earth had changed places and that the stars and all of the lights of the heavens were at my feet. The lights, the lights, and the lights— the incredible, passionate embrace of electricity and luminescence— when seen from above resembled nothing so much as an infinite array of constellations designed by the unfettered genius of an unseen hand.

At least that's what I remember thinking as I looked out of the window of an SAS jet coming into Kennedy Airport more than a dozen years ago. The lights were something more than a spectacle, however. To me they were an invitation to imagine the possibilities of my own dreams coming true.

I also found myself trying to imagine all of the millions upon millions of stories that were unfolding that very moment, even as the plane was coming in for a landing. If Oslo's nightlights were a shining coverlet, then New York City's made up a huge, multicolored duvet of gleaming possibilities and endless dreams.

Even though I had lived my entire life in Norway up to that point, I could not help but be aware of the "eight million stories that could be found in the Naked City." I had seen so many American movies I felt as if I had been to New York a hundred times prior to this, my first visit. But no book, no movie, no television show, no magazine, nothing prepared me for the sheer wonder of the reality that is New York City.

After the lights, after the spectacular spectacle that is visual New York City, after all of that, there is the city itself. And there are the people of the city. My first impression was that of being on a carousel while witnessing a bizarre bazaar of the greatest urban gathering in history, a gathering that resembled a psychedelic kaleidoscope.

As a visitor, I could take in the view or I could stay on board the carousel. I chose to get on board, and I had no idea of how much my life would change from that day onward. And I had no idea about how much I didn't know when it came to the people of New York City.

CHAPTER 2

Sture

Living for the City

As I made my way through customs and immigration at Kennedy on my first day in America, I had no idea that a dozen years later I would be the manager and part owner of Dorothy's By the Sea, a most popular restaurant on the western shores of Manhattan. Dorothy's—a restaurant overlooking the Hudson River, named after the great and tragic black movie star, Dorothy Dandridge.

I am fascinated that my partners felt that she symbolized all that should not be forgotten about blacks in America—spectacular possibility bound up in the limited universe of a constricted reality. And on that day at Kennedy Airport, I never dreamed that as the manager of that restaurant I would be a partner of some of the most prominent members of The Pride.

Many people are not familiar with the term "The Pride." I have heard it used in private gatherings and not so public conversations. My partners introduced me to the term and I have been told that it refers to a relatively select group of black professionals in New York City and elsewhere in the United States—African-American men and women who make their living as investment bankers, lawyers, entrepreneurs, and corporate executives. Many of them are graduates of some of the finest universities and colleges in America and all of them are impeccable professionals.

As an immigrant from Norway with limited dreams and even more

limited skills, there is no way that I expected to learn anything about
The Pride—I didn't even know of their existence. And, as I have come
to learn, most white Americans that I have met know nothing about
this fascinating group of men and women. And that is one more
thing I find to be so maddening and interesting and wonderful about
America—anything is possible.

Of course, when I settled in on the convertible sofa in the living
room of my sister Ilse's apartment in Queens later that day, I had no
way of knowing that I had begun an adventure that would teach me
about the restaurant business, the American criminal justice system,
and, of course, The Pride. All I wanted was sleep to wash the jet lag
off me so that I could wake up and begin the greatest adventure any
young man from Bergen, Norway, could possibly hope for.

I spent my first few days craning my neck in wonder, gazing at the
Statue of Liberty and the Empire State Building and the Twin Towers
of the World Trade Center and Rockefeller Center and Radio City
Music Hall. I made an effort to see every tourist site and all the sights
that I could find.

After a few days, however, Ilse made it very clear that, brother or
no brother, if I wanted to be able to keep craning my neck every now
and then, I needed to find a job. That was the only way I could maintain my legal immigrant status and my temporary residence on the
convertible couch in her living room. Having a very modest educational background, and discovering that my knowledge of Norwegian
history had limited value in the job market, I looked for and found a
job that fitted one of the few skills that I had that was in demand in
New York City in the 1980s—washing dishes in restaurants.

I worked in short order diners, hotels, and restaurants featuring
every kind of cuisine imaginable: Turkish, Slovenian, French, Egyptian,
Brazilian, Ethiopian, Italian, South African, Colombian, Ghanaian, and
Guatemalan. After a while, all scraps and leavings truly did look alike.
And then, by chance or fate, I got a job working at the world famous
Water Club.

Located on the banks of the East River and not too far south of the
United Nations, the Water Club is built on floating piers that abut the
East River Drive. It is, in effect, a huge barge tethered to the edge of
Manhattan. The Water Club gently floats on the multidirectional cur-

rents of the East River, offering spectacular views of New York's waterways, bridges, floating traffic and the East Side skyline. All of this is combined with great food, an exquisite wine list, and good service. The combination has made the Water Club one of the most popular and successful restaurants in the United States. Indeed, in operating Dorothy's, I always have looked at the Water Club as the standard that we seek to emulate.

One thing I knew from the time I got off the SAS jet at Kennedy Airport was that even though my sister Ilse loved me dearly, there was no one who was going to support Sture Jorgenson except Sture Jorgenson. So I used the one talent that I had discovered when I had my first job in Norway—I can work very hard.

And I worked very hard at the Water Club. I washed dishes on double shifts, weekends, holidays. I washed dishes when other dishwashers wanted the night off. After a while I became friendly with some of the waiters.

One evening, one of my new waiter friends called me over and, barely containing his excitement, told me of his great good fortune in securing a date with a double-jointed contortionist from Belarus who worked at the Barnum and Bailey Circus. The circus was leaving town in two days and she had the night off. My newfound best friend begged me to substitute for him.

I was only too happy to get out of the kitchen and see the Water Club itself. I couldn't wait to see the rich and famous of New York City and the world dining under the stars that shone through the skylight over the main dining area. It certainly didn't matter to me that the cacophony and madness that is any New York City restaurant on a Friday night made the place seem like Bedlam with good food. On that Friday night, as I served wine to actresses and appetizers to Wall Street wizards and entrées to CEOs and desserts to supermodels, I finally felt that I had arrived in New York City. And now I was sure that I never wanted to leave.

CHAPTER 3

Sture

Now introducing...

I remember the end of that evening. When the last guests had been served and all the tables had been cleaned and set for Saturday's brunch service, I sat in the now dimly lit dining room sipping some Felipe II brandy, and simply inhaled the wonderful, sentient experience of finally being where I wanted to be. The pianist in the bar just off the dining room was playing George Shearing's "Someone to Watch Over Me" in a haunting, yet lilting style, and the million billion lights of Manhattan reflected off the waters of the river. Off in the distance I could even make out the microdots of lights that were jumbo jets circling Kennedy Airport, bringing more dreamers like me to America at that late hour.

It was at this moment that I had my own personal revelation, an epiphany of sorts. The outline of my personal dream came to me. If I could have anything in this wonderful world amidst this explosion of humanity, I would have a restaurant like this. I would serve fine food and great wine and mingle with the best of the best in the world. I would bathe in the reflected starlight of my guests and friends and patrons and be more than happy. I would be fulfilled. At that point all I knew about the restaurant business was how to wash dishes, but one night in an actual restaurant told me that my dream was the right one for me.

And it was at that point the owner of the Water Club, Buzzy

O'Keefe, happened to come by, checking on his restaurant before closing up for the night. I later came to know Buzzy as a very smart businessman, who was able to build a successful restaurant based on his ability to understand people. That particular night he seemed to be able to read my mind, almost seeing my dreams as if they were being broadcast on a wide-screen television. I have never found out if he had the same dreams once upon a time.

Buzzy noticed me in my late night, after work reverie and told me that he had been watching me and that he liked my work. He offered me a full-time waiter's position and I accepted it in a heartbeat, afraid that he might change his mind before my dream started to come true and I wound up waking in the darkness of disappointment. And that turned out to be my true beginning in the restaurant business.

I didn't learn how to be a good waiter. I learned how to be a *great* waiter. I also learned how to be a *great* wine steward and a *great* *maître d'*. Our guests have to decide for themselves whether I have become a *great* restaurateur when they visit Dorothy's, just south of the Chelsea Piers and north of the World Financial Center, on the west side of Manhattan.

During the next decade of working my way up the ladder at the Water Club, I learned about a lot more than the restaurant business. I learned about life in the greatest city in the world.

Working in that restaurant was like having a ringside seat at the wildest, most bizarre and most beautiful circus ever. The Water Club was a veritable epicurean carnival. The supermodels and the tycoons, the actresses and the hustlers, the sycophants and the pseudo-hip, the has-beens and the wannabees, all were part of the cavalcade that I was privileged to observe and serve. There are many jobs that an immigrant from Norway could land in New York City. I have always felt that I got the best. I have no idea what second best would be, but it wouldn't even be close.

Even now, as I stand on the deck of Dorothy's, overlooking the Hudson River's shimmering wavelets, I reflect upon my good fortune. I also reflect upon the fact that the "Law of Unintended Consequences" controls so much of life. That "law" is a term used by my friend, benefactor and business partner, Paul Taylor.

Paul is a lawyer, businessman and a charter member of The Pride.

Indeed, it was Paul who first made me realize that there was something called "The Pride." And it was Paul who first introduced me to the Law of Unintended Consequences.

The law goes something like this—whatever your plan might be, there is always a strong probability that something is going to happen that is totally unplanned. To put it another way, one can be assured that something unplanned will occur as the result of any plan.

To put it yet another way—be prepared for the unexpected. And it was this law that introduced me to Paul in the first place. It was the law that resulted in my being a part owner and host of Dorothy's By the Sea.

Despite its cosmopolitan veneer and its ultraliberal reputation, when it comes to matters of race, New York City can be strangely conservative and segregated. As a schoolchild in Norway I read that there was a time in this country when there were signs on public restrooms, hotels and restaurants, restricting access to whites only. As an immigrant and an outsider I realize that it is easy for me to be critical because the ethnic and racial differences that we in Norway face are much greater.

Nevertheless, upon getting off my SAS flight in New York City in the late 1980s, I was certain that the racial divide about which I had learned was a thing of the past, especially in New York City. I was also certain that since all the civil rights bills had been passed there was true integration, certainly in a major international city like New York. I could not have been more wrong.

When I was working in the kitchens of various restaurants, I had no idea of what was going on outside in the serving area. A dirty plate needs washing. That was all I needed to know. However it was not too hard to notice certain realities when I started working the tables at the Water Club. The first time I could take a moment to look around it was obvious—the complexion and racial makeup of the patrons made me think I had made a wrong turn coming out of the kitchen and that I was back in Oslo. Where were the black people?

I often wondered why a question like this would even come to the mind of one of the finest sons of Bergen, Norway. And I realized that the answer was simple and so very obvious.

When I came to America, I had seen black people on virtually all the sports programs and in many movies and television shows. Black music, black fashion, and black style seemed to me to be very real aspects of American culture. As someone observing America through various media presentations, black people seemed to me to be a major and significant component of American culture, a far greater proportion than the 12 percent of the population that black people represent.

It was with a dawning realization that I finally noticed that very few black people came into the Water Club as guests. Over the years, I learned that it was not just the Water Club—it could be Lutece, the Gotham Grill, "21,"—it was almost as if someone had hung a "Whites Only" sign on the door that only blacks could see and read.

A dozen years later I am still trying to come to grips with this New York City phenomenon. Many books have been written and many books will be written about it. It correctly characterizes New York City as the most diverse and cosmopolitan city in the world. Yet this city is virtually segregated at the highest levels of commerce, culture and social intercourse.

True to the Law of Unintended Consequences, it would stand to reason that, at a place like the Water Club, the de facto segregation was noticeable. And, true to the Law of Unintended Consequences, and in a strange and almost predestined way, it would stand to reason that I would come to know Paul Taylor and learn about The Pride.

It would also stand to reason that meeting Paul and learning about The Pride would open yet another new and exciting chapter in my life.

CHAPTER 4

Paul

Mourning in the morning

I can't remember when I fell in love with the night. I know that I am a true night person. I have to work too long and too hard through too many daylight hours for that to be actually the case. But it must have been more than long ago that the night became a real part of my life.

I cannot tell you when I became enamored of reading and writing and thinking and loving and dreaming in the middle of the night. I just know that it is a part of me, and that nighttime will always be a part of me.

And so it is no surprise to me that I am wide awake, without the benefit of caffeine or anything else, considering the wonder of it all. I am not usually given to boundless introspection, but I have noticed certain changes in my life and myself as of late.

In another room, on an upper floor in the Harlem town house that is my home, is the absolute treasure of my life, my baby son, Paul Jr., now two years old—"the last gasp of the baby boom" some of my friends have called him—and yet, it was just over three years ago that my life began to change, forever. My story begins on a very specific day that I will always remember.

There was a memorial service scheduled for that day. But as I attended my friend Winner Tomlinson's memorial service on a cold

January morning, new beginnings and baby boys were definitely not on my mind. Far from it.

After all, I was a member of The Pride, that select group of black investment bankers, corporate executives, government officials, lawyers, entrepreneurs and assorted professionals who were determined to make it in America. We stalked the majestic canyons of Wall Street and prowled the murderous halls and treacherous boardrooms of corporate America. And we have more than survived, we have prevailed and succeeded, even beyond our wildest dreams.

And, although I have hated funerals and memorial services for my own personal reasons, I planned to attend the Tomlinson memorial service at the Riverside Church that day, because Winner had been my friend and because, as a charter member of The Pride, it was all about business. I simply had to be there.

Actually I am getting a little ahead of myself, and if I am going to tell this story right, I have to go back down the stairs of my Harlem town house and pour myself a proper glass of Graham's Malvedos Vintage Porto (1984). One cannot very well tell a good story without at least a few glasses of good port wine—that's a given.

Also, before starting, I want to look in on my son, just because that's what my father would do, and because it's what all fathers do—look in on their sons and daughters and make sure that everything is all right. Even when they know that everything is all right, it still makes sense to check.

Paul Jr. is resting comfortably and Miles Davis is going through his progressions of "Seven Steps to Heaven" on the CD player in his nursery. Paul Jr. has been listening to good music on a regular basis since the third month after his conception. He has been listening to Beethoven, the Soweto String Quartet, Cesaria Evoria from the Cape Verde Islands, Wayne Shorter, Horace Silver, John Coltrane, Gary Bartz, Dave Brubeck, Thelonius Monk, and Harold Melvin and the Blue Notes. It is no wonder that the boy loves music, as does his daddy (and his mommy, but to a significantly lesser extent).

As I go back to my study to savor the port wine and consider the beginning of my story, I feel very much in the mood for Stan Getz, "Desafinado" conjuring up the right mood. I have always found this

Stan Getz selection to be melodic and mysterious in a sambalike way.

It begins at the memorial service at the Riverside Church for Edwin "Winner" Tomlinson, undoubtedly the most successful black businessman of his time. And now, at the age of fifty-one, in the new-born infancy of his prime, he was dead.

Who was he? He was a black lawyer in New York City just like me. He was a friend, running buddy, drinking companion and sometime professional colleague. But he was so much more.

Sometime in the eighties, in the heyday of the capitalist era, Winner decided that billing life by the quarter hour and hunting and gathering clients was not the life for him. He left the life of ordinary lawyering to saps like me. And he never looked back. Not for a single solitary moment. At least that's how it always seemed to me.

With luck, consummate skill and the nerve of a one-eyed river-boat gambler, he managed to parlay his part-ownership of a barely profitable UHF television station in Charlotte, North Carolina, into a controlling interest in one of the largest home furnishing manufac-turing companies in the world, with facilities throughout the United States, Europe, the Caribbean, Latin America, and Asia. He died with plans waiting for his approval for plants in Nigeria, Indonesia, the Czech Republic, Morocco, Cuba, and South Africa on his desk.

I always believed that Winner's success was all the more remarkable because he accomplished his most important early corporate coups with the support and assistance of the now-defunct investment banking firm of Wilson, Pearson and Borderon. WPB, whose very own Master of the Universe, Jake Dusenberg, had gone down in flames before the onslaught of the myriad of junk bond transaction investigations directed by the then-U.S. Attorney, Rudolph Giuliani.

I remember the time well, and Giuliani was to junk bond traders what Attila the Hun was to the Holy Roman Empire—nothing less than "The Scourge of Christ." He left nothing but the bones and flayed skin of Wall Street bankers, traders and lawyers in his wake—a legacy that preternaturally ambitious Giuliani parlayed into becom-ing mayor of New York City.

Nevertheless, WPB sought to defy the mighty Giuliani—and the entire firm, with its 5,000 employees went down without a trace like a small stone in a big country pond. And at the end of the day, Winner Tomlinson was still standing.

I remain amazed by those particular facts to this very day. Indeed, the story almost defies the laws of nature as they exist in these United States of America.

There were some unattributed cocktail stories, the kind told after three or four free martinis, to the effect that Winner had somehow "cooperated" with the federal prosecutor's office in return for what amounted to immunity from prosecution. These stories were invariably based on no known facts, only the repetition of rumor giving credence to the first rumor in the first place.

Of course there has never been any proof of such an arrangement. And now that Winner is dead you can pretty much bet that any such proof went to the grave with him.

There were also stories about the enduring hatred that Jake Dusenberg harbored for his former favored client. I myself have heard many stories about how Dusenberg, after he paid a record $4 billion fine and served thirty months in a minimum security prison, plotted and planned a spectacular revenge against Winner, even as he, Dusenberg, worked on high profile charitable endeavors in black communities around the country as part of his court-ordered community service.

Once again, Winner came out the winner. He died before Dusenberg could implement whatever plot he might have been hatching. As was the case with a lot of things about Winner Tomlinson, the true story would always be the subject of conjecture, and much of that true story would be buried with him in the soil of his native Alabama, just outside of Birmingham.

It's strange how memory works. I can't remember the names of all the people that were on the conference call that I endured earlier this evening, but I can remember the details of that fateful day as if they were occurring this very moment. Almost like replaying a video.

Of course I did not know that it was a fateful day at the time. Then, it was just another day in the life of The Pride. It was a day full of the very routine and the very special.

I do remember that on that January morning it was cold as hell and that I had made myself get up at my normal time of 5:30 A.M. so that I could complete my morning workout and still get in some work time on my computer and telephone before going to Winner's memorial service. Getting out of bed that morning was a little more of an ordeal than usual due to one Lisette Bailey.

It would be hard for me to forget Lisette Bailey. She was twenty-seven, five feet nine inches tall, lithe and slender with a tawny, café au lait complexion that perfectly complemented her auburn hair. That hair was spread across my pillow as I strove to keep to my conditioning schedule despite the allure of her somnolent beauty.

"Paul, could you *really* have a reason to get out of bed so early?" A mischievous smile danced across her face, chasing the sleepy look away, replacing it with an expression that promised to awaken slumbering embers of passion. Fool that I was, I had thought that she was asleep.

"I am sure that I don't have a good reason darling, its just that . . ." to this day I am not quite sure what I was going to say next, but I am sure that it would not have really made a difference.

"Its just that what? That you have a reason to do something other than this . . . ? Is that what you are really trying to tell me?" and with that she threw back the bedcovers with a flourish, revealing her gorgeous body, entreating arms and long slender legs waiting to grapple with mine once more.

"Because if that's the case, I can just get up right now and start getting ready for work. After all, you aren't the only one with things to do this morning."

The sight of Lisette, naked, warm and luminescent, virtually glowing in the predawn rendered me temporarily speechless. For a few moments I thought that my routine would be broken. After all, I have always thought of myself as a man possessed of discipline and self-control.

I wish that I could tell you of the triumph of my remarkable discipline and that I simply continued with my workout routine for the day. Actually I returned to bed and Lisette and I continued our lovemaking from the night before. And let me say that, as always with Lisette, it was wonderful.

A word about Lisette Bailey: just a few words actually. She is not Paul Jr.'s mother, and she is not my wife. My wife, Paul's mother, is actually my ex-wife Diedre as well, and that is part of the longer story. Like one of those riddles that the Sphinx would tell.

It is enough for me to say that as this story begins, I was a single, divorced attorney, in his early forties, living alone in a luxurious, re-modeled town house in Harlem. My library bar is now a nursery, my gym has been replaced by a guest room, and I now exercise in an un-finished basement with no skylight to brighten my morning labors.

As a single man in New York City, I had an opportunity to enjoy the delights of the town, home to some of the most beautiful and sensual, intelligent and demanding women on the planet. But my story is not about my romantic escapades and sexual adventures. Let it suffice to say that I did not work all the time.

Later that morning, as the January sun actually began to insinuate its dull glow through the skylight of my town house, I began to push myself through the rigors of my typical morning exercises. For me there has never been an alternative in my universe.

I spend so much time sitting behind desks and luncheon tables, lifting nothing heavier than a telephone or a silver soup spoon or a martini glass, that without a regimen of regular exercise I am sure that I would have succumbed to stress or that I would have strangled an adversary, a client, a stranger, or all three by now.

The physical benefits of regular exercise were always known to me, but as I became more involved with my practice as a lawyer and a member of The Pride, I have found that I needed exercise to keep my brain clear and to have a chance at managing the stress attendant on being a lawyer *and* a member of The Pride.

Indeed, it has always amazed me that so many of my colleagues have been able to keep up the pace that they do without exercise. Of course, I was getting ready for a funeral of a colleague that morning, and I am afraid that there have been several more since then. And I know that there will be even more, sooner than later.

Interestingly enough, Winner Tomlinson didn't die from over-indulgence or lack of exercise. A week earlier he had died of liver cancer. No one saw it coming, least of all him. It had been diagnosed in August of the previous year. Quite simply, he was dead within six months and all the sit-ups and push-ups in the world probably wouldn't have helped him a damn bit.

It has been the intimations of mortality that have contributed to my general unease at funerals and memorial services during the past few years. And now that I had to go to yet another one I tried to exorcize my personal demons through exercise on that soon to be fateful morning, and Bob Marley's jammin' on the house sound system punctuated my movements. The sounds of Lisette showering in the master bathroom and the CNN announcer were barely noticeable as I started to enter that "zone."

Entering the zone had become more and more important as the years progressed. And it has been the mental health aspect that keeps me getting up at ungodly hours and doing certifiably insane things like leaving a warm Lisette Bailey in a warm bed.

Another reason I remember that morning is because I have such deep dislike for the ceremonies that celebrate death. So I felt like an extra surge of exercise would help me manage my way through what promised to be a particularly trying personal and professional experience. I remember that on that particular morning, I really pushed myself through a much more strenuous workout than usual.

Instead of one hundred sit-ups I did five hundred. Instead of bench-pressing for ten minutes, I battled those weights for almost a half hour. After thirty minutes on the StairMaster I added another fifteen minutes on the Nordic track.

I have my reasons for disliking death services. Almost two years to the day before Winner's funeral, my father had had "minor surgery" to correct a slight gallbladder malfunction. I will never forget the doctor telling me that with this corrective procedure, my father, then seventy years old, would live to be at least eighty-five.

I guess you could say that the doctor miscalculated somewhat. My father was dead within forty-eight hours of the first incision. I vaguely remember the doctor mentioning something about complications from the anesthesia.

I never bothered to listen to the complete explanation after I was told that my father was dead. I had been a biology major for my first two years of college and probably would have understood a good part of the explanation but I never saw the point in taking the time to clinically understand the cause of my grief.

My father was dead. What was the point of any further explanation? Like I said, I had my reasons for preparing for stress that day.

As I battled with the free weights that day, my brain felt like the "kaleidoscope" mode had been entered. I started working out at an almost frenzied pace as I thought about too much. I thought about all of the wakes, funerals and memorial services that I had attended.

I thought about how I used to believe that the worst thing that could ever happen to me was delivering the eulogy at my father's funeral. And, as the sweat poured off me that morning, I remembered that I had already found out that there could be something far worse.

By now any observer would have seen a six-foot-plus dervish, moving feverishly from floor exercises to machines to weights, like some gym-bound Sisyphus. I barely heard Bob Marley telling me to Lively Up Yourself.

I know I don't remember hearing Lisette leave, although I do remember that she had a seven-thirty conference call with London that she had to attend at the Broad Street offices of Goldman Sachs in the Wall Street district where she worked. Once the business day started, passion and romance and lovemaking had no place in Lisette Bailey's world. Of course, she was not unique in The Pride, or on Wall Street for that matter. As I moved into the final stages of my workout, Lisette was long gone, and that was O.K.

CHAPTER 5

Paul

What a tangled web...

It was O.K. because no number of sit-ups or push-ups or bench presses could make me forget that there was something worse for me than delivering the eulogy for my father. That's because six months after my father died, my younger brother died in a freak hang-gliding accident in the hills east of Monterey, California.

For almost a year, I spent almost all of my nonbillable time on estate matters, insurance matters, closing down residences, selling furniture and poring over endless piles of personal effects. There are certainly worse tortures; I just don't want any part of them.

A psychoanalyst might say that these serial deaths were the reason that I pursued such a self-indulgent lifestyle, but the truth is much simpler—I like to have a good time. And someone like Lisette Bailey could make a man forget almost anything.

It was almost as if she realized that there was a cloud, a burden, and she seemed to dedicate her time with me to make it all go away. At least that's how it seemed to me. She probably was just having a good time too. Her angelic smile and endless, eternally creative devilish desires always made me want to forget.

I could never forget the pain and sadness that I have felt in losing my father and brother that way. And she could never make me forget Samantha Gideon, although I never would have dreamed that Samantha would be gone from my life someday. Even today, married and with a son, a day does not go by that I don't think about her. I have grown accustomed to the reality that her memory will be with me as long as I live.

If Samantha hadn't gone away so suddenly, maybe she would have been the mother of my son. How different would my life be now? I have no regrets at this stage of my life, but still, I can't help but think about these things from time to time.

Finishing my shower, I still had time to get dressed and attend to my home computer and the attendant e-mail messages before leaving for the funeral, which was to be held at the Riverside Church, no more than a ten-minute taxi ride from my house.

Before going to my home office, which was on the second floor of the town house, I went down to the first floor kitchen, with its appointments of a Garland industrial range and a Norge refrigerator/freezer. It had a free-standing island with a marble-faced counter space, rubber tiled floors, and indirect halogen lighting. I had to begin my morning with a blended shake of yogurt, fruit juice, and soy powder to go along with a veritable pharmacopoeia of vitamins and herbal supplements. I took my cup of Kenyan mountain roast coffee back up the stairs and logged on to my computer.

In the relatively few years of its existence in my world, I have found e-mail to be virtually indispensable. There was a time in my life when there was no e-mail, I just can't remember it anymore. Just like I can't remember when there were no faxes or overnight mail. I must admit that I *do* remember Special Delivery letters.

When I sat down to check e-mail that morning, I had no idea that a note from one of my classmates at Harvard Law School would give me a perspective and then an idea that would change my life and the lives of many other members of The Pride.

Joel Rosenblatt was one of those people who saw public service as something more than an avocation. He had been in government since we graduated from law school, and he now worked as a senior staff member of the United States Senate Finance Committee's Subcommittee on Banking.

He worked there because he wanted to and liked it, not because he was looking for a platform for a partnership in some K Street or Wall Street law firm. And, he was a good guy.

Paul:

There is no easy way to put this—so consider this a word to the wise. The shit is really about to hit the fan for some of your investment banking colleagues "of color." The Securities and Exchange Commission and the Justice Department are working with my subcommittee to hold hearings about the rise of black investment banking firms and the correlation of that rise to their political campaign contributions to black politicians around the country.

Can you believe it? There would be no Merrill Lynch or First Boston or Lehman Brothers without all of the contributions, cash and otherwise, that they have made to various government officials over the years. But it looks like your people are going to have to play the game by another set of rules.

The worst part is that these hypocrites have wrapped themselves in so many veils of self-righteousness that going after these black firms is going to seem like a holy crusade, if they ever get any momentum going.

As I write this I realize that I should have some kind of advice or suggestions for you—and I don't. But I thought that you should know this, and I knew that you would know what to do with this information.

Take care.

Joel

As I have said, memory is so strange. It can be so unreliable and useless at times, and then there are other times, like now, late at night in my Harlem brownstone, when it seems like I am the only one in the world who is awake, that I can remember every detail of something that, at the time, I didn't even realize was so important.

For example, I remember that I stared at Joel's e-mail message, understanding it, and, at the same time trying to comprehend its greater meaning for a long, long time. While thinking, I sent an e-mail back to my former classmate and current friend.

Joel:

Thanks for passing on the information. I know that you have a lot more to do than worry about the fate of black investment bankers (and their lawyers) who don't know where their next BMW is coming from, but you should know (if you don't already) that it's a lot more important than that.

We both know that on a per capita basis, there are as many white knuckleheads on Wall Street as there are black knuckleheads. We also know that without some real power and influence and an institutional presence on Wall Street, the black experience in America will continue to be a series of parallel stories of individual achievements and collective frustration. You have to control sources of capital in this country to be able to play the game.

And, speaking of playing the game, it is so ironic that the moment black investment banking firms start to get a little traction that the SEC and Justice and the U.S. Congress (!!!!) start to jump on them for so-called ethical violations. What a crock of shit!

I guess that my clients can be more discreet in their future forays into the adjoining worlds of politics and municipal finance. But I would hope that I could give them more advice than that. If you have any bright ideas, let me know.

Hasta,

Paul

The note from Joel Rosenblatt set in motion a Rube Goldberg-like series of levers and pulleys in my mind that finally dredged up the bright idea that would change the life of so many.

As I logged off the computer, I remember thinking that Joel's note, while newsworthy, was hardly surprising. There were a lot of reasons for members of The Pride to be paranoid, not the least of them was that their very existence offended too many white people in the United States. There were otherwise intelligent, well-meaning and God-fearing white men and women in America who had lived their whole lives with a certain sense of the natural order of things.

In their universe, black men as principals and partners in Wall Street investment banking firms and law firms simply didn't exist. Black men and women who were chief executives and senior officers of major corporations simply could not exist. Black women with law degrees, MBAs and partnerships in major law firms offended the Laws of Nature as much as a flying pig or a talking mule. Some things simply could not exist in their world.

And their response upon encountering this unnatural reality—after the initial shock—has been to deny. And then, if denial did not reassert their conception of reality, then it was time to take more aggressive and even violent actions.

Sometimes those actions might be as simple as not hiring someone for a job for which they might be overqualified. It could be a peremptory "no" at the meeting of a co-op board in a particularly exclusive address on Park Avenue or Central Park West. Country club memberships and law firm partnerships and investment banking firm partnerships do not stay all white in New York City by accident or for the lack of qualified and interested black men and black women. All of these things are simply puny and pitiful attempts by some people to maintain the natural order of things as they had always known them and would like them to be.

If I had let the antipathy and hurt feelings of white people determine my fate, I imagine that I would be lucky to be pumping gas somewhere far from Wall Street. Still, Joel's note was not to be dismissed or ignored.

This guerrilla warfare against key members of The Pride could have disastrous results. Municipal finance-based revenues were an important part of the financial foundation of a number of black investment banking firms and law firms. Whether that business resulted in the sale of mortgage revenue bonds or the investment of pension fund assets, this income represented the base upon which other business could be built.

Or should be built, I thought wryly, because now it really was time for me to start getting dressed for the funeral. Going through the eternal ritual of selecting a dark suit, white shirt and subdued tie, I thought about the fact that too many of my friends and colleagues in investment banking were content to frolic in the high cotton of municipal finance, never heeding the commonsense thought that their success would eventually bring about serious institutional reprisals. But more than a few members of The Pride perceived the obvious—it was time to diversify and to solidify gains that have already been made.

That morning I finished dressing and called a local Dominican car service to send one of its seemingly infinite number of new Lincoln Continentals to come by and get me to the church on time.

I decided that I would make it my business to invite a few insightful friends to a postfuneral lunch. After all, Winner was to be buried near his birthplace in Alabama so there would be no need to endure an interminable ride to some suburban cemetery.

As I settled into the backseat of the car, salsa music gently tapping at the door of my consciousness, I started to think about a guest list. The right mix would be important as a plan started to take form in my mind. As I tried to sort these matters out, the always awesome and bold presence of the Riverside Church insinuated itself into view.

I was glad that I was early. This was going to be a very busy morning and, as the cliché goes, it really was going to be the first day of the rest of my life. Of course, at the time, I just had no idea how right I was going to be.

CHAPTER 6

Sture

Through the looking glass

In retrospect, it would seem that I knew about The Pride before I learned about it. After all, Paul Taylor was not the first or only black patron of the Water Club. However, since there were so few blacks who were customers of the restaurant, I would always notice them. And since far fewer were anything like regular customers, it was hard not to remember the repeat visitors. And in any event it would have been almost impossible to forget Paul Taylor.

Working at the Water Club was an education for me in many ways. I learned, for example, that clowns and idiots come in any and all colors—that there were as many black idiots and clowns as white idiots and clowns. There were the kinds who were too loud, too ostentatious, too ready to treat the waiters and restaurant staff as their own personal servants, or worse.

I always have thought that such people were insecure about something in their lives, but then of course, no one ever asked me. My job has been to see to it that my patrons are well fed and satisfied with sufficient libations. Their manners and deportment have never been my department.

And, since the Water Club (and now Dorothy's By the Sea) has always been an upscale establishment, during the past decade I have spent my working hours with people with decidedly high-income lifestyles—or at least pretending to do so. And, I have found that the size of the income and the amount of disposable cash that a person might have has nothing to do with having class or even knowing how to spell the word "decorum."

Paul Taylor always brought a certain amount of class with him when he came to the Water Club. He took the time to say hello to the coat check girl and was never superior or dismissive of waiters, sommeliers or the busboys.

I don't want to make him sound like Mother Teresa in a pinstripe suit, but he was always a classy and decent person. I remember he would come with his (then) wife Diedre, and they would celebrate anniversaries, birthdays and the like, and he was always solicitous of her without being a phony romantic.

When you work at a fine restaurant, you get to see all the types. And you get to know the pseudo-Romeos who want to be sure that the whole world sees that they are making a big deal over the woman who is their companion for the evening—wife, girlfriend, escort, it doesn't matter—regardless of whether any of the pomp and circumstance is meaningful to her. Paul was never like that.

I guess it was that something about Paul that gave me the nerve to talk to him about a serious problem that I was having at the time. And the way he helped me through it certainly gave me all the reason that I ever needed to talk to him a few years later about my idea which later became Dorothy's By the Sea. But that came later.

CHAPTER 7

Sture

A friend in need

I have found that most Americans think of Scandinavia as a region of four countries made up of the same people. Most Americans think that the difference between Finland and Denmark is like the difference between Los Angeles and Long Beach—not enough to spend time thinking about it. Clearly their ignorance is based on lack of information. The Danes hate the Swedes; the Norwegians hate the Danes, the Swedes hate the Norwegians, and nobody understands the Finns. Or cares.

After all, Finland is a country where the primary form of recreation is dancing the tango (!!), yet it has a suicide rate just below that of the local lemming community. Even within each of the Scandinavian countries there are serious differences, and that is where my story begins.

Norway has been a monarchy for centuries, and even though there is now a democratically elected parliament, there is an anti-monarchist movement that continues to believe that the institution is an anachronism that simply has to go. Before I dropped out of the university in Bergen, I was part of a student anti-monarchist organization and when I came to the United States I continued to stay in touch with my former colleagues.

I should add that, like many student protest organizations, the Norwegian Anti-Monarchist Movement, or NAMM, was not that serious and was certainly no threat to the monarchy of Norway. I re-member that when I was at the university, we used to spend most of our time sitting around drinking beer and smoking Turkish hashish, and telling sordid, bawdy jokes about the king and his family.

We composed an inflammatory pamphlet or two along with a few halfhearted demonstrations that hardly drew flies and certainly drew less attention. But we thought that in some way what we were doing was important, and we managed to maintain persistence about our point of view.

I guess that is why, when I got to New York, I continued to stay in touch with my friends from NAMM who, if the truth be told, were my only friends at school. And that is why I would send a few dollars back to Bergen from time to time to help support the activities of my friends in NAMM. And, when I say a "few dollars," I mean fifty dollars here, a hundred dollars there, since there was never a lot of money in the dishwashing business. It all seemed completely innocent and somewhat noble and righteous.

So you can imagine my surprise when two FBI agents were wait-ing for me at Ilse's apartment when I came home from work at two o'clock in the morning. Waiting for *me!*

It turns out that some of my erstwhile friends with NAMM had turned their infatuation with Turkish hashish into a commercial en-terprise, selling the potent product in more than a few neighbor-hoods in Bergen. And, not being satisfied with being minor league drug dealers, they had also accessed the internet and gotten instruc-tions for constructing a rather primitive pipe bomb which they man-aged to explode under a Carlsberg (the irony of it all, a Danish beer!!) beer truck in the vicinity of the king's palace in Oslo.

The FBI agents questioned me through the rest of the night, first at Ilse's and then at their headquarters in lower Manhattan. I was al-lowed to go with the very dire warning that I was in a lot of trouble and that I should consult a lawyer as it was very likely that I was going to be questioned again in the near future.

I remember as if it were yesterday. I dressed for work at the Water Club that late afternoon feeling absolutely adrift and in a haze. I had been stupid and I had been betrayed by stupid, stupid friends, a re-ally great combination in life. Now every hope and dream of mine was sitting on a tiny bubble of hope that sat in the FBI offices. A place where hopes go to die. I knew that I needed to consult a lawyer and had no idea where to turn.

In retrospect, I imagine I could have asked my employer, Mr. O'Keefe, to recommend someone. And maybe I should have. But something told me that it would have marked me forever in his eyes.

No boss wants to hear that a trusted employee is in trouble with the FBI. Just like no boss likes to lend money to his employees or hear about their marital problems. This problem was my problem and it was just too much of a problem to take to my boss.

As I finished dressing for work that evening and came out of the employees' locker room and into the restaurant area of the Water Club, I spied Paul Taylor at the bar, waiting for his date, as it turned out. As soon as I saw him, it was like an inspiration and a revelation. When people speak about an "epiphany," I now know what they mean, because on that early afternoon, seeing Paul Taylor was my epiphany.

I immediately realized that Paul was not only a lawyer, but he was devoid of obvious pretensions. He was not like a number of people who felt that owning a Platinum American Express Card gave them the right to look down their noses at other people and to act in any way they felt. I don't know how I knew that. I just did.

Maybe it was in the way that he remembered the names of the waiters and the bartenders, or maybe it was in the solicitous and sincere way in which he treated his guests, male or female. All I know is that all of my intuitive, lifesaving radar told me to talk to Paul Taylor. Now!

In the twenty minutes before his date arrived I was able to tell Paul my entire sad and sordid story. To his everlasting credit, he showed little or no reaction, but clearly understood the gravity of my situation.

He gave me his card, told me to call him the following afternoon to arrange an appointment to see him before the end of the week. Needless to say, at 12:01 P.M. the next day, I called his office and was given an appointment at 4:30 that day, which would give me just enough time to get to my job in a timely fashion since Paul's office was at 57th Street and Seventh Avenue, not exactly a stone's throw away from the Water Club. But, of course, I had no choice but to be there.

CHAPTER 8

Sture

Just like magic

To make a very long story very short, by the time I had gotten to his office, Paul had called one of his ubiquitous classmates from college (Dartmouth) or law school (Harvard), who in this instance worked for the FBI. As Paul put it, "Once I explained to him that you were a Norwegian knucklehead who posed no danger to the security or safety of the United States, it was a pretty simple conversation."

There was no plea bargaining, because there were never any charges. It was as if the entire nightmare had never happened and Paul Taylor was Mandrake the Magician. I mean it when I say that, from that moment on, I was eternally grateful to Paul, and he certainly has had my full faith, support, and loyalty ever since.

The best part is that, aside from not charging me a fee for an invaluable service, Paul has literally never mentioned this episode again. Ever. It was like it had never happened. And for that I am thankful as well.

There are too many people who want to lord their good deeds over you until you are sorry that they ever helped you in the first place. That was not the way with Paul Taylor. I simply consider it my good fortune that he has considered me a friend, then, and in all the years since.

And it has been through Paul Taylor that I learned about The Pride. After my NAMM episode, I could not help but be more attentive to him when he came to the Water Club. Of course he never had to wait for a table again. There were the other courtesies, the best tables with the best views, the complimentary cocktails and bottles of wine and champagne. As far as I was concerned, that was the best that I could do to make sure that Paul knew that I had a good memory.

A few years later it was Paul who suggested that we meet privately. By then I couldn't help but notice that he had a regular crowd of extremely impressive friends, most of whom were black, and all of whom seemed to have something to do with Wall Street, corporate America or the practice of law.

When I came by his office that spring afternoon, I simply couldn't imagine what the purpose of the meeting could be. I only knew that a summons from Paul Taylor, my American savior, was reason enough for me. I will confess, however, that there was this nagging, gnawing feeling that perhaps my idiot friends in Bergen had been acting up again. I whispered a long forgotten, brief prayer to St. Ursula, the patron saint of Norway, in the elevator on my way up to his office.

You could have knocked me over with a feather when Paul told me that he and several of his friends were interested in starting a first class restaurant and wanted to know if I was interested in managing it!

He told me the names of his colleagues, one of which was his ex-wife. He mentioned some numbers regarding the financing of the restaurant. And it was clear that these were big league players. And, as much as I loved Buzzy O'Keefe, I said yes on the spot.

Neither Paul nor I used the term The Pride that day, or at any point since. Indeed, I can't remember where I first heard it with reference to the coterie of accomplished black men and women in business in New York City. All I know is that as soon as I heard it, it seemed to fit. Lions and lionesses, aspiring to majesty and dominion in the hostile jungle called corporate America and Wall Street.

And, as soon as I heard the term, "The Pride," I knew instinctively that Paul Taylor and his partners in Dorothy's By the Sea were all charter members and that I was privileged to have a front row seat to be able to watch all of the inner workings and comings and goings of a truly unique group of Americans. When I was a young man in Bergen and Oslo, there was no one and no thing in Norway that could have prepared me for what I have learned because of my relationship with The Pride.

CHAPTER 9

Paul

Get me to the church on time

At some point, long ago in my professional development, I decided to be early for every appointment and function that I planned to attend — at least ten to fifteen minutes early. Aside from the fact that it means that I am *almost never* late for anything, it has provided an interesting advantage, one that I never expected at the outset.

Many of my friends and colleagues have told me that this particular habit is an overreaction to the legend/myth/supposition that black people are always late. Every black person knows the term "CP Time" and most have come to despise it.

As I have told my friends, my habit arose from my reading a biography of Lyndon Johnson by the Pulitzer Prize-winning biographer Robert Caro. In it, he refers to the fact that Johnson always arrived early to meetings in order to achieve a strategic advantage over whomever it was that he was meeting. This bit of logic struck me the right way and I thought that I would try it. And, believe me, it has worked.

Also, as I have told my friends, the truth is that almost every culture believes that lateness is a group characteristic. When I was in Tel Aviv I was introduced to the concept of "JP Time" (Jewish People's Time). And when I was in Tokyo, references to "JP Time" (Japanese People's Time) by my Japanese law firm hosts truly flew in the face of the myths and legends regarding Japanese efficiency and reliability. I know that many of my Italian friends use the term "IPT" (Italian People's Time") and are amused to find out that black people have a similar phrase. Clearly we all need a little help trying to be on time.

Being able to get to functions like Winner's funeral before the rest of the sheep gives me an opportunity to observe—who's in attendance, who is with whom, who is trying to align with whom—that kind of thing. I know that this has a certain *voyeuresque* aspect to it, but we all observe each other in one way or another, and being early simply provides me with my own peculiar perch. Kind of like sitting in the catbird seat, as the old Yankee broadcaster Red Barber was known to say on occasion.

As the car pulled up to the Riverside Church, I could not help but notice, standing like some mute, granite sentinel, Grant's Tomb. This final resting place of the alcoholic warrior, the frightfully, almost poetically corrupt president and his absolutely anonymous wife is a huge, silent, stone edifice built by humanity to the belief that there may be something more to life than life itself. At least that's my guess.

There has always been a lot of that going around, of course. We call them pyramids, burial grounds, burial mounds, skyscrapers, multi-use sports arenas. We all want to be remembered.

I know that I want my son to not only know me, but to remember me. Not just as a good father but as someone who is there for him on an absolute and unconditional basis. In this life and in all the lives to come.

And then I was in front of the Riverside Church, its massive doors facing the nearly frozen Hudson River. The service was scheduled to begin at ten, and it was just turning on nine. A few dozen people huddled in front of the church, speaking in low, almost frozen tones. While I saw the faces of a number of people that I knew, I didn't feel compelled to meet and greet just yet. I had come extra early for a reason—and funerals have really come to bother me anyway.

That morning I figured that a walk across the small park across the street from the church would give me the assurance that I could maintain my composure. It would also give me time to think about Joel's e-mail note and to rethink a strategy that was already starting to take form in my mind. And it would also give me time to think about Samantha.

CHAPTER 10

Paul

Taking that stroll down memory lane

Samantha Gideon was the lady of my life at that time. I would guess that if I were to have described our relationship then, I would not have objected to the use of the word "serious." In retrospect, if she hadn't died, there is every reason for me to believe that she would have been the mother of the little boy that is sleeping upstairs from my home office right now. Of course life is full of those elusive "might have beens" and "could have beens," when, of course, all that really matters is what is.

On that January morning, there was no way that I could see that far into the future. I just knew that I missed her. She was a singer, and quite a good one. She was just not fortunate enough to have experienced the life-changing serendipity that would get her the stratospheric recording contract that would have let her talent carry her to deserved stardom.

She did have a contract with one of the major cruise lines. So I am reasonably certain that she had been singing "Guantanamera" and "Impossible Dream" and "The Greatest Love" for the umpteenth time the night before.

She was way beyond adamant that I not use any of my contacts, friends and relationships in the music business to try to help her. I had once tried to surreptitiously arrange for her to have an audition and she found out. Even though the audition represented the chance of a lifetime for her, it was almost the end of our relationship—right there on the spot. She wanted to do it her way. Which meant no help from me.

On one level I understood her desire and need for independence. On the other hand, this was something about Samantha that I never really understood. After all, from my perspective I had (and have) helped people who have meant so much less to me. I have helped them because I could.

What's more, I know that Samantha could not have possibly believed the myth that *anybody* actually made it "on their own." I always thought that if I was simply an acquaintance, someone else in her life, Samantha would have permitted me to help her, and her life would have been so much different. Although I guess she would still be dead right now.

Instead, to the day she died, she stubbornly clung to the notion that she had to succeed without my help, assistance or participation. The only thing she would accept from me was my support. And that she had. The fact that she never let me be a contributing factor to her success is one of the few regrets that I carry in this life.

And so, I was walking away from the church, headed west toward the river, alone with my thoughts—thoughts about Samantha—thoughts about Winner. Thoughts about warm sheets that had cooled too soon that morning, thoughts about . . .

"Paul! I knew I would see you here."

CHAPTER II

Paul

Showtime on Riverside

As soon as I heard that shrill voice braying and careening over my shoulder, I knew who it was. Bonita Woolsey, Esq., the Corporation Counsel of the City of New York. In her role as the *de facto* Attorney General of the City of New York, she had a lot to say about which lawyers would write the legal opinions verifying the validity and probity of the billions of dollars of bonds that the City of New York sold every year. These were legal opinions that generated huge fees for the firms fortunate to be selected by the esteemed Ms. Woolsey.

And so, she was definitely someone with whom I had to speak. And, in the bizarre nature of my personal universe, she was also someone that I definitely could not stand. It was nothing specific. It was just something incredibly visceral and undeniable.

"Ms. Woolsey. It's always a pleasure. It's been much too long since we have had lunch or breakfast or drinks. How is life in City Hall treating you these days?"

"Mayor Dinkins has me on twenty-four-hour standby, or that's what it seems like. I thought that being a partner at Shearman and Sterling was hard work, but this job is eternal." Bonita smiled through teeth that would make an orthodontist retire to a monastery on a desert island, taking a vow of eternal silence upon entry.

I had to marvel at how, in one sentence, she managed to make sure that I remembered that she had been the first black partner at one of the top law firms in America, that she held a very, very important job in the biggest city in America, and that she was a confidante of the first black mayor of New York City.

Bonita Woolsey was one of those people that you could stand being around for about . . . ten nanoseconds. After that she seemed to be the manifestation of all annoyances. There was her braying laugh, her phony veneer barely covering the nudity of her hypocrisy and her unbridled ambition. And probably worst of all was her clear disdain for everyone and everything she surveyed. She was possessed of the unshakable belief that Bonita Woolsey was the undeniable center of the only universe that counted—hers.

What I remember most about her that morning was her . . . teeth. After all, I *had* to be cordial, my business, and that of some of my best clients, was connected to the peremptory whims of the esteemed Ms. Woolsey. I have always felt that I could stand the company of anyone if business was involved.

So I was prepared to converse with Bonita and to make sure that at the end of our conversation I had done everything to make sure that my business interests were unimpeded and unscathed. But her teeth! My God!

All of her front teeth seemed to wander in boldly independent directions, making her smile seem something straight out of a Salvador Dali painting, perhaps during his mescaline period. But on this particular morning there was—could it be?—something was clearly stuck between her two front teeth.

Was it this morning's whole wheat toast or, heaven forbid, last night's collard greens? There was no way of knowing, and that was information that I simply never wanted to know. There is such a thing as too much information. This was a living, breathing, braying illustration.

But her particle-ridden smile was hypnotic, and as we chatted, I felt myself trying to resist staring. It was like trying not to look at a hairy mole that resembled Mount Everest or a scar in the shape of a palm tree or a tattoo of the image of the Virgin Mary on someone's neck.

"If it was going to be an easy job, Bonita, Mayor Dinkins never would have needed to choose you." I felt my eyes wander tooth-ward.

I simply had to find a distraction. Anything would suffice. I could feel myself approaching the precipice of disaster, which beckoned, begging me to make the jump into the abyss of mockery and perdition. It was simply too early in the day for this kind of bullshit.

"Flattery will get you everywhere, Mr. Taylor. But to tell the truth, the private sector never seemed more appealing. When Mayor Dinkins gets reelected this year, I have promised him one more year and then I'm back at S & S, unless a better offer comes along."

"That's understandable, Bonita. You have certainly served your time." I remember thinking, why is she telling me this? And then I found out.

"I know that our conversations are always off the record, but this is really and truly off the record, okay?"

"Bonita, my lips will be sealed for eternity." A few more cars were pulling up to let off passengers in front of the church. The press was starting to stake out their positions for their television cameras and still photographers.

The sun was bright and it was still frightfully cold. I continued my silent, subliminal prayer for someone, anyone, to rescue me from the impending risk of embarrassment and professional doom. No one came.

"Frankly Paul, I am seriously thinking of going back to the practice of law. Of course my former partners at S & S will have been back in a heartbeat. But I think that I am ready for new challenges."

"You have already overcome so many challenges, Bonita (I suddenly, and with horror, realized that a subtle insult might be perceived and prayed that it would fly below her radar. It did.), what mountains are left for you to conquer?"

I must confess that at this particular moment I had not a clue that this conversation was about to take a more than serious turn. After all, I was just making conversation and trying to stay occupied until the doors of the church opened. I was also trying not to stare at Bonita's many and multi-angled teeth.

"Let me get right to the point, Paul. We can talk about this later.

But I want you to think about us being partners. With your experience and my contacts we would be quite a team. I think 'formidable' would be a good word, don't you? I can make money at S & S, but I don't kid myself, I can be there for one hundred years and I will be a partner in name only. To tell you the truth, I don't know if that is what I want anymore. What I *do* want is a chance to find out how good I can really be. I know that this is something out of left field for you, and that we have to make time to talk about this. But think about it for now, will you?

"Here comes Mayor Dinkins now, I have to go. Speak to you soon. *Ciao!*"

Bonita turned on her stiletto heels and I was truly one stunned buffalo soldier left in her wake. I was reminded of the expression from some old Stepin Fetchit-type film character, "Well slap my face and call me stupid!" And frankly, I could have not been more shocked if Bonita had done just that.

There was no way that I could even begin to fashion a response to her non-proposal. Although, I must confess that even that at that moment, despite my having something less than warm and fuzzy feelings for Bonita, the practical aspects of our alignment, as she so succinctly pointed out, had some real advantages. Of course, Winner Tomlinson's memorial service was neither the time nor place for such discussions. But given the flow of events in the near future, it was a discussion that I did not forget. But at that moment, it was time to go into the church.

CHAPTER 12

Paul

Now about that church . . .

The Riverside Church is a colossal monument to God built by the colossal fortune of John D. Rockefeller Jr. He was the eldest male heir of the greatest businessman and possibly the most rapacious entrepreneur in American history. We will never really know if he built Riverside Church to atone for his father's many sins. It may be that he felt that it was more important to fulfill an edifice complex, a construction/building disorder that was clearly transmitted genetically in its full glory to his son, Nelson Rockefeller, the governor of New York State a few decades later. Or maybe John D. Jr. just liked Gothic cathedrals. Or maybe he just felt like it.

It stands like some granite sentinel across Riverside Drive from Grant's Tomb. As I entered the church that morning, I couldn't help but think about medieval times in Europe when huge cathedrals were built as part of a socio-political effort on the part of the powerful to keep the powerless occupied.

After all, idle hands are the workshop of the devil and political dissidents. Revolutionaries and dissidents of varying pedigrees and radically differing degrees of success have been known to also show up when there is some of that nasty idleness lying around.

The royalty of a particular era would get together with the reigning religious leaders to declare the need for the construction of a monument to God and His everlasting glory. The church would openly and actively support such an initiative from the pulpit. In turn it would support the taxation and control over society by the State that royalty would have to impose in order to finance and complete such a project.

Since a project like the construction of a gothic church literally took centuries, this meant that generations of the poor and powerless would be employed as poorly paid, but busy, masons, carpenters, stonecutters, glaziers and bricklayers.

While the Riverside Church did not take generations to complete, there is no doubt in my mind that John D. Rockefeller Jr. and his inherited fortune represented a part of America that could be called royalty. After all, he was the son of the same John D. Rockefeller who engaged in price-gouging and shockingly monopolistic strategies that strangled any hint of competition. And he was the son of the same John D. Rockefeller who employed the rather interesting labor relations tactic of having his employees shoot and kill striking workers (along with their wives and children) at one of his silver mines.

John D. Rockefeller probably never felt the need to receive approbation from anyone. On the other hand, John D. Rockefeller Jr. had the luxury of reflection and contemplation. He did not need to build a fortune. His task was to institutionalize it, nurture it, and humanize it. And maybe, at the end of it all, maybe that's what building the Riverside Church was really all about. Only John D. Jr. himself knows, and he is certainly not telling anyone anything anymore.

CHAPTER 13

Paul

And so it begins

As I sit listening to Miles Davis riff his way through "Silent Way" with a young Chick Corea, I still can remember so many details of Winner's memorial service. I certainly remember how cold that day was. I don't think I will forget my sunrise dalliance with Lisette anytime soon. And it would be hard to ever forget that surreal and bizarre encounter with Bonita Woolsey.

As the doors of the church opened, the chilled early morning mourners eased their way past the massive wooden doors, searching for their assigned seats so that they could assess the status which had been accorded to them and to others. These things were important to some people.

I was simply looking for my seat, which I knew would be in a "special" row, given my relationship with Winner. As I turned to go down the center aisle, however, I happened to run into Ed Koch, the former mayor of the City of New York.

Ed Koch had been defeated by David Dinkins in his bid for a fourth term as mayor. He had been mayor for so long that some younger New Yorkers thought Koch's first name was "Mayor." When he was first elected mayor by a coalition of blacks and Puerto Ricans and liberals who found him to be far more progressive than the more "questionable" Mario Cuomo (who later became governor of New York), it was fully and absolutely expected that Ed Koch, the never-married Greenwich Village citizen and native New Yorker, would move forward in the liberal tradition of Robert Wagner, John Lindsay, and Robert Kennedy.

Ed Koch fooled everyone. He turned out to be the Democratic Mayor of New York who had no problems endorsing Ronald Reagan. He turned out to be the Mayor of New York City who actually bragged about closing the hospitals in the historically black communities of Harlem and Bedford Stuyvesant.

Ed Koch turned out to be the Mayor of New York City who *wanted* to be portrayed as the one white politician in New York City who would "stand up" to the swarming black and brown mobs who always wanted something, who always wanted more, more and more, who always wanted something for nothing. He was the one Mayor of New York City who would call a spade a spade (so to speak), and not bother to apologize. He was Rudolph Giuliani before there was Giuliani.

Koch was elected at the end of the Sordid Seventies in New York City. It was a time that had witnessed the President of the United States telling the town and its indomitable people to "drop dead" during its legendary financial crisis. It was a time when the moniker "Sin City" had replaced John Lindsay's "Fun City." Being the astute and seasoned politician that he was, Koch decided that he would found his administration on the twin pillars of High Ideals and Good Government. By getting the reformers and good government types on his side, he would be free to show his real colors when the time suited his purposes.

Prior to his actual inauguration as mayor, he decided to demonstrate his belief in Good Government by selecting only "The Best" as the commissioners who would preside over the Byzantine complex known as New York City government. He established an almost infinite number of screening panels, one for each of the over thirty departments.

These panels were composed of experts who, in many instances, were in serious need of a life. After all, the Parks Department panel was composed of people who spent their every waking moment worrying about New York City parks (to each his own). Each panel was supposed to interview every possible nominee to be commissioner of their area of expertise. It was not a pretty sight and only the brave need apply.

The final part of Koch's Good Government plan was that he would interview the top three survivors of this veritable Iroquois Gauntlet. As fate would have it, he found himself interviewing me, one Paul Taylor, a young, black, Ivy League-type, who was a candidate to be Commissioner of the New York City Department of Human Rights. In 1977, that position really meant something. Legends and leading lights like Eleanor Holmes Norton had held the job in the past. I had no way of knowing that Ed Koch had other plans for that job in the future—namely, evisceration.

I remember that we met in the basement of a nondescript office building on Park Avenue. I also remember that I was focused and locked in and ready for this job interview. At the time I really *wanted* to be the next Commissioner of Human Rights of the City of New York. I had come to feel that it was my destiny. I had already convinced myself that I was by far the best person for the position.

I had read everything about the job. I had done my research. I had already drafted a series of bold and brilliant new initiatives and proposals that I was going to put into effect in my first ninety days in office.

I knew *everything* about the job. I was ready for anything that the new mayor could ask me. I wasn't arrogant or cocky. I was just supremely confident. I was ready.

And then, after shaking hands and going through some perfunctory résumé questions, he asked his first substantive question, a question which I presumed was meant to begin his serious inquiry into my qualifications for the position of Commissioner of Human Rights for the City of New York.

"Do you have any white friends?"

There was a moment of shock, disbelief, and realization before I could say anything. I felt as if I had either lost my hearing or my mind. I tried desperately to recover my equilibrium.

"Excuse me?"

"Do you have any white friends?"

I have had many interviews and conducted many interviews before and since that fateful meeting. One thing I have learned is that there are times when you know that you have the job or client, no matter what, and there are times when you know that even if you could stand on your head and spit gold doubloons, you are not going to get the job.

Initially I was shocked that Ed Koch, someone that I knew, albeit tangentially, could ask such a stupid, asinine, bullshit, racist and idiotic question. I could not believe my ears! And then I composed myself and got a grip. I recognized the situation for what it was.

Ed Koch had no intention of appointing me to this job. His mind had been made up long before he came into the room. And then the perverse streak that I harbor and nurture, a side of me that is rarely exposed to the light of day slipped its leash and made its appearance on center stage.

"Actually Mr. Mayor, there are very few people who I call friends, and none of them are white But, I do know a few white people if that would help. I think I can actually remember their names if you give me a minute to think."

No response to the response. And I must confess to some disappointment as I was hoping to engage in a little rhetorical fandango with this knucklehead who presumed to dupe so many millions. Ed Koch had an agenda that would not be denied, and his mind-set was certainly not going to be disturbed, much less derailed, by a wisecracking nonentity who wasn't even going to be in his administration.

"What do you think is the reason for the high level of anti-Semitism in the black community?"

A Greek chorus in the back of my mind started chanting, "Oh shit!" over and over. The issue was no longer whether or not I would get the job. The question was would I have to fight my way out of the small cubicle in which this interview was being conducted? Koch was not a small guy. And I knew that his biography was lavish in its reference to his being a real deal combat veteran. But the perverse side of me was not going to back down. No way. The fun had just begun.

"Well, Mr. Mayor, it's not that we black people hate Jews. We just hate all white people and in many instances, particularly in the ghettos where we live, Jews are usually the only white people that we see. Actually, the black Jews in Harlem don't have a problem at all."

There were some perfunctory parting words and that was pretty much the end of the interview. Not only did I not get the job, I didn't even get a "regrets" letter thanking me for my interest. After that dance with the devil, nothing that Ed Koch did as mayor ever surprised me.

As I was escorted to my seat by a white-gloved usher (about five rows from the front, immediately behind the Tomlinson family members) there was not too much time to dwell on my Ed Koch saga. As visions of the former mayor evanesced into forgetfulness, I do remember thinking that Winner would have loved the white glove touch, although in his earlier years he had been nothing like a white glove type of guy.

It was getting close to showtime. It was time to absorb and observe. The memorial service for Winner Tomlinson was another occasion and another reason for The Pride to gather.

CHAPTER 14

Paul

Introducing Diedre and The Pride

The Pride is the term that I have used to refer to the black men and women, like lions and lionesses, who have risen to prominence on Wall Street, in corporate America, and in the canyons of its law firms, accounting firms and management consulting agglomerations. Being in New York, I am, of course, speaking of the New York version of The Pride. But The Pride is in Atlanta, Detroit, Chicago, Houston, Dallas, Philadelphia, Washington, Miami, New Orleans, Oakland, San Francisco, Denver, St. Louis, and Los Angeles. Actually, The Pride is to be found all over America.

As a charter member of The Pride, I know that we are the beneficiaries of the seismic changes that hit America in the sixties and seventies. It was a change that allowed some black men and women to actually achieve on the basis of their ability and some limited opportunity.

The Pride consists of some of the most interesting, talented, intelligent, bizarre, insufferable, heroic, treacherous and memorable people that I can ever hope to know. I don't kid myself, whatever I see in The Pride, the good and the bad, is in me too.

Many of them I genuinely like and some I love like brothers and sisters. Others are just too grasping, self-centered and opportunistic to suit my tastes. However, these are character traits that have virtually ensured success in the United States of America.

As I sit here now, pleasantly ensconced in my Sugar Hill town house, I know that I cannot afford to be too self-righteous or judgmental. After all, on that cold winter day, I sat in the sixth pew wearing a custom-tailored Giorgio Armani suit with a shirt sewn to my specifications by a Romanian shirt maker on West 43rd Street named Georges Tourvarian. My solid gold cuff links were from Zimbabwe and the tie that I happened to wear that day I had picked up at a little shop just off Bloomsbury Square in London. I know that The Pride is a part of me and I am a part of The Pride.

But as I sat there that morning, I couldn't help but feel that I was a participant in some kind of surreal game. I have always known a game when I saw it, and this was one of those times.

After all, most of the members of The Pride who were in attendance were certainly not there out of love or respect for Winner Tomlinson. They were there out of curiosity or speculation. They were there because there was business to be done, contacts to be made, acquaintances to be refreshed and refurbished.

I am not being judgmental. It's part of the American way of doing business, and there is no reason to begin to suggest that the charter members of The Pride would conduct their business any differently.

Consider this analogy: Dr. James Naismith put up a peach basket on a wall and "invented" the game of basketball. It was meant to be an exercise regimen for football players in the off-season. But after Oscar Robertson, Jerry West, Michael Jordan, and Fly Williamson got involved, the game became The Game.

Business and finance and politics have danced a dance for many years in this country. But the dance never saw the likes of Bonita Woolsey, Gordon Perkins, Edwin Tomlinson or . . . Diedre Douglas.

"Hello, Paul. No surprise seeing you here. You do seem unusually *thoughtful* this morning. I hope you don't mind if I join you?"

The always intoxicating fragrance of Ivoire de Balmain announced the arrival of my ex-wife as she slipped into the pew and somehow materialized next to me. I have always tried to pay attention at such events and to this day it still amazes me that she was able to appear at my side and surprise the hell out of me. I don't think of myself as some kind of all-knowing, ever-vigilant Yoda prototype.

Nevertheless, I would like to think that I would have some vestigial awareness of the fact that my ex-wife was in the house.

But then Diedre Douglas has always been something of a surprise. She has always been a luminous presence and a wondrous woman.

"Good morning, Diedre. Now I *know* this is an important event, if the divine Miss Douglas is making an appearance!" I spoke *sotto voce*.

"Don't yank my chain, Paul. It's too cold and too early for your usual nonsense. At least try for an original line or two."

It has always amazed me how Diedre could use words to cut to the bone. More amazingly, I have never seen or felt the blade, until it was too late. Every time, it has been too late. This was yet another one of those times.

"With all due respect to Winner, it looks like the usual suspects are filing in. No surprise there."

"No, Diedre, I guess there is no surprise. The surprise would be if the usual suspects didn't show for something like Winner's memorial service."

I couldn't help but notice the understated but entirely elegant black dress with purple trim that she was wearing. I am no expert on women's clothing, but I would have bet that it came from the St. John's collection. Of course, that would only be a guess on my part.

Even though the mink that she wore was understated, I am certain that it cost a year's salary for some midlevel corporate executive. Even now, when I think of her wearing that mink I have to smile at the thought of the next part of our conversation.

"Lovely fur you're wearing, by the way."

"How kind of you to notice, Mr. Taylor. What happened, did you take your "happy" pills this morning? Or is there a teenage cheerleader convention going on in town that has you in such a pleasant mood?"

"Ouch! You should be careful with that tongue of yours. You're using live ammo today."

"I'll thank you to leave my tongue out of this conversation."

Diedre has always had a way of delivering lines in an absolutely stern fashion with only the hint of a flash of humor that dances through those large and lovely eyes of hers for the briefest of moments. I thought that I saw that flash that morning. Was that *double entendre* or was it just my imagination, running away with me? There was no way that I could be sure. So I continued.

"Duly noted, Ms. Douglas. But have you noticed how many of your sisters are wearing lovely furs this morning? I mean, the fur is *flying* this morning!"

"No Paul, I did not notice. But now that you mention it there is some excellent taste in furs being shown here this morning. What's your point?"

We were able to carry on this conversation more or less freely, as the doors of the Riverside Church were now wide open and the invited guests were streaming in. Even as people tried to maintain proper decorum and solemnity there was a great deal of energy in the air. Our conversation was not particularly noticeable.

"Well Diedre, even my untrained and unsophisticated eye can see minks of every description—blackglama, what have you. I have seen beaver, sable, fox, raccoon, and ocelot. But doesn't it make you wonder why, at a high profile event like this, we haven't seen one animal rights activist. Doesn't that surprise you in the least?"

This was not the first time that I had raised this issue with a woman of color, so Diedre's response didn't surprise me in the least. However, even though I had known the woman for twenty years at the time, the crystalline gravity and sheer intensity of her response took me by surprise. As she arched her eyebrows I knew that I had trod on very thin ice indeed.

"Paul, my dear, you don't see any animal rights activists here because they *know* that they would have the living Jesus beaten out of them if they even *thought* about spilling paint on one of these sisters.

"I've got to tell you, as a black woman, I have to put up with indignities every day that you men can't even dream about. I have to take shit from white men, white women, *and* my beloved black brothers. I will be goddamned to hell if I would let some chucklehead who cares more about a glorified rat than black children in Harlem or Tunica put a drop of paint on *anything* that I own and have earned. Anything!"

There was silence between us as I absorbed what Diedre had told me and reflected upon it. In all the years of protests concerning the wearing of leopard, raccoon and mink furs, I realized that I have never ever seen even a tiny story or article about paint being thrown upon a black woman wearing a fur coat.

A few people spoke disapprovingly about Aretha Franklin after she wiped out an entire species of fox to get the fur for the outfit that she wore to Bill Clinton's first inauguration. But I don't recall any cans of Sherwin-Williams being opened in protest of her outfit. Talk is cheap and hospital bills are not.

In fact, ever since that conversation with Diedre, I have paid more attention to this subject. I am still waiting for the brave and noble animal rights crusader who loves those cute little minks so much he or she is willing to risk their lives by throwing a can of Malaccan Cinnamon Crimson Red Dutch Boy paint on a female member of The Pride in a mink coat.

The sense I get is that activist would be dead before the last droplets of red paint hit the ground as cunningly concealed scimitars, Uzis, stilettos and tridents were drawn from scabbards, holsters and other unknown and unspeakable hiding places. I have to confess that it would certainly be worth the price of admission at any price.

Diedre's comments rang sure and true. And on a very real level I could understand what she meant. Even after all the master's degrees and Perry Ellis outfits and American Express Platinum credit cards, as a black woman she had to stand guard over her dignity, her self-esteem, her *personhood*. There was no telling from which direction the next dignity-denying assault might come.

This was deeper water than I had anticipated in initiating this conversation. Maybe, just maybe, I thought, Diedre and I might have an opportunity to talk like human beings again. At the time I had no idea of what fate had in store for the both of us. For the moment, we both realized that it was best to just let the intensity of the moment pass so that we could resume our role as *voyeurs*.

CHAPTER 15

Paul

Watching the crowd

When Diedre and I were married, we would amuse ourselves by making the most outrageous comments about the passing carnival of life. Old habits die hard and on that cold January morning it was a mildly amusing way to pass the time. It wasn't long before Diedre started in and I followed her lead.

"You can't tell me that's her hair." Diedre was referring to one of our acquaintances who had very, very expensive extensions that flowed over her very famous shoulders as she virtually sashayed down the center aisle of the church.

"Of course that's her hair. I am sure that she paid for every single strand. Are you suggesting that she might be in arrears?"

"Let's not talk about rears." I followed Diedre's gaze and we had to keep ourselves from giggling like schoolchildren.

That's because one of our esteemed local elected officials, also a charter member of The Pride, and also renowned for having a huge butt, was waddling down the aisle, almost having to squeeze himself into what was not a narrow pew.

"I swear," Diedre whispered, "the back of his jacket looks like he has two pigs wrestling under there."

"I don't know about that, but I do know that it took a lot of pork chops, chitlings and cornbread to create that masterpiece!"

"Amen, brother Paul, Amen! Oh look, there's your girl, Bonita Woolsey. Should I invite her to sit with us?"

"Be merciful, Diedre. I have to work with that woman. Please don't make me have to sit through three hours of speechifying next to her and her teeth."

"I'll go easy on you this time, although the two of you seemed to be engaged in the most intimate conversation outside."

"You don't miss a thing, do you?"

"Clearly you don't remember a thing, do you?"

"*Touché, Madame* Douglas."

The reality was that while I tried to consciously pay attention to my surroundings, Diedre really "never missed a thing" and when we were together I always felt a half step behind. Her noticing my brief encounter with Bonita Woolsey couldn't possibly be a surprise to anyone who knew her, and I have known Diedre better than anyone for many, many years.

Because we were sitting in the fifth pew, we had to subtly shift so that we could get a view of our brothers and sisters, members of The Pride, as they walked a promenade down the center aisle of the Riverside Church. Since Diedre sat closest to the aisle, I was able to speak into her ear in low tones without getting so close as to risk a withering stare or a jab from the stiletto of her wit. She had to turn, just so slightly to reply or initiate a remark.

I would like to report that we sat there as the forty-something adults that we were, respectfully awaiting the beginning of the memorial service, all the while solemnly perusing the sixty-page (!!) program highlighting Winner's accomplishments and achievements in life along with the bereavement of his family, friends and associates. I would like to report that, but it would not be true.

It was almost as if we had reverted to junior high school for a few liberating and joyous moments. I am certain that all but the most astute observer would have thought that we were exchanging serious views. Not true. Not true at all.

"Will you look at the size of the ring that Bart Jefferson's wife is wearing?"

Diedre was referring to Bartholomew ("Black Bart") Jefferson, the former lawyer, funeral parlor owner and now media magnate. Black

Bart was known for being arrogant, self-consumed, and wealthy. He was escorting his fourth wife, a former airline stewardess, who was a third of his age.

"Well, all I can say is go Black Bart, go Black Bart, go. Mrs. Jefferson looks pretty happy too."

"Well, money can't buy everything."

"Well, Diedre, you do know that you can live pretty well with what money can buy though, don't you?"

"I heard that. Mrs. Jefferson is clearly feeling no pain in that department. But my, my. What happened to Mr. Militant-Going-to-Change-the-World?"

"He didn't like being poor, and begging didn't agree with him, just like you."

"*Touché*, Mr. Taylor."

The fact that Diedre even acknowledged a riposte on my part made me feel like I had just won a championship round on some interplanetary game show. I also thought it was best to quit while I was ahead and shut my acknowledged smart mouth.

"There's Arthur Lane. You know I heard that he was gay?"

Arthur Lane, better known as Arthur C. Lane, was the publisher of *The Dark Side of Business* magazine. He was six feet five, two hundred and forty pounds of muscle, even at the age of sixty-one. He was also a former Navy SEAL.

"Diedre, I am the first to admit that anything is possible, but where the hell did you hear that bullshit?"

"From my hairdresser," she said with an air of authority and confidence that was staggering coming from such an intelligent woman.

"Your hairdresser? I am afraid that I would have to bet that Henri or Pierre or Paquito is engaging in wishful thinking. But I have to admit that it is a hilarious concept. Let's get that rumor going. I would pay anything to see the look on Lane's face when he hears it.

At that point Diedre couldn't restrain a smile anymore. She had to bite her lower lip (a lovely lower lip at that, and the sight of her biting it brought back a flood of memories about . . .) to keep from laughing.

"Paul, I was hoping to get you to pass on that bit of 'intelligence' to see how far a ridiculous story could go. But I'm afraid that I can't keep a straight face on that one. But you are right; it would be a hilarious story if it ever got out."

And then, in walked Gordon Perkins. He was tall, heavyset, with a chip on his shoulder the size of an endangered redwood.

"My, my! A funeral just wouldn't be a funeral without Mr. Gordon Perkins."

"Well, Diedre, you know that Gordon carries a grudge that could break the back of a Bactrian camel. I would watch it if I were you." That occasioned laughter between us that danced on the precipice of truth.

In truth, Gordon Perkins could carry a grudge that would break the backs of a dozen Bactrian camels. As he strode down the aisle forcefully, anyone who bothered to notice could see that his custom-tailored Savile Row suit was amazing ill-fitting. Traveling in his considerable wake was his second wife, Kenitra Perkins.

Kenitra was a twenty-seven-year-old former model who was six feet tall, tawny with a face and figure and green eyes that would make Satan leave hell without leaving a forwarding address.

"It's a good thing that it's winter, that way Kenitra doesn't have to worry about people noticing her wearing long sleeves to cover Gordon's bruises and her needle tracks!"

"Diedre! You and I have both only heard those rumors. There's no way you can know that they are true!"

"Do you know them to be untrue?"

"I would expect a better answer than that."

"And I would expect a better question. Anyway, you know that too many of the stories about Gordon are true."

And I had to be quiet. Not that many years ago Gordon Stallworth Perkins had been a trader with Goldman Sachs. Legend has it that he had asked the head of his unit for a raise and had also inquired as to how much longer it would be before he became a partner.

When told in no uncertain and condescending terms that he would never be more than a mediocre trader and that he would never become a partner, Perkins called the man every kind of motherfucker possible and quit his job on the spot. With his life savings and a loan from his father-in-law at the time, he started G.S. Perkins and Partners, LLP. Gordon Perkins was now chairman and chief executive of the largest black-owned investment banking firm in the United States.

Since Gordon is something of a friend and a frequent client, I have had the mixed fortune of seeing how talent, genius and bad taste can combine to create . . . well, something different. Gordon was never a good man or a nice man. The only term that applies to Gordon Perkins is—a force of nature.

"Look, there's Jerome."

"I *knew* you had a thing for Jerome. I just knew it."

"Paul, you are beyond ridiculous. I thought that you knew class when you saw it. Now I am beginning to wonder."

Diedre's arched eyebrows and withering glance immediately made me feel as if I had somehow moved into the twilight zone of bad humor. I wanted to get out right away. That was for sure.

Jerome Hardaway was the Black Boy Wonder of Wall Street. He was the Anti-Gordon. Jerome was tall, athletic, good looking and impeccably well groomed without being fussy about it. Jerome was almost regal in his bearing without conveying the impression that he was impressed by himself.

He had established himself as a rising star at Smith Barney and, with the cooperation and support of the chairman of the firm, had established The Hardaway Group as a joint venture with Smith Barney. With that kind of firepower behind him and with his own skills and talent, he had built THG into the second to the leading black investment banking firm in the United States within five years. The competition between Gordon and Jerome was starting to get interesting, with the outcome of their competition having the potential of becoming legendary.

As Jerome pushed the wheelchair of his wife, Charmaine, down the middle aisle of the church, he nodded to Diedre and me. Charmaine, who was an internationally renowned biophysicist, had been afflicted by multiple sclerosis. The grace with which this ideal couple handled their adversity only made them more attractive. They were that real and that genuine.

Diedre and I both settled down at that point, trying to assume a more sober air. As the rest of The Pride filed into the church, three thoughts crossed my mind. First, it was amazing that I could be friends and laugh and joke and enjoy the company of my ex-wife. It made me wish that we would stay friends for a long, long time. Second, I wondered if anyone overheard our conversation, especially about Arthur Lane. I perversely hoped that someone did and that they would pass on that bogus story. Like I said, the reaction of someone as self-absorbed and self-important as Lane would certainly be worth the price of admission.

And finally, I wondered what kind of business opportunity could arise from this gathering of so many members of The Pride. It was an opportunity that I was determined would not let pass without trying to make something of it.

As the service began, an idea began to take shape that would change my life as well as the lives of many other members of The Pride.

CHAPTER 16

Diedre

Reflection on a winter's day

I purposely let my thoughts swirl and wander wherever they wanted to go as Paul and I brought our warm and comfortable foolishness to a close. We waited for the final preparations for Winner Tomlinson's memorial service to be completed. I have to admit that I thought about Winner who, though I met through Paul, I knew professionally and personally and on a *much* more personal basis once Paul and I were divorced.

I always respected Winner for what he had accomplished, not only in terms of his business success, but because of his desire and ability to be a positive force in the national black community. His financial contributions to the NAACP, the United Negro College Fund, and politicians like New York Mayor David Dinkins and Chicago Mayor Harold Washington were just a part of the story as far as I am concerned.

I believe that it was also important that he used his money to make major contributions to Harvard Law School (one of the largest in the history of that university) *and* Howard Law School (the largest in the history of that university). It always seemed to me that Winner was trying to send a message that over time, black Americans would be real players in all aspects of America. And I want to be one of those real players also.

As my mind continued to wander that cold January morning, I

couldn't help but think about how I had intended to start a national community development bank after I completed a few years at Citibank. This after I had gone to Mount Holyoke College to get my Bachelor's Degree in Fine Arts and after I had received my MBA from Columbia's business school. I remembered how it was not that long ago that all things seemed possible and that the rest of the world and I were young and full of hope and possibilities.

But it seems so long ago, really long ago, that Paul and I were married. We were joined in a marriage that crashed, burned, and died. A horrific crash occasioned by multiple causes. Some were Paul's, and if the truth be told, many were mine as well. We shared joint responsibility for, and custody of, the disaster that was our marriage.

And then an opportunity came for me to work in Citibank's offices in Paris. My girlfriends and family thought it would be good for me "to get away" in the aftermath, although I didn't think that self-exile was warranted. But I did get away.

First to Paris. Then London and then Tokyo. I also got so far away that my dream of a national community development bank got dimmer and dimmer until it was just a flickering light in a backroom of my consciousness. It was a backroom that I rarely visited.

By the time I returned to New York City six years later, I have to confess that, in all modesty, I was a polished, accomplished and outrageously smart global banker. Everyone knew that I was a brilliant rising star.

So when I was asked by the chairman's office at Citibank to take on a totally new assignment, I leaped at the chance. No valley was too deep, no mountain too high. The assignment: to set up a financial advisory unit that would advise pension funds, states, municipalities, and countries.

Within two years, I had made sure that my unit was a part of the bank's twenty-first-century strategy, a big part. In truth, I envisioned my career and the future of Citibank as being intertwined.

I was extremely loyal and extremely well paid. I made money for the bank and the bank paid me a lot of money. My unit was truly a profit center.

And then one day there was management reorganization at the bank. These came and went like the seasons and were of no real con-

cern to stars like me. The constellation where I dwelled had permanence like the sky itself. Besides, I had heard nothing that involved
my unit. So I had no real concerns.

I was summoned to the office of one of the most senior vice presidents at Citibank, one of the very few who reported directly to the
chairman. I just had to assume that the purpose of the meeting was
to officially announce my oft-rumored promotion to the upper tier
of senior management. My biggest concern was how I was going to
manage to look surprised when I received the long-awaited good
news.

As I took the elevator ride down to the third floor of 399 Park
Avenue, the nerve center of the empire that was called Citibank, it
was one of the few and last times that I have ever unfettered my
hopes.

As I recall, I actually allowed myself to worry about how I would
remain composed when the promotion was offered and how I would
celebrate with friends and family. I was in orbit!

I thought about the new challenges that waited. The ride down to
the third floor was dizzying in its possibilities and expectations that
day. It was a day that I simply will never forget.

The elevator ride back up to my office was not what I had anticipated. I encountered a scenario I never could have imagined because it was outside of the universe of my imagination.

CHAPTER 17

Diedre

More reflections

In a brief eight minute meeting, I was advised that my unit had been reorganized and that two of my rivals at the bank, one male, one female, both white, both younger, had been selected to run what had been my unit. My position was being phased out and I was offered an extremely generous separation arrangement.

In other words, I was fired. Sacked. Terminated. Shown the door.

As I sat in the Riverside Church that morning, I was amazed that I could still vividly and painfully remember that I was shivering with rage as I returned to my office, alone in that elevator in 399 Park Avenue.

The one thing I remember is that I made up my mind that no one would see my anger or my pain as I walked to my corner office with the panoramic view of Manhattan and closed the door behind me.

I also recall that the senior vice president with whom I had met had generously given me until the end of the business day to clean out my office and be out of 399 Park Avenue forever. And I remember that there was no time to waste crying or wondering why.

By early the next morning I was on a flight to Anguilla, staying in a private villa that I had rented from time to time. This was in 1985, and Anguilla was still a secluded getaway that only a fortunate, discriminating few knew about.

That has since changed now that Conde Nast and Regis Philbin have discovered the Cap Jaluca and Mallehana ultra-luxury resorts and other sybaritic pleasure palaces that didn't even exist when I made my journey into seclusion and self-discovery and renewal.

When I made my escape from the sheer and utter madness at Citibank, the only way to get to Anguilla was by hydrofoil from St. Maarten. Or, one could be really adventurous and take a five-mile flight from the same island in a four-seater airplane and land on a dusty strip of runway that had the nerve to call itself an international airport.

American Airlines has now figured out that it can make money shuttling wealthy tourists from Puerto Rico who are in search of something different. And Anguilla is certainly something different.

A former British colony, and still a member of the Commonwealth, Anguilla is a very small, extremely private, sparsely populated isle about five miles north of St. Maarten. Everything that St. Maarten has, Anguilla doesn't.

That is what always attracted me, even when the island didn't have central electricity. It is this special character of Anguilla that was one of the reasons why Paul and I went there on our first honeymoon.

Anguilla doesn't have casinos, it doesn't have large condominiums and discos and cafes and traffic jams. What it does have is some of the finest, quietest and most secluded beaches in the Caribbean.

And, because of a local law that declares that all beaches must be accessible to the public, there is none of the snooty, *faux* exclusivity that I absolutely despise in many of the top vacation destinations that I have visited. After the debacle at the bank Anguilla was just perfect for where my head was at, as the saying goes.

As I strolled along the bleached beaches, my newly liberated toes luxuriating in the sugary sand of that tropical wonderland, a plan began to glimmer, glow, and then gleam. It demanded that I grasp its reality and move with it right away. And I am glad that I did exactly that.

It wasn't about a national community development bank anymore however, it was a financial advisory firm that started to take shape in my mind. I would head it, own it, run it, and it was going to be a success.

I was determined that I would take everything that I had learned at Citibank—adversity, treachery, betrayal, strategic planning and expectation of success, and I would be a success. I would be a bigger success than I ever would have been at the bank. I was determined not to be bitter. I was determined to be better.

The totality of my experience at Citibank, and that ride back up the elevator to clean out my office had taught me a lesson that I will remember for the rest of my life. In business, it was simply never personal. It is always just business.

And that's the way that I have played it ever since. From that moment on the beach in Anguilla to that day sitting in the Riverside Church, business has never mixed with my personal life.

And as I sat next to Paul in the church that day, waiting for Winner Tomlinson's memorial service to begin, I couldn't help but think about all that had happened since that very special trip to Anguilla.

By the time I returned to New York, I had written out a complete business plan in longhand on the yellow legal tablets that I have always favored. I cashed in some securities that I had been holding, and made an insane number of calls to colleagues in the financial community. Within sixty days I opened the offices of DBD Financial Advisors in the newly opened World Financial Center in Lower Manhattan, right in the epicenter of my entire business universe.

I was able to hire away a few of my former staffers at the bank, the ones who saw the handwriting on the wall. When one has to choose between loyalty and opportunity, always choose opportunity. That's what the big dogs do every single time. Frankly, I really didn't care what their motives were. Again, for me it has been strictly about business—period.

As the crowd rustled and settled into the cathedral on the river, I couldn't help but reflect on the fact that DBD had offices in Los Angeles, Chicago, Atlanta, and Miami. The firm had over two hundred employees and it counted a number of Fortune 50 companies, cities, states and countries as clients.

As a matter of fact, I hired away so many people from the bank that now even my "successors," Mr. and Ms. Great White Hope worked for me. Again it was strictly business, nothing personal.

It is interesting to reflect upon the fact that DBD also has foreign affiliates in Tokyo, Paris, and London. At the time of Winner's memorial I was seriously considering opening an office in Johannesburg since the release of Nelson Mandela gave me reason to believe that there would be tremendous changes and opportunities in South Africa. I thought then that Johannesburg could provide DBD with an excellent platform to begin operations throughout the continent of Africa.

At the time, I also found myself reflecting on just how bizarre and interesting life could be. I know that Paul would probably have the mother of all apoplectic fits if he knew about the brief affair that I had with Winner just last year. To this day Paul has no right to have any kind of fit at any time. But Paul is a particular type of man, and I know that is how he would react.

A memorial service is a strange place for retrospection, but life is like that, too. It was funny how things started.

Winner was interested in becoming an equity partner in DBD and I figured that it wouldn't hurt to listen. Although we had known each other for years, we had never really spent much time together alone. I believe that we probably impressed each other with intelligence, wit and vision. And, there was something more.

And then one thing had led to another. Even now I can't remember exactly how. But very soon after our discussions began, my trips to Paris became more frequent, and they had not all been strictly business, that's for sure. Pleasure is the word that I am looking for here.

In some ways, it was a perfect affair. Both of us enjoyed the pleasure without the unwanted interference of unwitting and unbridled and uncontrollable romance.

I always knew that Winner was not going to leave his wife. Winner knew that I was not interested in being less than a full partner, and he was not interested in full partners in any aspect of his life and certainly not his business. But he was perfect for the kind of male companionship that I thought I wanted at the time. And then he had the bad taste to die.

As the last strains of Roberta Flack's rendition of "Amazing Grace" soared through the church, I began to focus on the services that were about to begin. It wasn't often that I contemplated my own mortality. I simply don't have the time.

But this was one of those times when I just couldn't help it. There was nothing that I could do but let the thought make itself known, bloom into my consciousness, and then wither and die.

CHAPTER 18

Sture

Yet another point of view

The reaction of Americans to cold weather has always been a real source of humor for me. The way some of them act and the layers of clothing that they wear upon the slightest sign of frost or a chill in the air, you would think that they had never felt cold weather before.

And, I must say, with all due respect to my black business partners and my many black friends and patrons of Dorothy's By the Sea, that many of my friends and colleagues of color seem to find that cold weather is a cue for them to vie for some kind of dramatic award—perhaps an Oscar for the Most Overdressed, or a Tony for Loudest Complaint About the Weather, or an Emmy for Greatest Number of Times for Exclaiming "Lord have mercy, it's cold."

As I left my Chelsea apartment that morning, taking the subway to attend Winner Tomlinson's funeral, I noted that it was a cold January day—at least by New York standards. In Oslo or Bergen, of course, the day would barely rate the wearing of a hat and gloves. Most Norwegians would not even dream of buttoning their coats.

Going down the stairs from street level to get on the subway, I saw a bizarre combination of fur coats, down jackets, scarves, hats, combat boots, cloaks (!!) and various combinations of fabric, the origins of which would be known only to the owners. My Norwegian compatriots would have been amazed at what New Yorkers considered to be cold weather.

I remember days in the heart of winter back home when Saab door handles would snap off in your hand like candy canes. And I remember seeing old men spit into the air and watching the spittle freeze in the air and bounce and roll on the street. One would imagine that New Yorkers would just curl up and die in weather like that. But, from my experience in New York, New Yorkers would figure out a way to survive.

Even though I have now been a resident of New York City for over a decade, I continue to be amazed at the qualities and character of the "New Yorker." I say "New Yorker," because the typical New York resident could be Chinese, black American, black Caribbean, black Dominican, Hasidic Jew, Irish or . . . Norwegian. What "New Yorkers" share as a common trait is the ability to deal with just about anything. That also happens to be one more reason why subways are my favorite mode of transportation. Just about anything can, and will, happen on the subways. Real New Yorkers manage to deal with it, and move on.

I have seen a blind old lady break the flintiest of hearts playing "Amazing Grace" on an accordion while wending her way through crowded subway cars at rush hours, the packed commuters parting like the Red Sea for Moses as she passed through. And I could swear that I saw her get off the subway and take off her dark glasses to count her change as the car full of chagrined passengers pulled out of the station.

I have seen newly arrived immigrants from Afghanistan, complete with turbans; robes and sandals receive barely a first glance from the jaded residents of the Big Apple. As a relatively recent member of the tribe known as New Yorkers, I have found myself wondering what would be going through the minds of my Afghan *compadres,* newly arrived from Kabul and camels and bazaars and casbahs, when they get into a steel tube and fly under the concrete canyons and stainless steel and glass mountains. It must be like traveling to another planet.

I took the subway to the 116th Street stop on the Broadway local and proceeded to walk past the Columbia University campus. I considered my environs as I walked the rest of the way to the Riverside Church.

Columbia is one of the oldest universities in the United States, being about three hundred years old. Centered on 116th Street on the west side of Manhattan, its current location was an absolutely rural location when it moved from Madison Avenue in midtown Manhattan about one hundred years ago.

Now, of course, Columbia stands on the borders of the Upper West Side and Harlem. It is as urban a college location as there is anywhere in the world. It provides not only a first class academic education and also yet another illustration of how New York City has always been in a constant state of change. It was a most remarkable place.

I imagine that I wound up living in Chelsea because it was affordable and close to the places that I was working, first the Water Club and now, Dorothy's By the Sea. It never occurred to me to consider the Maginot-Mason Dixon Line of Manhattan, 110th Street, as a factor in the location of my living quarters. Of course, not only am I from out of town, I am from out of the country, and there are those who would say that I am out of my mind.

I can honestly say that I have never had any thoughts, one way or the other, about going "uptown." I have too many white friends and black friends who wonder at the fact that not only do I go to Emily's on 110th Street, Sylvia's on Malcolm X Boulevard, and Londel's on Frederick Douglass Boulevard, but that I also go to the St. Nick's Pub on St. Nicholas Avenue for the late Monday night jazz jam sessions.

From the reactions of some of these friends, you would think that I had gone skydiving into some Hawaiian volcano or Rollerblading through some forgotten Bosnian minefield. In point of fact I don't know of any place on earth where I can find the combination of food, camaraderie and music. So I go uptown, to Harlem. For me, it is as simple as that.

But these are the United States. And nothing ever seems to be simple. After all, the *losers* of this country's only civil war seem to think that it is a point of pride to be able to fly the flag of a lost cause.

Indeed, I have read that in particularly desperate political times some people run for the office of President of the United States defending the righteousness and correctness of being able to fly this flag of a lost cause over government buildings.

This is also a country where black people can be positively adored for their athletic and musical accomplishments and arrested for "Driving While Black" on the very same day, with a gratuitous beating thrown in for good measure. This is a fascinating country indeed.

As a matter of fact, I must confess that while I truly admire, respect and enjoy the company of my black friends and colleagues, I have not, for one minute, ever wished that I were a black American. This is not the kind of thing that I would announce during Sunday brunch at Josephine's, but as a matter of self-preservation and survival, it is not a wish that I would ever make or ever want to come true.

To tell the truth, I sometimes wonder how black people in this country are able to cope with the obvious and the discreet affronts to their very humanity on a daily basis. They see people, like me, come from all over the world, with no claim to citizenship or any special rights, and we immediately receive better treatment, and more importantly respect, than most of them will ever receive.

In some ways, it is what makes The Pride all the more amazing to me. It is difficult enough to be successful in America, no matter what your color or ethnicity. I have traveled extensively through Europe and I can state without fear of contradiction that on its slowest day the United States is a hundred times more competitive than any aspect of its European counterpart. To paraphrase the song, if you can make it in the United States, you can make it anywhere.

There is something about the American ethic, the American psyche, the American mind-set, which makes being the biggest, the fastest, the best, to be the most important achievement of all. It's almost as if Americans intentionally disavow the concept of mortality and race headlong into tomorrow, trying to win, buy, and own everything, as if there is some permanence to these achievements. The U.S. is not a slow racetrack—it has never been, and it certainly will not be slowing down anytime soon.

I spend some of my leisure hours reading American history and it was interesting for me to find out that in the late sixties and early seventies the United States was actually lagging behind the Europeans and Japanese in terms of productivity and modernization. The decline of the American "empire" was predicted by many an observer. This so-called decline was probably born of the indolence and complacency that can affect any competitor that is so far ahead of the field—which was certainly the case for the U.S. in the period after World War II through the sixties. What a wake-up call the so-called decline turned out to be.

Since that time American industry in all of its aspects—financial services, construction, and manufacturing—has retooled, retrenched, restructured and rethought itself into an incredible economic engine. Further, all the Americans in business that I know seem to pursue success and tomorrow's dollar as if there will never be enough, as if someone is chasing them, as if another "decline" is always around the corner. That deep-seated, well-hidden, never-articulated fear must be a tremendous incentive because it has manifested itself in a frantic, frenetic business fury that I have never seen in Europe. Maybe it exists in Japan or China, but I doubt that it could be so deep-seated in the culture and so maddeningly pervasive.

And that's a real long way for me to say that for black Americans who face some form of prejudice, bias, and discrimination every day of their lives to be so successful in the face of such obstacles in such an incredibly competitive environment, is truly amazing. Like the members of The Pride.

I can tell you I stand in awe of these men and women who have "made it" in America. I sometimes wonder if they must be supermen and superwomen. I know that they are not, but I also know that they are very special. I have also come to learn that they are very human, subject to the same frailties and failings as possessed by those who would try to stop them and keep them down. After all, it must be hard to try to overcome your adversary every day of your life without finally becoming very much like your adversary in the process. How ironic, indeed.

CHAPTER 19

Sture

A view from the pew

Take the guest of honor at the memorial service—Winner Tomlinson. I only knew him through Paul and Diedre and through his being a guest at the Water Club and at Dorothy's. But I also came to learn of his incredible achievements by paying attention and reading the papers.

His ascent to the very pinnacle of business achievement in this country was nothing short of amazing. It was almost as if he willed it to happen and it did. He was a force of nature, and if only out of respect, I wanted to attend the memorial service that morning.

But there was more. I had also heard the comments of some of the less than discreet white patrons at both restaurants when they assumed that they were out of earshot of anyone who would care when they referred to Winner as a "black-assed nigger" and a "colored buffoon." My blond hair, blue eyes, and Scandinavian accent give me the perfect camouflage in these kinds of situations. Most of my white friends, colleagues and patrons just cannot imagine having a close, personal friendship with a black person and it came as little surprise to me that many of these same whites would utter the most foul and tasteless comments about black Americans. Even about the members of The Pride. Even about Winner Tomlinson.

Experiences like that have helped me to realize that in the boardrooms and executive suites of Wall Street and corporate America, there were minefields, booby traps and trapdoors waiting for the members of The Pride every day. Somehow many of them foiled their adversaries, at least enough times to keep up a winning percentage. Personally, I have found that singular and collective achievement to be absolutely incredible.

Clearly Winner had prevailed and it just could not be too cold for me to come and pay my respects to him and his family. His feet of clay would be something to contemplate on another day but not this one.

As I entered the church I could see Paul and Diedre engaged in an animated discussion about . . . ? Well, who knows? While they are my business partners and friends, I have been determined to stay out of their personal life.

But one could not help but observe what an "interesting" non-couple they were. Of course they had been married and of course they had been seriously estranged for years. That is, before the completion of the "Paris Peace Talks."

Legend has it that after he and Diedre had been divorced for about ten years, Paul appeared at Diedre's condominium apartment door with a bouquet of Sterling roses, a bottle of Pommery champagne and round trip Concorde tickets to Paris with a suite at the George V waiting. Legend also has it that he simply refused to take "no" for an answer and that they spent a weekend in Paris sorting out their differences. They had become human and humane to one another ever since, acting something akin to the way civilized couples behave once they are no longer a couple.

What most people didn't know, because they don't pay attention, or because they are easily deceived, or because they believe what they want to believe, is that Paul and Diedre danced around the slightly glowing embers of passion and love almost daily. They tried to pretend that there was nothing there but friendship. They dated other people. They were strictly about business in their business together. And somehow they just managed to sit together at the memorial service for Winner Tomlinson.

But if you really paid attention, you could see arcs of some nameless energy pass between them from time to time, usually for a reason apparent only to the two of them. I make my living knowing and understanding people, and it has always been clear to me that if Paul and Diedre live to be a hundred years old, they will still be "a couple" no matter what.

Though I do have to confess that it is fun watching them pretend that there is nothing going on between them. And once you know, it is hilarious watching them act as if they are just pals, just friends. And on a serious note, it is reassuring to know that real love can never die and that it never really goes away. It may wear many disguises and hide from the misguided and the deceived, but true love never goes away.

It was comforting to think about such things that winter morning as the crowd in the Riverside Church started to settle down. Soon the Tomlinson family would file in and take their appointed positions in the first two rows of pews. And then it would be time for the services to begin.

CHAPTER 20

Gordon

Make way for Mr. Perkins

Iwas born in New Rochelle, New York. New Rochelle is the home of the mythical Rob and Laura Petrie and the legendary Coalhouse Walker. I don't really give a shit about it one way or another, but it passes for a conversation piece in some circles.

I have to admit that attending Winner's memorial service made me feel strange in two ways. First, it always unnerves me when contemporaries die because it could always mean that I could be next. That is a concept I just don't like. Never have. Never will.

Second, there is nothing I can do at a memorial service except be there. I really don't give a shit how it sounds, but the truth is that there is nothing that I can do for the "dearly departed" and most of the crying and moaning and wailing is phony anyway. And in any event, there are deals to be done, money to be made, and none of that is happening at anybody's memorial service. I feel like I am losing money every moment I am sitting at one of these jackleg events—just like the dinners, banquets, and receptions that I have to endure so often.

I knew that this was one of those functions that I "have" to attend, so I was there, with my knucklehead wife, Kenitra. She is a great decoration for the arm and I know I have everybody's attention with that pretty bitch in tow, but she has really been getting on my nerves lately. But that's a story for another time.

Like I mentioned, I was born in New Rochelle, historically one of the first real suburbs of New York City. I was an altar boy at the Blessed Sacrament Roman Catholic Church in town, and went on to New Rochelle High School where I graduated with honor.

In grade school, I was the fat boy that you always teased. I grew up almost thinking that my real name was "Fat Butt" or "Melon Head." No one ever thought that I had feelings that might merit consideration. It was a tough lesson, but I learned—no one is on my side but me.

By the time I got to high school the fat started to redistribute itself around muscle and mass. I became a star fullback/linebacker on the football team. I still love to hit, I just don't get the chance very often.

I was also an All State wrestler in the heavyweight division. No one dared to call me "Fat" anything, of course, but I never forgot that the people who are kissing your ass today might be kicking your ass tomorrow. It's a lesson that my father never let me forget. And I have always tried to take his advice, even though he has been dead for ten years now.

My father was a master sergeant in the United States Army and served in the European theater during World War II. One of the lesser known facts about American history is that the threads of racism have been so deeply woven into the fabric of the American heart and soul that, even during the course of the life and death struggle with Nazis and rapidly spreading world fascism, the American armed forces had serious official restrictions regarding black soldiers participating in combat. Combat was the domain of The White Man. Any other approach would defy the Forces of Nature.

Although many young black American men wound up serving and dying in combat anyway, there were many like my father, Master Sergeant Julian Perkins, who were deemed fit only to handle supply and support functions. This resulted in an illustration of what my erstwhile buddy, Mr. Smart Ass Paul Taylor, calls the Law of Unintended Consequences.

The intent of the policy of segregating black and white troops during World War II was hardly benign, in that it was created in the wicked pit of racism and hatred. The unintended consequence was that not as many black soldiers died in World War II as might have been the case if the more "enlightened" policies of the Vietnam War had been in effect. Ain't that a bitch?

And there's more. As a result of that bullshit policy, a lot more black men survived the war, and a lot more black children were born into the time of the First Great American Baby Boom and the era of unlimited possibilities that was the United States after World War II. Going even further with the absurdity of Paul's Law of Unintended Consequences, the young black men who survived World War II were self-selected—many of the brightest, most ambitious, law-abiding citizens with the greatest potential of the pool of young black people in America at that time.

Another "unintended" result was that Julian Perkins, a young man just up from Charlotte, North Carolina, didn't learn any specialized combat skills that wouldn't have had any utility in the real world anyway. Instead, he learned skills related to supplies, logistics, record keeping, and accounting. In other words, he learned skills that would be much more important than shooting, demolitions or bayoneting in the coming peacetime business/boom environment.

After the war my father completed the requirements for his high school diploma, went to Hampton University, courtesy of the G.I. Bill, yet another illustration of Paul's law. Ultimately he became the comptroller for a small trucking firm in Westchester County and there he met and married my mother, the former Aretha Patchett, the only daughter of lifelong schoolteachers in nearby Mount Vernon. And it was in Westchester County that I was born.

My mother and father told me that everyone knew that I was special, almost from the time that I was born. I was speaking before I was a year old and reading before I was three. I entered Blessed Sacrament Elementary School in New Rochelle at the age of five and by November of my first year in school I was in the second grade.

My father may have been the initial beneficiary of Paul's Law of Unintended Consequences, but I know that my father was a *summa cum laude* graduate of The School of Hard Knocks. He and his family had survived the Great Depression and World War II and white people by being tough—always tougher than the other guy. And from the time I knew anything, I knew that there was no other way.

I know now that my father was tough on me because he wanted

me to be ready for anything. And tough is what I became. At a very early age I knew, just knew, that I didn't give a shit about anybody, nobody but my mother, my father, and myself. After that, everyone just had to get in fucking line. That's just the way it is with me to this very day.

But you can ask anyone. I do not bullshit. I cannot bullshit. I don't try to trick and smile and weasel my way into anyone's good graces. I am who I fucking am, and I don't really give a shit whether you like it or not. Just don't fuck with me. Because, simply put, I am not someone to be fucked with.

Just ask my ex-boss who used to work for me. You heard me right. This asshole was the head of the municipal bond trading unit at Goldman Sachs, which was where I worked when I first got out of business school. After a couple of years of being one the top performers I asked this idiot about a raise and what kind of time frame I could anticipate before I would be considered for partnership.

I will never ever forget being told in no uncertain terms that there was "no fucking way" that I would ever even be *considered* for partnership at Goldman Sachs. I also recall being told that if that was on my mind, I should just pack up my shit and get out right then and there. I have to tell you, for one of the few times in my life, I was just stunned into stone fucking silence.

I don't remember all of the details of what happened next except that I did call my soon to be ex-boss every kind of motherfucker I could think of while packing up my shit and going out the door. At that moment I had no idea of what I was going to do next.

Of course what I did do next is borrow some cash from my now ex-father-in-law and set up G.S. Perkins and Company. Initially, we got our business doing the same municipal finance deals that a lot of other black firms were doing. But I could see that diversification was going to be the wave of the future and that the white folks were going to try and strangle the municipal golden goose as soon as possible.

So G.S. Perkins is also into asset management and we are currently negotiating with Merrill Lynch about co-managing an investment fund that focuses on biotech industries. I am also in serious discussions with Bear Stearns concerning co-managing another fund that focuses on the internet. As the Chairman and CEO of G.S. Perkins I can tell you that we are doing very well indeed.

So well that about three years ago I hired that dumb asshole from Goldman Sachs who told me to pack my shit. One of my most pleasant experiences in recent memory was calling him up while he was in Akron, Ohio, on firm business and telling him that he was fired and that all of his corporate credit cards were canceled. So he would have to get home the best way he could.

I also absolutely relished telling him that the only severance money he would ever get would be by counting the change in his pocket. After making him go to court and spend a fortune on attorney's fees, I ultimately settled his lawsuit for peanuts, courtesy of Paul Taylor. Of course, this was an instance where the consequences were intended.

CHAPTER 21

Gordon

More about me

My father died in a car accident as we were coming home from a New York Giants football game. It's a long story and one that I save for another time. All I will say is that it taught me a lesson for life—you had better always look out for yourself. I say that because after my father was killed it seemed to me that it was my mother and I against the world. And as far as I was concerned, even in high school, the world was never going to win.

I got an academic scholarship to Columbia (so I could be close to home) and after graduating from the college, I immediately got an MBA at the same school. In the process of going to school and working part-time for six years, I learned, and then knew, that Wall Street was my destiny.

I wanted to be in charge of my life and to have no one in charge of me. The only way that was going to happen was with M-O-N-E-Y, and I was going to get all that I needed, and then some. And that is exactly what I have done.

At that is why I am the Chairman and CEO of G.S. Perkins. And that is why I was sitting at that dumb-ass memorial service for Winner Tomlinson. It's part of what I do.

Smart-ass Paul Taylor refers to "The Pride" to describe what he calls successful blacks who have prevailed in New York and elsewhere. If I buy into his theories on the subject, and I must confess that I do to a very limited extent, then I am the baddest lion in "The Pride." And there was certainly no question after Winner kicked the bucket. So, like I said, I have to be at this service. But I don't have to like it. And I don't.

First of all, since my father died, I have been to exactly one funeral. And that was for my mother. Second, I have a lot better things to do than to sit around and listen to people lie about someone who is dead and is going to stay dead. And finally, if the truth were told about the Winner Tomlinson that I know, half the people in Riverside Church would have run screaming into the frosty morning air.

But I was not there to tell lies, or the truth, about Winner, I was just going to sit and listen to this endless stream of chicken-leg-shaking preachers and gladhanding politicians preach and preen and lie. I do this because I have to and only because I have to. I do a lot of things that I don't particularly like. But, because I am Gordon Perkins, I do a lot more things that I do like.

CHAPTER 22

Paul

Meanwhile, back at the church

I am savoring this late night reverie as I reflect on the changes that took place that winter morning. I guess I should not be surprised that, at the time, none of us, Jerome, Gordon, Diedre, me—none of us realized that at that particular moment in time we were about to be a part of something so very important.

What I remember most about that morning was that there was a strange and completely incomprehensible feeling that came over me as I sat next to Diedre. And like a rabbit hypnotized by a cobra, I could almost observe my feelings and emotions flowing around me like some strange river. But I could do absolutely nothing about it. It wasn't until several months later that I had even the remotest clue as to what was going on in my heart and in my life.

That January morning in Riverside Church was one of the most fascinating days of my professional life as you will undoubtedly agree as this story goes on. My life changed on that day. But it wasn't because of Gordon and Jerome and all the bright ideas that surfaced that day. It turned out that it was Diedre who made the difference.

In fact, it was all that I could do to try and pay attention to the names and faces that floated by in a very special universe that only included her and me. It was strange and confusing and wonderful and baffling, all at the same time.

By way of some further explanation, you should understand that when Diedre and I had been a couple, we had had one of those miraculous, magical, mysterious relationships that you remember even when you forget your teeth in a glass somewhere that you can't remember. The kind of white hot passion and crystal clear connection that stays with you even while sipping vodka martinis on a Caribbean beach in your sunset years.

We loved, we fought, we hated and we charmed and enchanted each other for over a decade. At one point it was as if our beings had melded and PaulDiedre, or DiedrePaul, was our name.

We lived in each other. We lived for each other. We loved each other with a passion and urgency that defied time, and, as it turned out, defied common sense as well.

And then, it was over. And it had been over for over a decade. To this very day I can't even remember the precise reason that we came apart at the seams. But we did.

We did so with a spectacular vengeance that made most breakups seem like the Easter Parade on Fifth Avenue. I am pretty sure that the passion that brought us together also tore us apart. And, in what seemed like an instant of time, as close as we were, that's how far apart we became.

In the early years after we had parted ways, we quite sensibly took pains to avoid each other and to spare ourselves each other's company. But we were members of The Pride and neither of us was going anywhere anytime soon.

So we found a way to get along, and after a time, the bitterness and grief and pain that we had caused each other was no longer a part of our story. We were acquaintances, then colleagues, and then, in a manner of speaking, friends. After all, no one knew us better than we did.

We had reached an accommodation of sorts by the time of Winner's memorial service. We were long past the point of being uncomfortable around each other. Indeed, our past made us extraordinarily compatible and since, given the vaporizing dissolution of our marriage and earlier relationship, neither of us perceived the possibility of romance between us in our future. And so, we found ourselves in the position of actually being friends.

And that is why I have no earthly idea why thoughts came to mind that day that had nothing to do with The Pride or Winner Tomlinson. My eye was drawn to the heavenly valley that began with that wonderful point on earth where her breasts made themselves known under the DKNY blouse that she wore.

I could barely restrain myself from caressing the line of her jaw and my mind was helpless in recalling all of the times that she permitted the tips of my fingers to float along the almost perfect symmetry of her unforgettable face. Her legs, prominently in view and wonderfully poised on wonderfully stylish heels, formed the demarcation of a universe in which I lived and died a thousand lives of pleasure many millennia ago.

We lived as boyfriend/girlfriend, man and woman, and husband and wife. In all of my experiences with women, before and after Diedre, I have never experienced such wondrous passion and sensuality and physical expression of love. And so, as I sat in *church*, all I could think of was kissing and licking and hugging and holding and sucking and loving—and how wonderful it had all been.

I could literally feel my breaths shorten, my pulse quicken and I could feel myself getting hard—right there in the church, for goodness sakc. I had been with Diedre too often during the ten plus years after our breakup to have these feelings now, I thought. I begged and pleaded with myself not to think the thoughts that had me wanting her in the worst way.

To this very day, I believe that at that moment I only loved Samantha. And I cannot believe that there will ever be a time that I could forget Lisette and all of the sexual wonder that she introduced into my life. Yet, at that moment in time I truly wanted Diedre. It was the first time in a long time and, as it turned out to be, not for the last time.

CHAPTER 23

Paul

Wading in the water

My only escape was to try to somehow pay attention to the proceedings at hand and try to engage her in small talk. My only hope was to try not to think about how I wanted to once again let my tongue and fingers explore that wondrous body under that so elegant St. John's business suit. I struggled mightily and it was only by the grace of the barely subtle carnival that was Winner Tomlinson's service that I was able to succeed.

"Here comes the ringmaster," it was almost as if Diedre was reading my mind. The carnival analogy was hard to miss, if you were paying attention.

She was referring to the Reverend Quincy Holloway, the presiding cleric at the service. If there were no such thing as carnivals and circuses they would have had to invent them for Reverend Holloway. He was the prototypical Jesse Jackson wannabee, dozens of whom proliferate throughout the country, magically sprouting in the glow of television lights and under the penumbra of clustered microphones.

Like any person who dares to reside in the public eye I am sure that Jesse Jackson deserves some of the criticism that has been leveled at him over the years. But few have ever doubted his intelligence, his vision, and his ability to transcend the opinion that others might hold. And, at the end of the day, Jesse Jackson can point to real, substantive accomplishments. He can say that he has helped many people as a part of his life's story.

Reverend Holloway was Jesse Jackson Lite. He simply aspired to be more than he could ever be. And though he was smart enough to know that, he didn't let that hold him back for a nanosecond. He aspired to be more than a local celebrity. He aspired to be more than the national figure that he was. He wanted to be global, he wanted to be intergalactic. He wanted to walk the earth like Cane, the Kung fu icon.

"He certainly doesn't seem to be suffering this morning," I whispered into Diedre's ear. This caused her to gasp in an effort to hold back the paroxysm of laughter that she barely kept from dancing past her lips.

"Perhaps he found a way to ease the pain," was the response that she was barely able to whisper as she grappled with a gale of laughter that would have been slightly inappropriate, to say the least.

We were both poking fun at one of the more bizarre aspects of the legend of Quincy Holloway. Reverend Holloway rose to prominence in the late sixties by claiming to have been hit in Memphis by one of the bullets intended for Dr. Martin Luther King Jr.

For years he ended his speeches with the tearful refrain, "If only I could have taken another bullet." During speeches, sermons and even television talk show appearances, he would regularly and dramatically rip open his shirt and show the scar that still coursed across his magnificently rippled chest.

It was a routine that was a guaranteed crowd killer. Men wept. Women swooned. And I had it on good information that it was more than a rumor that more than a few women, after recovering from their swoon, would be sure that the Right Reverend Holloway got a phone number and an appropriate invitation to "ease the pain" (another surefire line that he regularly used in his speeches). Quincy Holloway had had his pain eased all over the world.

And then one day, about ten years after the death of Dr. King, *Time Magazine* printed a story, complete with hotel receipts, which proved that on April 4, 1968, Quincy Holloway was in Monterey, California, comfortably lodged at the Seven Gables Inn as the very private guest of the notoriously wild and sexy toy industry heiress, Rachel Steinberg.

Most people would have been destroyed and obliterated. Most people would have been erased from the consciousness of the public for all time, except as the object of ridicule and scorn. Most people with a shred of decency or an ounce of self-respect would simply never show their face in public again.

But Quincy Holloway was never like most people. And that explains why Quincy Holloway "kept on keeping on," to borrow one of his pet phrases. I must admit he deserves some perverse credit for his ludicrous tenacity in the face of absolute adversity. *Time Magazine* simply did not understand the nature of their prey and the hunter wound up being captured by the game.

First, Holloway denounced *Time* as being party to a racist plot. Then he tried to organize a nationwide boycott of the publication as punishment for its daring to doubt his veracity as well as its mortal sin of casting aspersions on his credibility.

Then, demonstrating an almost supernatural, gravity-defying ability to confound his tormentors, he called a press conference and tearfully admitted that indeed he was in Monterey on that fateful day. He also "admitted" that the shock and trauma of Martin Luther King's death had so profoundly affected and disturbed "his very soul" that in wishing that he could have been in Memphis he believed that he had been in Memphis.

Amazingly, he managed to trot out two nationally renowned black psychiatrists who confirmed that his story was a classic manifestation of a phenomenon known as "Black Grief." The scar was simply explained as an extraordinary psychosomatic reaction to trauma akin to the stigmata that some Catholics manifest on their bodies when visiting Lourdes or other holy sites. Clearly, all things were possible for Quincy Holloway.

Even some of the most cynical members of the press bought this story. Actually, most black reporters covering this story could barely keep a straight face when Reverend Holloway stood before the cameras with this myth. However, some white writers relied upon the supposition that the mystique and unknowable mystery of black Americans could conceivably include the heretofore unknown malady of "black grief."

Holloway proved once more that, if you are going to tell a lie, make sure to tell a BIG lie. Many people liked his new and improved story better than the original one. From the day of his "confession," Quincy Holloway was bigger than ever. And that's not all.

A few years later, a U.S. Army Ranger on a training mission off the coast of Brazil became disoriented during a parachute jump and landed in the middle of the Amazon jungle. After a few days it was learned that the hapless Ranger was being held captive by an aboriginal tribe that had yet to be "discovered" by Western civilization until this hapless pilot in full battle regalia happened upon their ancestral burial grounds. Understandably, the locals took some offense to this intrusion and were preparing to sacrifice the pilot in order to appease their understandably enraged ancestors.

Up to this point the story was an ordinary twentieth century flight of fantasy. And then the story took on the stuff of which legends are made. The Lost Ranger was black. The Lost Ranger's mother was black. And the Lost Ranger's mother was still young and stunningly attractive.

She was also one of the blessed people of this planet who believed absolutely in whatever it might be that the good Reverend Holloway might say. When it came to Quincy Holloway, she was an impassioned zealot.

As soon as Reverend Holloway laid his eyes on the gorgeous and distraught mother of the Lost Ranger he knew he had found his new cause. He also sensed that he had found yet another way to ease his pain. After meeting privately with her in his suite at the Waldorf Astoria, he had the mother of the Lost Ranger join him in announcing to the hastily assembled press corps that thrived on Quincy Holloway stories that he would immediately fly to Brazil and negotiate the release of the Lost Ranger.

For almost a week CBS, CNN, PBS, BET, NBC, and ABC and the entire world held its collective breath waiting for some word, any word, about the Right Reverend, Very Reverend Quincy Holloway. The last verified word about his rescue mission was that he had parachuted into the Amazon jungle armed only with a cellular telephone and an incredible amount of nerve.

Somehow the cell phone broke during his landing and for one of the few times in the prior twenty years; there was an entire week without any news about Quincy Holloway. This occasioned innumerable prayer vigils and huge crowds staring at phalanxes of television sets in the picture windows of appliance stores throughout the country.

But time did not stand still for Quincy Holloway. As the facts were revealed much later, Reverend Holloway's parachute was blown off course and he wound up landing at a luxury resort in Salvador, in the Bahia province of Brazil, several hundred miles north of Rio de Janeiro. More importantly, he landed far, far away from the aboriginal tribe that was hosting and preparing to roast the Lost Ranger.

I came to learn from some of my contacts at *Ebony* and the *New York Times* that the good reverend not only landed at this luxury resort, but that he rested there for several days. He spent his time having his pain eased and didn't bother to call anyone, not even the grief-stricken and smitten mother of the Lost Ranger.

Eventually he commandeered a jeep and headed toward the fringes of the Amazon jungle. That was when, by pure serendipitous accident, he occasioned upon the Lost Ranger on a dusty road. It turned out that the aboriginal tribal leaders decided that their ancestral gods could be appeased with an act of mercy and he had been released over a week earlier, unharmed and none the worse for wear.

When news of the Quincy Holloway's "rescue" of the Lost Ranger hit the wires it seemed like the entire planet erupted. The world rejoiced. Once again the Reverend Holloway was a true hero. He was now a hero of epic and mythical proportions.

He had found the Lost Sheep. He was indeed the Good Shepherd. When the Reverend Holloway announced the Good News at a press conference at JFK Airport, no one had the nerve to question what had really happened. Of course it may have been that Reverend Holloway just never heard any questions on that subject.

The mother of the Lost Ranger continued to be understandably appreciative. And her gratitude served as a useful explanation of her presence in the hotel room adjoining Reverend Holloway's as he toured the country on his never-ending speaking tours. For years she could be counted on to be a part of the crowd on any podium where Holloway was speaking, leading the trademark Quincy Holloway chant of "Zoom, Quincy, Zoom!"

I knew the real Holloway story. Part of how I have been able to get ahead and stay ahead has been by learning the real story, and it is not always an easy task.

I caught myself about to make a joke to Diedre at the expense of the good reverend as I realized that many people perceived his hambone and chicken leg antics as being real and worthwhile. Many people, black and white, thought of Quincy Holloway as a real leader, a true and reliable spokesman.

But it was impossible for me to say nothing. I used the excuse of the birth of yet another witty, pithy comment to lean close to Diedre and whisper closely into her ear.

"You have to admire the right reverend for the discreet way in which he always gets more bacon with his eggs and gravy with his biscuits." I could immediately see that my comment had hit home as she yet again was forced to stifle a laugh. And then, to my surprise, she turned to speak in *my* ear and made a comment that I found more than interesting.

"Now Paul, you know that at the end of the day that's what we all are doing. Or did Dartmouth, Harvard, and that Armani suit come with a high horse as an accessory?"

I didn't have the good sense to let it go that morning.

"Diedre, please . . . Quincy hasn't had something original to say since Muhammad Ali was Cassius Clay. He has been an opinion maker even though the only opinions that I know of him influencing have been the ones belonging to members of the press."

"And you know as well as I do, that the only thing that keeps Quincy going are contributions," Diedre responded, "many of them from your clients. And I wouldn't be surprised to find out that a few of your checks have helped him make his payments on his suite at the Waldorf!"

"*Touché, mon cherie. Touché.*" Her perfume and her very presence were intoxicating. I remember wondering how that could be. It would be later that I came to understand.

She was right, however, and there was nothing more for me to say. At the end of the day Holloway and his crowd were looking to be a part of the action. And he was a part of the action, a player in the game, no matter what anyone might say about him.

Frankly, I did not have any more time to think about this latter day Knight of the Mystic See Me. As solemn as Winner's memorial service might be, there was business to attend to and there was never enough time. I started to focus on how this event might be something more than just a time to renew acquaintance.

And that's when the vision began to take its nascent shape in my mind. After all, Gordon Perkins was there. Jerome Hardaway was there. Diedre was there. We were all in the same room, although on very different missions.

I thought, when was the last time that the four of us had a serious discussion? We had been at innumerable dinners, bars, nightclubs, fund-raisers and cocktail parties. But when was the last time the four of us had a serious conversation? It had been years, if ever.

And then I thought—by the time the service was over and all of the hellos and goodbyes were uttered, most of the day was going to be shot anyway. Certainly the meaningful part of the business day would be gone by the time they got behind their respective desks.

A late working lunch was not the product of any grand inspiration at the time; it just seemed like a good idea. Later I would learn it was one of the best ideas that I ever had.

CHAPTER 24

Sture

Standing in the shadows

The memorial service ended pretty much the way that I had expected. Although this is not my native land and I was not with my Norwegian brothers and sisters, there is no way someone could work at Dorothy's By the Sea and not have a good idea of the order of the day. There were the speeches by Reverend Jackson and Reverend Holloway—and the mayor and the governor as well as a letter from the president that was read by Ed Bradley of *60 Minutes*. There were the obligatory tears from the family, but no wailing or rolling in the aisles.

As an immigrant to this country, I had learned from experience to always expect the possibility of extreme histrionics at black funerals. I was, therefore, somewhat surprised at how quiet and dignified the Tomlinson service turned out to be. The Winner Tomlinson that I knew would probably have been disappointed.

I also noted the obvious wheeling and dealing that was going on among the "mourners." As the manager of Dorothy's By the Sea, I knew many of the mourners by face, if not by name. I knew their ways and their habits, their likes and dislikes.

It was no surprise to me that there was a cynical, businesslike aspect to the post-mourning. By the end of the service, it was as if the mourners were at a reception or fund-raiser and business was taking place like it was high noon at the stock exchange. After proper respects were paid, there was a clear need to take care of business, and as I stood on the steps of the Riverside Church that time was clearly at hand.

There was Paul Taylor, noticeably elegant yet understated as usual, gliding through the crowd. He seemed to be using the "Zen" approach that he had told me about, moving without moving, through the crowd. I could not help but see him speaking with Gordon Perkins first, then Jerome Hardaway, and then easing back over to Diedre Douglas.

I don't really remember Diedre and Paul being separated, even with all of his moving about. At the time there was nothing to take note of and I suspected that it was just my imagination running away with me, as the song goes. In retrospect, after all that would happen in the coming months, I realize now that I was watching the magic of romance and the miracle of business creation taking place at the same time.

At some point I found myself watching one of our former employees from Dorothy's, Alexander Lapidoulos, holding the car door, waiting for Gordon and Kenitra Perkins to get into the Mercedes Benz sedan for which he was the driver. In the blink of an eye I saw Gordon roughly grasping Kenitra's wrist as they headed to the car.

I had heard that for several years Gordon had used a car service. But Gordon hated waiting for anything. And even the best car service might have to have their best clients wait every now and then. And finally there was a point when Gordon decided he needed a car and driver. And so now he had a car and driver.

Ultimately that car was a Mercedes. And instead of a service, there was an employed driver whom Gordon could hire and fire at will (Alexander was Gordon's fourth driver in two years. On this January day that driver was the former headwaiter at Dorothy's, and my friend, Alexander Lapidoulos).

From conversations with him I knew that for Alex, working for Gordon Perkins meant getting out of the daily grind of being a head waiter while retaining a basis for having his green card renewed so that he could stay in this country. He was still a long way from citizenship. It was after only a few weeks into the job that he discovered that his biggest problem and the greatest benefit to the job was . . . Kenitra Perkins.

What do you tell a friend when he is playing with dynamite, plutonium and the Ebola virus at the same time? Not a lot when that lethal combination is wrapped up in a package as gorgeous as Kenitra Perkins.

Alex might have been an immigrant waiter from a small town two hundred miles north of Athens, but he was not blind, although clearly he was an unredeemable fool. He could recognize a lonely, neglected and needy woman, and Kenitra was certainly all of that . . . and a whole lot more.

He later told me that glances returned in his rearview mirror turned into innocent conversation, which turned into double entendre, which turned into not so accidental touching, which turned into lovemaking in the backseat of the Mercedes station wagon, the penthouse, his apartment—whenever and wherever they could.

It was a recipe for disaster. They both knew it. And when Alex told me, I knew it as well. And I tried to tell him. Of course he wouldn't, couldn't listen.

But Alex was not a complete fool. He knew the dangers in making love to the wife of a rich and powerful and mean and violent and vicious man. I know. I told him too many times myself. But when it came to Kenitra Perkins, he could neither help himself nor stop himself. He guessed that he was in love and that she was too.

But he didn't know about her "helpers." In fact, he had no idea. He naively thought that the pills that she took so regularly were vitamins. After all he was in America where everyone was so ostentatiously health-conscious.

In truth, even if he knew, it probably wouldn't have made him act any differently. You would have had to have seen Kenitra Perkins in a simple black dress, high heels, and a simple strand of pearls around that most gorgeous of necks to understand. Eighteen months of marriage to Gordon Perkins had not defeated her beauty, her aura. She was still the most gorgeous woman that most men had ever seen.

She was tall, she was lithe. Her body was so simple, so limber; she seemed to enter a room on the breath of angels. She had skin the color of soft, warm caramel on a sunny day. Her hair was a light brown that was an absolutely perfect complement to her skin and her gray-green eyes gave her the look of some wonderful alien from the planet Aphrodisia.

And then there was her smile. When she smiled that genuine, real, 100 percent pure smile, it seemed to light a thousand rainbows in the beholder's universe. Her smile gave promise to every hope that a man could have. In a word, she was gorgeous.

She was not perfect. A perfectionist would say that her breasts could have been larger. Some of the cattier tongues meowed that her naturally undulating hips would one day be too wide.

As a native of Norway I can tell you that in Oslo there are no ugly women. They are all beautiful. And also I know that all the men in Oslo would leave home forever just for the chance to spend a day or a night with Kenitra Perkins. Beauty is never perfect. Beauty just is. And Kenitra was the literal embodiment of real beauty.

Moreover, she willed herself to be even more beautiful. She spent the time, the effort, the money, perspective to make herself as beautiful as she could possibly be. As a result, her teeth, her hair, her skin, her nails, her clothes, her shoes—were all perfect.

I watched that day as Gordon led, almost dragged Kenitra to the car where Alex was standing at the ready—the door to the backseat already open. Anyone who was looking could see that they dared not look at each other in Gordon's presence. Of course, Gordon was not paying attention. He practically threw Kenitra into the backseat and ordered Alex to take her home.

"Alex, get your fucking ass in gear! I've got business to take care of, take this bitch home," was all that Gordon said.

"I'll see you when you get home," was something Gordon never heard Kenitra say. The dawning smile on Alex's and Kenitra's faces was something he never saw. It was probably just as well.

I have to believe that there was a cauldron of rage, jealousy and pain boiling inside Alex. He was a man, after all.

But I have to hand it to him. He never revealed his true feelings. Not a bit. He simply tipped his hat and bid his employer a good day. Alexander simply and carefully pulled the car away from the curb in front of the Riverside Church, looped around Grant's Tomb and headed downtown on Riverside Drive.

During his time working at Dorothy's, I came to know Alex pretty well. As one immigrant to another, I understood his heart, his spirit. As you might say here, "I knew where he was coming from." I can't say that we were close friends at the time, but after he left the restaurant to work for Gordon Perkins (with my recommendation, I might add), Alex would share quite a bit about his affair with Kenitra Perkins.

It was a fascinating story, and he had to tell someone. I guess that's why he told me. He later told me about what happened after he drove down Riverside Drive. I have every reason to believe that it's true.

CHAPTER 25

Alex and Kenitra

Stolen moments

As she sat in the backseat of the car, Kenitra watched the world go by in a barbiturate haze that somehow made her mostly miserable life a little better. It was a life that had seen her on the cover of *Vanity Fair*, *Cosmopolitan*, and dozens of other magazines just two short, miserable years ago. And now she was sneaking quickies in the backseat of her husband's car with her husband's driver—and no other life to speak of—aside from her "helpers."

The "helpers," various barbiturates, antidepressants and other pharmaceutical miracle pills helped her to survive. She was also not averse to cocaine when she could get it. Kenitra Perkins was a survivor. She even planned to survive Gordon Perkins.

For the moment Alex helped make her life better. He was her husband's driver, her lover and her friend. He helped her to survive.

That day, she found herself focusing on the back of Alex's head, thinking and reflecting. She thought about her life. She reflected on Gordon, her husband/abuser/tormentor. She thought about Alex, her husband's driver. She thought about sex.

Alex was twenty-three at the time. Six feet, four inches tall and built like the proverbial Greek god. Being that she was a few years older than Alex and a lot more experienced in the ways of sex and love, she naturally fell into the role of mentor in their relationship. In the few months that they had been lovers, she had taught him all that she knew. In other words, she taught him a lot. Probably even more than Gordon Perkins ever knew.

"Did you miss me?"

"You know that I did."

"I don't know a damn thing. You haven't said a word since you were dismissed by your master."

"I wish you wouldn't play these games, Kenitra. You know that I missed you. You know that!"

"I'm not playing, Alex. Did you miss me? It seems like a pretty simple question to me."

"I won't play your games anymore, Kenitra. You are driving me crazy. You know how I feel."

"Oh really? Tell me, darling. How do you feel?"

"You know that I miss you. I need you. I live and breathe you, Kenitra. The thought of that son of a bitch putting his hands on you, makes me want to . . ."

"How noble, Alex. How very, very noble. So very noble coming from a *driver*. And very Greek, I must say."

Alex didn't find out until later that the latest barbiturates that Kenitra had taken were just starting to take effect. Kenitra figured that she would say damn well whatever she wanted to say—whatever was on her mind. At that moment, she wasn't quite clear as to what that might be. But that was not her problem. It was bad enough that she had to take shit from Gordon day and night, night and day. Alex would just have to deal with it.

"Why do you speak to me so? You know how I feel. You say that you have feelings for me. Don't you?"

"Of course I have feelings for you, Alex. I recall telling you that right here in the backseat of this car . . . just the other day. Do you want me to tell you again?"

"You know that I do."

"Are you really *sure*?"

"Why do you play with me so?"

"Okay darling, no more playing. Really. We are at 86th Street, correct?"

"Yes, Kenitra."

"Good. Pull the car into the parking area by the 79th Street boat basin. I know you remember the place. I'll say it again when we get there."

It was all that Alex could do to control himself and the car as he headed to the 79th Street ramp off Riverside Drive. He certainly did remember the place and also remembered all the things that Kenitra could do with her hands and lips and tongue and seemingly every other part of her body.

They had made love at that particular spot several times. It was never busy during the middle of the day. It was amazing how somebody could hide in broad daylight in the middle of Manhattan.

He carefully maneuvered Gordon Perkins's car and wife into a parking place that was discreetly distanced from the other cars that were there, probably for the same reason. It was a cold day. But it was not too cold to even begin to chill the burning embers in his heart, his soul and his groin.

Alex recalled that he took his hat off and placed it on the passenger seat. He began to unbutton his tunic as he got out of the car. By the time he opened the door to the backseat he realized that Kenitra had not been idle.

She had already unbuttoned the front of her dress as he closed the door behind him. Kneeling before her beauty and lowering his head into the hot and moist wonderland that was offered to him, he realized that she hadn't bothered to wear anything under that dress. As her long and tapered fingers held her lips apart his tongue entered her and they both died and went to heaven once more.

CHAPTER 26

Paul

Step by step

I noticed Gordon walking back to the crowd in front of the church. While he seemed to have been born with a perpetual scowl, I had learned long ago that it was usually for effect. Gordon was at his most dangerous when he was smiling.

"Paul. What's going on?"

"Not much, brother. You look particularly bereaved and mournful. I know you are going to miss Winner so much."

"Fuck you. Don't start with me, motherfucker. What's on your mind?"

Gordon actually said that smiling. Gordon was now presenting what had to suffice as his most genuine and sincere expression of "friendship." Actually, in the universe of Gordon Stallworth Perkins, there were no real friends. Nevertheless I was probably one of the few people who Gordon might think of as a "friend." So that's where his smile was coming from. At least that is what I thought.

"You know, I was thinking . . . it's already after noon and not a lot is going to get done in the office today. What do you think about a few of us having lunch?"

"Who the fuck is 'us'?"

"I was thinking you, Diedre, Jerome, and I might head over to the Water Club and grab a bite and talk things over. I have a few ideas that I want to bounce off you guys."

You could almost see a frenzy of calculation and strategizing going on in Gordon's brain as he processed this information. Where was the advantage for him? Where was the advantage for anyone else? How could he take advantage? Would he miss something if he didn't go?

I know that Gordon knew that I had better things to do than to waste his time. If I suggested a lunch meeting like this one, there had to be something to it. He just couldn't figure out what it was right off the bat. His curiosity alone demanded that he go to lunch that day. I knew that.

I also knew that he was not crazy about either Jerome or Diedre. He thought that Diedre was a stuck-up bitch who was always looking down her nose at him as if she smelled something foul. He thought of Jerome as a holier-than-thou phony who couldn't be as good as he pretended. No one was perfect, of course.

It drove Gordon crazy that he could not figure out who Jerome Hardaway really was. That was just pure Gordon Perkins.

But Gordon also knew that Diedre was smart. And, in his universe, Jerome was even smarter. It was also pure Gordon Perkins to acknowledge reality to himself.

"I'm game. I just have to be somewhere by four, so if we are going to do this, let's get going. I don't have all fucking day, even for a smart-ass motherfucker like you."

This would have to pass as an RSVP from Gordon. I had already spoken to Jerome and Diedre about lunch and they were on board. The train was getting ready to leave the station. My first job, finishing the guest list, was complete. My next challenge was to get all three into a car and on to lunch sometime soon. It was like herding cats.

CHAPTER 27

Diedre

Slowly I turned, step by step

I found myself wondering what this lunch that Paul had mentioned was all about. And then I was looking at Paul walking toward Mayor Dinkins. With all the business that he did with the City of New York, and hoped to do, it made sense to me. He was paying homage. At the very least, he was paying attention.

And then I found myself, for reasons that to this day I still can't quite explain, wondering if my hair looked all right. At the time of Winner's service, my feelings about Paul were more than decidedly mixed.

With my heels, I am about five feet nine inches tall. I had just celebrated my fortieth birthday in the Fiji Islands. With the help of my personal trainer I would like to think that I kept myself in pretty decent shape.

I am a banker and a business owner. For me, gorgeous is a considered decision. When I dress for the day I have to think about what a man would think. If my clothing plays into the Woman-as-Whore mind-set that too many men live by, any meeting would be ruined for me.

On the other hand, if my appearance is too severe, then I play into the Woman-as-Bitch mind-set that the rest of the men live by. Again, any meeting that I would be at would be ruined. I have some fishnet stockings and some black decidedly mini dresses and impossibly high stiletto heels at home, but that will remain an unknowable fantasy for most of the men I know.

I have had to walk the fine line between the two extremes. It wasn't easy, but frankly, I am glad that is still the case. Too many men I meet are wondering how they can fuck me and the rest have decided that they don't want to and spend time trying to deal with their own, counterintuitive, decision.

But I found myself thinking about my hair. I live in an eight-room duplex in SoHo. And my "Wall Street" office is in midtown. There are a lot of hair salons that I could use, nevertheless, every Thursday afternoon or Saturday morning I get a car to take me uptown to Leila's on St. Nicholas Avenue in Harlem.

At Leila's no one cares that I probably have been the most successful black woman to ever walk Wall Street. At Leila's, a *real* black woman's hair salon run by women from the Dominican Republic, I am just another well-dressed sister coming to get my hair done. And that's good enough for me.

And then I saw Paul and found myself wondering about my goddamn hair again. And then he started walking toward me. And, if I live to be one hundred, I will remember every word that was spoken for the rest of that day.

At the time having a legitimate excuse to be around Paul was all I needed. But I would have thrown back a dozen cyanide shooters before I would have let him know that at the time. Even now he doesn't need to know that.

"Paul, I'm willing to wait until lunch to hear about your 'bright idea.' After all it is your treat. But what does goddamn Gordon Perkins have to do with it?"

Not surprisingly, he was prepared for this. He knew that Gordon was not particularly popular with anyone in The Pride. His was not the favorite person with anyone on the planet Earth for that matter.

"I'm shocked at what you say, Diedre. Gordon speaks so highly of you. I know how you feel, but you know I wouldn't waste your time."

"You've wasted enough of my time, Paul."

"Ouch, Diedre! That was way below the belt."

Frankly, as I look back on that conversation, I realize that I was harsher than I intended. As I looked at the expression on Paul's face,

I realized that I had gone too far. There was nothing I could say or do, however, except move on and try not to dwell on my too obvious *faux pas*.

"All I have to say, Paul, is that I know that you wouldn't waste my time. I have to assume this is about business."

"It's not about the Fiji Islands, darling," Paul said, as he headed to another packet of Friends of Paul.

It didn't seem as if my comment bothered him one way or the other. Who would know? But how the hell did he find out about the Fiji Islands? Damn!

Paul had spotted Jerome and Charmaine Hardaway. He had had a chance to mention this impromptu luncheon on the way out of the church. As Jerome and his wife were heading for the black Chevy Suburban that had pulled up to the curb, he spoke to Jerome. I knew that Paul believed that confirming never hurt. After all, he wouldn't get a chance to get the four of us together at a luncheon table for a long time.

As her battle with multiple sclerosis got worse it became increasingly difficult for Dr. Charmaine Hardaway to attend, and endure, events like the Tomlinson memorial service. It was not just the time and energy. It was the reminder of what she could no longer do. She couldn't even just walk across the room and engage in a casual conversation.

She also had to ignore the pitying glances that somehow she always saw, even if it was only out of the corner of her eye. She always saw. And she was always racked by the guilty feeling that somehow, someway, because of her infirmity, she was holding Jerome back. She just didn't know.

It was always amazing to me how patient and caring and devoted that Jerome could be. Way past any reasonable expectations.

But, if Jerome felt frustrated, cheated, burdened . . . he absolutely never showed it. Not to Charmaine. Not to their children. Not to any member of The Pride. Not to anybody on the planet. Not a glimpse. Not a flash.

Cynics, many of whom were charter members of The Pride, just had to come to the conclusion that he was that improbable being, the Good Man.

I always figured that, as far as Jerome was concerned, he had given his word to a good woman and that was that. Not everyone understood that, and Jerome really never gave a good goddamn.

As I walked up to Jerome and Charmaine, I knew that Charmaine had enough trouble in her life without having people hovering, feeling sorry for her. I put her disability as far out of my mind as I possibly could. I have to confess, however, I always wonder when I see the two of them—how would I handle such a situation if my life was like Charmaine's? I listened to Paul.

"Charmaine, Jerome, always great to see you! Sorry it has to be under these circumstances—but you both look great. Actually, not you Jerome, but Charmaine, you are as gorgeous as ever. You must have a pact with the devil. You sold your soul so you would never grow old. Right?"

"Paul, you are a liar, but don't you dare stop."

"Charmaine, you are going to hate me for this . . ."

"Again?"

"Charmaine, I'm crushed."

"Sure, Paul. Where do you need Jerome to be this time?" At least she was smiling.

"Well, Charmaine, I need to borrow your devoted boy toy to lunch, right now, for just a couple of hours. You know I wouldn't take him from you if it wasn't important."

"You know I understand, Paul."

Up to this point Jerome had not said a single word. For a man who was so loving, caring, and all of that, he spoke his next words without a single degree of warmth. I knew as I heard the tone of his voice that Jerome was exactly the right choice to be at this luncheon.

"Paul knows that I can get my own meals. So I know that this lunch has to be important. How are we traveling?"

"I have a car picking us up in about ten minutes."

The look in his eyes told me that he had a lot of questions about this luncheon. First there was the "Gordon" factor. Plain and simple, no one liked him. And the road to his success was littered with the bones of his partners.

As far as I knew, he and I were O.K. But having lunch with Paul and me was not reason enough for Jerome to change his plans of spending an afternoon at home with his wife.

"See you in a few minutes. Charmaine, please let me know when your lost twin sister comes back to town. You know she is the answer to my dreams." There wasn't much point in Paul trying to dance with Jerome. Either he was coming or he wasn't.

As I was walking off to engage in a few "maintenance" conversations before the ride to the Water Club I heard Jerome speaking to Paul over my shoulder.

"By the way, Paul, Ray Beard is going to come with me. That won't be a problem, will it?"

Paul turned to object. He clearly had a plan in mind. One look in Jerome's eyes told me that it would be useless for Paul to argue.

"No problem at all. See you in a few minutes, Jerome. I'll let you know when our car gets here."

Paul's face did not betray his momentary frustration. In due course, Jerome would regret having invited Raymond Russell Beard II. But at the time, who knew?

CHAPTER 28

Diedre

Come one, come all

Watching Paul go to get Gordon, Jerome, myself, and now Ray Beard, in the same vicinity as the area where the limousine was pulling up was a hoot. I have heard Paul use the expression "herding cats." Paul was herding cats. Except I think cats would have been easier.

All of us had something to say to somebody. Or so it seemed. I almost felt sorry for Paul. He seemed like he had the job of social director on the SS *Pride*.

He finally got everyone into the car and we headed off to the Water Club. This turned out to be a good thing. And then again, in retrospect, maybe it was not such a good thing.

On the one hand, this meant that everyone who was going to be at lunch was in the same car, contemplating their own personal strategy, their reason for coming, the counterstrategy of their fellow passengers. And most important, all of us were trying to figure out what the hell Paul had in mind by inviting us to lunch.

I wasn't in the habit of biting the hand that fed me. But none of us needed a free lunch. Something important was going on. That was certain.

On the other hand, this meant that all of the passengers had to be regaled by a literally endless stream of bizarre, mindless, quasi-off-color jokes that seemed to be Gordon Perkins's sole purpose for living. Here's the only one that I can remember but it gives a pretty good idea of what we endured during the thirty minute ride from the Riverside Church to the Water Club:

> *A traveling zoo went out of business and a farmer bought one of the young female zebras that was put up for sale. He brought her back to his farm and let her out in the field to meet the other animals on his property.*
>
> *The zebra goes up to the chicken and said, "I'm a zebra, what do you do?" The chickens explained that they laid eggs and that the farmer picked up their eggs every day, ate some, and took the rest to market.*
>
> *Then she went up to the cow and said, "I'm a zebra, what do you do?" The cows explained that they gave milk and that the farmer drinks some of the milk and takes the rest to the market.*
>
> *Then the zebra goes up to the old bull and says, "I'm a zebra, what do you do?" The old bull appraises this exotic, young, nubile creature and says, "If you take off those striped pajamas I'll show you what I do around here!"*

The alleged punch line to the joke was accompanied by an incredibly loud, "Har, Har, Har!" courtesy of Gordon Perkins. His laugh sounded like sand in a garbage disposal by way of Ralph Cramden. But he sounded like he was enjoying himself so much that some people have said that his laugh was infectious. But then, so is typhus.

I hope that I didn't look like I felt that my flesh was crawling—although that is exactly how I felt by the time I saw the East River. Jerome laughed in a semi-polite fashion, I guess because he figured that if he didn't laugh there might be an encore. Raymond Russell Beard II just smiled a smile that meant whatever anyone wanted it to mean.

Gordon, of course didn't give a damn. One of his traits that I both hated and had to grudgingly admire. He knew that almost everybody found him to be annoying and obnoxious. If you worked for him or with him, he could be hell. But he really didn't give a damn. He didn't care what anybody thought about him. And not too many people can make that statement.

By the time our car pulled into the driveway of the Water Club, I believe that Gordon had told what was probably his fifth joke. This one was about a midget rabbi, a lesbian acrobat, and a Mexican priest with a cleft palate and a club foot. Mercifully, before some vile and unspeakable punch line, the car stopped and one of the valets opened the door, cutting Gordon off as everyone got out of the car, barely concealing our collective relief.

As Jerome's right-hand man, Raymond Russell Beard II, exited the car and headed for the entrance of the Water Club, I couldn't help but reflect on what I knew, and didn't know about him. He was the son of a prominent Atlanta minister who in turn was a scion of one of the leading black families in that city.

He graduated from Yale at the age of nineteen. He graduated from Stanford Law School at the age of twenty-two. After clerking for a United States Supreme Court Justice, Ray decided to defy convention and come and work with Paul rather than join any one of the number of major New York law firms that was clamoring for his services.

Ray wound up working a lot on the Hardaway firm account that Paul's office was handling for Jerome. As a result he and Jerome came to know each other quite well.

Stevie Wonder could see that Ray's star was on the rise, and after a couple of years Jerome made Ray an offer to join his firm as a senior vice president. I also know for a fact that he cleared all of this with Paul.

Now, making about a half a million dollars a year with the Hardaway firm, everyone knew that the best was yet to come for Raymond Russell Beard II. Ray Beard was on the path of myth to legend to eternal star, at least in his own personal universe.

With the build of an athlete, movie star good looks, and a mind like a computerized steel trap, Ray was the kind of man that women loved to love and men loved to admire. It was almost biologically impossible to dislike Ray. And he knew it.

Yet, there was something about Ray that just didn't ring true. It was almost as if he was just too perfect. To me, it was as if his perfection was masking some grand imperfection that was impossible to discern if you got too close. It was a flaw that you would never see from afar.

I couldn't figure it out. At least I couldn't figure it out at the time of our luncheon at the Water Club.

I had been to the Water Club many times, mostly during the time that Paul and I were together. Since we had parted ways I had not frequented the place as much. I did not see the need to dance on cold ashes.

But I knew, from casual conversations with other members of The Pride, that Paul continued to escort his "ladies du jour" to the restaurant. It was understandable; it was always a great place to dine.

As Buzzy O'Keefe came to the front of the restaurant to greet the luncheon party, I saw him cast an almost quizzical imperceptible glance toward Paul. It happened so fast you really had to pay attention to catch it.

I guess I could appreciate Buzzy's concern regarding the possibility of an awkward moment. But of course, Paul and I were long past all of that.

Buzzy led our party through the restaurant to a table in the northeast corner. An excellent choice as it turned out, as all of us had an excellent view of the East River and its eclectic *mélange* of aquatic traffic—yachts, barges, oil tankers, speedboats, and the occasional J-24 testing its sails in the dead of winter. The table also afforded our conversation all the privacy that was possible in such a public place.

"Thanks, Buzzy. Much appreciated."

"Great to see all of you. Paul, if you need anything just call me. I'll send a waiter over right away."

Buzzy discreetly nodded to me as he headed away from the table. I doubt that anyone at the table even noticed.

Probably not, particularly in light of the sideshow that took place next to our table. It was a fitting prelude to the main event.

There is an old expression about it being better to be lucky than good. On this particular day, Ray Beard was both.

At the table closest to ours were three women celebrating the birthday of one of their party. The birthday girl was Monique Lafarge Jefferson, the newly arrived evening anchor on the Fox television affiliate. She was a native of New Orleans, and I have to hand it to a girl-friend, she was an extremely attractive woman.

She was as gorgeous as the sky was blue, with the kind of attractive Creole charm that could make the monkeys want to throw down their bananas and come down out of the trees. She looked that good.

And then she looked at Raymond Russell Beard II. And he looked at her. Even now, "Wow" is the first description that comes to mind.

It was like being at Alamagordos or the Bikini atoll. It was nothing short of being a witness to a nuclear reaction. When Ray looked into Monique's hazel orbs he was helpless. You could almost hear his heart carrying the drumbeat of *The 1812 Overture,* his hands morphing into the front paws of a willing lapdog. Forever.

But I could tell that Monique was also in deep water, with the *Jaws* theme playing loud and clear. Ray Beard was no shepherd boy just off the farm. It would take another woman to see it—girlfriend was trying to be cool—but she was one step from having that facade just dripping and dribbling away, pooling at her feet.

I have to hand it to Ray. He was helpless but not hapless. As Paul, Jerome, and Gordon began to notice that there was some interaction between our table and the adjoining one, Ray found a way to ease himself into the consciousness of the birthday table.

"It seems that it's somebody's birthday," he said, his eyes focused on Monique Jefferson like a laser-guided missile. I remember that listening to him that afternoon, the first impression that came to mind was warm maple syrup on hot new waffles.

"As a matter of fact it is," a voice piped up. It was Summer Spring Winters, a leading gossip columnist for one of New York's competing tabloids. Her mission in life was to dish the dirt.

She had seen Ray Beard come in as part of a luncheon party. And, as best I could tell, and fortunately for Ray, she immediately succumbed to her overwhelming desire to be an intergalactic match-maker.

Ray displayed skills that made it clear why he was a star on the rise. He did not "diss" Summer Winter, but he did stay focused on the prize.

"Forgive me for being inquisitive. I was hoping that I could send the birthday girl a drink, perhaps later today, since I can see that she is busy right now." All the time never taking his eyes off Monique Jefferson.

I may have been born at night. But it wasn't last night. Ray was praying, really praying, that Summer was not the birthday girl, celebrating her fortieth birthday for the fifteenth time. And then, his prayers were answered.

"It would be my pleasure, Mr. . . . ." Monique spoke with a voice that reminded me of peach ice cream on a Georgia farm. When she spoke I could almost taste the cream, the bits and pieces of fresh succulent peaches with just enough sugar to last a lifetime. I can only imagine the effect that it had on Ray Beard.

"Ray, Raymond Beard. Happy birthday, Ms. Jefferson. Even Stevie Wonder would recognize the newest star in New York City. It's my pleasure."

His combination of flattery, adoration, and appreciation would be devastating to most women that I know. As I remember, Monique handled his rhetorical charge of the light brigade with a smile and a business card that would precipitate a call later in the day. I knew that call would not be about the latest headlines.

Good fortune was with Ray. All of this happened within a few brief moments. While Gordon, Paul, and Jerome may have noticed the exchange, they paid no attention whatsoever, what with the shuffle of tables and chairs and the to and fro of waiters, busboys and all of that. But I remember. I did not realize the significance of the encounter until much, much later.

And then we were all settled at our luncheon table. And, thankfully, Paul and Jerome were able to keep enough small talk going to prevent Gordon from relaunching into his seemingly infinite series of raunchy jokes. It is hard, even now, to convey my feelings of relief.

Everyone ordered their cocktails, appetizers and luncheon entrées. I somehow remember that Paul ordered a Long Flat Australian wine for the table. The first meeting of The Pride in the post-Winner Tomlinson era was about to be called to order. Paul was presiding.

Just as Paul was getting ready to speak, I caught Ray stealing one last glance at Monique Jefferson who, while getting up from her table with her luncheon companions, boldly (I thought) returned the stare. If one looked closely, you could almost see the beams of psychic energy tracing the path from one soul to another. Then it was time to get to work.

Even at the time, before I knew what Paul had in mind, I had a premonition that this was one of those historical moments. At the time I did not know how right I was. After the appetizers were served, Paul cleared his throat and I can remember most of the conversations of the day as if they were yesterday.

"You know, this is a sad and serious moment. Before we begin we should at least raise a glass in a toast in memory of our friend Winner."

"Where I come from, we pour a libation for the brothers that can't be here."

And then I heard Jerome Hardaway. The voice was unmistakable.

"Paul, you pour your drink on the floor if you want to . . . I'm going to toast the brother, have a drink and move on."

If it had been anyone other that Jerome Hardaway no one would have had a second thought. But Jerome chose that moment to reveal a harder edge than most of us knew existed. As things turned out, we all had a lot to learn about each other.

CHAPTER 29

Paul

A journey of a thousand miles begins

As I recall that afternoon, there was no real point in trying to make things too formal. This had to be something more than just another "friendly" luncheon, with nothing accomplished but running up the tab on someone's Amex card. It was getting quiet in the Water Club, as it was getting toward the end of the weekday lunch hour. I don't recall that any of us noticed the noise of waiters bustling about, clearing tables and moving dishes.

Jerome, Gordon, Diedre, Ray, and I placed our orders, and there was almost an internal silence that we experienced. It was as if we all realized that there was a real purpose for our coming together that day.

We simply failed to notice the sound of the East River high fiving the moorings of the barge on which the Water Club perched. We barely took note of the appetizers as they were being served. I would imagine that there was something about my tone, demeanor, and my choice of words that made everyone know that somehow, someway, this could be a very special moment. Somehow, on this sunny winter afternoon, it all seemed different. I know that I felt different that day.

I don't recall exactly what I said that day. But I do know that, even though I had not prepared remarks, there were some points that I had to get across, and I think that I did.

"Listen, I know that you probably have been trying to figure out exactly why I asked all of you to lunch today . . ."

"Not really. A free lunch on your tab is good enough for me." Of course that would be Gordon.

"You look like you haven't missed too many meals without my help, that's for sure."

"Don't be so mean, Paul. You're about to make me cry!"

"Gordon, Paul—I am sure that we would all *love* the full length version of your Amos 'n Andy routine, but I think we all might have something better to do." I knew that I could count on Diedre to keep us somewhat focused.

"When you are right, you are right, Diedre. Gordon, with your permission, let me get to the point."

"I thought you would never get around to it. Carry on my brother, carry on."

It was at about this point that the waiters brought the entrées and the wine was served. This all took a few minutes which provided the perfect break before getting to the serious part of the discussion.

After the various sorting out of condiments, sipping of wine, tasting of entrées and savoring of the various components of the meal, I knew that it was time to get the discussion back on course. I took a few bites from my plate and tried to resume. My meal could wait.

I am used to articulating my thoughts using the spoken word. I have spoken before thousands at bar association meetings (both the American Bar Association, which used to have an absolute ban against black lawyers, and the National Bar Association, which was formed by black lawyers in response). I have spoken in boardrooms and courtrooms and I truly believe in my ability to explain and persuade. But this time was going to be different—challenging and interesting.

I remember that as I cleared my throat I wished that I could somehow read the minds of some of my closest friends and colleagues. I felt like I was sprinting through a familiar room while blindfolded—and with the furniture having been moved, if only slightly. One false move and I might break a toe, or worse.

"I have a plan that I want all of you to think about. I think I know all of you well enough to ask you to consider what I am going to say with your minds, not your feelings.

"All of you will probably think that what I am about to say is making no sense—at least at first. But I am telling you, this plan can make history, and a lot of money, for all of us."

"How much money, Paul?" It was Gordon again. Of course.

"I'm going to get to that, Gordon. Give me a minute."

"I'm listening too." It was Jerome. It was good to know that I had his attention. It was time to press on.

"Gordon, Diedre, Jerome—we are all friends and colleagues at this table, and we can be honest. We all have a pretty good idea as to how well each of you and all of you are doing in business these days. Ray, your contribution to Jerome's business is well known, so we can move on.

"I happen to know that each of you receives a couple of offers to sell or merge every year. If you had taken any one of these offers, you would never have to work again. And neither would your grandchildren."

At this point in the luncheon I *really* wished that I could have read minds. Glances flashed across the table like invisible lasers. Everyone's mind was working in overdrive. If I had to guess, my bet would have been that the unspoken thoughts of my guests went something like this:

Diedre: I haven't seen Paul like this in years . . . maybe ever. What *does* he have on his mind? I just can't figure out where he's going with this . . .

Gordon: What *is* this motherfucker talking about now? If it was so fucking important, why the fuck is he telling all of us, including that faggot Ray Beard? . . . Damn, that Jefferson bitch is fine . . . great set of lips too; I bet she gives great head.

Jerome: As usual, my best bet is to be quiet. I am not quite sure what Paul is getting at, but I would bet that he wants all of us to work together on something. . . . what? He is going through a whole lot just to get us to support somebody's campaign. It's got to be more than that. But what crazy scheme could involve him, Diedre, me, *and* Gordon. Jesus, what a lowlife son of a bitch! I will never understand how someone who is so successful and smart can be such an asshole. Amazing!

Raymond: I guess it's a good thing that Jerome wanted me at this luncheon—actually, I'm damn glad, since I got to meet Monique over there. Damn, that's one fine female! And why is Gordon looking at me like that? I can't stand that motherfucker, and I guess the feeling is mutual. What the hell is Paul talking about? I just cannot follow where he is going with a luncheon speech to an audience of four.

"As I was saying, I don't want to make a luncheon speech. Not that any of you would let me. But I need to get a few things on the table for all of you to consider. After all, and please excuse me for getting a little dramatic, but it's rare that you know that history is being made while it is being made . . ."

"A little dramatic?" I knew that I could count on Diedre to keep all of this in perspective. And, I have to believe that the look on my face let her know that this was not a time to play around. An apology would have been too much to expect and unnecessary as well, but the look on her face told me that her full arsenal of smart remarks would be retired, at least for the moment.

"As I said before, and I will not belabor the point—all of you are doing well as individuals and through your respective companies. Whether you stay independent or sell to one of the larger white firms, no one will be holding a benefit for any of you any time soon."

I took a moment to take a sip of my wine and let my words sink in. A small smile made its way around the table. It was not what I would call a "dramatic pause," especially since the moment came and went quickly. But as I recall, there was enough time for everyone's thoughts to shift focus from personal agendas to the subject of the luncheon and the reason for my invitation.

In a few moments Jerome would understand why Ray Beard was not a part of the original invitation list and Gordon would know that I was not wasting his time. Diedre would know that there was a good reason why I wanted her to join a private luncheon at which Gordon Perkins was a guest.

There were a lot of loose ends to tie up. It was time to get busy. While I had not planned on Ray Beard being present, I decided to speak as if he were not there or as if I always had anticipated his presence.

"As professionals and as friends, I have the greatest respect for all of you. As individuals and as people who have accomplished so much, particularly as black people, you are history makers.

"But you know, and I know, that in the big picture, it's all minor league. At least up to now. You know it and I know it. You know that I am speaking the truth."

As I looked around the table I could see that I now had everyone's attention. I would never describe Jerome, Gordon, or Diedre as being vain. They all had their personal sense of self-esteem, and they certainly did not need me for any validation of their achievements. Yet, no one could enjoy hearing their life's work being described as "minor league."

I was now tap dancing on thin ice. And it was exactly where I wanted to be. Now they were truly listening to what I was saying. Personal dislikes and estimates of the length of Monique Jefferson's skirt and considerations of her other talents would have to wait.

"The folks at Merrill Lynch and Blackstone and Wasserstein Perella do not wake up in the morning wondering what any of you are going to do. That's just the facts of life—today. We all know it.

"The next merger that changes an industry, the next financing that bails out a country, the next acquisition that makes the front page of the *Wall Street Journal*, we may hear about it before Joe and Moe Shmoe, but we read about it just like everyone else."

I paused for a moment to look around the table again. I was off into uncharted territory. Either this was going to work or it was going down in flames. There was nothing to do but to keep on keeping on. There was simply no time to hesitate or reconsider.

"Obviously I did not ask you to come to lunch just to present you with the realities of the world at the end of the twentieth century. You don't need me to tell any of you what you already know.

"But everything that I have told you gave me an idea the other day, and I wanted to see what each of you thinks about it. So bear with me for just a few more minutes."

"A few minutes is about all you've got, brother." It was Gordon. No surprise there.

"Your patience is going to get you into heaven, Gordon," Diedre spoke with a smile that wasn't really a smile at all.

I am sure that a perfunctory "fuck you" was on the tip of Gordon's tongue. But it seemed that for some reason Gordon just did not feel like getting into it with Diedre that afternoon. It was a consideration for which I was extremely grateful at the time.

"Jerome, you are the scientist at the table, could you please . . ."

"Former scientist," Jerome corrected. He had been physics major in college, going to business school instead of pursuing an engineering doctorate. His correction was gentle, however, with a smile on his face that was as puzzled as that of every other guest at the table.

"Duly noted, Jerome. Now, could you please explain to everyone the difference between a physical reaction and a chemical reaction?"

Jerome could not possibly have anticipated where this discussion was heading. Nevertheless, he carefully put his fork down and fastidiously dabbed at the corner of his mouth with his napkin. Then, having considered what he would say, he spoke quietly and gently and with overwhelming intelligence despite the simplicity of the question.

"A physical reaction involves the combination of several items, but the items themselves remain essentially unchanged. Sugar in water for example—the sugar and the water remain separate and distinct even though they are mixed together.

"A chemical reaction, on the other hand, involves the combining of two or more items to create a new and different substance. For example—a piece of iron, some water and some oxygen, mixed together, *creates* rust, the result of a chemical reaction. Striking a match, the spark of energy caused by friction combined with the sulfur and phosphorus in the match head, causes a chemical reaction, energy is released and we get fire."

Jerome had pointed us in the right direction. He couldn't have done any better if we had rehearsed his lines beforehand. Now was the time.

"The match and the fire is exactly what I am talking about, Jerome. I am suggesting that we start a fire, right here, right now, at this table!"

"Paul, what on earth are you talking about?" This time it was Diedre. She was probably speaking for Jerome and Gordon as well. Everyone was more than a little curious as well as being anxious for me to get to the point before they started feeling like they were on some rhetorical ride to nowhere.

"Diedre, Gordon, Jerome—I want you all to think about a chemical reaction involving your respective firms. As three separate entities, you will all almost certainly continue to do well and make money.

"But, if your firms merged, the synergy would be absolutely incredible. And if you think about it for a moment, all of you know that I am right. The combination of the resources of your firms, together with your collective energy, drives and smarts . . . it would be a chemical reaction. It would be big, hell, it would be huge.

"If your three firms merged, on day one you will not only be co-owners of the largest black-owned investment banking firm in the world, it will also be one of the hottest new firms on Wall Street.

"Everyone, and I mean everyone will want to know what you are doing and what you are going to do. The folks from Merrill, Blackstone, Goldman—all of them, will be calling you every day. The three of you can create a chemical reaction in the world of finance. I am not exaggerating one bit when I say that the three of you will be in the center of a virtual business tsunami that you will create, control, and direct."

I paused and let my words sink in. They were all very quiet. I looked at the faces around the table. Whatever it was that Gordon, Diedre, Jerome, and even Raymond thought I was going to say, merging their three firms was not it. My idea was from another galaxy of thought, another universe of perspective. They could not have been more stunned if I had started speaking in Urdu.

But they were all very smart. I knew that. Indeed, I was counting on that. They had not gotten to where they were in life and business by dismissing good ideas simply because they were not their own.

And so, not even Gordon Perkins—loud, always first with the smart remark—had anything to say at first. I had achieved my initial desired result. I had shocked them into deep thought and serious and immediate consideration of my proposal.

They simply had to consider my idea. It was that outrageous and it had the tantalizing potential of fabulous success. I didn't expect Ray Beard to have anything to say.

This discussion was heading into the deep water and he was still on the shore. That much I knew. I figured that Jerome would be contemplative, and the question was, would Gordon or Diedre speak first.

CHAPTER 30

Paul

Stepping up to the plate

"Paul, let's cut to the chase. There is no way any of us would say yes sitting here at this table. You couldn't possibly expect that. So what is it that you want us to do with your bright idea?"

It was Diedre breaking this whole situation down to its basics, as I hoped that she would. I correctly figured that the group dynamic would be critical during the next few minutes.

However, we all have our strengths and we all have our weaknesses. The key factor affecting relative personal success is the number of times that we can use our strengths and how often we can control and divert attention from our weaknesses. I have a tendency to make the "smart" remark and to be sarcastic. I have to call it a weakness as it usually serves no good reason, and even my closest friends have to choose to ignore those comments, as they are rarely enjoyable.

For some inexplicable Tourette-related reason, the smart aleck imp in me decided to make a guest appearance. In retrospect I have no idea how that happened. I am just glad that I was able to leash the little beast down before irreparable harm was done.

"As a matter of fact, Diedre, I don't have any documents in my briefcase, although I could whip some up by the close of business—if that's all you need to get moving on this."

The quiet table got quieter than a confessional in a whorehouse. I immediately realized that the imp that had hopped out of my sub-conscious had almost immediately returned to his dark cave, hidden deep in my psyche. Of course I was left facing the absolute collapse of everything that I had planned. I had to think and move fast. I smiled and tried to make it clear that there was no animus behind the stupid, snide comment that I had made. Of course, at that point all I could do was press on.

"Seriously, I think that your idea makes sense. You are absolutely right, Diedre, in saying that the most that you can do is think about it. But I think that the next step is for all of you to decide to think about this and we can get together in a few days to talk about a specific game plan, if you decide that you want to play this game."

"Okay, Paul," said Gordon. Finally. "Let's just say that before we go along with your really bright idea, we might have a few questions. Like why do you think this idea is such a bulletproof, gold-plated winner?"

Gordon had a smile on his face. But this time he was not trying to be funny. And there was no laughter forthcoming. He was taking this very seriously. And that was a good sign. But I had to be very careful. Gordon, despite his crude ways, had a great mind and he would be the first to spot any weakness in my proposal.

"Let's just think about it for a moment, Gordon. You are doing just about as much public finance business as the major white firms. You are in just about every major city in the country. There isn't a major agency finance director, state comptroller or city treasurer who doesn't know you and your firm.

"Even with the tax changes of the past few years and the shrinking margins, you are at the top of the heap. But let's think about this a little bit more.

"Diedre, you have been making huge strides in the asset management field. More than most folks on the street know right now. At some point soon your firm will be a brand name on the street, and then most of the major companies, unions, and states will be banging at your door. You know it, and the rest of us at this table know it too.

"Jerome, your firm is getting corporate finance deals going in industries that are only going to get bigger—high tech, internet firms, biotechnology, international structured finance. Your best days are definitely ahead of you. Again, we all know it. After all, we have agreed to be frank and honest this afternoon, haven't we?"

I was on a roll. Gordon, Diedre, and Jerome were fully involved in what I was saying. Ray Beard was along for the ride. It was a critical moment. I could see each of them computing, figuring, speculating, extrapolating—trying to figure out their next move in this floating, shifting, three-dimensional chess game, when I had just changed the rules.

They now knew where all of this was leading. The question was, could they, or rather would they, buy into this idea, right here, right now. If we walked out of the Water Club without some kind of threshold agreement I didn't think that anything I suggested would ever happen.

It was clear that Ray Beard was the fifth wheel and from the look on his face, he really didn't like it. He was used to being in or near the center of attention. He was seething—almost visibly. But he simply was not a player in this game. He was just a part of someone else's team. And frankly, I could not worry about that. I had to move on.

"These are all the good points. But, like most things in life, there is another side to the coin.

"The other side of the coin goes like this—Gordon, the profit margins in municipal finance will never be any better than they are right now. You and I both know that there will be a steady decline in the profitability of this part of your business. What is your solution? Get more business and diversify simultaneously. If you join in this merger, you get to do both."

Gordon did not say a word. You could see his brain weighing all the possible aspects of what I was saying.

"Jerome, if you get these new hot deals going, you are going to be a real star on Wall Street . . . for about half a minute. Because that's how long it will take for the bigger firms to ramp up their own units to do the same deals . . . only bigger. Or, they will just buy you out. And we all know that can happen.

"If you do this merger, however, you will be part of such a highly visible operation that you will get more business than you can ever hope for on your own, and even the big boys will have to think twice about just taking you down. Basically, this merger offers you protective cover as you move forward with your existing strategy.

"And then, Diedre, there is you and your firm."

Diedre shifted almost imperceptibly in her chair. Probably no one noticed but me. My comments were hitting home. As I looked at the faces of Gordon and Jerome, it was clear that I had spoken the truth. It was also clear that Diedre did not welcome an analysis of her business in front of others. But there was no stopping now.

"By any possible standard, you are doing real well. Your asset management business is moving forward. But think about it. If you had Gordon's municipal contacts and Jerome's corporate contacts, there would really be no stopping you.

"If you don't merge, it's only a matter of time before all of you will be fighting tooth and nail to keep the business that you have as other small firms come after you.

"So you see, if you merge, you create history with the chemical reaction of your combined presence. If you don't, you will miss an opportunity to move into the truly big time. And, you may even find your existing businesses in jeopardy and at risk over time.

"Either you adapt, or people will be talking about who you used to be. You won't wind up in the Wax Museum, but you will most certainly be referred to in the past tense as the coming charge of the light brigade of Harvard/Yale/Chicago/NYU Business School graduates goes right after your franchise in the business. The choice is yours. Gordon, Jerome, and Diedre—the opportunity is right in front of you."

When I stopped and sipped some wine, it was eerily quiet at the table. No one spoke. It felt as if my words were like the assault of a demented and possessed archer savant—shooting arrow after arrow, hitting the bull's-eye every single time. Everyone at the table was used to plain talk. But this was something different.

By now the Water Club had started to clear out. As the waiters cleared the luncheon plates, everyone considered what I had said while they ordered some refreshments to end the meal. As I recall, Gordon and I ordered Delamaine, Diedre order Sambucca, Jerome had Amaretto di Saronno, and Ray Beard had some Sandeman's port wine, a pretty decent vintage as I recall.

The winter sun had given all of the heat and light that it was going to give for the day. At this point, the light had begun to fade almost perceptibly. The only question I had at this point was who was going to speak first. The three of them simply had to see that this idea would work. My task was to help them make it happen. That is, if we ever got that far.

CHAPTER 31

Paul

Oh happy day

"**P**aul, I really have to hand it to you this time. If anyone but you had suggested something like this I would have told them to go fuck themselves . . . excuse the language, Ms. Diedre," said Gordon. "But, of course, if we are going to be business partners as Brother Paul suggests, we are all going to have to . . . adjust."

Diedre acknowledged Gordon's comment with a grim, tight smile. But I knew that her mind was clearly beyond Gordon's eternal mind games.

As I looked at it, in this very special chemical reaction, all three of the components were critically important. Gordon was important because of his nationwide network of contacts. Also, even though profit margins in the municipal finance business were shrinking, the name of Gordon's firm would give the new enterprise instant credibility and a pipeline of deals that would almost guarantee that the new firm would be listed on the financial pages of newspapers around the country every week.

It seemed to me that Gordon had bought into my idea. But with Gordon, one never really knew what he might be thinking or what his real plan might be. Clearly, if this new partnership was going to work it was going to be tricky . . . to say the least.

We all waited as he sat back in his chair and cradled a balloon of brandy in his very large hand. He savored the aroma and he also seemed to be savoring the attention from everyone around the table. This was clearly his moment. He took another sip, considered its flavor and then continued to speak.

"Paul, as I have said before, when you are right, you are right. Your analysis of my business hit the nail right on the head. My educated guess is that you hit pretty close to home with Diedre and Jerome as well."

The absence of comment was all the confirmation that I needed. Gordon continued to carry the ball on this play. I silently cheered him on.

"Everything you say makes sense. If I had Jerome's corporate contacts and Diedre's asset management operation I would be kicking even more ass up and down Wall Street.

"And I have to believe that if Diedre had complete and unlimited access to the state and city finance officers that I know, and the municipal union leaders that they know, her business would grow exponentially.

"As far as you are concerned, Jerome, we all realize that with my deal flow, and cash flow, you could go after even bigger and better corporate deals, and have the financial wherewithal to buy your way into new deals. But, there is no way that I am going along with this one."

I felt myself deflate. I felt that everyone could hear the whooshing sound of air leaving my body. I could not believe that this was happening. A moment ago, it was too good to be true. Now, it was too bad to be real. What the hell was wrong with Gordon?

"At least, not right now." Gordon was really enjoying himself. His melodramatic pause had everyone very focused.

"If this thing is going to work, a big if, then we are going to have to find out if we can work together. After all, it doesn't make sense to go through all the bullshit that a merger entails and then find out that we can't work together. I think that we should date a little before we start heading toward the honeymoon suite."

"Well, Gordon, what would you suggest? After all, if you think that this idea has any merit, then we all need to start somewhere, right?"

I was doing all that I could do to maintain momentum. Now I knew that I had to be quiet and hope that there was some momentum in all of this. I did, of course, have some ideas on how this undertaking could get off the ground. But it was really important that Gordon, Jerome, and Diedre came to some of those same conclusions.

If everything went in the direction that I hoped, we would leave the Water Club agreeing to some trial cooperative projects while I drafted a preliminary Letter of Intent as a prelude to an actual merger. I noticed that Jerome was about to speak and it was clear that the best thing that I could do was to keep quiet.

"Paul, I have to agree with Gordon this time. You have come up with an idea that is wild and great at the same time. And you know something? It just might work. It is so outrageous and logical in its concept . . . it just might work. But you are right. We have to start somewhere." At this point, Jerome looked at Ray Beard, seeming to realize for the first time that Ray was very much out of place. He seemed to start to ask Ray for his opinion, just so that Ray would have something to say. But at precisely that moment, Diedre had something to say and Ray had to stay bolted to his second tier role.

I watched Diedre take a deep breath and then exhale—very slowly. Clearly, her mind had been going a million miles an hour ever since I had hatched my grand scheme. I knew that she liked and respected Jerome and I also knew that she absolutely could not stand Gordon. And as for my involvement—I hoped that we had been ex-spouses for too long to let anything personal get in the way of business. And this was certainly business of the highest order.

I also knew that ever since she had left Citibank, building her own firm into a success had been the prime motivating factor in her life. Whatever was second place wasn't even close. I also knew that she was on the verge of making that firm into something that was not only going to be successful for the long term, but that it was on its way to becoming an institution—in other words, it was going to last. Knowing Diedre, she already had a plan—and now this. She thought long and hard. And then she spoke. Another pivotal point in this most interesting of afternoons.

"I really don't know where to begin with you guys, but I guess I am going to have to try. Paul, you are the last person in the world from whom I should take advice, but what you are saying makes a hell of a lot of sense, in a very bizarre, but very real way.

"Gordon, let's be frank. The truth is the truth. We have simply never gotten along. Not even a little bit. But business is business. Enough said.

"Jerome, with you it's something else again. You are truly one of the very special people that I know—you are a gentleman and you are a man of your word. But Jerome, I have never seen you be anyone but the man in charge. I am not about to be in second place at this point in my life either. And Gordon, we all know about you.

"So, gentlemen. The question is, given the facts of life as we know them, where are we going to go with Paul's oh-so-brilliant bright idea?"

"Goddamn good question, Diedre." It was Gordon again. But he was being surprisingly human and practical. This was one time he was not trying to get under Diedre's skin.

"We can chew on this thing until it is mush, or we can try and make it work. I don't have time to waste, and my guess is that neither do any of you. So, if we are going to do something, let's try and figure it out right now."

And with that, I was amazed that the group just got down to business. Plain and simple. Gordon was, and would always be, a lout, an idiot, and an asshole, but no one would ever, ever say that he was stupid. Certainly no one sitting at the table that day. He quickly and concisely outlined a plan of action that could have been downloaded from my brain.

He correctly pointed out that if the three principals had any hope of working together, two things had to take place. First, they would need a basic outline of the principles of a merger which, logic dictated, should be contained in a Memorandum of Understanding or Letter of Intent that I would draft within thirty days for the group's consideration. Gordon also suggested that each of them commit $10,000 to fund the legal fees that were inherent in such a task.

The whole afternoon had taken a turn which amazed and exhilarated me. I could only observe as they took their first collective acts based on this proposed joint venture. It was not the commitment of the money that was meaningful. After all, it was not a lot for them. It was their commitment to work together that marked this day as being very, very different. And we would all remember this day and this moment for the rest of our lives.

Gordon then went on to make another suggestion. He pointed out, again with compelling logic, that the only way to truly find out if the threesome could work together would be for them to select some cooperative projects that would determine empirically the extent to which their combined efforts could be successful in the long run.

Gordon went on to suggest that each of them select a project that was currently of personal interest, and present it to the group to see if it could be the basis for a cooperative effort. The true proof of all of this synergy would be the success of their collective efforts.

This would of course require that each of them reveal confidential and private information about their firms and their strategies. A leap of faith to say the least. "You show me yours and I will show you mine" at a big league level. Gordon, Jerome, and Diedre all realized it.

Ray continued to sit, stewing in the juices of his extremely obvious irrelevance. For a moment no one said anything. This adventure had more than one Rubicon. That's for sure.

It was really clear to me that this whole thing had taken on a life of its own. I was now along for the ride like everyone else.

CHAPTER 32

Diedre

She who hesitates . . .

I could have conjured up a million guesses as to why Paul wanted us to have lunch that day, but his merger idea still would not have occurred to me. It was that amazing it was shocking, it was surreal, and it was great. And it was also moving a lot faster than anything that I might have expected.

I had decided to come along for Paul's luncheon because the group that he was assembling seemed to be entertaining, at the very least. And Paul seemed to care so much. And I have to confess that spending time with Paul had started to be more enjoyable than I cared to admit at the time.

But my wildest ideas would not have come close to his proposal to merge my firm with Gordon's and Jerome's. And now, here we were, sitting at the Water Club, talking about how to make it happen.

I remember all of us sitting around the table waiting to see who would take the first leap of faith in this nascent undertaking. It did not take long.

"All right, God dammit!" You would have to be deaf, dumb and blind not to know that it was Gordon. In some ways he could be so predictable. A strength and a weakness, as time would tell.

"If we are going to play, show me yours—I'll show you mine, I don't mind going first. But I am going to say this one time and one time only. If anyone takes anything from this table and tries to fuck me, it will be the worst decision that you ever made."

I have never taken threats well, and I was going to be goddamned if I let the likes of Gordon Perkins pull a grandstand play like this. As I started to speak I saw a similar thermonuclear reaction emanating from Jerome. This whole thing was about to go bastard ballistic. No question about it.

It was at this very moment that Paul stepped in. His sense of timing was unerring that afternoon. I remember thinking that I wish he could have been that way more often in the past. But it was a thought that was almost a subliminal blink. And then it was gone.

"Everyone please just simmer down . . . please." Paul had his hands extended, palms down, in the universal gesture of the peacemaker.

"Jerome and Diedre, you know Gordon and the way he is. If you want to work with a diplomat, I should just pay the bill and we can all go on up the river to the U.N. and find us some diplomats.

"Gordon, you know good and goddamn well you can't go around threatening Jerome and Diedre if you are going to work with them. So why don't we just move on? O.K.?"

There were swollen thunderheads of temper floating on the horizon of the luncheon table that afternoon. One spark of tantrum lightning and it was all over. For more than a few moments there was total silence. Sunshine and monsoon hung in the balance. And then there was Gordon again.

"That's fine with me. I'm just telling it like it is. But you're right Paul. Let's move on. Jerome, Diedre, no harm intended."

It was the closest thing to an apology I had ever heard from Gordon in his entire life. Sincerity was another thing entirely. But with Gordon you could never ask for too much.

With that semi *mea culpa* Gordon began to explain how he conducted his business. We all knew that Gordon was big in public finance. But as he began to "open the kimono," it was clear that none of us knew the half of it. His Rolodex and firm database was chock full of the names and numbers of state comptrollers, city treasurers, mayors, city council members, and very influential "consultants." And Gordon wanted much more.

"Listen, later this year, the City of New Orleans is holding its mayoral election. There is an opportunity there that is ours for the taking. It's just sitting there."

I remember listening and thinking that the incumbent, Prince Lodrig, was young, black, and progressive. In four short years he had engineered a near miraculous change in the *laissez-faire* approach to government, introducing honesty and fiscal probity to a political lifestyle that had created the caricature of New Orleans that existed in the minds of too many people.

I also remember thinking that Mayor Lodrig was a son of the Crescent City and exceedingly popular. He clearly needed a second term in order to truly institutionalize many of the changes that he had begun to initiate. There were too many weak, venal and corrupt people, in and out of government, that were used to waiting out an occasional hurricane or tidal flood of reform. To them, Prince Lodrig was just some more bad weather. He would be gone soon enough. Gordon continued.

"Mayor Lodrig's opponent is this knucklehead Percy Broussard. He used to be a radio commentator and, to tell the truth, he is probably receiving more than a little of his campaign financing from the Oliver North-Gordon Liddy-Pat Robertson wing of the Republican Party.

"Here's where it gets good." I had never seen Gordon express such glee before, and I was not sure that it was such a good thing. Over time I would become sure that Gordon laughing never presaged anything good.

"On its face it looks like Lodrig should run Broussard right into the bayous. But I have it on very good authority that Broussard is going to come into some very serious campaign money and that Lodrig will not have anything like a cakewalk into his second term. I don't care what you have read in the papers. That's the real deal and the real story.

"Now, I have known Prince for a long time. I gave him money when he won his election for mayor, and I gave him money during his two earlier campaigns when he lost. This is going to be his fourth campaign for mayor of New Orleans and I can tell you that he doesn't intend to lose this time.

"Prince is a reformer and a progressive and all that good shit. But he is also a realist. He absolutely hates to lose and he knows that money is the 'mother's milk of politics.'"

It was absolutely fascinating listening to Gordon. As loathsome as I found him to be as an individual, he was undoubtedly one of the most impressive and intelligent people that I ever met. When he knew what he wanted, he knew how to get it. And clearly, he usually did. Lunch that day taught me a lot about what I knew and didn't know about Gordon Perkins.

"Right now I am locked in as a part of Mayor Lodrig's campaign. As a matter of fact, I am Co-Chairman of his Finance Committee and I am going to have a lot to say about what happens in New Orleans after Lodrig wins. It's fair to say that I am going to flat-out control all of the municipal finance business in New Orleans.

"Now I know that it is a small market. But it's a major American city, and I plan to leverage that control into influencing my business in a dozen other markets across the country within the year.

"Diedre and Jerome, if you can contribute some money to Lodrig's campaign, it will help make my plan work. If you actually show up and are visible in support of the mayor, I am certain that a number of people we know will be attracted and give Prince the momentum that he needs to derail Percy Broussard before his campaign really gets up a full head of steam."

Basically, Gordon proposed that Jerome and I would work together to raise money, give money and generally support the mayoral candidacy of Prince Lodrig. Upon his victory at the end of the year, the new firm that Paul had proposed would have a key position in the municipal finance industry throughout the country. It was pretty heady stuff for a firm that didn't even exist. It would clearly be an important foundation for a new business operation.

"And I'll tell you this. Even if we don't wind up making this merger work, if you work with me on this I will figure out some profit-sharing plan for you that will make all of this worth your while. It's that big!"

With that Gordon sat back, cradling his balloon of Delamaine once more. He had said a lot. It was clear that he didn't need to say much more. I was trying to compose in my mind how I would introduce my firm's latest plans. While I was doing this, Jerome began speaking.

CHAPTER 33

Diedre

The revolution will not be televised

It was clear that he did not need a lot of prompting. Although he had been largely silent during lunch, Jerome clearly had been sizing up everyone and everything. Almost everyone thought of him as being cautious and reserved, but clearly Jerome was not averse to taking risks. After all, he had left a great job with a major firm on Wall Street to start his own firm.

He was not a man who was afraid of seizing his own destiny, that was for sure. And now, in the Water Club, on a cold January afternoon, Jerome once again saw an opportunity to seize his destiny—by the throat. And I had that sense that he believed, as I already did, that Paul was right.

"Okay, folks, you all know that the Hardaway Group has been trying to get more involved in the corporate side of the business. We do asset management and municipal finance, but let me tell you a few things that you may not know about our little shop.

"Our long term strategic plan focuses upon the changes that are taking place in the biotechnology industry. And believe me, these changes are taking place at mind-bending speed.

"I know everyone is talking about the internet and e-commerce, and where all that is going. And I say God bless them. I am not sure about the internet-based businesses. I am sure about biotechnology. I have seen work that is being done right now. And I have read and analyzed extrapolations that would absolutely blow your mind."

I had never seen an animated Jerome Hardaway. I doubt that anyone at the table had, including the ever-sulking Ray Beard. This luncheon was turning out to be memorable for more reasons than one.

Jerome Hardaway was a graduate of Yale University. Through the networks of friendship, association, and affinity that develop out of schools like Yale, Jerome had been contacted two years earlier by one of his classmates who was senior vice president of one of the leading biotech firms in the country.

It turned out that this classmate, Dr. Barry Herzog, had read in the Yale alumni magazine about Jerome's accomplishments and thought that he needed to speak with an investment banker who wouldn't necessarily eat him alive on the first meeting. Herzog had sense enough to know that if he went to one of the big houses the odds were that they were already in touch with the board and senior management of his company, dancing the dance that was to be the prelude to an incredibly lucrative public offering. Jerome went on to explain the reason for this rather unorthodox business connection.

"Herzog needs help because he has developed an amazingly successful successor to AZT that enhances the quality of life for HIV patients. He has managed to position himself as the sole owner of the patent. And frankly, he is pissed off because he has been passed over for promotion and a larger equity share in the company where he works.

"It's pretty clear to me that if he walks with the patent for this new drug, he could start up and finance a company that would fly. Absolutely fly. Soar would be a better word.

"Of course all of you can see the potential in Dr. Herzog's dilemma."

Jerome had never been known for being much of a talker, but his story was riveting. We all leaned a little closer to the table so that we could hear every word that Jerome was saying, oblivious to our collectively synchronized fascination.

"The challenge is to organize Herzog's move and implement his plan for him, securing the financial structure to make all this work without divulging details. Of course it is critical that we maintain a continuing and permanent equity interest in any resulting deal or deals."

We all understood the horizon of opportunity that lay in front of Jerome. If he could be adept and agile enough to pull this off, every science jock and computer geek with a hint of ambition would be banging on his door. And, in this New Jack world of technofinance, every major investor would sing his praises and fill his pockets.

"Jerome, this sounds great, but I am hearing a lot of 'ifs' and 'buts'." I didn't want to rain on anybody's parade, but I felt that I had to speak up.

"I mean, if Dr. Herzog does receive his proper recognition and compensation from his current company, including equity, do you think he would still leave and follow through with the plan you are putting together?

"And, if you are able to structure this deal, how do you know whether 'loyalty' is simply a disposable noun in the vocabulary of the good doctor? How do you know that he won't cut you loose as lead banker the first time the Merrills and Goldmans start whispering sweet nothings in his ear?"

Jerome sat silent for a few moments. I knew that he had already thought of these things. All of us were curious as to what his answer would be. We didn't have to wait long.

"The reason why I brought up this deal is that I think that if we worked together, our joint efforts might really make this thing work.

"The way I see it, access to institutional investors and public pension fund managers would make a huge difference. Gordon, if you can get some of those pension fund managers to invest some of their capital into so-called high risk ventures like Herzog's, we can all make a killing. We can feed like lions on the Serengeti." Jerome smiled a smile that made me hope that we could always be on the same side.

"And Diedre, your access to institutional investors can clearly help move this deal forward. And with this kind of firepower, you can be sure that I will put this deal together.

"And by the way, Diedre, don't you worry about Herzog. You can be sure that he already knows better than to backstab me." Jerome said this in a way that revealed, just for that moment, a tougher, harder, stronger side of him than I ever knew existed. And I just knew without actually knowing that I did not want to be near Barry Herzog or anyone near him if he ever dreamed of double-crossing Jerome. I took some real comfort in that knowledge.

There were still a lot of if's and but's. But everyone at the table understood the import of what Jerome was saying. And we all started to truly realize the awesome potential that lay within Paul's proposal.

As individuals we all had confidence in our respective strengths and ability to succeed. Frankly, it had never occurred to me to have the same level of confidence in anyone else. Now, at lunch at the Water Club on the most improbable of winter days, that all changed. I could almost see everyone's mind working, processing data, and arriving at what would be one of the most important decisions that each of us would ever make. At least that was becoming clear.

And now it was time for me to say something. I have never been a big believer in unnecessary drama, but I must say that at that moment I did hesitate. Not for dramatic effect, but because I knew that I was diving into deep waters, and a moment of contemplation was necessary.

CHAPTER 34

Diedre

Don't go breaking my heart

As I took a breath and gathered myself, I felt Paul's eyes on me. I looked up, and for a moment I thought I could read his mind. I could see his very real powers of self-control straining to keep him from saying anything that might throw this discussion off-track at a very critical phase. I could almost hear him—

It's happening! It's really happening! That's two down and one to go. But two won't do. It's got to be three. Come on, Diedre! Come on, get with the program! Please baby, please! I am sure that it was just my imagination, but I could have sworn I heard his voice in my head just then.

It was, of course, just a matter of chance that I was the last one to speak and render some kind of decision on this proposal. In point of fact, I was probably the first to decide—I have always known opportunity when I see it, and this was not opportunity knocking, it was trying to kick the door down. I was reaching for that door as soon as Paul laid out his plan.

But being the last to speak on the subject had its benefits. Even though I was sitting with some very controlled individuals, there had to be some anticipation with respect to what I was going to say. I thought that I could see a glimmer of a glint of expectation in the eyes of Jerome, Paul, and Gordon.

Ray Beard was something else again. I remember a look that reminded me of a laser fueled by cold fusion. In retrospect, I am surprised that no one else noticed the almost palpable resentment and barely controlled rage in his eyes that we would all have cause to remember in the months to come.

At the time, Ray Beard was not the issue. And at the time I could not also have cared less that Jerome's wonder boy had hurt feelings. It was time to move on. And I took another deep breath and watched the marvelously diverse aquatic traffic on the East River float by our table. There was a barge filled with refuse that could have been from outer space. There was a luxury yacht, about eighty-five feet long. There was a police cruiser. There was yet another oil tanker. There was a ferry plying its way across the East River with some commuters getting an early start home. It was definitely time.

"Well, gentlemen, I have been working on a project that I think you might find interesting. I have been talking to the heads of several of the major municipal employee unions throughout the U.S. I want these unions to form an investment fund that my firm would manage.

"Once I have the fund in place, I would establish a traditional portfolio, but—and here's where it gets interesting—this investment fund will work with the World Bank to finance inner-city development projects right here, much in the same way that the World Bank guarantees loans in Azerbaijan, Bosnia, Vietnam, Brazil, and South Africa.

"And get this, the reason why this works so well is that the municipal employee unions would be investing in their own futures by assuring their retirement income. And at the same time they are investing in the future of their own jobs, they will be financing development projects in the various cities that could stabilize and enhance the future of these cities. Of course, this would also assure their future employment.

"The way I look at it, it's a classic example of doing the right thing and making the right business decision at the same time. Now, Gordon, it's pretty clear to me that with your contacts with the various public employee unions around the country, as well as your relationships with all the municipal and state officials in the country, you could help put this concept over the top.

"Jerome, you have a staff of bright young technicians that can help structure the World Bank component of this project. This whole thing has to go from concept to reality. Getting this concept into a format that we can take to the World Bank is something more than a notion. But Jerome, I have a sneaking idea that you and your people could do it." Jerome never said a word, but I thought I could see undistilled assent in his eyes.

"I have lost a lot of sleep trying to figure out how I was going to get this done. And, you know what?

"To tell God's honest truth, Paul's idea of the three of us working together was the farthest thing from my mind when we sat down to lunch today. But now I know that it would certainly get my plan off the ground, and I think it would do the same thing for you, Gordon, and for you too, Jerome. I am sure of it!"

I like to think of myself as being someone who rarely gets carried away, but this was an opportunity of a lifetime. And I wanted to be sure to get my point across. And that afternoon, I was sure that I did.

At a luncheon punctuated by silences and pregnant pauses, my little talk precipitated one more. The movement of the waiters and busboys had simmered down to a point that was hardly noticeable. The Water Club barely rocked and rolled on its moorings. The winter sun had just about completed its half day's work.

Everyone seemed to be momentarily lost in thought, everyone contemplating the dreams and aspirations of the others, wondering what might really be possible if this merger were to make the transition from contemplation to reality. Call it woman's intuition, call it what you want. I had a very real feeling that day that there was a growing sense that this was one idea that might really work.

CHAPTER 35

Diedre

We're on the right track now

All that was left was for somebody to say something to get things moving in the right direction. On that day, that somebody was me.

· "Paul, on behalf of all of us, I have to hand it to you. You have hit the home run of home runs. Jerome, Gordon—unless you feel differently, I think that it's fair to say that we have the beginnings of a deal. Congratulations to you, and to all of us!" And, with what I recall was a dramatic flourish, I lifted my glass in a toast, as did Jerome, Gordon, and Paul. Even Ray Beard glumly joined in.

"Paul Taylor, if you can figure out how to merge our three firms so that each of us thinks that we are still the one in charge, you are truly the genius that we think you are. For once you will have earned the exorbitant fees that you usually charge everybody in town. Or was this going to be one of your pro bono projects for which you have become so famous?"

I think that this was another time that I caught Paul off guard. Things had been so intense and serious that lightening the moment was the right thing to do at that particular time. Everyone laughed. Everyone laughed, except Ray Beard. There was an aura of ill humor about the man that day that I will never forget for many damned good reasons.

"Diedre, anything that you and this esteemed group of tycoons might consider as compensation for my services would be greatly appreciated by my paternal great-aunt in New Bern, North Carolina." Paul was smiling, and in the euphoria of the moment I could have sworn that I could see the light dancing in his eyes.

"Who are you calling a coon?" Gordon chimed in with his typical brand of humor, but again, the lightness of the moment carried even his heavy humor and we all laughed again.

The euphoria eased into reality, and it was not surprising that at a table with one lawyer and four bankers they would get back to pragmatics once more, no matter how high spirits might be soaring. Our collective attention centered once again on the task at hand and that alone. After all, it was getting late, and since we were of one mind with respect to Paul's idea, there was no need for more small talk.

We agreed that, as Gordon had suggested, Paul would get a draft Memorandum of Understanding out to us within two weeks. We also agreed, business being business, that we would send retainer checks to Paul and that he would have a new client, "Project DGJ," and that he would bill for work on this proposed merger.

Jerome came up with the idea that we should each outline our respective cooperative projects and circulate them as soon as possible. This way, when we got back together we could actually come up with some plans of action to see if this thing could really work and how we could practically and actually contribute to the success of the specific projects that had been mentioned during our luncheon.

"When we meet again why don't all of you come to my place for dinner? As this whole thing moves along, the fewer people who know about it, the better. Meeting privately will keep the rumble on the grapevine to a dull roar."

Everyone immediately understood that I was right. Even though we were comfortable with many of our friends and colleagues, there was no good reason to broadcast our plans at this point. Nothing good could come of that.

Also, it became clear to all of us that even though we all knew each other well enough we had to treat this entire matter just as we would treat it with people that we didn't know. That meant formally scheduling meetings and keeping to commitments to complete assignments in advance of the meetings. We all knew the drill.

The luncheon meeting was now drawing to a close. As Paul settled the bill, we all took a few moments to consider the path that we had chosen. It was a sobering thought. And that was when Paul proposed a final toast.

"Diedre, Gordon, Jerome, Ray, if I can be serious for just a few more minutes."

"Paul, you're killing us! Goddamn! Is there any way we can get out of this? We already agreed to pay your ass." It was Gordon again, of course. But he was speaking with what passed for good humor and Paul pressed on.

"I want to thank all of you for truly listening to me and for taking my suggestion seriously. I had no idea how all of you might react to this, and I am truly gratified, and to tell the truth, I am more than a bit humbled by it.

"If I was really smart I would know how this was going to turn out. As it is, I know that with your three firms, we have a chance to make history and see something spectacular take place. So, here's to all of you . . . and history."

Probably for one of the few times in his life, Gordon didn't have a smart remark. We all toasted, finished our drinks, and it was time for us to go.

In settling his bill, Paul had asked Buzzy O'Keefe to arrange for a couple of cars—one to take Jerome, Ray, and Gordon downtown, the other for Paul and I to go to our respective midtown offices.

It was now getting close to half past three and we all wanted to get back to our offices to get some work done before the end of the day. Since we all knew each other well enough, there was no need for formality in bidding each other farewell. Within a few moments, hats and coats were collected, goodbyes were said and the luncheon party split up into two cars and departed, one car going to midtown, the other heading to Wall Street.

As Paul and I settled into the backseat of the car there was not much to say. I can't speak for Paul, but I truly wanted to savor the moment. I think that he did too.

Between Winner's memorial service and the luncheon and the incredible plans that were discussed, it was a day that I will never forget. And, as it turned out, it was a day that changed my life. Forever.

CHAPTER 36

Gordon

Slipping into darkness

Drugs have been a part of my life for over two decades. Of course I should be clear. Not all drugs. Cocaine and marijuana are the only drugs that I use. That is, along with alcohol and an occasional cigar.

When I say they are a part of my life, I mean that getting high whenever time and circumstance permit is a part of what I do. I can't remember the last time I attended a business meeting when I was seriously under the influence of any of that, but there have been more than a few mornings where the night before was not a faint memory.

I have always thought that all of this talk about "drugs" is just that much bullshit, since I don't know what the difference is between a shot of whiskey or a couple of lines of Colombia's best. The only difference I am aware of is that one is legal and one is not. Of course, seventy years ago, alcohol was illegal and cocaine was not. So go figure.

The way I see it, what I do when I am not on duty is nobody's fucking business. Actually, its no one's fucking business what I do, period. I started getting high in college. And I have been getting high ever since. And nobody has ever given me a good enough reason to stop.

I don't even want to think about whether I am "dependent" or "addicted" or a "habitual user." Basically I do what I want to do when

I want to do it. I don't get high every day, and have never had a desire to do so. I have gone months without even taking a drink or a joint or a line, but what the fuck does that prove?

Life is too short and I can never have enough good times. So, when I get a chance to get some smoke and some coke and get crazy with a couple of freak bitches, you can bet your fucking ass that I am going to jump on it with all four feet.

I do find it interesting that I have found a new friend over the past few years when I get high on coke. I call him the Dark Lord.

I find that after running through a few grams of blow in a night, my mood changes drastically. That is when the Dark Lord comes out and hangs around with me through the night. He doesn't leave me until all the coke is gone and I can't get him to go away. The more coke I put up my nose, the longer he stays around.

But when he goes away I don't give a fuck about the Dark Lord anymore and I will get my man to drop off another half ounce with the doorman at my co-op on Park Avenue. And the Dark Lord will be waiting to meet me again.

And there is always a next time. Some people smoke cigarettes, some drink bourbon, some eat Oreo cookies. I do coke and reefer. What the fuck. I have kicked too much ass in my life for me to worry about what anyone might think.

As I sat in the car with my man Jerome Hardaway that day, there was a fucking carnival running through my head. Paul had really blown my mind with his merger idea, and to tell the truth, the more that I thought about it, the more it made sense. Frankly, I never would have suggested something like this. I also know that no one would ever go along with it if I had.

But now the concept was on the table and everyone had to acknowledge its power and potential. I just had to figure out how to make all of this shit work for me. Gordon Perkins always comes out ahead. That's my first and only rule.

I had originally planned to fuck this knucklehead "aspiring actress" that afternoon, but when the lunch ran into overtime, that plan was pretty much blown to hell. No matter, the last thing I have to worry about is getting some pussy.

Hell, I have money, my own company, and my own time and a

dumb-ass wife who knows better than to so much as think about giving me static about what I do and where I go. Besides, I was glad to have a chance to spend some private time with Jerome. I am probably one of the few people in the crowd that Paul calls "The Pride" who knows that with all of his refined ways, Jerome has a lot of street in him.

We were out drinking one night, and he let it slip that he used to run with a gang in North Philly while he was in high school. It was only one of those "save the inner-city youth" programs that got him to Yale and all of the good things that resulted in the persona that is now known as the esteemed and respected Jerome Hardaway.

That night he told me about the gangbanging and gunfights that were a part of in his early days. While he did not say it in so many words, I gathered that Jerome had kicked much ass in his Philly gang days and that he was not so high and mighty that he wouldn't kick ass even today. But I also got the impression that he kept his temper and his street tendencies on a very short leash. I have always been impressed by Jerome's personal control.

That kind of self-control has just never been a strong part of my life. Obviously, I have always been able to set goals and accomplish them. But I have always gone out of my way to indulge myself when I have felt like it—liquor, women, drugs—whatever the fuck I have felt like doing, I have done. And will keep doing. I just wish that I could keep that goddamn Dark Lord from fucking with me so goddamn much.

"So, Gordon, what do you think of all of this? Are you really in on this deal?" said Jerome.

"Shit yeah! Paul is one smart motherfucker."

"I think you're right. But there's a lot that we all have to give up if this is going to work. We are going to have to share control. Do you really think that we can all do that, Gordon?"

"I can do anything that I need to do if it's going to make me money. After all, we aren't talking about some run of the mill Mickey Mouse motherfuckers here. You and Diedre are top of the line. You know me. Everybody knows what I can do and what I will do to anyone that fucks with me.

"I know that if we get together we will have one bad motherfucking firm. After all, we already are three bad motherfuckers."

Jerome smiled and I could tell that he knew that I was right and that he agreed, although he would probably choose a slightly different vocabulary. We both sat back for a minute and since we had known each other for so long, we didn't have a lot to say at that moment.

As a matter of fact we both used our cell phones to check with our offices for messages. Nothing spectacular was going on. As we headed down the FDR Drive towards the Wall Street district we were both pretty much talked out. That's when, after a few quiet moments, Jerome spoke again, and with his words he woke up the Dark Lord.

"I hope that you and Kenitra enjoyed being out on the Island last weekend. I wish that Charmaine and I knew that you two were coming out. Maybe next time we can have dinner or drinks."

"What?"

"I almost forgot that Charmaine mentioned that she saw your car in the driveway of your house out in Sag Harbor. But believe me, I know how it is, sometimes we leave the children with neighbors, and Charmaine and I go out there and we don't see anybody."

I could feel the blood start to freeze in my brain. I remember the chilled feeling that I got only when the Dark Lord paid me a visit. I just didn't expect him in the backseat of a limo that afternoon. Especially since there was no cocaine around. This was something new.

Jerome just kept talking. I am positive that he was oblivious to my reaction. He could not possibly have known that the Dark Lord had joined us for the rest of the ride, and the rest of my day and night.

"You know, we really enjoy Sag Harbor in the winter with the snow, the ice, and the quiet. I never thought of you as a peace-and-quiet man, Gordon. Let us know the next time. O.K.?"

"Sure, Jerome. Next time I will be sure to get in touch. It will be great to see Charmaine. No shit, she really is a great woman. She clearly has bad judgment to be with a sorry motherfucker like you, but aside from that, she is absolutely a wonderful woman."

We both laughed at my little bit of bullshit and that was just about that. Except for the fact that the Dark Lord was kind enough to remind me that the previous weekend I was in Los Angeles fucking a couple of actresses whose names you would know, one black and one Asian. Those two bitches, a suite at The Mondrian, a case of champagne and a bag of coke, you can be goddamned sure I remembered where I was that previous weekend.

CHAPTER 37

Gordon

Life's little pleasures

I was goddamn sure that I was not in fucking Sag Harbor that week-end. And I was sure that my fucking whore bitch of a wife Kenitra had told me that she had stayed at our place on Park Avenue with the flu. She hadn't mentioned a motherfucking thing about going out to goddamn Sag Harbor.

The Dark Lord helped me pole-vault immediately to the conclusion that if that fucking bitch would lie about where she was that weekend, then sure as shit she was lying about a lot more than her whereabouts. Like if she was fucking around, spending my money on some broke dick hustler motherfucker . . . who knows what the fuck she has been doing? The Dark Lord was kind enough to mention that she might have been selling pussy. I remember him mentioning that she might be giving head in the men's room at the Harvard Club. How the fuck would I know?

I felt the anger start to rise and then magically evanesce into some universe that I would never see. I felt fine. Everything was very clear. We were pulling up to Jerome's offices on Broad Street.

"You know, Jerome, I am sure that we will be getting together a lot more in the future. Paul's plan can work I am sure of that, all bullshit aside."

"Well, you know I am going to do all that I can to make it work. This is going to be one hell of a year, Gordon!"

"That's for sure. Have a good rest of the day, Jerome. I'll speak with you tomorrow."

We shook hands as Jerome got out of the car and he headed into his office. That's when I let the driver know that there was a change in plans. We would not be going to my offices in the World Financial Center. Instead we would be going to my apartment at Park Avenue and East 72nd Street.

That's when the Dark Lord whispered a suggestion to me. I used my cell phone and made a certain call to a certain number at a certain address in Greenwich Village. I always carry a good bit of cash and within minutes I had the half ounce of pure Colombian cocaine that I suddenly wanted more than usual. I am sure that the driver didn't notice that my nose was starting to run and that I was getting a little jumpy.

But I wanted the coke and now I wanted the Dark Lord to be with me when I had a very special conversation with that bitch-wife of mine. I wanted to be in a very proper frame of mind. Beating her would not be enough. That would be the dessert for the meal that I had planned for her.

I have beaten Kenitra many times, sometimes a slap, sometimes I have had to punch the shit out of her when she just would not get out of my face. Never in her face, though. Never. She is a pretty motherfucker and I have always enjoyed making her give me some head after I beat all the bullshit out of her. The only thing that she understands is total and absolute domination and humiliation.

I knew how I would dominate that bitch this particular afternoon. But I wanted to think up some special ways to humiliate her, break her down, and make her beg me to beat her, fuck her—make her beg me to do anything and everything to her. And that's just what I planned to do. The Dark Lord was whispering suggestions to me in a steady stream that just went deeper and deeper into the planned degradation.

And that's when the Dark Lord had a stroke of pure genius and shared his inspiration with me. I picked up my cell phone and called home. Kenitra picked up on the second ring.

"Hey, baby, what's going on?"

"Not much, Gordon. Just relaxing."

I could tell from her voice that she was wary. But she had to front it off. She couldn't even begin to act guilty.

"Listen, I was just thinking. My meetings are pretty much over for the day and I am on my way home. Why don't you let Colleen go home and call Alex and let him know that we won't need him for the evening?"

"You can chill a couple of bottles of champagne and put on that short, tight red dress with the four-inch heels. I'm bringing some refreshments that I am sure you will enjoy."

I know that Kenitra didn't know what the fuck to say. The Dark Lord was an absolute genius.

"O.K. Gordon. Sounds like you're in the mood for some fun."

"You got that right. I am definitely in the mood for fun. And Kenitra?"

"Yes, Gordon?"

"Be sure to turn the lights down and the music up. The way I like it."

"Whatever you say, baby. You the man!"

"Don't you know it. See you soon."

Real soon, bitch. Real fucking soon. The Dark Lord was inspired and Kenitra was going to get schooled that night. By the time that night was over she was going to wish for the worst day of her life instead of what had happened to her. That was a promise I made to the Dark Lord as I settled into the backseat of the car and thought about what I was going to do to Kenitra first. I couldn't help but smile.

It had been a good day. It was going to be a great night. The Dark Lord would see to that.

CHAPTER 38

Jerome

Don't look back

I stood watching as the car carrying Gordon Perkins headed down Broad Street. It was cold as hell, getting colder now that it was getting dark. But something made me stand there and just think about it all for a moment. Down the street was the headquarters of the Rolls Royce of investment banking firms, Goldman Sachs. Up the street stood the building that once housed the now-departed buccaneer investment banking firm, Drexel Burnham.

Man! Sixty Broad Street, Drexel's headquarters address, used to be the center of the high flying investment banking universe. It was the ultimate definition of the fast lane. Boesky, Milken, Kluge, Perlman, Tomlinson and so many, many more, found that the end of the rainbow was less than fifty yards from where I was standing.

I knew the firm well. I have a busload of friends, colleagues and associates who literally found themselves on the street thanks to a nondecision by the United States Secretary of the Treasury that let the firm die.

I still find it amazing that no one found it a little interesting that that Secretary of the Treasury was the former head of Dillon Read, one of the white shoe investment banking firms that considered Drexel Burnham to be anathema. Everyone knew that the key players at Drexel were arrogant, aggressive and most importantly, largely Jewish. Supposedly this was never an issue. Yeah, right!

As I walked into the lobby of the building where my firm's offices were located, a variety of thoughts stampeded their way through my consciousness. Here I was, the chairman and chief executive of my own Wall Street investment banking firm. Surpassing the wildest, most hopeful, most insane dreams of my mother and father and Charmaine.

I had to wonder about what those unseen powers had done to Drexel Burnham. What on earth might they do if the plans that we discussed at the Water Club ever came to reality?

I had to smile at that. The unseen powers certainly did not scare me. I knew that they were there, so that was half the battle as far as I was concerned. I have certainly seen worse in my time.

You should know that I am a graduate of Yale University and that I received my MBA from Columbia. Most people in The Pride know that I began my professional career as an analyst at Merrill Lynch and that I was considered something of a "star" at Salomon Brothers before founding my own firm.

What is also true, and what very few people know, is that there is a whole other side to my life. I am sure that nobody in The Pride knows except that damn Gordon Perkins. And sometimes I could kick myself dead in the ass for drinking with him that night and running my mouth.

The truth is that I have been arrested so many times that I lost count. I was in jail on numerous occasions as a teenager in Philadelphia. The truth is that I was present at several homicides and assaults, although I was never convicted of any crimes related to those events. And the truth is that I was involved in any number of petty crimes before the age of seventeen.

My mother and father and Charmaine and Gordon are among the few people in my current life who know anything about this side of me. There is no explaining my past behavior. No broken home. No abusive treatment by my parents. No dysfunctional family.

My father was a postal worker and my mother a hospital maintenance worker. They worked hard to provide me with a comfortable home and all the educational opportunity that they could afford and then some. They tried hard to raise me in a proper and steadfast fashion in a small home on Osage Avenue in West Philadelphia.

I am told that I was a unique child. I was very bright, "whip smart" they called me. When I spent time on academic endeavors, I excelled. No matter the school, no matter the subject, no matter the competition. But I was also an absolute knucklehead, doing the wrong thing, just because it was the wrong thing. There was no sense in my own particular universe. It was kind of an inner-city Dada approach to life.

I am more than thankful that my sons are nothing like me and a lot like their mother as far as their conduct and deportment is concerned. I would have had to absolutely strangle the young Jerome Hardaway. In fact, I realize how much my parents must have loved me because they didn't just throw me off a bridge or send me to my Maker in some other fittingly Philly fashion.

Nothing seemed to work on me in those days. Threats, punishment, bribes, entreaties, beatings, made no difference. I cringe when I think of how perverse I must have seemed to my mother and dad. A hundred years of my success won't make up for the pain that I caused them.

I was a frequent visitor to the juvenile courts of the city of Philadelphia. I am sure that anyone who gave a damn about me as I backed into my senior year of high school figured that a penitentiary or a cemetery was waiting for me in the near future. No need to confirm the reservation.

I can't help but be reminded by Paul's theory about the Law of Unintended Consequences. The notion that all kinds of things happen that have nothing to do with the original intent of the actors is an interesting concept. I can testify to it playing a major, indeed pivotal, role in my life.

CHAPTER 39

Jerome

Welcome to the Law of Unintended Consequences

Jonathan Bedford Samuels was an illustrious graduate of Yale University (Class of 1949). He was an extremely successful businessman (steel, petroleum, precious metals) and a renowned philanthropist. It was not surprising that Mr. Samuels was such a success in business—he was born to take his place in the hierarchy of American business. His mother was part of the Bedford family, a Maine institution. His father, Charles Wilson Samuels, was part of a family that had owned a good part of northwestern Connecticut for at least two hundred years.

His philanthropy was to be expected as well. Most of it was directed to Yale. It was part of his family tradition.

But just as certain evolutionary changes—the first amphibian, the first beast to walk upright—take place for no reason, Jonathan Samuels just changed his approach to philanthropy and life, and in the process, changed my life forever. If you asked him he probably could not tell you where his bright idea, his revolutionary idea, came from.

It is said that a moment of inspiration occurred to Mr. Samuels while he was sitting on his yacht on Long Island Sound. He considered the notion that the same leadership and organizational skills that were the hallmark of generals, presidents and corporate chairmen, were also the leadership and organizational skills that were the hallmark of successful gang leaders and heads of criminal syndicates. His musings continued.

If his theory was valid, then it should only be a matter of giving the gang leaders and criminal syndicate heads an alternative that the smartest of the group would comprehend as an avenue to greater and safer wealth and success. And, if that were true, then finding a way to channel and focus the energy and intelligence of young people headed in the wrong direction could produce outstanding citizens, could indeed change the world. And those musings begat the Star Search Foundation.

Operating on Jonathan Samuel's moment of inspiration, and his generous philanthropy, within a few years the Star Search Foundation had scoured the school records and national achievement test results of thousands of inner-city high school students. A network made up of the administrators of the best public and private schools in major cities began with New York, Chicago, Washington, Los Angeles . . . and Philadelphia. Clearly it's always better to be lucky than good.

Star Search was looking for extremely bright young men and women who were clearly headed in a direction that absolutely and positively did not include college. Star Search was looking for the kind of young people that Jonathan Bedford Samuels had in mind on that yacht on Long Island Sound that day. Young people who, with guidance and opportunity, could become some of the leaders and achievers of this country. And that's how Star Search found my sorry ass and changed my life forever.

I can tell you that I absolutely did not believe or trust the first couple of letters that I got from the Foundation. I do remember throwing the letters out with a nagging curiosity growing in the back of my consciousness. I also remember throwing the third letter into the trash and not tearing it up. And then I remember taking the letter out of the trash, smoothing it out and calling the Star Search Foundation. I will never know what made me do it. I am just glad that I did.

I picked the right time to change my life. It was also the right time for Star Search to "suggest" some applicants to the Class of 1971 at Yale University. By the way, I later learned that Jonathan Samuels actually *increased* his financial support of Yale when he founded Star Search, making it almost impossible for the university officials to say no when Star Search made the "suggestion." And that's basically how I wound up at Yale University.

In later years, Charmaine would ask me whether I felt intimidated by my freshman year in New Haven. In response I would have to gently remind her about my past, and how nothing that might be at the Yale University colleges could compare to the sociopaths, knuckleheads, gangsters, hustlers and killer bitches that I knew and hung with in Philadelphia. Compared to bullets, knives, fists and bad intentions, the achievement tests were a breeze. Plus, I always enjoyed taking those standardized tests.

As it turned out, I tested off the charts when I attended the July 1967 orientation session for Star Search students. As a result the only freshman class I took was French, and I began my double major in economics and engineering.

Considering what I had seen in my short eighteen years, there wasn't a whole hell of a lot that I had in common with my Yale classmates. I didn't fit in and at the time, frankly, I did not feel the need to fit in. I have never been about that.

And it wasn't simply a racial thing. I certainly did not have very much in common with the white graduates of Choate, Croton, and Deerfield. Similarly, I sure in hell didn't have much in common with my black classmates who called Baldwin Hills, Shaker Heights, Teaneck, and Long Island home. It was simply a matter of perspective.

Of course there were the inevitable knuckleheads who either believed the hype about white superiority or had been duped and bamboozled into believing that black people don't know about intimidation and retaliation.

And so, there was that day, in my freshman year, when I found myself face-to-face with a drunken member of the world-class Yale swimming team. I was about six-three and 190 then, and I remember him being significantly taller and bigger than me. Probably six-seven and 230 pounds would be about right.

On this night, Mr. Swimteam found that he had an uncontrollable urge to rub the head of a black man for good luck. And, as fate would have it, the head that he just had to rub was sitting on my shoulders.

I later found out that Mr. Swimteam, in his sophomore year at Yale University, had literally never had any substantive, challenging contact with a black person except the housekeeper at his home in Wellesley, Massachusetts. So I guess one could say that his desire to rub my head was understandable and certainly worthy of forgiveness.

Unfortunately for Mr. Swimteam, I did not share this perspective. To be succinct, I blew Mr. Swimteam up. Kicked his stupid ass.

My fighting skills had no formal orthodoxy. I learned through survival and trial with no error allowed. Let's just say that my skills were sufficient to put Mr. Swimteam in the hospital. And when he did recover he could compete in some swim meets only on a limited basis in his senior year.

As you can imagine, the result of this particular incident had its humorous aspect. In the first instance, after that, no one, absolutely no one, no matter how angry, drunk, racist, high or insane, ever thought it was a good idea to mess with me. As a result, the rest of my time at Yale was remarkably free of these types of incidents.

The unintended result was a remarkable degree of racial peace and harmony that existed at Yale during the late sixties and early seventies. I later learned that my incident with Mr. Swimteam, who is now a United States senator, became of the stuff of Yale campus legend. The tale of our encounter was retold over many a beer, joint and glass of wine. Many of the white students were not sure which of the limited number of black students was me. So, rather than engage in the harassment of a black student who could have turned out to be me, most white students determined that the best course of action was to simply leave the black students alone.

Since, as black students, we were already infinitely outnumbered in New Haven, in the state of Connecticut, and America, most of us had the good sense not to instigate or participate in nonpolitical confrontations that could turn unpredictably physical. Some wrestling, shoving, a few minor league punches. That was one thing. Throwing down with no mercy, that was another thing entirely. And something to be avoided if at all possible. It was a great recipe for survival, and it allowed me to continue with a personal transition that I never would have believed.

To my parents' never-ending wonder, satisfaction and amazement, there was something about the challenge of being at Yale that struck just the right chord with me. My contrarian impulses took over once again.

I could tell in the tone of voice of counselors, in the barely hidden condescension of instructors and students, that I was expected to fail. I decided that was exactly what I would never do. I would succeed just to drive these people crazy. But then something happened that I could never have expected.

I actually began to enjoy school. I began to pursue my studies with a passion that I used to reserve for gangbanging and ripping people. I discovered that I actually enjoyed learning. I couldn't stop reading Fanon, Sartre, Dickens, Baldwin, Wright, Virgil, and Musashi Miyamoto. It was like popcorn, once I got started, there was no way that I could stop. And I have never wanted to stop since then. Since then all I have wanted to know is everything.

I learned later that my success at Yale was considered to be the ultimate validation of the founding premises of the Star Search Foundation. My life story was the real-life laboratory results for which they were searching. Lucky me.

By my junior year I was on a track that looked pretty good. I was on schedule to graduate ahead of time, with honors in all my subjects. My double major in economics and engineering was demanding, but it occupied my time and my life. I had no complaints. As far as I was concerned, life was O.K., as complete as it could be at that stage in my life. But I was wrong.

CHAPTER 40

Jerome

Charmaine

Charmaine Leslie Cumberbatch was the daughter of Dr. Lionel Cumberbatch and Mrs. Mattie Hatfield Cumberbatch of Shaker Heights, Ohio. When they first moved to one of the finest suburban towns in America in 1961, the Cumberbatches were one of the few black families to live in that exclusive residential enclave.

Now that I know the man, I am absolutely sure that it mattered not in the least to Dr. Cumberbatch that he was the first black any thing, anywhere. He expected, demanded and got only the best for his family. It was simply a non-negotiable point in his universe. In his view, Shaker Heights was the best place to live in the Cleveland area, and that was essentially the end of the discussion as far as he was concerned. Prejudiced real estate brokers, appalled neighbors and puzzled friends just had to learn to live with it.

Charmaine, one of the three Cumberbatch daughters, went to the local Catholic school system through junior high school, and then she went to Shaker Heights High School, which, at the time, was ranked among the top private schools in America in terms of the academic achievements of its students.

Charmaine attended with her sisters, Beverly and Cynthia. Beverly later went on to Stanford University and graduated from Harvard Medical School. Cynthia attended the Fashion Institute of Technology, and is now a noted women's wear designer in Milan. Charmaine, for all of her accomplishments was very different, and pursued a very different life even before she met me.

I am sure that it's pretty clear that, given my background, just showing up on the Cumberbatch front porch to take Charmaine to the movies would have precipitated paroxysms for Dr. and Mrs. Cumberbatch. But the truth of the matter is that Lionel and Mattie have always been pretty cool with me once they understood that my feelings for Charmaine were sincere.

Charmaine has the soul of an artist and the brain of a scientist. She has tried to pursue both passions with equal energy and vigor. So it must come as no surprise to learn that she was a National Merit Scholar in English literature and biology. At Mount Holyoke College for Women, she was the lead in all the Drama Club productions and also one of the top students in the pre-med program. As far as she was concerned, it didn't have to make sense to anyone else. It made sense to her. And, as far as I can tell, that's the way it's always been with Charmaine.

I suppose that it was a sign of the times that schools like Yale and Williams, Dartmouth and Wellesley, Mount Holyoke and Harvard all had black student organizations. While they all had sociopolitical objectives, the social agenda was never too far down on the list. This was especially crucial in light of the fact that so many of the young black men and women attending these schools felt socially isolated at the time, despite their presumed familiarity with white America.

So, just like their white counterparts, these groups and organizations scheduled mixers and other social events. It was a fairly reliable way for young men and women in college to meet. And then, of course, nature could take its course.

And so it came to pass, on a late autumn day in New Haven, a busload of about forty young black women from Mount Holyoke arrived on the Yale campus. By then Charmaine was a sophomore, majoring in organic chemistry. She has always told me that she went on the trip because her best friends teased her into going. They seized upon the fact that up until then she had not been very "social." I now know that the furthest thing from her mind was the idea of meeting the love of her life.

At the time of our meeting I considered myself very successful with the young ladies. When I was running with the gangs in Philly, there were very few women who would say no to me. At Yale, I was truly busy with my studies, but I was not a damned monk. I rarely felt myself feeling lonely or neglected.

In the late sixties and early seventies, there was a certain black militant chic that pervaded many of the college campuses. I guess it was a kind of precursor to the gangster chic that gallops through young black America today.

Back then it was important to have a big Afro. Military jackets and sunglasses were *de rigueur*, combat boots were optional. Being somewhat aggressive, assertive and possibly combative were also part of the effect that many young brothers adopted.

Not trying to sound immodest, the fact is that, at the time, I had been there and done that. I had been as tough as the toughest and had backed down from no one when there were no ivy-covered walls or campus police to back my play. I saw no need to advertise. I was very happy being myself and there was simply no reason to prove anything to my relatively privileged black classmates at Yale.

Nevertheless there were a couple of occasions that were reminiscent of the "Mr. Swimteam" episode. I remember the time a couple of my black classmates saw it as their righteous and holy mandate to make sure that somehow, someway, I would feel that I did not "belong."

As a result, a few of my more knuckle-headed classmates left Yale University with a double degree. One taught them all about the nuances of their major and the other taught them to never, ever, mess with me. In that aspect of their degree they graduated *summa cum laude*.

Oddly, none of this had anything to do with that particular autumn Saturday night in New Haven. It seemed a no brainer to go to the mixer with scores of black women from colleges throughout New England being in attendance. My motivation for going that night was, frankly, hormonal. If anyone had told me what was about to happen next, I would just have had to laugh at the sheer, unabashed, shameless romanticism of it all.

I can still visualize the entire beginning of that evening. I was at one end of the gym where the mixer was being held. I was just beginning to sip some absolutely nonalcoholic punch as I looked for a place to sit and take in the proceedings that were about to begin. That's because at these events, at least in the sixties, black "mixers" at schools like Yale and Harvard and Princeton and Dartmouth served as the setting for cultural clashes as distinctive and meaningful as anything found along the Gaza Strip.

You could see brothers from the projects of Detroit trying to talk a hole in the neck of some Jack & Jill alumna from one of the "finer families" of Baltimore. You would find Alabama ingénues bewitching Los Angeles *bon vivants*. You could make a movie about it all.

As I was getting ready to sit down I was bumped by a gasp of loveliness that boldly looked me in the eye and immediately let me know that she knew that I knew that she knew . . . that our meeting was destiny and history . . . and love.

"Excuse me. Can I get rid of that pesky punch bowl that seems to be in your way?" was the wittiest *bon mot* that I could offer, given that I was at ground zero of a nuclear emotional explosion. I still cannot put into words the ebb and flow of currents that reshaped my heart and soul in that very moment.

We were still in our late teens so there was no Richard Wright or William Shakespeare dialogue. But the poetry of our first encounter is eternal as far as I am concerned, and I would bet my life that Charmaine still feels the same way too.

As my comment faded into infinite banality, our eyes met, as the saying goes. In truth that is what happened. And at that moment I knew a feeling that I had never felt. Love? Lust? Desire? Surrender? All of the above?

But, at that very moment, we were both stunned into silence. Anyone who has ever experienced love at first sight knows what I am talking about. Tongue glued to the roof of a Sahara-dry mouth. Sweaty palms flowing with ever-growing rivers of perspiration. Speed-racing heart and a galloping pulse worthy of the Kentucky Derby. A tingling in the fingertips that presaged the collapse of the dam that held back all emotions and feelings.

Frankly, with all my "experience" I did not know what to say. Charmaine, with all of her "upbringing and breeding," did not know what to say either. A pure romantic would say that we just stood there staring into each other's souls. We were overjoyed to be drowning in a whirlpool of love and desire.

I felt like Sir Edmund Hillary on his very best day. Charmaine later told me that she felt like Althea Gibson at Wimbledon. Witty commentary was not going to happen that night.

"Would you like to dance, Mr. . . . ?"

The first strains of "I Heard It Through the Grapevine" by Gladys Knight and the Pips coursed over the loudspeakers. The dance floor started to fill up immediately.

"As Mary Wells would say, 'you beat me to the punch.'" It was the best that I could muster as a response, and I headed to the dance floor with an angel on earth. I didn't have time to calculate the damage, but I knew that I had been seriously smitten.

And so we danced, and danced, through the night. In later years, we would both have to admit that we would never give the Soul Train dancers a run for their money. But we enjoyed ourselves thoroughly. And we enjoyed each other. It was like the whole world had disappeared and there was no one but Charmaine and me.

By the time the disc jockey played Smokey Robinson's "Ooh Baby Baby" as the last dance, Charmaine told me that she decided to go back to my room since she was going to spend the rest of her life with me anyway. And the strangest thing was that I felt the very same way. And what is most amazing is that in the last twenty-five years, nothing has really changed between us. It is like we just met over the punch bowl in New Haven last night.

Charmaine moved in with me in New Haven after the Christmas break, much to the horror and disappointment of her parents. But after Dr. and Mrs. Cumberbatch met us together they realized that they were in the presence of inevitable, unconquerable, irreplaceable love. To their credit, they have supported and loved the two of us ever since. We got married at the end of the spring term of my junior year.

The plan was for Charmaine to resume her studies after I finished business school. Aside from bringing the everlasting brilliance of love to my life, Charmaine also has been my best and most trusted advisor. She convinced me that my future lay in the business arena. To use her words, "you can always hire an engineer if you feel like changing the world." And she has always made me feel like changing the world, which is one more reason why I liked Paul's idea so much.

But in the latter part of my senior year, Charmaine started falling ill, repeatedly. At first my chest puffed out with pride as I thought that this was the first signs of pregnancy. But that pride was soon snuffed out as we realized that it was not pregnancy, but something entirely different.

Various specialists at Yale Medical School simply did not have the answer. Dr. Cumberbatch called upon his entire national network of experts and specialists, and still, no answer. And then, we finally got an answer, and a diagnosis.

It turned out that Charmaine was experiencing the first stages of multiple sclerosis. And there was no cure. And she would never be the same.

Just like that, our lives changed once more. But Charmaine was not afraid or shaken by the diagnosis, because she knew that I would always be there for her. And I have been there for her from that day to this very minute.

When I heard the diagnosis I can honestly say that I never felt shortchanged, cheated or cursed by fate. I have always looked upon her health challenges as an opportunity to show her how much I love her and how special she is in my life. And I know that I always will.

As Charmaine's situation stabilized and we learned to live with it, I went to Columbia Business School, and it was to an apartment on Morningside Drive that we brought our first child home. And despite Charmaine's health challenges, we have had two children, Jerome Jr. and Hannibal. I went on to work on Wall Street, and five years ago, I formed my own firm.

Now Charmaine and I live in Hastings-on-Hudson right outside New York City. We have cars and maids and drivers and our children live a life of privilege and comfort. We like to consider ourselves down to earth, but in reality, our feet rarely touch the streets that I knew as a teenager in Philadelphia.

CHAPTER 41

Jerome

Raymond Russell Beard III

The chill of the January evening snapped me out of my reverie as the arctic winds began to prowl the serpentine streets of the Wall Street district. I started into the building where my offices were located. It had been an interesting day, but it was not over.

As I got into the elevator to my thirty-second floor suite of offices, I considered the future. I did not survive and prevail in Philadelphia, Yale, and Columbia by being a fool. I have always paid attention.

From the first day that I met Raymond Russell Beard III I knew that there was the possibility of a problem. He was extremely bright, one of the smartest people that I had ever met. He was always ambitious and self-assured, right up to the precipice of arrogance, with a few toes poking over the line. And he has been just the kind of person that I wanted in my organization. Up to the day of Winner Tomlinson's funeral and the luncheon thereafter, he had been perfect.

I think that Ray's problem was that he came from one of those special black families in Atlanta. In that city there is a coterie of families that has kept to themselves. The members of these families have thought of themselves as being better than most black people primarily because of the high incidence of preachers, lawyers, doctors and undertakers and light-skinned relatives in their midst.

As a child of that world Ray grew up believing that he was entitled to the best of everything. And, if he was not recognized as the first, the best, the brightest, in whatever forum, something was fundamentally, institutionally wrong.

After meeting Ray I learned that he was entitled to more than a few ass-whippings during his early days at Morehouse College. His attitude, however, sustained him through Harvard Law School and his first few years on Wall Street.

By the time he came to work for me he seemed to have his attitude problem under control. But I must confess that, at times, I had the eerie feeling that not only did Ray Beard feel that he was better than everybody else, he felt that he was better than me. It was a bizarre feeling that I have never really been able to explain.

I am not an insecure person. I have always welcomed the company of bright and brilliant and incandescent people into my personal universe. I never worry about how brightly my light shines. I can honestly say that at this stage in life I am comfortable with being me.

Nevertheless, there is an uneasiness that I have always had when it comes to Ray. The instincts that helped me survive and prevail in Philly, Yale, Columbia, and Wall Street tell me that I should always, always keep a close eye on Raymond Russell Beard III. And on that particular winter day in January I watched Ray. I did not miss a thing.

I am pretty sure that neither Gordon nor Diedre noticed a particularly nasty confrontation between Paul and Ray just before we left the Water Club. As best I can tell, it was Ray's attitude to which Paul took offense.

I don't know what was said, except it was clear that Paul took Ray by the arm and in that immobilizing act promised to beat the living shit out of him. And Ray clearly backed down.

I had seen how over-proud Ray had been at Winner's memorial service. I had watched Ray's over-proud play with the young TV reporter, leaving me to wonder once again why women would find a man so in love with himself to be attractive. I had watched him barely hide his discomfort as Paul set forth his plan for us. And frankly, I was very disappointed that Ray could not understand that he would be a part of whatever plan Paul described.

What I saw take place between Ray and Paul was Ray backing

down. Basically he rolled over and surrendered. There could be a lot of reasons why Ray might do all three of these things, beginning with the fact that Paul could kick his ass. Nevertheless, I really did not like seeing my so-called protégé back down and skulk out of the room, pouting like a girl.

I have known fear many times. But I rarely show it. And I never show it to an adversary.

But Ray Beard's pride and arrogance were just for show. They weren't real. And since I am sure that Ray knows that, he has always found a need to overplay his hand. The problem with that *modus operandi* is that on occasion you get your feelings hurt when someone calls you out.

As I exited the elevator and entered the lobby of my office it was close to five o'clock and so I simply nodded hello to the receptionist. I was at work now and for as long as I was here I would rule, I would decide, I would control.

That's just the way it had to be.

CHAPTER 42

Jerome

Berta's story

As I walked into my office, my secretary and personal assistant, Berta Colon, had all my messages and she told me everything I needed to know. Berta had an interesting story all by herself. It all starts with me believing that I had been condemned to Secretary Hell during the first ten years of my professional life.

I have had secretaries with men problems, child problems, weight problems, pet problems, butt problems, religious problems, allergy problems and sometimes just plain old madness. I had secretaries who could not spell. I had secretaries who could not type.

I had secretaries who did not know how to answer a telephone in a remotely professional fashion. I have had secretaries who had carried around an attitude as a matter of personal principle. I have had secretaries who thought that their job description included wearing short skirts with no underwear, bending over to pick up "dropped" pencils throughout the workday. And then came Berta.

Berta was a forty-something-year-old Puerto Rican woman who had been through several lifetimes of experience. Looking at Berta one would see a raven-haired beauty, with sparkling coal black eyes well on the way to their destiny as eternal diamonds. She had defied Father Time both in her appearance and in her spirit.

As I came to learn over time, she had grown up in East Harlem and was enrolled in the enriched school program in the best public school in that part of town in those days, Benjamin Franklin High School. Berta was accepted at Mount Holyoke College, Charmaine's alma mater, where she was supposed to go after graduating as class valedictorian. But Berta found out that she was pregnant right after graduation. The father was one of the Young Lords.

Not having the baby and going on with her education and her dreams was simply not an option for this young Catholic girl. She dutifully married Hector Colon, and they had a little boy, Hector Junior. For two years she worked as a bookkeeper at a bowling alley and tried to make a home life. She put her dreams of going to Mount Holyoke and becoming a lawyer on a back shelf in the cupboard of her mind.

And then Hector Senior discovered heroin. Or perhaps heroin discovered him. It really didn't matter. Whatever the case, he became hooked to the Boy Who Made Slaves Out of Men. The deterioration and destruction of this bright, ambitious and committed young man was dramatic and shocking to Berta and Hector Junior. Within a few months Hector had moved out of their apartment and it did not surprise Berta in the least when the police came to tell her that Hector Colon, formerly a dynamic and charismatic leader of the Young Lords, husband of Berta, and father of Hector Junior, had been found dead of an overdose on the rooftop of a movie theater in the South Bronx.

To her credit, this did not beat Berta down. She knew that grief was not going to pay the rent. Her heartbreak did not put shoes on Hector Junior's feet. The bowling alley job was not going to be enough and right after the funeral she started looking for a new job.

She found a position working as a personal assistant to the talent agent who represented Latin music stars like Celia Cruz, Ray Barretto, Willie Colon, and Tito Puente. Berta was bright, loyal, talented and personable, and she has always been able to take care of business. And it was not long before she was managing the business affairs for some of the biggest names in the Latino music world.

This work required her to go on the road a lot more than she wanted. Of course this meant that she had to spend time away from Hector Junior. Too much time as it turned out.

The money was good and for twelve years she would wake up too many mornings in hotel rooms in Miami, Paris, Los Angeles, or San Juan. She would be by herself wondering what the hell she was doing so far from her son.

And then one day she received a call in Atlanta from the headmaster of the boarding school in Connecticut which Hector Junior attended. She was told that Hector was about to be expelled for fighting and starting fires.

Berta called New York and told her boss that she was quitting immediately. She flew back to New York that afternoon and was in Connecticut picking up Hector Junior within ten hours of the wake up call that changed her life.

Within the week Berta had found an apartment in Riverdale in the Bronx and enrolled her son at a Catholic school three blocks away. She obtained work with a temporary secretarial services agency. That way she could set her own work schedule and have as much time for Hector Junior as he needed.

Before too long, thanks to Berta being with him, Hector was just fine. He got into very few fights, his academic record improved. And there were no more fires.

Over the next few years Hector grew up to become a fine young man. Berta's heart was full and fulfilled because of this remarkable transformation. She had plenty of work as a temporary executive secretary. Paris and Los Angeles and San Juan seemed a million miles away.

But the one constant in life is change. Her son continued to excel at school and he received a full academic scholarship to Temple University in Philadelphia. He was close enough so that Berta could see him often and conveniently. But he was far enough away so that she knew that in many ways she was alone. And she came to know that in many ways she was alone for the first time in her life.

It was about this time that I was going through my eighth (or ninth or one hundredth) secretary since I had started my firm. I was giving serious thought to resigning myself to working with temporary secretaries for the rest of my life. And then the agency for whom Berta worked assigned her to me for a month.

In our professional roles, we were made for each other. Berta was the smart, intense, loyal and intuitive assistant that I had needed and had been looking for. She has always seemed to just understand what I am trying to do without my having to say a word. Someone once said that watching us work together was like watching Magic Johnson and James Worth working on a fast break that would lead to the inevitable slam dunk.

I know that I can always take care of myself. Nevertheless, I have to confess that Berta's protective nature clears a few minefields in my daily life. There is something about her that makes me feel that she would stand between me and the doors of hell. And it has been this silent, brutal, gentle velvet ferocity that I have valued the most. And this is what has made her the most trusted person in my organization.

West Philly, Yale, Columbia, and Wall Street have taught me one thing, if nothing else. Always watch your back. Berta always has watched my back.

CHAPTER 43 ·

Jerome

Bad moon rising

And as I walked through the doors that led to my office suite I could tell by the look on Berta's face that there was a problem that she couldn't handle. But this was a problem that I had been expecting since the luncheon at the Water Club.

"Good afternoon, Mr. Hardaway." The arch of Berta's eyebrow confirmed that my intuition was correct.

"I guess it is evening, Berta. Obviously lunch went a little longer than I had planned. No need for you to stay late though."

"Anything I need to know regarding the lunch? I didn't see it on your schedule." Berta completely ignored my lightweight attempt at humor regarding her working late. And she would wear gold lamé curl-toed slippers to work sooner than she would leave the office before the work of the day was completed.

Her comment regarding her surprise at my unexpected lunch meeting was discreet and I heard her loud and clear. Berta knew that I would always tell her everything that she needed to know. When it came to work we had no secrets between us.

"Please make sure to remind me to tell you all about it tomorrow. Paul had some interesting ideas to share with Gordon Perkins, Diedre Douglas, and myself over lunch.

"I am going to need your help in putting together some information that I need for the next meeting that we have scheduled. I already put it in my personal book. You can copy the details later."

I was leafing through Berta's file of notes, correspondence and other papers while speaking with her. I noticed that the door to my private office was ajar. I always like to keep it closed. Berta knew that. Something was up. Again, I was not surprised in the least. I kept on with the business of the day.

"By the way, I have to attend a dinner at Diedre Douglas's home the Thursday before President's Day weekend. Paul, Gordon, and Ray will also be there."

"Do I need to make arrangements for Mrs. Hardaway?" This was Berta's way of asking whether the event was social or business. I could also sense her tensing.

"No Berta. Charmaine will not be attending."

"By the way, speaking of Mr. Beard . . . he's in your office right now, waiting for you. Mr. Hardaway, you know I know how you feel about people in your office when you are not around. Let's just say that Mr. Beard was very insistent.

"I might have stopped him from going in there. But I also *know* how you feel about anyone causing scenes in your office."

I had to keep myself from smiling at the thought of Berta booting Ray Beard out of my office. Berta worked on Wall Street, lived in Riverdale and had been to Paris and seen the world. But Berta had never left East Harlem behind. Ray would never know how lucky he was.

"Like I said, he was very insistent. And, he seemed upset. I have never seen him like this before. So I made a judgment call. And I know how much special interest that you have shown to Mr. Beard. So I let him wait in your office."

There was something about the way that she gave me all of this information that let me know about her ambivalence regarding my very high opinion of Ray. I certainly picked up on it.

Ray was my protégé, that's for sure. Some people thought of him as my *alter ego,* even though that certainly was never the case.

He was somebody whom I thought to be very, very special. And I wanted to make sure that he was being groomed for something very special in the future of my firm.

In my view special people deserve special treatment. Just his being in my private office was special treatment in my book. That was for sure. But I do recall the moment when the coats of finishing provided by Wall Street, Columbia, and Yale almost fell away, leaving the original West Philadelphia to surface, and I was ready to jump all over young Mr. Beard. Fortunately for both of us, it was only for a nanosecond . . . or two.

I could tell that Berta could tell, however. Ray was his usual oblivious self, simmering and stewing in my office. But Berta and I both knew that Raymond Russell Beard III was a very lucky man.

I composed myself. I knew what kind of conversation Ray and I were going to have. I really wasn't in the mood.

"Thanks, Berta. If there's nothing else, why don't you plan to leave for the day? It would seem that I should take some time to consult with Ray."

This time it was me arching an eyebrow as I said "consult." I know that Berta appreciated the rather subtle humor that I was employing to help me get myself together.

"Thanks, Mr. Hardaway. Have a good evening and I will see you in the morning."

"The morning will be just fine Berta. Get home safely."

With that Berta went to straighten up her desk and I turned toward my office. I took a deep breath and walked in. At least Ray wasn't sitting at my desk. I had to smile to myself at the thought of what my reaction would have been.

CHAPTER 44

Jerome

Something about Raymond . . .

"Good afternoon, Ray."
"I sure as hell don't know what's good about it."

As I headed toward my desk, I could see Ray was standing near one of the picture windows that surrounded my office. I could have sworn that he was actually pouting. At the time I just couldn't believe it. Later, I realized that it was true.

"I'm just not following you, Ray. What seems to be your problem?"

"Jerome, do I have to spell it out for you? Do I have to paint a picture? You saw what happened at the Water Club this afternoon."

"I was there, Jerome . . ."

"Then you know."

"Ray, obviously you are agitated. We are both tired. We are both busy. I sure as hell have better things to do than play Twenty Questions with you tonight. And I would hope that you have better things to do on my time than to tell me something that we both already know.

"I'll tell you what I know. I didn't see or hear any problems for you, me or the firm this afternoon. So I'm giving you a few more minutes so that you can tell me about your problem and then we can both get back to work."

I knew for a fact that Raymond Russell Beard III was a thoroughbred. He came from excellent stock as the saying goes. He was trained at Morehouse and Harvard to prepare him for The Big Time. But at that moment in time he was just another angry thirty-year-old who was dangerously approaching that perilous province called Out of Control, nostrils flared, lip poked out, eyes blazing. He was a poster boy for the Angry Young Brother Syndrome.

On that particular evening I was simply determined not to get caught up in Ray's attitude or antics. I had a lot on my mind, and Ray's attitude did not make the Top Ten. On the other hand, Ray had become important to the firm and me, and so it made sense to at least pay attention to Ray for another few minutes. His allotted time was running out, however.

"Jerome, you saw what happened!"

"Ray, now you are repeating yourself. And you are getting much too loud." The last part of my comment was delivered with a look that even an enraged Ray Beard was smart enough to decode imme-diately. I could tell in the immediate change in his attitude and tone that he realized that he had come as close to the line between com-plaint and confrontation as it was wise for him to do. He was angry. But he was no fool. At least he was not a complete fool.

"I apologize, Jerome . . . it's just that for two hours, Paul, Gordon, Diedre, even you . . . ignored me! Treated me like I was just part of the furniture. It was humiliating. I felt like a fool."

"Ray, I am going to ask you once again to calm yourself down and think about it . . . just for a minute. You were there because I invited you and I wanted you there. Gordon, Diedre, and Paul went along with my request. It's just that simple.

"If you were going to be ignored, believe me, I could have let you spend your entire time at the Water Club talking to that TV reporter. I wanted you at the table. I didn't think that you required an en-graved invitation to realize that."

While I was not in danger of losing my temper, I suddenly got the feeling that I needed to tell Ray a little bit more about the facts of life and at least have him contemplate the fact that I might lose my tem-per with him. I looked him right in the eye as I continued to speak.

"To tell you the truth, Ray, I first asked that you come along to lunch as a courtesy. But as Paul spoke this afternoon, it was clear to me that if this deal was ever to come through, I would need your help in making it work. You were there because I *thought* that you were ready to be a prime-time player.

"Now, if I need to hold your hand and pat you on the back all the time to let you know that everything is O.K., just tell me. But I will tell you Ray, I need people who can help me. I am not looking for anyone that I have to help. Just remember that."

I could tell that Ray was totally taken aback—rocked on his heels, as it were. I am sure that he thought that he was taking the offensive by waiting for me in my office.

But whatever tactical advantage he thought he might have must have evanesced for him once I started to tell him about his place in the real world, at least his place in my real world. To Ray's credit, he did have the presence of mind to know that he had gone just about far enough on his excellent adventure into Temper Land. And I had come about as close as I cared to on that January evening. It was time to lighten the tone.

"Ray, if you have something to add about today—Paul's idea, Gordon's suggestion, what the agenda should be at Diedre's next month, just tell me. Of course. If you just want to vent, knock yourself out.

"But I will tell you, Raymond Russell Beard the Third, your best bet would be to use that phone number you got from that TV reporter before it gets too late in the day.

"I know that if I were in your shoes, I would be on the phone right now instead of doing a flamenco dance on my desk. As I recall, she does the eleven o'clock news so I am sure that she has time for dinner beforehand. It's your move, Ray."

Ray now had a look on his face as if I had been reading his mind. Particularly with respect to the comment regarding the TV reporter. A dopey, sheepish grin began to stroll its way across his grim visage. I never would have believed his resentment continued to burn, probably deeper even more than he realized.

"You are definitely right, Jerome. What can I say? I guess I should listen to my big brother and make that call. I guess I just read the whole thing all wrong today. All wrong. I don't know what I could have been thinking. Thanks for setting me straight."

"Listen Ray, if you never venture into foolish territory, you will never know what smart is all about. Don't worry about it. Let's just move on. O.K.?"

"That's fine with me, Jerome. I am going to take your advice and make that call now. See you in the morning."

"Enjoy your dinner. I have a feeling that you will. Monique Jefferson seems like a lovely young lady. I am guessing that it will be a good way for you to spend your evening. Try not to be too late tomorrow morning." That last comment was followed by a wink and an exchange of smiles that felt sincere at the time. I remember that at that point we embraced spontaneously. That was very interesting in that neither of us were the hug-your-brother type. I thought that I had allayed Ray's concern. As it turned out, he had simply decided that it wasn't time for him to show his true heart.

He would do that later. He would do that much too soon. In any event, time would prove that it was all meant to be.

CHAPTER 45

Sture

Meanwhile, some things never change

Running a popular bar and restaurant that also serves as a hangout for very special people in New York City is just a magnificent experience. There are so many stories that I have from working at Dorothy's that I almost don't know where to begin. I do know that I am often reminded that I am a long, long way from Bergen.

I remember noticing that after Winner Tomlinson's memorial service Paul Taylor, Gordon Perkins, Diedre Douglas, Jerome Hardaway, and Ray Beard started meeting for lunch and drinks more frequently than I had noticed in the past. Not all five together, just in different combinations—Ray with Jerome, Diedre and Paul, Gordon and Ray. This was not particularly noteworthy since they were all friends and colleagues. But they were clearly meeting on purpose and not just bumping into each other.

One of the reasons why I really enjoy working at Dorothy's is that there is a never-ending stream of fascinating, delightful people who come through there. Sometimes it's the superstars of The Pride, people like Mayor Dinkins, Will Smith and Jada Pinkett Smith, Wesley Snipes, Ken Chennault, Jesse Jackson, Oprah Winfrey, Gordon Perkins, Denzel Washington, Edwin Tomlinson, Robert Johnson, and others of the same type of personage.

And then, there are the personas that are not the centerpiece of The Pride, but they are charter members nonetheless. They might be lawyers, advertising executives, consultants, community organizers, investment bankers. The one thing that they have in common is that they are fascinating.

I remember running into a few of that crowd at the bar of Dorothy's early in the evening after Winner's memorial service. There was Trinidad "Trini" Satterfield, five feet two inches of absolute foolishness and simultaneous genius. Trini was a practical joker of mythic proportions and also one of the most brilliant advertising executives in New York City. Although he was nearing sixty, Trini had the temperament and energy of someone thirty years his junior.

To hear Trini tell the story, he was born in Trinidad (where else?) and came to the U.S. with his parents as a child during World War II. His father was one of the first West Indian politicians in New York City, having been a close associate of the inestimable, historic and legendary Silver Fox, J. Raymond Jones. Trini grew up a privileged child and was one of the few West Indians to attend Morehouse College in the early 1950s.

An improbable fullback on the college football team, Trini was an excellent student who also honed his social skills for all time. One of his close friends was a spoiled, indolent black prince from one of Atlanta's leading black families, Martin King Jr.

The stories that he told about Martin Luther King Jr.'s college days would have resulted in the possible recall of the Nobel Peace Prize if they were ever made known to the general public. The women, the parties, the liquor was almost too much to believe. And I'm from Norway.

Then there was Ralph Watson. Ralph was a third-generation undertaker. His family had been running one of the leading funeral homes in Harlem since Adam Clayton Powell Senior moved the world-famous Abyssinian Baptist Church from 42nd Street to its current home in Harlem.

While the family business paid for his yacht and home in Sag Harbor, along with his home in Pelham Manor and his condo in Atlantic City and his teenage mistress in the East Village, he seemed to spend more time at the bar in Dorothy's than consoling bereaved families. Of course, this is just my observation. In any event, it's really none of my business.

Ralph, as a member of one of Harlem's finer families in the fifties and sixties, also had an absolutely privileged childhood leading to his absolutely privileged life. His feet never crossed the threshold of a public school, and his pre-college résumé was filled with names like Collegiate, Horace Mann, and Deerfield.

He went to Williams College and then Stanford University for his MBA. I am told that he really did not want to go into the dead body burying business and that his father had to fly out to California after the Stanford graduation and literally drag him out of a luxurious pleasure loft that Ralph had in the Mission District of San Francisco.

Rumor has it that when Ralph returned to New York he had at least one more rebellion in him. He hooked up with a couple of entrepreneurial types and started a talent management agency. One of their first clients was an all-girl rhythm and blues band that consisted of five gorgeous young ladies who could actually play their instruments and carry a tune.

One of the first gigs that Ralph's agency arranged for the band, I believe it was called Bad Gurlz, was at the women's facility at Riker's Island, New York City's jail. Not exactly a *primo* engagement, but Ralph and his colleagues figured that this would be a tough crowd and would give them a chance to find out if the Bad Gurlz were for real.

And, they figured, since the performance was going to be in the minimum security part of Riker's, they would be seated in an audience among women who had not been with a man in months, sometimes years. There should have been all kinds of "collateral benefits" in attending this performance. Ralph and his friends figured that these women would not be able to keep their hands off them and they would have some big fun while watching the Bad Gurlz try out their material.

Wrong.

Ralph and his colleagues left Riker's Island that evening with their virtue absolutely intact. Not only did the female inmates *not* put their hands (or anything else) all over them, they barely noticed them.

It was a different story with respect to the Bad Gurlz, however. They were a hit at Riker's. In fact they were almost too much of a hit. Their performance drove the women inmates into such a frenzy that security had to escort the Bad Gurls out of the prison auditorium. Ralph had not thought about the lesbian influences that surface in many women's prisons.

Bringing the Gurlz to the Riker's women's unit was like bringing Vanessa Del Rio and the Playboy Playmates of the Year to a Marine base at the end of basic training. Ralph and his buddies skulked out of the auditorium that night, as anonymous and as out of place as nuns in a strip club.

I am told that it was soon thereafter Ralph decided that the talent management business was not for him. And, obviously, he found a way to reconcile his love of living the high life with burying dead bodies all day. And that explains why he had the time and inclination to sit around the bar at Dorothy's By the Sea whenever he had the chance.

Completing the trio at the bar was the one and only Jerry James. Jerry's story was also pretty interesting. Orphaned before he was five, Jerry had grown up on the streets of the Bedford Stuyvesant section of Brooklyn until he was arrested and convicted of attempted murder and arson at the age of seventeen. By his own admission he was pretty much a "knucklehead" up until this point, well on his way to a dead-end appointment in maximum security or the cemetery.

However, while in prison Jerry got his high school equivalency diploma and in the process found that he had an aptitude and appreciation for academics. When he was released on parole at the age of twenty-two, a special MacArthur Foundation-sponsored program arranged for him to be enrolled at Williams College in Massachusetts. Upon graduating from Williams, he got an MBA from the University of Pennsylvania's Wharton School and he had worked in various positions in state and local governments since then, almost exclusively in New York.

Aside from being a brilliant government administrator, it was commonly thought that Jerry was pretty interesting in other ways. He had worked for Governors Rockefeller, Carey, and Cuomo. He worked for Mayors Lindsay, Koch, and Dinkins. As I mentioned, he was absolutely excellent as a government administrator.

But he also was reputed to be notorious in his use of all kinds of drugs although I have heard him say that alcohol was, and always would be, his best friend. Anybody who knew Jerry James has heard him say that he would never go out with a woman over the age of twenty-four, even though he himself had had his fiftieth birthday several years earlier.

It would be a semi-amusing throwaway line except that Jerry was serious and seemed to run his love life by this bizarre credo. He adhered to this rule even if that meant terminating otherwise satisfying relationships with young women who had the misfortune of reaching the quarter century mark.

As with other brilliant people that I have known, Jerry was erratic and unpredictable. His profanity was beyond any that I have ever heard from anybody. And another strange aspect of his social life was his "Five Per Cent Rule," a rule that requires further explanation.

This was the group that was sitting at the bar the evening of what turned out to be a most memorable day, drinking Belvedere vodka martinis and telling stories that most surely were born as lies. I remember a few of the tales that were told by that crew that night, and I still have to laugh at them. Jerry James started. While I make it a habit not to hover over my patrons, I will tell you that more than a few martinis had died noble deaths at the hands of this trio prior to the commencement of the storytelling.

"Did I ever tell you about the time I modeled in this men's magazine? It was *Ebony Man* actually."

"No, goddammit. And I don't feel like hearing any more of your motherfucking lies this evening. No one wants to hear how someone made a mistake by putting a picture of your tired ass in a magazine." Trini Satterfield was never one to mince words.

"Shut up, old motherfucker! Let me tell my story. It's the truth. I swear to God."

"Know we know you are lying. The truth couldn't mean anything coming from a lowlife like you." It was Ralph Watson's turn to chime in.

Now I have to mention that, if you just happened on this conversation, you might think that this kind of banter and insult presaged a possible outbreak of fisticuffs. I happen to know for a fact that these charter members of The Pride actually admired and respected each other in their own way. The insults and banter were just a part of how they got along. And I have found that no matter how sophisticated and successful some members of The Pride might be, this kind of banter and insult could surface during any moment of relaxation.

"If you knuckleheads would just listen for a minute. About fifteen years ago a college classmate of mine started working as an editor with this new magazine, *Ebony Man*. You may remember it. Johnson Publishing wanted a sophisticated magazine to appeal to black professional men. Obviously they weren't thinking about you two motherfuckers.

"Anyway, my buddy decided that he wanted to do a fashion issue without using professional models. Instead he wanted to use good-looking professional brothers like me."

"Your friend must have owed you a whole lot of money. Or did he just feel guilty about you finding out about him and your momma?" Trini was determined to stay on Jerry's case throughout his entire story. I wondered how he could keep his train of thought. That turned out not to be a problem.

"As I was saying . . . they asked me to pose in an Armani suit in one of those pseudo-hip poses—foot on a stair, elbow resting on leg, thoughtful yet promising facial expression. You've all seen the pose at least a million times."

"So what happened, Mr. Model Man? I don't have all goddamn night to listen to your bullshit stories." You could always count on Trini to keep firing no matter what. Jerry just pressed on, seemingly oblivious to hoots and catcalls from his own private audience.

"What happened is that I figured that this was going to be a great way to meet women. Even though it was a new magazine, I just *knew* that thousands of women would look at the magazine and my picture, and at least a half a dozen would call. If half of them were cute, I would have myself a good supply of bitches for the year.

"You all know my Five Per Cent Rule. Applying it to this situation seemed to be one hell of a smart move. As soon as the magazine came out, I couldn't wait for the phone to start ringing. It was spring time and I was expecting to have a hell of a summer harvesting a new crop of females."

"Since women rarely call your rusty black ass, this must have been a big goddamned deal for you. You are probably lucky you didn't wet your pants." Ralph Watson picked up on his role in this mini-Greek chorus.

"Fuck you, man. I am telling you this was a damned good plan. It was a great plan actually. There is no way that I wasn't going to be just swimming in women as soon as this magazine hit the stands. And you know what? The phone started ringing almost immediately."

"So, Soul Casanova, what happened with the phone calls that your tired ass got?" Trini could always be counted on for an unkind remark or two or three.

"Believe it or not, the first call was from some faggot in Baltimore named Bruce."

With that, Jerry's friends at the bar started laughing so hard they almost fell off their bar stools. I have to admit that by now I was laughing pretty loudly myself.

"You must be bullshitting! Please tell me you are bullshitting!" Ralph spoke these words with tears of laughter streaming down his cheeks.

"I wish I was, simple motherfucker. But the truth is that I received five stupid ass calls. Four were from faggots like Bruce and the fifth call was from some jailbird motherfucker serving time in Angola Prison in Louisiana. You talk about a waste of time. More importantly, talk about busted hopes and dreams!

"But you know what?"

"What? You Simple Simon motherfucker. I'm already tired of hearing about your sorry ass modeling career." Trini finished his comment and went to order a reinforcement for his rapidly disappearing martini.

"I am still trying to find a way to get in the *Ebony* "100 Most Eligible Bachelors.""

"What, you want to hear from your sissy fan club again?" Once again, it was Ralph's turn.

"No, dumb-ass. Listen to my theory, you might learn something. About eight million people read *Ebony*. About five million are women.

"Now if one out of ten of these women actually reads the Eligible Bachelor's article, that's 500,000 women. If one out of ten actually looks at the pictures and notices me, that's 50,000 women. If one out of ten of these women actually like my picture and bio, that's 5,000 women. If one out of ten of *these* women really like my picture and bio, that's 500 women.

"Now, if one out of ten of these women like my picture enough to try and contact me, that's fifty women. And if one out of ten of those women are fine, that's five women. And that's a lot of women. Certainly enough to tide me over for the year."

By the time Jerry finished his theory, Ralph and Trini were trying to survive the paroxysms of laughter that seemed to have possession of their very souls. Laughing and pounding their fists on the bar, tears of laughter streaming down their faces and peals of laughter echoing off the walls of Dorothy's. By now I had fully joined in the laughter although I knew better than to try and join in the banter so as to avoid being verbally sliced and diced to ribbons. Being from Norway there are some American skills that I just have not developed as yet. But I am trying.

Several people at the bar who found themselves to be unwitting eavesdroppers started to laugh as well. It didn't seem to bother Jerry James at all. He had kept right on with his out-to-lunch theory as if he were giving a soliloquy at Yale Drama School.

Trini was the first to compose himself enough to provide a response. He put his glass down and cleared his throat.

"I have always known that you are a dumb-ass motherfucker. But that has got to get the Olympic gold medal for stupid. I can't believe that you wasted Ralph's time and mine with that stupid shit. Remind me to tell you to shut the fuck up the next time you start speaking."

With that they ordered another round of martinis and continued their hardball bantering. It was time for me to check on some of the other prized patrons of Dorothy's By the Sea. But I knew that I would have to return to hear another story or seven before the evening ended.

CHAPTER 46

Paul

My mind is a camera

About a week after the luncheon meeting at the Water Club, Diedre and I spoke on the phone. By then I had started working on the merger project and I was starting to think that this was something that could really come to pass. It was fantastic, it was a ninety-nine yard pass to win the Super Bowl, but I could see how it could happen.

I was reviewing a memorandum to the file that I had written when Diedre called. My secretary knew to put her calls through. I recall scanning the memo as Diedre and I spoke: it basically summarized everything that had transpired at the Water Club. I have always found that contemporaneous documentation helps me keep track of what the hell I have been doing.

"Having a good day, Paul?"

"It's always a constant struggle to stay behind, you know that." It was an old line that I had used for years, but I always felt comfortable using it with Diedre.

"Paul, I hesitated to mention it on the ride back from the Water Club, but you really should have seen your face when you snatched Ray Beard."

"That son of a bitch had a lot more than that coming to him, that's for sure."

"Paul, I can't believe how angry you still are. Is this male menopause we are seeing or midlife crisis come early?" I could see her smiling broadly in my mind's eye as we spoke.

To tell the truth, I started to deny the entire reality to which she referred. But something came over me and I realized that I should just deal with what she was saying . . . it was true. And there was no need to try and hide my feelings from Diedre. She could always read me like a book.

"All I can say, Diedre, is that there is something about Ray Beard, his attitude, his way of being, who he is. Let's just say that his super-cilious pompous stuck-up pretentious conceited attitude got in the way for just a moment or two."

"I'll say." Diedre's enjoyment of my discomfiture virtually and mirthfully bubbled through the phone.

"Seriously, it's hard to put into words, but you know as well as anyone that when we got out of school and hit Wall Street, there was nothing, absolutely nothing that was handed to us. I remember too many idiots asking me if I played basketball while I was standing there in a three-piece suit with a briefcase, just because I am black and over six feet tall.

"I remember being told that there was no way that I could be smart enough to be partner at the white shoe law firms while they hired my less bright white brothers and sisters.

"And how many times have *you* been mistaken for a secretary or an assistant or an intern or a hooker, anything, and I mean anything, other than a banker who had some knowledge and some authority?"

"You know that I don't believe in crying the blues. I've done pretty well, as have you and Gordon and Jerome and a lot of people that we know. But we *worked*, really worked to get where we are. For a long, long time. Not as long as my parents and your parents, but I don't mind saying, I have paid my dues. As have you."

"And then you get some half-ass punk like Ray Beard sashaying down the boulevard. A Grade A knucklehead making serious six fig-ures just by showing up on Wall Street. And then, a certified star like Jerome Hardaway takes him under his wing and makes him his pro-tégé. And this idiot has the nerve to cop an attitude with me!"

"I am sure that the Paul Taylor that I know couldn't possibly be whining, but I sure feel like getting you some cheese to go with that whine."

"Whining? Diedre, what on earth are you talking about?" It was impossible for me to think of myself as whining. But I made myself listen.

"I am afraid so, my dear. You sound like a very old and windy fart, complaining that the young folks have it easy these days. The next thing you know you will be telling me about how you walked to school through five miles of snow every day."

"You and I both know that the truth is that there will always be someone who comes after us who will have it better than we did, just like we have it much, much better than our parents, and a lot of others who came before us."

There was no way that I could disagree with what Diedre was saying. She was speaking the truth and all I could do was listen. But this was a case where the truth didn't hurt. And sometimes it helps to look reality in the eye. This turned out to be one of those times.

CHAPTER 47

Diedre

E. Frederic Morrow

"Tell me, Paul, have you ever heard of E. Frederic Morrow?"
"Can't say that I have. Who is he?"

"Was, Paul. E. Frederic Morrow was the first black person appointed as an assistant to the President of the United States. He worked for President Eisenhower in the fifties when the White House had a relatively small staff, and working in the White House really meant something. And it was a time when D.C. was still a segregated southern city. For a black man to be on the staff of the President of the United States was truly extraordinary at that time.

"Mr. Morrow worked at the White House for most of the two Eisenhower terms. He opened doors that black people didn't even know existed. He mediated, interposed, networked, and did a hundred things that never made the headlines or the history books.

"Do you want to know how I know about Mr. Morrow?"

By now I had Paul's full attention. He was through whining and was wondering where this story was going.

"Actually, Diedre, I do want to know. You are telling me something I just never knew. How did you meet this man?"

"I met Fred Morrow when I started working at Citibank. He had recently retired from Bank of America as an assistant vice president if you can believe that! Here is a man who worked in the White House, for the *President of the United States* and he winds up as an AVP at Bank of America.

"We were talking at an Urban Bankers Coalition dinner when he told this story about his White House years and how even President Eisenhower himself had difficulty helping him find a job when he left government.

"There were no pickets, protests, sit-ins or boycotts to protest this injustice. Even the people who he had helped, and they were legion, stayed quiet. But you know what? I can truly say that Mr. Morrow was not a bitter man. He was not angry. He felt that he was part of history, a process of change that was inexorable."

Paul was now absorbing and enjoying this. I think that I was telling him something that he really needed to know.

"And do you know what this man told me before we left the luncheon that day? He said that while he could never truly forgive the white people who ruined his career, his final victory was the progress that all the young black people had made since he had come along."

"Now we both know that Ray Beard is Blue Ribbon asshole. But he and thousands of other young brothers and sisters wouldn't even be within shouting distance of Wall Street if it wasn't for you and me and Gordon and Jerome and a lot of people who were at Winner's memorial this morning."

"I certainly agree with the 'asshole' part."

"Sure. But we can't expect that every young brother and sister that comes along is going to be perfect. Sly Stone wasn't right. Everyone is not a star. Ray just needs more guidance than he is getting from Jerome. I am sure that life will teach him all that he needs to know. And from the looks of things, I am betting that he is going to get some extra schooling real soon."

"I still should have kicked his ass," I heard Paul mutter.

"My, my! I must have dialed Mike Tyson's number by mistake. What has brought on this bodacious attitude? Oh wait . . . I know. Samantha must be out of town."

I have always known where to put the needle into Paul especially when it came to his relationships with women. I could immediately tell that I had scored once again.

"You should get yourself a crystal ball and really make some money."

"I just know when you are on edge, Paul. You know I know you too well. I am sure Ray Beard will be glad when Samantha is back. Perhaps then it will be safe for him to walk the streets again."

We both had to laugh at this point. It was great having a chance to just talk with him. He had always been one of the smartest people I ever knew. And I always considered myself lucky to know him, all of our differences notwithstanding. This little conversation of ours was a wonderful break in the day.

"Paul, I have to go. But we should talk again. Soon. I would really like that." I tried to speak without the New York Pride attitude, or sarcasm, or wit. It was just words from someplace inside that I needed to say.

"I would like that too, Diedre." I could have sworn that I picked up some ever so slight hint of sadness or longing or something. It was like a small cloud that hides the sun for a moment or two during a summer picnic and then moves away.

CHAPTER 48

Paul

Remembering Bobby Coles

As we hung up I picked up the scent of Ivoire de Balmain, the scent that Diedre always wore. I don't know how that could have happened. Magic would be my best guess.

And then it was time to go back to work. And the scent of perfume dissipated and freed me from the reverie that it created. As I hung up the phone there was literally another call coming in.

It was from the vice president of a machine parts manufacturing company that wanted to work out a deal with the economic development officials of the Atlanta city government. I took the call and worked out the preliminary details of how I would get the information that I needed before I flew down to Atlanta for the first round of meetings. I was already sure that I could work something out.

The next call was from the managing director of an investment banking firm whose client was looking for a joint venture with a client in Detroit that I represented. Again it was manufacturing. This time the deal concerned machine parts. It was nothing glamorous. But it kept the lights on and the bills paid.

Right after that, one of my law school classmates who had been in Congress for the past twelve years was calling me for some career guidance. I tried to let him know that the grass was always greener on the other side, but he was determined to make the jump. I really couldn't say that I blamed him.

Public service, especially elected public service could be real hard on a person. My classmate was getting to the point that the aggravation, hassles and loss of a personal life was outweighing fame, the semblance of power and an ability to help a few people.

The next call was from the vice president for development for a major Hollywood studio. The studio was interested in the dramatic rights to a novel written by one of my clients.

I had to smile at the thought that suddenly black writers and stories about black people were deemed "interesting" to mainstream media. It was even more amazing when these books were found "interesting" even when no one got killed and the word "motherfucker" was not in the title of the work. I still keep hoping that maybe times really do change.

And then there was a break in the action and I started to sort through the mail and memos and bills that are all a part of the business of practicing law. And that's when it happened. A memory, like a wraith, made an uninvited appearance in my consciousness with no warning and no introduction. I thought of the name of one of my good friends from college about whom I had not thought in years . . . Bobby Coles.

Bobby had this madcap idea that he could major in English literature at Dartmouth College during the week and work on the weekends as a professional actor with the Harlem-based New Heritage Repertory Company, directed by Roger Furman. At the time there were two major black drama companies in New York City, New Heritage and the Negro Ensemble Company. For whatever reason, Bobby thought that his best opportunity was with New Heritage.

In any event, when it came time to graduate, Bobby saw his career choices as going to graduate school to get a doctorate and teach English literature at some university, or acting professionally on stage, in New York City. At least that's what Bobby perceived as his options. Life is rarely that simple, however, and it wasn't that simple for Bobby.

In the early seventies almost the only roles that were available for black actors and actresses involved singing and dancing—the all-black versions of "Hello Dolly" and "Guys and Dolls" come to mind.

And, with all of his talents, skills and abilities, Bobby could not sing or dance his way out of a wet paper bag.

And as far as the movies were concerned, most of the roles that were available to black actors in those days were in such timeless classics as "I Shot My Mama, Part I," "I Shot My Mama, Part II," and "Touch Me Again and I'll Kill You." Television offered opportunities to be a part of such cultural classics like "I Can Dig It, Can You Dig It?" and the universally acclaimed series "I Shot My Mama."

As it turned out, Robert DeNiro, Dustin Hoffman, Robert Redford, Al Pacino, all contemporaries of my friend Bobby Coles, had one less competitor to worry about. Bobby was a dreamer, an artist, a madcap brother with a heart full of hope, but he was not stupid. He did not see an opportunity to do anything but starve, so he shelved his dreams and went to graduate school and became an English professor at Oberlin College in Ohio.

And then I remembered the rest of the story. After we graduated, Bobby and I did not see that much of each other. Every now and then some conference would bring him to New York City and we would get together for drinks or dinner.

And then one morning I read in the *New York Times* that one Robert Coles, a distinguished professor of English at Oberlin College, was found in his car, dead from carbon monoxide poisoning. It was a presumed suicide.

I knew at once that it was a suicide. No question in my mind. I knew that every real dream that Bobby had was stomped to pieces and thrown in the gutter called procrastination. He simply had never found happiness in his life or in what he had to do for a living.

He went through all the motions. He got that PhD and became a professor. He had a wife, children, house, car, professional organization memberships, and vacations in faraway places. He simply never had any of his dreams come true in his life or in what he did for a living.

And then, one day, he just got into his car and didn't bother to open the garage door. He started the engine and waited for his last dream to come true. I learned from his wife that the "Pieces of a Man" album by Gil Scott-Heron was on the CD player in the car when they found him. Somehow that struck me as the perfect note to end the symphony of his life.

Thinking about Bobby, I thought about so many of our friends and colleagues and classmates of that era. When we were in school, discovering our blackness, our manhood, womanhood, personhood—we believed that all of our dreams could come true and that all things were possible. And we were absolutely right at the time.

It was only later that we found out that this is never true forever. And black, white, Hispanic or Asian—growing up is about learning how to practice the art of the possible. But there is a certain cruelty in learning that some things were impossible, just because . . . just because you were born black, just because no one black had ever done it before—just because you were born a little too early to ride the wave of monumental change that was now rolling across the country, from coast to coast.

Everyone I know has a way of dealing with these kinds of frustrations. Some people just buy their way through life. I know too many people with too many shoes, suits, homes, boats, cars and jewelry. Some people drink, some smoke marijuana and some snort cocaine. Some do all of those things and more. And many just live their lives and keep their heartbreak and frustration in a place so secret that they can't even find it if they tried. And then some people turn on the car with the garage door closed, and listen to Gil Scott-Heron forever.

Thinking of Bobby Coles got me to thinking about myself. I know that I used to have a lot more hopes and dreams than I do these days. In fact, it's getting harder to remember exactly what those hopes and dreams were.

I guess that at this point in life people would say that I was successful, completing college and law school. I now have my own law practice with work that takes me all over the country and all over the world. I work in the greatest city in the world and walk with the rich and the powerful without question or pause.

So what could be the problem? It's just that I wish I could remember a few of those hopes and dreams. What the hell were they? And I remember those almost dreamlike yesterdays when Diedre and I were together, a million years ago, a billion billion dreams ago. I certainly couldn't ask her about those dreams anymore. It was just not possible.

My melancholy reverie was mercifully interrupted by more phone calls. I also recalled an appointment for which I would be late if I didn't snap out of it and get back to work.

But I couldn't get Bobby Coles out of my mind. And I couldn't get those hopes and dreams back into my mind.

And I just hoped that Bobby had found out where his hopes and dreams had gone and that he was finally enjoying them coming true.

CHAPTER 49

Paul

Welcome to my world

"The mind is a terrible thing to waste." It's also a terrible thing to lose your mind. I am reminded of both of these sayings as I take another sip of port wine and listen to Andy and the Bey Sisters to their vocal version of "Round Midnight." My little boy is dreaming in Baby Land which is exactly where he should be, and his dreams make my life real.

Why is everything about those times a few years ago so clear in my mind? I have no idea. But the more of this story I tell, the more I remember. I can't remember what I had for lunch on a given day last week, but I can remember some of the days during that time as if they happened just moments ago.

After that enlightening conversation with Diedre and my reminiscing about Bobby Coles I finished up my calls, correspondence, memos, all that. Since my offices were on West 57th Street, it was a pretty simple matter to just take the A train up to 145th Street rather than wait for a car service to come and pick me up. During the ride up to my town house on Hamilton Terrace in the Sugar Hill area of Harlem, I started thinking about how I wound up living there in the first place.

A few years ago the *New York Times* called my neighborhood "one of the finest residential streets in New York City." Every Saturday and Sunday, no matter the season, no matter the weather, dozens of buses disgorge hundreds upon hundreds of tourists into the neighborhood, looking at my home and that of my neighbors. They come from France, Holland, Italy, Japan, Mexico and sometimes Greenwich Village.

They come to see this legendary Harlem neighborhood of which they have heard so much but never seen. They come to see the architecture of homes built over one hundred years ago, when this part of Manhattan was actually a suburban community. It lost its suburban status, however, when the subway came into this area in the first part of the twentieth century.

I guess I will never cease to be amazed and amused by the flow of sightseers. Of course, some of them come by their curiosity naturally, coming to Harlem much in the same way that they would tour the Left Bank in Paris, the Ginza in Tokyo, Trastevere in Rome or the Wilhelmstrasse in Berlin.

I am sure that for others, the real attraction was going into a "black" neighborhood and leaving safe and sound and intact. Huddled together, hoping for safety in numbers, these "explorers" are always hilarious and entertaining. The only thing missing are the pith helmets.

I am sure, however, that they regale their sheltered friends back home with the tales of their brave expeditions into the heart of darkness in Harlem. These visitors seem to walk through the neighborhood with well-remembered instructions not to speak to or feed the natives under any circumstances. They are herded along the street by guides who clearly got their training from Border Collie school.

On a particularly perverse day, I might pass one of these tour groups and suddenly shout out "Buon Giorno" or "Konichi Wa" with a perfect accent to really give them something to talk about when they returned home. This kind of greeting would usually leave these neo-explorers stunned and wondering what they had really heard.

The distance between Columbus Circle, where I boarded the A train and 125th Street, the next stop, is the longest distance between two stations in the entire New York City subway system. The train moves faster than anywhere else in the city, but it still gives you time to think. And I started thinking about my introduction to home ownership in Harlem.

CHAPTER 50

Paul

This old house of mine

At the time of this story, I had been living in the town house for over ten years. Diedre and I had just decided to call it quits for real, and while living in a furnished apartment I read in the *Amsterdam News*, Harlem's newspaper of record, about a vacant dilapidated brownstone that was located on Hamilton Terrace. I was representing a general contractor by the name of Cecil Roberson back then, and I asked him to come and take a look at this bricked-up, boarded-up wreck of a former Pleasure Palace.

It was a four-story limestone town house built over one hundred years ago. As soon as I saw the corrugated iron braced against the remainders of windows, and the chain over the steel plate where there should have been a door, I was ready to go.

"This house is beautiful," I thought I heard Cecil say. His words rudely interrupted my planning where I was going to get a Bombay Sapphire gin and tonic. The house was already headed to the delete file in my mind.

"Cecil, all I can say is that your sense of beauty is more than a little different from mine. You can be sure that there is no way that I am spending any more time looking at this train wreck of a house."

"Oh man! I thought you had vision."

"Vision? You're damn right I have vision, 20/20 with these glasses on. That's why I can see that there is no way in hell that I need to be spending any more time messing around with these . . . these ruins.

"Brother, I am gone. Blink and you won't see me."

Needless to say, Cecil talked me into "taking a look." It was another one of those days that changed my life. Again, I had no way of knowing it at the time. I was simply annoyed and starting to get more than a little pissed off with Cecil as I continued behind him for this impromptu tour of modern urban dilapidation. Cecil continued to run his mouth, and in retrospect, I am thankful that he did.

"Paul, you need to take a look at this place. I am telling you, if you can just allow your imagination to get control of that tight-ass lawyer brain of yours for a few minutes, you could see a palace."

"Palace? Man, all I see is a beat to shit shell of a house that does not need to be introduced to my hard-earned money. This house is a problem looking to be adopted."

We moved forward and I remember that after we unlocked the padlock and pulled back the alleged "door," the one that was made of a steel plate, the vision that greeted me was a combination of the basement of the house in the movie *Psycho* and some miscellaneous scene from an Indiana Jones movie.

When we walked into what might have been a parlor we saw . . . well, we saw enough to make a sane person turn on their heel and walk right out. There were dead animals representing several species. There were all kinds of garbage of indeterminate origin. And, in a particularly bizarre and kinky twist, there was a wheelchair lying on its side, one wheel idly spinning, keeping track of endless time, I suppose.

Experiencing a minor epiphany, I realized that I was out of my mind to be standing there with Cecil. I also realized that there was no way that this used-to-be, never-going-to-be-again house was going to see a nickel of my hard earned money.

That's when Cecil started talking. And given the fact that I am writing to you from my private office in that house, you had better believe he was goddamned persuasive.

"Paul, I know what you are thinking . . ."

"Then let's just get the fuck out of here."

"Just listen."

"You just listen . . . let's get the fuck out of here now."

"A bit of history, brother."

"Fuck history. Let's go, now."

"At the turn of the twentieth century, a French architect was commissioned to design an enclave of suburban town houses. In 1900, the streets that are now in Harlem were considered the rural part of the island. Hell, The Dakota apartment building on 72nd Street got its name in the late 1800s because it was considered so far uptown it might as well be in the Wild West, like the Dakotas, North and South.

"The houses that you are looking at were all built at least one hundred years ago. *One hundred years.* These buildings are sturdy, well designed and well built. They simply don't build houses like this anymore.

"As far as I can tell there has been no fire damage or water damage. That means that, structurally speaking, you have before you the same residence that was built over a century ago! You simply can't walk away from that!"

We walked through the wreck and Cecil helped me to understand the potential for converting it into a palace. By the time we saw some successful rehabilitation jobs, I was ready to buy. And I did. And I hired Cecil to handle the contracting work.

Buying the house was a great idea. Refurbishing the house was a great idea. Hiring Cecil was a terrible idea.

A job that should have taken six months took eighteen. I lived in that furnished studio apartment for so long I forgot what it was like to have more than one room.

After about a year I had to cut Cecil loose as it turned out that my construction loan money was going up his nose to satisfy his growing cocaine habit. Cecil became another ex-friend in my life's menagerie of ex-friends. But, after eighteen months and three more contractors, I moved into what turned out to be an urban palace, right in the middle of Harlem. Cecil was right about that after all.

When the house was finally finished, it had a formal dining room that could seat sixteen and a professional kitchen with Garland appliances. That was the ground floor. The second floor housed my home office, complete with the paraphernalia of the New Age—computer, modem, fax, scanner, etc.—that I needed for the days that I decided to conduct business from home. There was also a library and mahogany bar with a brass rail and a TV/ movie screening room that could seat a dozen guests quite nicely.

The third floor was dedicated to pure sybaritic indulgence and pleasure. There was actually a guest bedroom and adjoining bath on that floor. But the main feature was a Jacuzzi bathtub that could comfortably seat four settled under a skylight through which the sun or the moon could shine through two stories of the house.

On the top floor, half of the space was dedicated to a complete gym with weights, treadmill, sauna and Nautilus equipment. A smaller skylight illuminated this space.

On the other side was the master bedroom. Another skylight there. Off the bedroom was a master bathroom with a tub six feet in length to accommodate my long legs. The wreck of the house that Cecil had seen did have the soul of a palace after all.

My description of the house is in the past tense due to the fact that since I got married and my son was born, the house has been transfigured once again. The gym is his nursery. The TV/movie theater is now a "family room." Life changes.

CHAPTER 51

Paul

Something's cooking

By the time I got to the front door of my house I was thinking about the very long day and getting ready for Samantha, who was coming back into town that night and was coming straight from the airport to have dinner and take me on a short trip to heaven. I closed the last vestibule door behind me and walked into my kitchen, checking voice mail and snail mail.

The rest of the day required a plan and it had been on my mind all day. I had had some fresh red snapper marinating in white wine and garlic oil since early that morning. Another hour of marinating would be perfect before blackening it using a special Cajun recipe that I had picked up on one of my many trips to New Orleans.

Actually, I have enjoyed cooking for years and would have cooked a meal like that for guests or just for myself. However, since Samantha was taking a flight out of Chicago that would put her at my place around 9:15, I had about an hour to work on some lingering office items and projects before preparing a dinner that would be a choreographed culinary prelude to mutual seduction.

When it came to Samantha, I was never quite clear who seduced whom. I just knew that the very thought of her being with me excited me beyond description. This schoolboy reaction always amused me and puzzled me. But who was I to go against the wind?

I set the cooking range on low so that it would be just the right temperature to warm the rice and peas that I would be preparing along with the blackened red snapper. I also selected a bottle of 1990 Far Niente Chardonnay so that it would have time to cool slowly, the way that Samantha liked it. Then I went upstairs to go to work.

It was certainly the end of the day for most human beings but I did not think it out of order to go into my home office with a well-made Belvedere vodka martini. I rarely order martinis when I am out because I am so particular about the way that my favorite cocktail is prepared. So when I am out it's usually a gin and tonic for me. Plus, it's hard to mess up a gin and tonic, as long as the gin is Bombay Sapphire and the wedge of lime is fresh.

I know what quality to expect when I prepare a martini for myself. I walked over to that mahogany bar that had been custom-designed for this house, and took out the sterling silver shaker that Samantha had given me for my birthday (Valentine's Day) and then I got busy.

In 1993 not many people had heard of Belvedere vodka. Quadruple distilled from Poland, it is the smoothest, finest and most expensive vodka that is commercially available. I always keep a bottle in the freezer and, having placed some ice and water and vermouth into a martini glass so that it would be properly chilled, I poured the vodka into the shaker on top of crushed ice and a few slices of fresh lime. I poured some vermouth into the shaker and after some vigorous shaking a perfect martini was born and was poured into a properly chilled glass that had received a last few sprays of vermouth. After a twist of lime (not lemon) was added, the drink was complete. It was now time to catch up with my work of the day.

I have always been blessed with the ability to work quickly and efficiently when I focus my attention. So, with not much time being available, I sat down to my computer with my martini and checked all of my e-mail messages and gave appropriate directions to my three associates and my secretary.

I spent a good bit of time on a memorandum to Byron Cruick-shank, my most reliable and trusted associate. Byron was very bright, even brilliant, but he had no sense of self-promotion and had no ability to maintain a relationship with a client. But he was excellent in completing the assignments that I gave him and I tried to fill him in on the details of the Water Club meeting, because Byron would do a lot of the heavy lifting when it came time to draft the inevitable documents.

I reviewed the message to Byron, made a few grammatical changes and pushed the Send button. The making of The Pride into an institution had begun. Byron would start working on the necessary documentation that the Water Club meeting required first thing the next morning.

I checked my watch. It was now going on eight. I knew that I had to start working on the meal for Samantha, but as I took another sip of my rapidly diminishing martini, I knew I had to make one more call. It wouldn't take that long, that was for sure.

"Sudden" Sammy Groce was one of those mythic New Orleans characters who would have had to have been created if he didn't already exist. He used to be a disc jockey on the local black radio station and a Freedom Rider. Rumor had it that he had something to do with the Bay of Pigs fiasco in Cuba but nobody could prove it.

Sammy was one of my best contacts in New Orleans. He knew everyone that mattered and everything about them. He could tell you about high society and he could tell you where to get a bag of reefer and where the "clean" hookers hung out.

Bobby was one of those people without any visible means of support, but he drove a Mercedes Benz and wore Armani and Versace. And he was an excellent source of intelligence of all sorts. All he ever asked of me is that I share with him any New Orleans information that he didn't already know. It was a pretty good deal for both of us.

I was absolutely certain that Jerome, Diedre, and Gordon did not disclose everything they knew about their respective projects. It would make no sense for them to do so. But I knew better than to ever trust Gordon Perkins. And there was something about his talking about the New Orleans mayoral race that raised my antennae. That's why it made sense to call Sammy Groce. I dialed his number

"Sammy here. What's the word?"

"Sammy, it's Paul, here in New York."

"My big man in the Big Apple! What's happening? You must want something or you wouldn't be calling little ole me. You never call just to say hello."

"Sammy, you are breaking my little ole heart. Next thing you'll want to give back the ring I gave you. Just listen up for a minute. To get to the point, what's the story with Prince Lodrig and Percy Broussard?"

"Point? There ain't no point! Prince is going to kick Percy's ass from here to Mardi Gras!"

"That's it? Don't bullshit me, Sammy. Tell me what you know."

I knew in advance that dealing with Sammy Groce required a certain amount of patience and a certain attitude. I took another sip of my martini and leaned back in my chair. This might take a minute. I was glad that I had put John Coltrane's "Ole" on the house sound system. It provided just the right kind of background for this conversation.

"Well, there is a little bit more. Just a teensy weensy bit more."

"Sammy, I have to tell you. I am not surprised in the least. What's up?"

There were times when I felt like taking the next flight down to New Orleans and kicking the living shit out of this Peter Lorre look-alike. But Sammy served a purpose. And the purpose was best served with patience and persistence. I listened.

"Well, Paul. Everyone here figures that Prince is going to flat-out win the election. But there is some word that Percy Broussard has some really wealthy friends, friends with some seriously deep pockets, and that he is planning some kind of surprise just before the election.

"I have to tell you that I have no fucking idea what that surprise could be. Prince is pretty clean. He has had a couple of girlfriends, but no drugs, no bribes, no larceny, no real bullshit. And believe me, I would have heard about it."

"I know that, Sammy."

I was speaking the truth. In some ways the scum of the earth could look down on Sammy. However, Sammy was an incredibly reliable source of information, especially the type that people didn't want known. If Sammy said that Prince Lodrig was bulletproof insofar as an election in New Orleans was concerned, then he was definitely bulletproof.

After all, this was a city in a state where a governor was elected while under indictment. And the man was quoted as saying that the only way he could lose the election was if he was found in bed with a dead woman or a live boy. And he won.

"So what was this goddamned surprise about? Sammy, you know I don't believe in Santa Claus or bullshit. What the fuck is going on?"

"All I can say is that the word is out that although Prince is kicking Percy's ass in every poll from Lake Ponchartrain to the Superdome, Percy is supposed to have something up his sleeve that he is going to spring on Prince just before the election.

"Nobody seems to know what the hell it's all about. But I will tell you something else."

"I'm all ears, Sammy." Sometimes, listening to Sammy was like trying to do the *New York Times* crossword puzzle backwards. The answer was somewhere in what he was saying. But where?

"Like I said, the word is that there is some serious out of town money backing Broussard. And, when the bomb drops on Lodrig, it's going to be a motherfucker, plain and simple. And that's all I know."

I tried to assemble the bits and pieces that Sammy was giving me as he occasionally repeated himself. On the one hand, there was Gordon, saying that the new team should collaborate in the re-election of Lodrig. That strategy seemed to be supported by what Sammy was saying. On the other hand, this talk about a "surprise" just before the election worried me—a lot. Especially since no one knew who was behind this "out-of-town money."

"So that's all, Sammy? Are you sure?"

"Absitively, posilutely! Those of us who know anything are trying like hell to find out what this "surprise" is all about, but I can tell you that Lodrig's people aren't losing any sleep over it. He is as strong a candidate as you can get in this part of the world, and he and his people know it for damn sure."

"Well, Sammy, if that's all you know, I sure appreciate it. Thanks for now and remember, it's my treat at Petunia's when I come to New Orleans."

"I heard that, brother. Just don't start getting forgetful on me when you get down here."

"Don't worry your nappy head about that. But Sammy, if you hear anything more about this, anything at all, you call me right away, O.K.?"

"You got it, Paul. You take care now. Bye."

As I put the phone down, I thought more about what Sammy had told me. Sammy was real good when it came to scuttlebutt and back-door information as he had just given me. Sammy might be comfortable with the scum of the earth, but he could find a pearl of truth in a mud hole.

And, I knew that Gordon Perkins could never be totally trusted. After all, he was Gordon Perkins. If there was a way to use this entire plan to his own advantage at the expense of Jerome, Diedre and myself, I was sure that he would find it and use it, in a heartbeat. That was Gordon, plain and simple.

Gordon was a man with no moral compass at all. His sense of right and wrong was totally self-centered and devoid of concern for anyone else. Once you knew that about Gordon, he should never be able to hurt or disappoint you. At least that was my theory. It was just the kind of person he was. Snakes bite, sharks attack, and Gordon will always scheme and plot. But at the moment, there was nothing to connect Gordon to the plot against Lodrig, and how could that make sense since Gordon was supporting Lodrig? So I just filed that information away. That's all I could do at the moment.

Checking my watch I realized that Samantha's plane was about thirty minutes outside of LaGuardia, moving toward New York at about four hundred miles an hour. She would be at my door in about an hour. It was time to start preparing my special meal for her. Heaven would be on the menu for dessert.

CHAPTER 52

Paul

Someone's in the kitchen . . .

Among my true confessions, I must admit that cooking is one of my favorite pastimes. It's so different from what I do for a living it provides me with an escape any time I can get near a stove and some pots and pans. Actually I got into cooking quite by accident, literally.

When I was twelve, my mother was in a car accident—sideswiped by a drunk driver. For eighteen months she was confined to the house, in traction for the entire time. My father had to continue in his work as a traveling sales representative for IBM throughout the entire Northeast. That meant I suddenly became responsible for all housekeeping duties, including grocery shopping and cooking.

During those eighteen months I learned all that I needed to know about what to buy in a supermarket to maintain a household. I learned everything from soap to butter to detergent to eggs and tuna fish and peanut butter. In the process, I learned to do some rudimentary cooking during my mother's lengthy convalescence.

I used to say that I began cooking as a survival skill. But the truth is that, as a bachelor, married to Diedre and then single again, I learned to enjoy cooking. I tried to mask my enjoyment by telling people that I had to learn to cook "since I end up begging women for so many things, I don't want to have to beg for food." It was always a surefire laugh line.

But the truth has always been that the diversion, the opportunity for creativity, the aromas, the spices, the sauces, the avenues of originality limited only by my imagination intrigued and attracted me. And it has attracted and interested me over the years.

To this day, I pride myself on being able to cook three meals a day for a month without ever repeating myself. Crawfish *étoufée* (when Sammy Groce could get it together to ship some fresh crawfish up from Louisiana), chocolate chip waffles, honey-dipped fried chicken, *ichi-ban* tuna, Bananas Foster, stir-fried vegetables, pasta sauce with soy grits that takes two days to prepare . . . these are a few of my favorite things.

A turning point in my attitude toward cooking came about in the late seventies when I began reading the works of Jorge Amado, the Brazilian novelist and author of *Dona Flor and Her Two Husbands*, *Shepherds of the Night*, *Tereza Batista*, and many other enjoyable tomes.

Aside from his great writing, I couldn't help but be entranced by Amado's continual references to various cooking styles found in Brazil. His descriptions of the spices, the oils, the seasonings, the combinations of fruits and fishes and poultry and vegetables could set a mouth watering after just a few pages.

I like to think that, thanks to Jorge Amado (*Obrigado, Senhor*) I became a true artist in the kitchen. Palm oil, cloves, coriander and cinnamon have become standard features in my dishes. I now combine cooking wines and Turkish peppers and Mauritian sea salts to create evanescent masterpieces.

I checked my watch and realized that I really needed to start to focus on preparing this meal for Samantha. Any more delays and I would be cutting it close. Samantha was a jewel, my own personal goddess, and I was her most fervent worshipper. And she was a lot of fun.

When she was away for several days, like this trip, I missed her lips and hips and mouth and arms and endless legs. But in a bizarre and counterintuitive and interesting way, I enjoyed our separations because our reunions were so wonderful.

There was the time, for example, that she returned from an unusually long trip to Italy. She appeared at my door one Saturday afternoon in the spring wearing a drop-dead designer raincoat that she had picked up in Florence. It looked like a fortune, especially in the rain. But it was not until she entered the foyer of my house that I realized that, under that raincoat Samantha wore absolutely nothing but a pair of fishnet stockings and a garter belt, the better to complement the stiletto high heels that she wore. I did my very best to welcome her to America well into Sunday afternoon. The phone and the doorbell simply went unanswered.

I dared not think of the treats that might be in store for us that evening; it would certainly have distracted me from my preparing dinner. And it would have just overloaded my precarious circuits. The mere anticipation of Samantha's arrival was arousing enough.

As I prepared another martini and contemplated the exact steps that I would take to prepare our meal, I had only two objectives in mind—to present a meal that would unlock her appetites and passions—first for the meal and then for me.

I had decided on a meal that was, in my view, imaginative, but fairly straightforward in its preparation. As the Far Niente Chardonnay continued to chill, I contemplated the coming meal of blackened red snapper, rice and beans and spring broccoli imported from the Cape Verde Islands that would be steamed with Sandeman port wine (most appropriate given the broccoli's Portuguese origins).

As I started to heat the pans and season the foods, I had a few minutes to think about Samantha Gideon and me and what had come between us in just a few years.

CHAPTER 53

Paul

Samantha on my mind . . .

I remember when we met. I was waiting to meet a client in the lobby of some midtown hotel, The Palace, I believe.

In one of those very strange concatenations of truth and fable and chance and circumstance, the client called down to the lobby to tell me that it would take him about forty-five minutes to join me. He asked that I have a drink in the hotel bar while waiting for him.

It was certainly not the best news of the day for me, but business was business. I dutifully trudged over to the lounge, fully intending to have yet another in a long line of Bombay Sapphire gin and tonics while listening to some forgettable lounge singer or pianist. At least that was my plan. That was my plan until I saw Samantha for the very first time.

The songwriters and poets say that love can begin with a smile, a touch, a sigh or the lyrically impossible symphony of a shared laugh. I guess that sometimes it can be the proverbial gaze across the proverbial crowded room. All I can say is that in my case, I never knew what hit me.

I remember sitting at the bar, starting to sip my drink when I heard the first strains of "The Man I Love" being sung. Not remarkably well, if the truth be told, but in a memorable sort of way that grabbed my attention. But for some reason that I could explain right after I get around to explaining the origins of the Law of Gravity and the

Law of Unintended Consequences, I happened to look up and right into the face of an angel whose name turned out to be Samantha Gideon. She was gorgeous and more important, she had the grace and affect and chemistry that made me feel like I had died and gone to heaven. At that moment she was my angel, singing to me and only me.

The fact that she was an early evening lounge act at a midtown Manhattan hotel was in no way reflective of the quality of her singing. The truth is that you can go into the leading Baptist church in almost every major city and you can find at least one or two people in the choir who could sing as well as Aretha Franklin and who can make Mariah and Brandy and Whitney and Salt *and* Pepper want to go back home and start all over. It has always been about packaging, opportunity, ambition, fortune and circumstance. Clearly the stars had not properly aligned for Samantha Gideon just yet.

Samantha did not have a major label record contract and she did not have expectations of being in the big-time anytime soon. But she loved to sing and she sang whenever and wherever she could. In this case, on that particular day, it turned out to be in a hotel lounge where I was waiting for a client.

Samantha had charm and personality, but she would definitely take no shit from anyone. And that was probably one more reason why she was singing in a hotel lounge in Manhattan instead of in one of the main rooms in Las Vegas. But she also had the charm and style and personality that made every man in the room feel that she was in love with him, and just him. I know I felt that way.

When I first heard her sing, her voice had the quality of Brenda Russell. Or was it the lead female singer for Hiroshima? Everything But the Girl? Swingout Sister? Her voice had the ability to make me smell colors and hear bass lines clearly for the very first time.

As it turned out, Samantha also labored under a misconception not unknown to unusually beautiful women. Men did not ask her out much because there was an unspoken assumption that there must be a man in her life. How could there not be?

So Samantha spent many nights at home alone. There were a lot of reasons that she was glad to be working that night. Not having to be alone was one of those reasons.

It defied logic that nobody was waiting for this woman after the show, at the stage door or at home. But logic and reality only have a nodding acquaintance in my world. I gave a waiter twenty dollars to take my business card and a note to Samantha when her set was over.

It was going to be another twenty-five minutes before my client came downstairs and amazingly, Samantha came out from her dressing room fifteen minutes before he was due to arrive. It turned out to be the shortest fifteen minutes of my life.

Actually, it was more like the shortest fifteen seconds. She came over to my table just long enough to sprinkle the pieces of my card and my note on my table, give me a smile that was imported from somewhere near Antarctica and walk away. It took an entire week of phone calls before she would agree to speak with me and another two weeks before she would meet me for drinks.

I must say that, when we finally did meet on purpose, there was a certain magic, electricity and chemistry that neither of us could deny. It would be our loss to try to fight it.

It was as if we both knew that there was *something* right away. Whether we acknowledged it or not was going to be the only question about us, as there was already an "us." I cannot deny that I originally pursued Samantha for the sheer interest and pleasure of it all. After that first date, I needed to be with her. It was that simple.

One morning in bed, a few months later, I remember Samantha saying, "Paul, I decided to go out with you because I really didn't have a lot else to do. But darling, the truth is that after spending some time with you, something happened that hadn't happened in a long time. I started to feel reactions like longing, desire, a very real suspension of time and space."

Our love affair began with that cosmic starburst of energy and longing so characteristic of those first days of true romance. Our own special brand of magic became known to us when, after several months, we found that we felt the same way as we had at the very beginning.

I couldn't wait to see Samantha when she was away. She would tell me that she would wait in her hotel room anticipating my next phone call like a lovesick teenager. I would find myself fussing and fuming like some jealous schoolboy, cursing myself for even caring if another man would show her more than perfunctory attention. To put it simply, we were hopelessly in love.

As I turned my attention to the finishing touches of the meal, I couldn't help but think about the Water Club luncheon again. It had really gone well I thought. Getting Jerome, Gordon, and Diedre together for lunch had been a hunch. A correct one as it turned out—the three principals had bought into the concept. The devil would be in the details.

First of all, Raymond Russell Beard III was going to be trouble. And then there was Diedre. Unbelievably I found myself trying to understand the hint of feelings that seemed to surface during our conversations. I could not understand how that could be possible after so many years of having reached an accommodation of sorts—a working arrangement. What could that be about?

As I lit the candles on the dining room table the doorbell rang. It was Samantha. All the thoughts of the Water Club and the merger and Sammy Groce and The Pride blew away like wisps of smoke on a windy day.

It was time to take the first of my seven steps to heaven.

CHAPTER 54

Paul

This is my beloved

As I went to the door I thought about how much I looked forward to seeing her. And I really had to laugh at myself as my sophomoric heart skipped a beat. Greeting Samantha was always a pleasure and even after having dated her and loved her and romanced her for almost two years, I still experienced a very special thrill every time I saw her at my door. Every time was almost like it was the very first time.

As I opened the foyer door there she was. She was wearing a mink coat that was the color of black diamonds seen through the waters of a bottomless lake. But she could have been standing in a denim jacket for all I cared. Samantha was about five feet ten inches tall, incredibly erect, slender, with hair the color of dark clover honey and a complexion that reminded me of a cup of *café con leche* that I once had on the Avenida Castellana in Madrid.

Her eyes were dark, not black and not brown; they were the bottomless color of dreamless nights that seemed to go on forever. And she had a graceful delicate air that absolutely changed the universe in which she walked.

"Good evening, Mr. Taylor."

"I'm sorry, miss, do you have a reservation?"

"Actually, I do have reservations about coming to see a man that I have dated for almost two years who won't give me a key to his front door and makes me stand out on the stoop like a delivery from some cheap escort service."

"Cheap? I'm prepared to pay good money! Hell, I'm willing to go up to twenty dollars."

As I said that, opening the door to escort her inside, her smile appeared. Her smile was always my personal beacon of happiness. It lit up my world and made all the shadows of doubts and cares disappear in the warm embrace of its brilliance.

This exchange continued as I took Samantha's luggage from the driver who had brought her in from the airport. As we walked up the steps from the foyer Samantha had to get in the last word.

"Twenty dollars doesn't buy what it used to, Paul Hiawatha Taylor. You may be a very sad brother by the end of this evening."

I recall being desperately glad that the conversation had magically moved away from that "key" thing. In my mind and heart, I absolutely loved Samantha. I dreamed of a life with her. Loving her and being loved by her made hope and happiness bloom in my heart. But giving her the key to my house . . . !!

She already had the keys to my heart. And I would think that would be enough. I would be a fool to have the Lisette Baileys of my world come to visit my private pleasure palace once I gave a key to Samantha. And while I truly loved her, I was not sure that I was ready to abandon the occasional dalliances and fun-loving frolics that had been a part of my life for so many years. But at that point all I could do was embrace that woman in my arms, having missed her for so long. For a few moments we held the whole world within our arms. I kissed her with a passion that probably surprised the both of us. Maybe it was the excitement of being together again after being apart for too long. Maybe it was the stress and colliding influences of the day.

Maybe it was the martinis. I just know that I kissed her like the photo of the Navy sailor kissing the nurse in Times Square at the end of World War II. And for those wonderful moments we were the only two people in the world.

"Whew! Mr. Taylor! You should let a girl know if she needs to brace herself for that kind of greeting! Is it going to be like that all night?" Samantha threw that last line with a smile that let me know that my passion was a shared treasure.

I helped Samantha to remove her coat and it was like unveiling a masterpiece at the Metropolitan Museum of Art. She could have been wearing sweatpants and a torn T-shirt and it would have aroused me beyond the horizon. But she was not.

She was wearing a "simple" black dress that was cut three inches above the knee and displayed a pair of legs that were like stairways to heaven. The fact that she was wearing black mesh stockings (not pantyhose) just added to the hypnotic effect. With her four-inch heels she could almost look me in the eye. And in her eyes I could see yearning, desire, appreciation and a love that bordered on desperation. Dinner had to wait that evening.

In a whirlwind of kissing and holding and fondling and embracing and sucking and undressing we found ourselves on the living room couch. Time only permitted me to take off my pants and shorts, and as her dress rose up her thighs as she lay down, I removed the lovely black silk panties that were the only thing that stood between me and an eternity of passion and mad happiness. Somehow my shirt disappeared along the way and then we were both naked, except for Samantha's stockings.

There were all kinds of foreplay . . . I pleasuring her and she pleasuring me, all I can remember are the moans and begging for more. And then we made love on the couch with the gentle passion that was just the storm before the hurricane of sex and passion that would be part of our dessert.

At some point we roused ourselves from the trance that we had entered. I put my slacks back on without bothering to button my shirt. Somehow we found her panties rumpled in a corner of the couch cushions and her dress was not too far away. Samantha went to freshen up in the powder room and I went into the kitchen to find that mercifully, dinner was still in good shape (the heat was low in the kitchen while it was up high in the living room).

By the time she sat down to the dining room table I presented her with a martini and a kiss and then . . . it was time for dinner.

CHAPTER 55

Paul

Getting to know all about you

Iwent back into the kitchen and within minutes appeared with a teak wheeled serving cart—blackened snapper, pasta with a soy and ginger sauce, broccoli steamed with port wine and a perfectly chilled bottle of Far Niente Chardonnay (the last twenty minutes of chilling must have done the trick). Just like I planned it. A perfect meal for a perfect evening with the most perfect woman I knew.

I could tell that as I served the dinner at the table the stress of her moving halfway across the country in the course of a day had started to fade. I could only hope that Samantha could sense and appreciate the attention and attentiveness that truly came from the heart.

As our Mikasa crystal glasses clinked I virtually sang out a toast to Samantha, my desire for her simply had no bounds.

"*Salud, amor y dinero y el tiempo para gozarlos.* Health, love and money and the time to enjoy them." We sipped and then we dined.

And, as two people who had really started to know each other very well, we really didn't need a whole lot of conversation, even though we had been apart for weeks. Being together, the wonder of being close again, that was enough for the moment. But we both knew it was only for the moment.

"Paul Taylor, I swear I feel like I may have died and gone to heaven. That was simply an excellent meal. You have truly outdone yourself this time.

"I swear, if you don't marry me soon, I may just have to hire you as my personal chef . . . and consort."

"If I don't marry you soon, I would be a fool. . . ." As soon as the words left my lips I knew that I had said a lot more than I had intended to on that particular evening at that particular time. I remember cursing the hell out of the Belvedere vodka that I had been drinking. Or was it the Far Niente Chardonnay? Perhaps it was the black mesh stockings.

"What was that?"

"I said, Ms. Gideon, I would be a fool if I didn't marry you soon. But right now I have a custom-made serving of Bananas Foster waiting to seduce your mouth and tongue."

Samantha and I knew each other very well. She knew better than to press me with respect to anything important. That was the best way to get me to do the opposite, even if it was against my own best interests.

Besides, Samantha was a lot of things, but she was never, never, never stupid. I knew that she knew what she had heard. And I could feel her heart smiling. Samantha knew that she was the love of my life. And while marriage was not in the top five on my "Things to Do" list, it never seemed to be at the top of Samantha's either.

As I headed into the kitchen I now recall hearing her stifle a cough. It didn't seem like anything resembling a problem at the time.

At the time, having been married to Diedre, and having had that marriage implode and explode, I had sworn off permanent relationships. Of course that was before that night in that midtown hotel lounge. I found that despite the profound nature of the difference between our lines of work, I truly felt that she was that ever elusive soul mate, and she was very, very good for me.

I had to admit to myself, if to no one else, that I did want my house to become a home, not just a funhouse. But at that moment I couldn't help thinking about that cough.

I remember thinking, as I sliced the warmed bananas and began the simmering of the rum and brown sugar glaze, that I had been hearing that cough for more than a little while. Actually, since the Halloween party we had attended in Malibu, and by now it was January.

Being the totally dedicated performer, Samantha never missed a gig. She also found a way to not go to the doctor. Again and again. Since the cough didn't really interfere with her singing, she always acted as if it was no big deal. And I wanted to make sure that I didn't "control" her or "direct" her. So I said nothing.

By the time I served the Bananas Foster the chardonnay was gone and the entrée was on its way to Memory Land. All that was between us and heaven at the top of the stairs were two plates of one of the greatest New Orleans desserts that has ever been devised for the human mouth. And as we had our dessert and gazed into each other's eyes, we finally knew that it was time to go upstairs and go play in heaven again.

"Would you like to see my etchings, Samantha?"

"No, but I would like to see your . . ."

With her laughter wreathed around me like garlands of joy from some strange enchanted isle, I walked with Samantha up the stairs of the town house, heading toward the master bedroom. The dishes would simply have to wait until morning. Samantha was in the house.

I remember that we neither of us ever commented on that cough again. But, as we went up the stairs to head to the stars, I couldn't help but wonder.

And worry.

But that night my worries just had to wait. And what was there to worry about anyway? Heaven was two steps ahead of me on the stairway to my bedroom. And I certainly didn't intend to keep heaven waiting that night.

But in the morning it was pretty clear that it made sense to worry about Samantha. That cough seemed to get worse by the moment. So bad that I could have sworn that I saw flecks of blood on the sides of her mouth when a particularly serious attack hit her. I was afraid for her, especially since it was next to impossible to tell Samantha to do anything.

She was the kind of person who operated according to the principle of mind over matter. If she didn't mind, it didn't matter. So even though Samantha *had* to know that something was wrong, she simply refused to acknowledge it.

She considered the increased huskiness in her voice a part of the maturation of her vocal talent. Even though she knew that she would have had to smoke two packs of cigarettes a day to sound anything like she did. And she had never smoked in her life. Still, she carried on.

I truly valued my relationship with this woman so I tried to avoid obvious points of conflict. She would visibly bristle at the suggestion that she see a doctor.

She always acted as if my solicitousness was offensive. So I tried not to be a pain in the ass in conveying my concern.

And then, a few weeks later, a few days before Valentine's Day, Samantha woke up in my bed, coughing violently, almost choking on her own blood and phlegm. I could not worry about conflicts any more.

"Samantha, you can get mad all you want, but you have to see a doctor!"

"Paul, I love you loving me and caring, truly . . . I promise I will make an appointment first thing in the morning. Just please, please, help me."

I held her in my arms. I remember feeling desperation and affection, love and fear. She felt feverish and cold at the same time. I only hoped that the depth of my concern didn't show on my face. I was truly worried.

"Do you really promise?"

"Cross my heart and hope to die."

It was a jarring choice of words. And it only made me worry more. I knew that while I was worried sick about Samantha, I was also being selfish in being worried about my feelings if I were to lose her. But the herd of feelings that stampeded through my heart could not be stopped.

I was glad that she had agreed to see a doctor though. That was progress I thought.

I thought wrong. In the morning her agent called and told her that she had a job in Las Vegas as the last minute replacement for an act on Valentine's Day. She would be gone for a week.

And when she returned, we were scheduled to go to Anse Chastenet in St. Lucia. Somehow the doctor's appointment lost priority in the light of the day.

After all, the morning after that attack she was feeling and sounding much better. The agony of the previous night seemed like some kind of nightmare. Best ignored and forgotten.

I continued to worry about her, however. But no one but a doctor would really know, and Samantha did not want a doctor telling her something that she did not want to hear.

Samantha was not the first or last person with this wrongheaded, ostrich head in the sand, approach to health.

Nevertheless, every time I think of it, it still saddens me. And it always will.

CHAPTER 56

Gordon

The Dark Lord

After making my brief stop, it didn't take me long to get to my eleven-room apartment on Park Avenue. Kenitra and I lived in a co-op building that was notorious for scrutinizing and rejecting applicants. I remember being incredibly polite and responsive during the interview with the co-op board.

I got word, however, that the board was less than "enthusiastic" about my application, even though it was impeccable and my net worth exceeded that of everyone in the building. So, prior to the final vote I was able to arrange a private breakfast meeting with the chairman of the co-op board.

Only two people actually know what happened at that breakfast meeting in a small diner on Madison Avenue that morning.

As we left the breakfast meeting accomplishing little that satisfied me, we started walking back to the building where I now live. I took out my seven-page personal financial statement and promised the co-op board chairman that I would shove it down his throat if I wasn't admitted to the building.

I was prepared to tell him what I was going to do to his wife and dog, but the paper down the throat threat turned out to be enough. Within two weeks we were living in the building. The co-op board chairman and I actually got along pretty well, at least until he moved to a farm in Australia a few months later.

I enjoy the building. It's stylish, understated, discreet and elegant. It's all the things that I am not. I could give less than a shit about what Kenitra thinks, but the truth is that the both of us have enjoyed living on Park Avenue.

But that evening, as I went up the elevator, riding with my new best friend, the Dark Lord, style, understatement, discretion and elegance were far from my mind. I had to smile to myself when I remembered that I had the apartment soundproofed soon after we moved in. Perfect for what the Dark Lord and I had in mind for Kenitra this particular evening.

By the time I entered the apartment I had a real plan in mind. Part of it involved the call that I had already made to Kenitra telling her to get dressed and ready to have some fun.

I know goddamned well that Kenitra is a gorgeous woman. And that night she was dressed in sheer stockings, high heels and a short, tight red dress. I could feel as she moved against me as I came into the hallway of our apartment that she was not wearing anything except that dress. And I knew that the passion that she was conveying was in anticipation of the goodies that she knew I would be bringing.

"Are you glad to see me, or are you just horny?"

"Actually both," I recall saying. I also remember smiling and seeing a puzzled look on Kenitra's face. I know she preferred this persona as opposed to me having a foot up her ass. I also know that sneaky bitch was also trying to figure what I was up to. She would find out soon enough.

"What brought this about? It's not my birthday, it's not . . ."

"Does a fellow need a reason to celebrate life with his wife?"

"I guess not . . ."

I always knew that Kenitra was a survivor, first and foremost. So I am sure that her red alert bells were ringing, I was that goddamned nice. But I guess her defenses were down. Or maybe she was just glad that my foot wasn't up her ass as soon as I came in the door. It was the treatment to which she had become accustomed.

She had asked the maid to leave as I had requested. So it was just the two of us in the entire apartment as we walked into the entertainment room with its wide-screen television and state-of-the-art sound system. It was a great place to sit and relax. We sat down and it took Kenitra a few moments to realize that I had spread about a half an ounce of pure cocaine on the glass tabletop. The cocaine was the reason for the stop that I made on the way home.

"Would you like to join me?"

I remember that she still had that puzzled expression on her face. If she knew what the Dark Lord and I had in mind she would have run out the door and not looked back. But she had a weakness for fun and a weakness for cocaine. She was not a slave to it. But she enjoyed it and I guess it represented what little liberation she could get. I had never known her to say "no" to coke. And she certainly wasn't saying "no" that evening either.

It just did not occur to that bitch the real reason why I would show up in the middle of the week with enough cocaine to last us the weekend. Except that tomorrow was Thursday and she never figured out the whole deal until it was too late for her. Plenty of time for the Dark Lord and me to do what we needed to do.

To make a very long story short, we started drinking the Pommery champagne and consuming many, many lines of what was some very excellent coke as I recall. Snorting it, licking it off of each other, sprinkling it on our tongues. We had a ball. And all the time Wynton Marsalis was playing in the background.

And then things started to get interesting. This was also around the time that the Dark Lord made his surprise appearance. The second bottle of Pommery brought about an atmosphere that I am sure Kenitra thought was amorous.

Now there was lots of kissing and sucking and fondling and licking. I am sure that she thought that ecstasy was right around the corner for both of us. She was half-right.

Kenitra was a survivor. But her defenses were down. The champagne and the cocaine and the attention kept her from staying focused on Point Number One—If you fuck with me in any way, any way at all, you better always be on guard. Because I will fuck you up. Plain and simple. The motherfucking bitch knew that she was wrong and just didn't think. It was too bad for her.

She didn't think when I encouraged her to keep drinking the Pommery in long, greedy gulps. She didn't think when I kept putting more and more cocaine up her nose, down her throat, all over her breasts and nipples. She certainly didn't think when I playfully suggested that I tie her arms to the legs of the sofa on which we were sitting—which would, of course, require her to lie down on the floor on her back.

I set that bitch up real good. I poured champagne over her breasts and licked it off. I sprinkled coke between her legs and licked it off, being sure to spell my name on the inside of her thighs . . . with my tongue. And then I punched her in the nose. Very hard.

Then the Dark Lord suggested that I slap her on both sides of her face as the blood gushed from her nose. And then I punched her in one of her wide-open-with-shock eyes. I just let the Dark Lord take over. He was real good in these kinds of situations.

"You bitch! You stupid motherfucking bitch! Did you really think you could go out to our place in Long Island and FUCK while I was away?"

(SMACK!)

"What, you thought I wouldn't find out?"

(SLAP!)

"Jesus, Gordon. What are you talking . . . ???"

(PUNCH!)

"You goddamned better tell the truth, bitch. Then, maybe I won't kill your ass."

(SLAP!)

"Gordon, I swear to God . . ."

(KICK!)

For the next hour the Dark Lord and I took turns beating the living shit out of Kenitra. She had to have figured that she had died and gone to hell. I hope so. But she had the instincts of a true survivor.

If she had told me who she was fucking I would have killed her for sure. And despite a really terrible ass whipping, the motherfucking bitch did not talk. Not a word.

"Did you think I wouldn't know? Bitch, I know everything!"

(PUNCH!)

"Did you really think that I wouldn't find out that you were fucking some motherfucker in MY house?"

(SMACK!)

Now I know that Kenitra was drunk and wired on cocaine. But she held on to the knowledge so that she might have a chance of surviving. So while she could not control the grunts and moans and groans that my fists and feet elicited, she never said another word. Not one fucking word. The Dark Lord and I were both amazed.

And so he and I beat and kicked and punched her until we got bored. So then we thought of truly creative ways to abuse her which she would have to remember with disgust for the rest of her life. I really tried to fuck her up. And finally, we untied her and left the room. The bitch should have been glad to have been alive as she staggered into the kitchen to get some ice and then into the bathroom to vomit and try and bathe away her disgust and her pain.

CHAPTER 57

Gordon

Night hunting

But the night did not end for us. I took the Dark Lord up on the suggestion that I put on my leather pants, leather boots and leather jacket and leave the apartment to take a taxi up to the Hunts Point section of The Bronx.

Now, the last thing I needed was to be out on the streets of New York City with the Dark Lord. But he could make things like that make sense. So I went out for an adventure with my only real friend.

Now, most people are not aware that almost all of the meats, vegetables and produce that feeds New York City comes into the Hunts Point section of The Bronx, north of Manhattan. The largest produce market in the world is located there and every night, hundreds of trucks loaded with tomatoes, lettuce, milk and everything else comes rumbling over highways and streets through this neighborhood of warehouses and garages.

And, to serve the market of bored, lonely, horny truck drivers, are strip joints, topless bars and hard-eyed whores who have abandoned any hope of self-respect and dignity as they sell themselves to absolutely anyone with a few bucks. And I had more than a few bucks.

The Dark Lord and I got to Hunts Point pretty quickly that time of night. A hundred dollar bill to the taxi driver ensured that he wouldn't give a fuck what I did in the backseat of his cab. After all, there was another hundred waiting for him when we got back to Park Avenue.

The driver was from Afghanistan. He didn't care that I was snorting a few more lines with the Dark Lord as I looked for a likely bitch. And I found one. She was probably sixteen, blonde, probably from Minnesota or some fucking where like that.

Negotiations were swift. She got into the taxi. She was glad to have a few lines of coke. I remember putting a small rock under her tongue. And then we engaged in a truly bizarre orgy of passion and pain, the passion was for me, the pain was for her, the fun was for the Dark Lord.

When it was over I shoved the bitch out of the door with a few hundreds and a kick in the ass. Her curses fell short of the taxi as she wiped the blood from her mouth and other places as I headed back to Manhattan. And I remember wondering if the Dark Lord would ever leave me alone.

The Dark Lord always lets me go to work. And by the morning I was in my office, in charge, as usual. But I wondered what would happen if the Dark Lord didn't let me go back to work. In a hundred different dingy, dirty and depressed neighborhoods I have seen junkies and derelicts, the flotsam and jetsam of society.

Sometimes I have wondered, could that ever be me? Would the Dark Lord take me to one of these places and just leave me?

It's probably the closest that I ever come to feeling fear. I remember on the cab ride back from The Bronx feeling depressed, degraded, frightened, miserable and exhilarated all at the same time.

And I have to tell you, in all honesty, that despite all my money and prestige that there are times when I feel like it's all a myth. And, I must confess, if the Dark Lord were to stop being my friend, it would all be a myth.

Sometimes I wonder why I feel the need to gamble with my life and career with such wild behavior. Sometimes I wonder why I have to go so deep into the gutter that I have to look up to see down. As I rode down Park Avenue I literally could not remember what I had done to Kenitra. Nevertheless, I was sure that Kenitra would never forget and that was what was most important. The Dark Lord would remind me if I needed reminding.

And as I tried to banish the memory of the Hunts Point whore out of my mind, I could see her laughing at me. I felt like my brain was bathed in misery and confusion.

By the time the taxi pulled up to my apartment building the Dark Lord was long gone. I was alone. And I was a part of The Pride once more.

As the first streaks of sunlight prodded the city into reluctant wakefulness, the rest of the members of The Pride stirred—in Harlem, in Brooklyn Heights, in SoHo and Scarsdale and Park Avenue.

Along with the millions of others who lived and worked in New York City, the members of The Pride began their private rituals before donning their uniforms and heading into the fray.

CHAPTER 58

Diedre

She works hard for the money

The next few weeks sped by with the familiar rapidity of life. One moment can seem so very important and then, the world just continues to fly by at the speed of life. That's how it was after the luncheon at the Water Club.

After all, Jerome, Gordon, Paul, and I all had lives and independent businesses long before that day. And I know that while I was trying to arrange that deal with the unions and their pension funds I was still running my day-to-day business. And running my business included paying bills, checking on payroll, collecting fees, checking on new business prospects and generally dialing for dollars every day.

Paul was kept very busy drafting and redrafting a seemingly endless number of versions of the joint venture agreement between the three of us. You can believe that between Jerome, Gordon, and me there was a truckload of comments and revisions.

I think that at one point Paul called it an "organic" document. A useful and apt choice of words. I also remember him referring to the process as being similar to someone trying to herd cats, whatever that meant.

Each of us wanted to be the boss. Nobody wanted to be Number Two. And despite all of the expressions of goodwill, there were issues of protection and safeguards that made it clear that complete trust had not blossomed just yet. Sometimes the suggested changes were creative and substantive. Frankly, many times they simply reflected the personality of whoever was suggesting the changes.

Nevertheless, some serious progress was made. And some six weeks after the Water Club luncheon, we were close enough to an agreement that it made sense to have the dinner at my place that we had originally agreed upon. We were all pretty sure that we had the basis for making an agreement.

And then, just like that, it was the day of the scheduled dinner at my house. Thursday had been chosen because of the President's Day weekend. The Black Ski Summit was going to be in Vail, Colorado, that year and I know that I was planning to head out by noon on Friday.

The Black Ski Summit was an interesting manifestation of a number of forces, trends and foibles. In some ways it represented a national convention of The Pride, unintentional though it might be. The Pride was not limited to New York. Members of The Pride lived in Baldwin Hills and Shaker Heights and Buckhead in Atlanta and on the Gold Coast of Chicago. While New York City might be the capital of The Pride, the constituency was national.

Whether it was Sag Harbor or Martha's Vineyard or Vail or Washington, during the Congressional Black Caucus Weekend, the members of The Pride found new and innovative ways to get together and to network. And it was a network with awesome potential if it were ever truly harnessed and focused. But, at the moment, like a lot of the people who were going to the Summit, I was simply looking forward to having a good time in Vail.

The previous year the Summit was held in Lake Tahoe. I missed it, but I heard that by the time all of the participants had departed, there was literally not a liquor bottle left in the entire town. The Pride could be incredibly thorough on occasion.

I am hardly one of those Martha Stewart types who obsesses over every detail of an event at my home. But I do have standards. Very high standards.

While I enjoy cooking, I was not even going to pretend to cook for a gathering like this one in the middle of the week. I called Butterbean.

Butterbean is a truly elite catering service that had been started by a former Broadway star, Chiquita Henry, who had been a star several years ago, singing and dancing and acting her way into a niche of fame and a little bit of fortune. Broadway and Hollywood had never been particularly kind to Chiquita, however, so she was smart enough to have come up with a Plan B long before her entertainment career came to a *denouement*.

Butterbean was not just a catering service. Chiquita also arranged for the best waiters and waitresses to serve her excellent fare. For the harried host or hostess who wanted to do things right, Butterbean was a godsend.

The Butterbean staff scurried around setting the table, chilling the wine and preparing the bar in my 5,000-square-foot SoHo loft. It was a loft in a building that was a converted factory space. I had worked with a very eclectic interior decorator to maintain the illusion and reality of space while creating different living environments with as few walls as possible.

While areas like the kitchen, exercise area and bedroom were partitioned off and the bathrooms, Jacuzzi and wardrobe were demarcated by walls, the rest of the space was wide open, with the dining area, living room, entertainment area and study spread throughout the rest of the sprawling space that was my urban hideaway.

With track lights, ceiling fans and hidden speakers, my interior decorator and I had created my own personal refuge in the middle of the busiest city in the world. It was my refuge and my home.

I found myself worrying and fussing over every detail like some kind of diva hostess. Jerome arrived on time, promptly at seven. Paul arrived a few moments later. And I could have sworn that I heard the Butterbean staffers sigh with relief because I could no longer bother them.

Greetings between Paul and me had been comfortable for years. We had come to an understanding and moved on with our lives. But the warmth and comfort that we had experienced recently was puzzling. I just did not know what to make of it. It was not unpleasant, just unsettling.

"Paul, I'm not surprised that you are late. You, of all people."

"Late? Wasn't dinner scheduled for seven?"

"But Paul, aren't you the one that is always ten minutes early?"

I made this last remark with a smile to let Paul know that I was just jerking his chain. I meant my smile to convey something more than politeness. What that was, even I didn't know. We looked at each other, continued to smile, and entered the living room area where Jerome was already seated.

The three of us had cocktails and made small talk while waiting for Gordon. During the weeks since the luncheon we had communicated by e-mail, fax and conference calls. As a result there was no real news to report as we chatted.

We had already understood that the plan that night was for Paul to review the key elements of the merger of the three firms and to outline the steps that would need to be taken in order to actually complete this deal. Additionally, Gordon, Jerome, and I were to report on the three projects that could be the basis for cooperative efforts that we had mentioned at our first luncheon meeting.

The plan was to finish dinner by ten as everyone had something to do the next day. Paul was going to St. Lucia, I was going to Vail, and Jerome was going to the Finger Lakes region in upstate New York. We were all there to take care of business. This made Gordon's lateness all the more noticeable and annoying.

Gordon could be crude, surly and undeniably offensive, but when it came to business, he was as reliable as the sun coming up in the morning. He was never a no-show when it came to business. But by seven thirty, with no Gordon Perkins, I thought it best to ask the Butterbean staff to start serving the appetizers. No one commented on Gordon's absence.

And then the doorbell rang.

It was Gordon, of course.

CHAPTER 59

Diedre

Dinner is served

I remember thinking that it was bad enough that Gordon was a total sleaze, actually the word asshole came to mind. I was also thinking that it was also bad enough that I was planning on working with him. I didn't think that it would be too much to expect that he would be on time! It took me awhile to catch on to the real deal when it came to Gordon.

As soon as he came in and got settled and apologies were dispensed, Gordon was constructive, positive and insightful in his comments. In other words, he was acting totally out of character. He was also a little jumpy and not the least bit hungry.

It actually seemed to me that he had to force every morsel of the catfish with watermelon relish into his mouth with a supreme effort. And he was certainly drinking more than a little of the champagne that I was serving.

Now that Gordon had completed the dinner party, we made small talk while the Butterbean staff unobtrusively removed the appetizer plates and replaced them with entrées featuring Chiquita's signature dish of Afro Cuban Black Beans and Broiled Salmon à la Negril. I had chosen a very nice Riesling to accompany the meal, and with the exception of Gordon we all enjoyed the food, the wine and the ambience before getting down to business.

When we had finished with dinner, coffee and dessert was served.

It was time for Paul to deal with the business of the day. As Paul began to speak, I couldn't help but notice that Gordon seemed distracted, as if there was some other plan on his mind, a plan other than the one that we were discussing.

"I know that all of you have read the latest version of the documents that would put this merger together. Lord knows I have received enough comments," said Paul.

"All that is left is for the three of you to commit to a confidentiality agreement. I would also suggest a six month time frame to get this deal done, and, of course, the standard due diligence provisions.

"If the three of you sign this Letter of Intent, none of you are bound to do this deal. But it is a hell of a big step. Like I said at the Water Club, this could be very big. If the three of you can work together you will make all of Wall Street sit up and take notice."

"Paul, are you going to be our lawyer or our P.R. man?" It was Jerome, providing some useful levity. We all laughed although I remember that Gordon, whose nose seemed to be running incessantly, was rather halfhearted in his laughter.

"Jerome, I am sure that you pay your P.R. people better than you pay your lawyers. That's just a cross we poor lawyers have to bear. But, if that was an offer, I may take you up on it. But I have to tell you that I hear that you are a hard, hard man to work for."

"You must have heard that from Ray Beard." I couldn't resist. No one had mentioned his absence, and his pompous nature deserved his being the butt of a joke or two. A brief laugh passed like the wind riffling the leaves of the forest, and then we proceeded to get serious again.

"There is not a whole lot more to do with the document tonight. If it makes sense to all of you, all of you should sign it and we can move on. If there is anything new to cover with the Letter of Intent itself, we should talk about it now." Paul continued to try and keep us on course.

The ensuing silence was a blessing. I could see that it was a relief to Paul as well. We were a strong-minded group. No one had been unreasonable, and now the Letter of Intent was essentially a done deal.

In the moment or two of silence I had to really hand it to Paul. From a seemingly spontaneous luncheon at the Water Club to now, he had taken a bright idea and turned it into a real, live deal with the clear possibility of success.

He had been able to persuade some of the strongest-willed and aggressive people that I know to work together and not for just a little while. If everything went as planned, this would be a permanent life-changing arrangement.

I couldn't help but think about the fact that Paul had always been a student of history. More than most, Paul realized that the history of black people in America was complicated and complex in texture. I had heard Paul speak on many occasions about the fact that despite the passage of civil rights bills and the election of black mayors across the country there still remained a chasm between black America and white America. We all knew without saying that this chasm would not be bridged and could not be bridged, as long as there was such a tremendous disparity between black and white in the financial sector.

This was not a matter of personal income. All you had to do was to look around the dinner table for confirmation of the many Urban League studies that found that the gap between black and white family median income was shrinking at a rapid rate.

But the key to power in America was access to capital. The key to real power in America was the ability to raise money, large sums of money, in order to advance various business objectives. That was the key to real power. We all knew that if Bill Gates were black, there simply would never have been a Microsoft. If Steve Jobs were black there would be no Apple.

More to the point—even being white, the fact that Bill Gates's father was a partner with a prominent Washington State law firm that represented venture capital companies made the real difference in Bill Gates becoming the wealthiest man in the world. It was common knowledge in the world of corporate finance that Bill Gates's original strategy was to build Microsoft to a point where he could sell it to IBM. IBM didn't buy and Bill Gates raised the necessary capital, through contacts that included his father's network and became the leader of the Corporate Free World. Being white and utilizing strategies that most certainly included priceless paternal counsel certainly made all the difference in the world of one Bill Gates.

This was the reality that Paul was looking to change. In our own way, we had all been looking to change this implacable reality. And we all believed that it could be changed if a black controlled firm on Wall Street had power, capital and influence.

CHAPTER 60

Diedre

Getting down to business

"From where I sit, I would think that the three of you will be working together sooner than later."

"Brother Paul, I think that you got it right this time and you can count me in. All the way." I would not have guessed that Gordon would be the first to formally get on board. But Gordon was always full of surprises.

"Now if you all will excuse me for a moment, I have to go to the little boy's room." As Gordon rose from the table and headed down the hall to the guest bathroom I could hear myself thinking on another, subconscious channel: *Jesus Christ. I can't believe that Gordon showed up late and high. I knew he had his bad points, but what the hell are we going to do with him if drugs are part of his package (no pun intended). Clearly we are all going to have to keep an eye on him.*

As Gordon disappeared down the hall toward the bathroom for what seemed like the tenth time, it seemed that everyone was thinking the same thing. This was one of these times when no one wanted to say anything. The fact was, to say anything at all could have been tantamount to blowing the whole deal sky high. We had invested a lot of time and hope in this project and we were all used to overcoming obstacles. Gordon's obvious problem was just going to be one more obstacle for us all to overcome.

Of course this was not a meeting of church deacons. None of us were saints when it came to our pleasures. Whether it was wine, Cuban cigars, reefer, vodka, coke or gin, we all knew about and enjoyed many of the vices of life. And, of course, this was also the case for so many other members of The Pride.

The Pride is most definitely not a bunch of drug ridden, alcoholic bacchanalians. The members of The Pride are people who are just like other Americans trying to make it in this hard world. We have our weakness and our vices and foibles, so what is new?

Of course, there is a time and place for everything, and you can't try to succeed in the United States of America as a black man or woman if you don't know that. The question was whether Gordon knew about the right time and place for his various vices.

And just then, as we started to engage in some more small talk about plans for the long weekend Gordon returned to the table. Amazingly, it was the same Gordon that we all knew, not the disoriented impostor who had come to dinner earlier. He was just a little more subdued than usual.

"I really have to apologize to all of you, especially you, Diedre, since you are our hostess." I could hardly believe my ears. This simply was not the Gordon Perkins I had come to know and loathe.

"I should tell you that I have been taking this sinus medication and sometimes it really throws me for a loop. I guess I seemed to be pretty out of it, but I think I'm O.K. now."

To say that we were stunned would be like saying some people like fried chicken on Sunday. I was floored at being introduced to this almost human side of Gordon. Under the circumstances I really had to give him the benefit of the doubt regarding my suspicions as to what really "threw him for a loop."

I may have been born at night, but it wasn't last night, and I was not prepared to accept his excuse completely. After all, knowing Gordon, his story was probably bullshit. But the Gordon Perkins I knew and loathed usually didn't care what people thought. So for him, this was progress, however slow, on the road to humanity and decency.

In any event I had enough to worry about without wondering about whether Gordon was sober or not. He was a big boy and he had done pretty well without any of us looking after him. Frankly, I figured that whatever the case, as long as it didn't interfere with our business, I didn't care and didn't want to know.

And, looking at Jerome and Paul, I could see that Gordon's *mea culpa* certainly put them at ease. At least they were sufficiently at ease that they were not ready to bolt from the table and crash the deal.

The Butterbean staff cleared the table and cleaned up the kitchen and I saw them to the door. I do recall thinking that being able to host a catered dinner was truly a blessed luxury. I returned to the dining room with four glasses of some thirty-year-old port wine that a client had brought back from the town of Porto, Portugal.

Johnny Hodges was playing a solo on a Duke Ellington album that I had put on my sound system and the rapture of his music seemingly came from a galaxy far, far away. Despite the rapturous melody that oozed comfort and relaxation, I knew that Paul would make sure that we got down to business. And he did.

CHAPTER 61

Diedre

We're on the right track now

"I think that the best thing that we can do for the rest of the evening is to see how each of you can provide support or assistance to the three projects that are supposed to get the merged firm off the ground. Diedre, would you mind starting the progress reports?" Paul got things started, which was exactly what he should have done under the circumstances.

We were all at ease, but not so relaxed that we had lost sight of the reason why we had gotten together. Butterbean had provided us with an excellent meal and the Gordon *contretemps* was seemingly resolved, at least for the moment. As I took a sip of the port wine and looked around the table at my future partners, I had the feeling that I was moving down a road that made sense, even if I couldn't see all the way to the end.

I have never thought of myself as one of those overly intuitive women. I need hard facts, data and information in as much detail as possible. But every now and then I have to trust my inner voice, and this time my inner voice was saying that this was the right time and place.

"I have been able to get some real movement with a couple of the public employee unions and the managers of their pension funds. I am supposed to make a special presentation to them—they are going to fly into New York to meet at my offices in about a month. I am looking at about five billion dollars in assets that I will be managing if everything goes according to plan."

"Diedre, here is a list with the names and phone numbers of the chief financial officers of six Fortune 500 companies that we do work for." It was Jerome. And as well as I thought I knew him and despite my high expectations that evening, I was still momentarily taken aback. He was handing me pure gold.

"Call them next week. They are expecting your call and of course they all have huge pension funds. They have each already told me that they want you to make a presentation to their investment committees."

As Jerome took a sip of the port and passed the list to me, I hoped that my face did not reveal my total surprise and pleasure. Otherwise my eyes would have been as big as saucers and my jaw would have simply been on the table. As it was, Paul and I exchanged the briefest of glances and we knew—this merger just could work after all.

"Jerome, this is just great. I am going to have FedEx packages going out to these people in the morning and I will call them Wednesday. At dawn! Thank you very much, Mr. Hardaway."

"Nothing to it, Diedre. If we are going to be partners, this is how it's going to have to work. Right?"

"Brother, when you are right, you are goddamn right!" Gordon seemed to have revived to become his normal self. A subdued Gordon was simply too good to be true. And speaking of Gordon, I had to wonder what he had up his sleeve.

It was almost as if he were reading my mind. Not that Gordon could sit on the sidelines of any conversation for too long, in any event. The next words that came out of his mouth answered that question in full.

"I guess it would be a good idea for me to add a word or two. I don't want to be dead weight. After all, I always try and do my part."

Gordon paused for dramatic effect. Pure Gordon, that's for sure. He then explained what he had been doing to advance the cause of what would be The Pride's newest investment banking firm.

"Diedre, in the morning you will receive a fax from my office with the names and contact information for the chief financial officers or comptrollers for the cities of Newark, New Orleans, Oakland, Detroit, and Birmingham.

"I have spoken to all of them and they know the deal and are expecting your call. Their investment committees are prepared to meet with you and they just have to decide the amount of assets that will be put under your management. I think we are talking about somewhere between two and five billion dollars at a minimum."

"Gordon, that is just amazing."

"Just taking care of business, Diedre. But I'm not finished. California, New York, Oregon, Illinois, and Ohio all have pension funds with venture capital components.

"Jerome, here is a list of the venture capital fund investment officers. I have spoken to all of them about your biotech project and they want to talk. No promises, of course, but I really think you want to make these calls." He handed the piece of paper to Jerome and sat back and smiled. Now we all knew that this could work.

All I could think was that Gordon was sick, twisted, arrogant and a true pain in the ass. But I could see now why he had been so successful so far. When he put his mind to taking care of business, he was just awesome!

CHAPTER 62

Diedre

Flying high in the friendly skies

Within moments we were all engaged in conversation about how we could work together. The team was starting to come together. Any reluctance or reticence was left way behind as we came to realize the true value of our working together.

"Gordon, I have gotten the public employees unions in Detroit, Denver, and Minneapolis to agree to host fund-raisers for Prince Lodrig. You just need to have the mayor's people call me so that these events can be coordinated. He will have to fly to all those cities, but I am sure that it will be worth the travel." I was fully on board now and there was no point in holding cards too close now.

"While we are on the subject, Gordon, I have spoken to the political action committees of several of my largest corporate clients and they are prepared to support Lodrig. As Diedre said, if you have Mayor Lodrig's people call me I will work out the details." Jerome was clearly prepared to do his part to make this venture work.

"That sounds great," said Gordon. "Thanks, Diedre, and thank you, Jerome. And by the way, Jerome, you should know that I spoke with the economic development officers in New Orleans, Oakland, Seattle, and New York City. They are all anxious for your friend Barry Herzog to locate his new biotech plant in their city.

"All of them have all kinds of tax incentives, tax abatements, employee training, free office space and low cost construction loans. All you need to do is call and let the bidding begin! They will certainly dance to your tune on this one." And then Gordon continued with what seemed to be his one-man surprisathon.

"Paul, I think that I speak for the three of us when I thank you for bringing us together. And, we thank you for your great idea in the first place. And I also think that I speak for all of us when I tell you that if you don't agree to be our counsel now and after the merger, we will just have to gang up on you and kick your long, black ass!"

We all laughed. Hard. It was a great feeling that night. It was a feeling that we were all part of something special. That is why, to this day, I cannot explain this undercurrent of a bad feeling that I had that night. It was a strange and funny feeling. And then Gordon continued.

"I don't know how much you all have been reading about the mayoral race in New Orleans, but my guy, excuse me, *our* guy is winning this thing in a cakewalk. Now, even though it's only February, his campaign people want to start a media blitz at the beginning of next month.

"I think that if we can contribute about $100,000 it will make a big difference to the mayor and it will make a big difference for our new operation after the election. They have excellent memories in that part of the world, you know." Gordon smiled as he looked at the three of us. Gordon smiling was always an enigma, and this was one of those times.

Given the euphoria and the good feelings of the moment, Jerome and I were only too happy to write out checks right on the spot. After all, the contacts that Gordon had given us were worth a lot more than that, and given the circumstances, it was the least that we could do. We all knew that you have to pay to play, and none of us have ever minded paying, as long as we got to play. We were all in this game to win. Second place was not an option.

We spent the rest of the evening taking care of what business was left. We passed our checks over to Gordon. Paul passed around copies of the Letter of Intent and we all signed them.

As we finished our drinks, Paul reviewed the status of the three projects. There was Gordon's mayoral race in New Orleans, Jerome's biotech project, and my asset management business. We all understood what needed to be done next. Now it was just a matter of following up.

Following up was something at which we all excelled. And that was one more reason why I felt that when we were working together completely, the results would be phenomenal.

"As far as these projects are concerned, I figure that it's going to take anywhere from three to six months to get any real traction going. Real progress takes time, we all know that. But you probably want to keep the momentum going on this merger."

Paul was correct in this regard. Even though he would be the counsel for the new firm, each of the three principals had to have their own counsel acting for us in our individual capacities. It was nothing personal, just business.

And there were all kinds of details that the lawyers would have to address. Issues like due diligence review, audited financial statements and a mountain of documentation that would be needed to make something like this happen.

We had already agreed that there would be no cash exchanged in the deal and the Letter of Intent was clear in making Gordon, Jerome and I equal partners. Since Gordon and Jerome had nominal partners, they would have to deal with those situations on their own. The new firm would have three and only three owners.

"Paul, I agree with your estimate on the timing, so let me suggest this. You know that every year I host a Labor Day party at my place in Sag Harbor. Why don't the three of you plan to come out that Thursday evening?

"By then we should have everything under control and we can have a dinner meeting to finalize the details and get everything signed, sealed and delivered before partying through the weekend. What do you think?

"The party isn't going to be until Saturday night and we can spend Friday on my yacht taking in the sights while Paul finishes up the paperwork." Gordon's last comment was made with a sly look in Paul's direction, meant in good humor.

His invitation and plan made all the sense in the world. Jerome and Charmaine had a place in Sag Harbor and Gordon's place had eight bedrooms and a guesthouse, more than enough to accommodate Paul and me.

We all agreed and finished our drinks and said our good nights. Paul, Jerome, and Gordon left in separate cars and I went to sleep dreaming of the million possibilities that this evening had introduced.

Within twenty-four hours Gordon and Kenitra were in Switzerland and I was at the Black Ski Summit in Steamboat Springs. Paul was walking on a beach in St. Lucia with Samantha and no doubt Jerome was pointing out the constellations to his children on an ice cold clear night on the Finger Lakes in upstate New York.

By the following Wednesday we were all back in New York City and we were all doing exactly what we said we were going to do. Following up was something like a religious calling for all of us. And working on the deal started to make more sense every day.

In the weeks and months that ensued, we saw each other numerous times. At wedding receptions, parties, fund-raisers and dinners— it was part of life in The Pride. There was no need to constantly refer to our pending deal. Indeed, an outside observer would have observed nothing special. It was as if our deal was in another dimension, another reality.

But I know that I thought about it every day. And I know that we all knew that a dramatic moment in our personal history was coming. And that it was not far away. We made a tacit decision to keep quiet about the whole thing. It was important for all of us to keep doing the work that we had been doing before all of this started, but Labor Day was getting closer every day.

CHAPTER 63

Paul

All the news that fits . . .

It will never cease to amaze me how the mind can go in so many different directions during times of stress. There are times when the mind wanders aimlessly down halls of thought. And sometimes a bright spot of humor will be found that will keep you sane, at least for the moment.

As I reflect on that Friday morning in the middle of August, I was sitting on a USAIR jet, flying to Gary, Indiana, of all places. I was listening to the hypnotic sounds of Cesaria Evoria while sipping a gin and tonic with a wedge of lime that the flight attendant was kind enough to get me as soon as we took off. I have found that being in first class did have benefits other than leg room on occasion. The plaintive Cape Verdean sounds seemed terribly appropriate that day as the 737 made its way through a remarkably cloudless sky.

I certainly didn't have any reason to smile that morning even though the deal with Diedre, Jerome, and Gordon was moving forward better than I could have ever planned or dreamed. The deal was coming together without as much as a hiccup. The "test" projects were proceeding apace and none of the principals had raised any serious objections or problems as the structure of the merged firm started to come together.

Still, ever since that dinner at Diedre's, I couldn't help thinking that there was something that I was missing. I just didn't know what it was but I certainly felt that there was something else.

That call to Sammy Groce in January came to mind, as did the election "surprise" to which he referred. But what the hell was that?

Frankly, I didn't have a lot of time for doubts and second thoughts. All I have ever been able to do is make the best decisions that I can and then try to live with the consequences. The last thing I was going to do was to try and crash this deal because crazy Sammy Groce had a hint of a thread of a piece of a bit of information about this and that, or because Gordon looked funny. As a veteran member of The Pride all I could do was move on.

And then there was the deal itself. It was time-consuming and complicated in many ways. There were three sets of lawyers who had become a seemingly permanent part of my life. There was the rest of my practice which, thankfully, was growing and thriving. And then, there was Samantha and her health.

CHAPTER 64

Paul

It's the same old song

As the plane banked over the concrete mountain ranges of Manhattan Island, I did find myself smiling as I thought about a prospective client who had come into my office just a few days earlier. "Prince" Albert Olajide was referred to me by one of the members of the Ghanaian Mission to the United Nations.

The prince was supposed to be from a royal family based in Kano, a state in northern Nigeria. He was also supposed to be in need of legal services with regard to a "major" financial transaction in Nigeria.

Now normally, the words "Nigeria" and "major financial transaction" would be enough to send me running the other way. I had heard way too many stories about Americans going to Nigeria and being lucky to be able to leave town with their underwear.

I have thought it incredibly ironic, in a flukey sort of way, that the African country with the highest literacy rate would be the home of some of the most intricate and effective cons, scams and schemes seen anywhere in the world. Nigerians could teach gypsies and three-card monte dealers a thing or two.

Of course, many of these cons, scams and schemes have been exported to the U.S. And some of the subterfuges that I have heard about are simply awesome in their simplicity and effectiveness.

For example, through the most routine inquiry, anyone, including some Nigerians with bad intentions, can get the name and home address of a targeted victim. It is then a simple matter to file a change of address form with the U.S. Post Office routing the victim's mail to an address selected by the scammer.

Within a week or two, the scammer can have the victim's banking and credit card information. This data could now belong to a cabal of Nigerians of dubious virtue who would obtain new credit cards, drain bank accounts and generally create pure havoc in the life of the victim.

This was one reason that I was more than a little wary about meeting with "Prince" Olajide. In fact, I was doing so only as a courtesy to my Ghanaian friends. And, there was always the possibility, however remote, that the prince was an honest person with a legitimate business proposition.

Prince Olajide turned out to be a well-groomed African brother, probably in his late twenties. He was immaculately attired in what appeared to me to be a custom-tailored Savile Row suit.

The prince was sleek and ebony smooth in appearance and style, exuding nothing if not confidence and absolute sincerity. He was clearly a man who was used to impressing and, although I don't impress easily, he certainly got my full attention as he came into my office.

After we greeted each other, shook hands, and sat down in my office, the basic formalities ensued. I served espresso to the prince and rooibos tea from South Africa to myself. We exchanged business cards.

The card that the prince handed to me with exquisitely manicured hands had only his name and a London phone number. After the basic pleasantries were exchanged, the prince took another sip of his espresso, sat back in his chair, and got down to business.

As the jet reached its cruising altitude, I just had to smile at the rest of the story. I decided to replace Cesaria Evoria with Sonny Rollins to give some balance to the reverie that my recollections had brought on. The "Alfie" album will always be a classic as far as I am concerned.

"Mr. Taylor, you were highly recommended by our mutual friends and I want to thank you for honoring me with an appointment."

As he began to describe his business proposition and his need for representation, there was something about the prince's speech patterns that struck me as odd . . . for no good reason. It wasn't until later, when I found out that he had attended school in Edinburgh, Scotland, that I realized that I had been listening to a Nigerian-Scottish accent. Once you hear it you could never forget it.

"Mr. Taylor, my uncle is a senior official in the Ministry of Finance in Nigeria. As you are no doubt aware, due to the significant sums of money generated by my country's oil reserves, the Ministry of Finance is called upon to invest huge amounts that arise as the proceeds from the sale of oil into Grade A investment accounts throughout the world.

"Currently, there are accounts amounting to two billion U.S. dollars which need to be invested outside of Nigeria immediately. The interest revenues are critical toward funding services that the government must provide to our people."

"Prince Olajide, pardon me for getting right to the point, but what service can I offer in all of this? I am a lawyer, not a banker. I don't see how I can help you in this situation."

I try not to display impatience or make impolitic statements as a matter of personal choice. But sometimes it's important to interrupt and this was one of those times.

And I was pretty sure that I had heard this story before, probably several times over. During the previous ten years, thousands of Americans, some of them members of The Pride, had been approached by phone, e-mail, fax or mail with a Nigerian story that sounded very similar to the story that this prince was telling me.

The basic scam was based on a story that some Nigerian government agency, like the Ministry of Petroleum or the Ministry of Finance needed to invest huge sums of money. If the targeted recipient of this information were to pay a modest servicing fee, usually between $5,000–$50,000, they would receive 2 percent of the multimillion-dollar investment for their trouble in facilitating the transfer of funds from Nigeria to their personal bank account.

Needless to say, no one has ever seen one thin dime. Yet the scam has persisted, obviously prospering among the terminally gullible.

For some reason many of these Nigerians have targeted members of The Pride. It seems that they were targeted because they were somewhat prominent and were perceived to have some access to capital. And, because they were of African descent, they might have a tendency to want to do a deal like this—working with the Motherland, as it were.

By now Sonny Rollins and Oliver Nelson were deep into their collaboration on the "Alfie" album. I asked the flight attendant for another gin and tonic with the mandatory wedge of lime. For the moment, it was better to think about Prince Olajide than the reason why I was flying to Gary on a Friday morning.

CHAPTER 65

Paul

Don't play that song for me

"I am glad that you asked that question, Mr. Taylor. I like a businessman who gets right to the point." The prince definitely had a plan. But I couldn't get over his Scottish accent. It was like seeing Michael Jordan in a kimono. The dissonance was simply hard to ignore.

"I have to make it clear Mr.—Prince Olajide that I am an attorney and I am not usually involved in any business transactions for my own account."

"Of course, of course. That is the reason I have come to see you and not some other lawyer." I had to hand it to him, he was smooth and cool, if nothing else. I could not imagine butter melting in his mouth.

"You see, in order for the sum of two billion dollars to be invested in the United States, I will have to pay a servicing fee of five million dollars. While my personal accounts in Switzerland and the Isle of Man could easily cover this cost of doing business, recent exchange control regulations in Switzerland and the Isle of Man are making that kind of transaction somewhat complicated, if you know what I mean.

"It would be so much easier to simply raise that paltry sum here in America and share the profits with my co-investors . . . and with my counsel."

The prince flashed a knowing, conspiratorial smile. I halfway expected him to wink and nudge me in the ribs with his elbow.

And it was at that point I knew that this was all complete and utter Grade A bullshit. I had guessed that was the case when the prince first started to talk. Now I was sure.

"Excuse me, sir. Would you happen to have a mirror?"

"I beg your pardon?" The prince was truly baffled by my question. And, months later, at 25,000 feet, I still had to laugh. There was not much else to smile about at the moment so I had to savor that moment from the past.

"I asked you for a mirror because I need to take a good look at myself."

"I am afraid that I just . . . don't . . . understand."

"I just want to see if I look as dumb as you must think I am."

The prince began to stammer and stutter and sputter. He found himself in the unfamiliar position of being able to say nothing as he was truly taken aback.

"Look, I am sure that we both know bullshit when we see it. And your Savile Row suit and Scottish accent notwithstanding, this whole deal is bullshit. And we both know it.

"Now I mean no insult. Some of the most successful business people that I represent are hustling day and night. I just have a problem with you trying to hustle me.

"I don't know what our mutual friends from Ghana told you about me, but they could not have told you that I just fell off the truck from the country. Did you really think that you could just moonwalk into my office and get me to fall for this?"

In retrospect I had to hand it to the prince. Once he had been busted he did not try to breathe life into a dead con. He knew when to hold them and he knew when to fold them.

"Mr. Taylor, it appears that we will not be able to conduct any business today . . ."

"Or any other day, my friend."

"I understand completely and I apologize for taking up your time. I trust that you will not be offended if I don't finish my espresso?"

"Under the circumstances, no offense taken. Please have a good rest of the day."

And with that, Prince Olajide walked out of my office and out of my life and into the record book for the top bullshit story of the year. It was the only thing that happened during that time that made me smile.

Sonny Rollins continued to play. I continued to sip my Bombay Sapphire gin and tonic. My big dilemma was whether I should put on James Carter or Mark Whitfield next. Of course, there was always Shabba.

At that point, on that flight, on that day, music was my salvation and my lifeline.

CHAPTER 66

Paul

If I ever had a dream before . . .

Samantha died exactly ten days after my meeting with the prince. It was not sudden and it was not a surprise. The doctors were very clear in their diagnosis. Nevertheless, her death was a shock that would stay with me for the rest of my life.

A few weeks after our trip to St. Lucia, I was finally able to persuade Samantha to see a doctor about her cough and nagging throat problems. One week later she was diagnosed as having throat cancer. One month later, after intensive radiation and chemotherapy, the doctor told Samantha that she might not live to see Christmas. She barely made it to August.

The diagnosis was a shock. The prognosis was disaster. Her death was expected. And when it came, she embraced it with grace and dignity. And I cried bitter tears alone. Again.

First my father had died unexpectedly. Then my brother had his fatal accident. And now the love of my life was gone forever. For more than a few moments I felt as if my brain had lost its moorings and that my soul was hurtling toward eternal darkness and hopelessness. All the good works and success and money that I had didn't mean a goddamn thing. My life was being torn apart by what? Fate? Destiny? Bad luck?

There was nothing to do but laugh to myself as I decided on Oscar Peterson as I finished my drink. Gary, Indiana, was about a half hour away, and the coffin containing Samantha's wonderful and gorgeous body was in the hold of the jet. I was flying in to attend her funeral in her hometown.

As the jet continued on its sad journey through the skies over western New York State, I was glad that I had met some of her family before—her mother, father, a couple of sisters and her younger brother. But I knew that there was nothing in my life that had prepared me for the pure and exquisite agony of having to witness Samantha's family, consumed with grief, having to bury her long before her appointed time.

The recollection of the Prince Olajide story was the only light moment in an awful awe-filled day. By the time the plane landed in Gary with its tragic cargo, I knew that as overwhelming as my grief might be, it simply could not compare to the pain felt by her parents. A father should never have to bury his daughter. A mother should never see her child's coffin.

I was Samantha's lover. In a different world and in a different time and place she would have been my wife. But my pain and loss was dwarfed by what I saw in the eyes of her mother and father. And we all wept, without shame and without control.

The funeral services were held at Mount Nebo Zion Baptist Church in the heart of Gary. The minster was Reverend Wendell Wesley. I learned that he had been pastor of the church for thirty-five years.

I have to confess that I have a very cynical view reserved for some black Baptist ministers. I had seen too many of them use their position as the source of spiritual guidance to take advantage of their congregation, to make money and to seduce vulnerable widows. I know that there are many ministers who truly believe in their work and are spiritually dedicated and I am sorry that their rapacious brethren diminish the reputations that they work so hard to maintain.

I know a game when I see it, and in my mind, too many of them cared not a damn for the Bible and worshipped at the wrong altar all the time. I will always be glad, however, that I reserved judgment before meeting the pastor of Mount Nebo Zion Baptist Church.

I will remember his eulogy for Samantha for the rest of my life. In fact, in the days and weeks after her funeral, it was Reverend Wesley's words that would sustain me through the pain and hurt that came with the realization that I had lost her for all time.

Indeed, it still surprises me that I can actually replay the Reverend's entire sermon in my mind, like some kind of haunting videotape. It is not unwelcome, just haunting and beautiful, like my memories of Samantha.

Reverend Wesley spoke in the traditional cadences of a Baptist minister. But he did it with exquisite drama and class, and without the bombast and pretension. He was eloquent and elegant. His words over Samantha's casket were perfect.

Dearly beloved, and we are all beloved in the eyes of the Lord; To the Gideon family in this time of your great loss, please know that you have our prayers and that our tears flow with yours. There are times of great tragedy that can also be times of great hope. A time of great pain can also be a time of great pleasure. I know, I know, right now all you can think about is the pain. And we lift our voices to heaven and ask, where is the pleasure?

We are here to celebrate the end of a wonderful and glorious life. And at the same time that we mourn the loss of our dear sister, our dear daughter, Samantha Gideon, we must believe, we just have to believe, that she is in a better place now. She is receiving the blessings that she so richly deserves, and the glory. She has gone home. Her father's house has many mansions. And she is there now. That we know.

Can I hear an amen?

The pain and the suffering that we expect at birth is a cause for tears and sadness. But a soul has been saved, Samantha's soul, Samantha who believed in God in her heart and soul and is experiencing the glories of paradise now. Angels are washing away all her tears and protecting her, and she will not be crying for the rest of eternity. Everybody, say amen.

And, even as we stand before her casket, as we gaze at what is left of her presence here on earth, we are tempted to ask God, Why? Why now? Why Samantha? Why, God? Please tell me why? But you know what? We are asking the wrong question at the wrong time. I don't believe you heard me the first time. I said, we are asking the wrong question at exactly the wrong time.

We didn't ask, "Why?" a beautiful child was born to wonderful and loving parents who cared for her with kindness, affection and compassion from the very first day that she was born until now.

We didn't ask, "Why?" she grew into a beautiful and talented woman who could charm a smile from the meanest man in town. And we didn't ask God "Why?" she was given the voice of an angel who could sing so sweetly that she could make the monkeys come down from the trees. Can I get somebody to say amen?

No, nobody asked "Why?" then. So how can we have the nerve to ask God "Why?" he would take her back so that she could join the heavenly choir and sing for the pleasure of all the blessed ones forever? She belongs to God. She always belonged to God. We all belong to God. We have to remember that. She didn't belong to any of us, not even her mother and father. She always belonged to God.

He was kind enough to let her visit us for a little while. And we must be thankful that he let one of his angels walk with us, touch us, love us, smile at us, if only for a little while. But it could never be time enough. And it was never going to be forever.

As we remember Samantha, the warmth of our smiles should dry our tears of sadness and grief. The angel called Samantha is gone from us, for now. But in a little while, just a little while, in the twinkling of an eye, I know that we will all be listening to the sweet sounds of her voice once more. One by one, God will take us all away and we will be a part of that heavenly chorus. Even those of us who can't sing a note here on earth . . . don't worry, we will be singing in heaven.

So let's turn this funeral into something else. Let's change it from a time of sadness and tears into a time of thanksgiving. Let's change the day from one of grief to a time of wonderment and expectation and celebration of the life of Samantha Gideon.

We are so sad that Samantha is gone. Nothing can change that. And Mr. and Mrs. Gideon, you know that this whole congregation extends its hands and hearts to you. But we also join you in giving praise to God, in giving thanks to God for the wonderful gift of having had Samantha in our lives.

Mr. and Mrs. Gideon, we are going to grieve with you right now, but we too anticipate the day and the hour and the minute and the second and the moment when we will all stand in the glorious light of our Lord and Savior. And then we will see all our loved ones once more. Can I get an amen?

Now I will tell you, Mr. and Mrs. Gideon, you have lost a daughter, but right now, someone has lost a sister. Someone has lost a mother or a father. Tomorrow someone will lose a wife or a son. But with God's mercy, we will all be reunited in the sweet green pastures that are just on the other side. Some day soon. Very soon. Believe it, brothers and sisters. It is the way of God's world. Let everybody say amen. And now, let us pray.

For the first time in over three decades, I did pray. I didn't pray the way they taught me in catechism or Bible school, but I prayed. I prayed to God, I prayed to That Which Is Greater Than Me. I really tried to give thanks for having had Samantha in my life.

I prayed that Mr. and Mrs. Gideon would find some comfort at this awful time. And I prayed that somehow, some way, this loss would somehow, some way, make some sense in my life. And I prayed that it would be soon.

CHAPTER 67

Paul

Shared pain—shared tears

After the funeral, there was her burial in a cemetery not far from the church. The family had a number of people come by the house for the tradition post-funeral meal. It was a hot August day in Indiana, so a lot of the people who came by wound up eating their ham sandwiches and fried chicken on the lawn in the backyard while Mr. and Mrs. Gideon quietly and with enduring nobility received condolences from their guests in the parlor.

I had endured the sight of Samantha's casket being lowered into her grave. The family was kind enough to let me place a single long-stemmed purple Sterling rose on the casket. It was her favorite flower and to this day I cannot look at one without thinking of her and loving her all over again.

When I got to the house, I waited until the appropriate time to have a few words with Mr. and Mrs. Gideon. There was not a whole lot to say. I promised to stay in touch and that I would complete the shipping of Samantha's personal effects back to Gary. I also promised to visit again during some holiday season. And then it was time for me to go.

I had already decided that I was simply not going to spend the night in Gary. I arranged to rent a car and drive to Chicago and catch a late evening flight back to New York.

As it turned out, the one hour drive to O'Hare Airport was the absolute perfect therapy. I didn't even bother to turn on the radio to listen to music. I drove in absolute silence so that I could gather my brain and organize my spirit and my thoughts.

I thought about the last month of Samantha's life. To say that it was brutal would be an understatement. It was beyond hell. She was never in much pain, the technology of modern medicine and pharmacology being able to do that much for her.

But there was never any doubt that she was going to die, so once we had some kind of acceptance of that awful truth, she and I had a chance to say all the things to each other that loved ones rarely get to say before one or the other is gone. And then, of course, it is too late.

At least we had the good fortune of knowing when the end was coming. And for that I will always be truly grateful.

But knowing that every day was closer to our last day almost drove me out of my mind at the time. I raged at fate and God. I cried for no reason and for every good reason there was. Despite my trying not to, I kept thinking about a few words that I read in something called *Five Rules of Life*.

The rules referred to the fact that, if we are lucky, we will find one person in life who will love us as much as we love them. And, if you find that person, you should do everything you can to keep that person in your life. And then I would just weep.

And sometimes I would sit at her bedside, while she was sleeping, and I could swear that I could see her actually fading away. She started to disappear right before my very eyes.

At the end, she passed away quietly. She just went to sleep. Just like that. Despite the pain, it's a moment I will never forget.

CHAPTER 68

Paul

Pieces of a man

Now, driving to O'Hare Airport, on the way back to New York, I tried to take stock of my life. I felt that I needed to take a look at myself.

The woman that I had come to love was dead. The love of my life was gone. The woman whom I had loved, Diedre, was now a client. She had loved me, very well I believed, but now it was strictly business. At least that is what I tried to believe.

Lisette Bailey was still a treasure and a source of pleasure and enjoyment. We both always had fun. But was there anything more? I doubted it.

As far as Lisette was concerned, I was almost sure that it was only about fun. Her career, her life, her future, came many places ahead of anything having to do with me or any other man.

Since Samantha had died I was sure that I wanted something more than fun. Sure, I still wanted to have fun. But I also wanted what I had with Samantha.

There I was, forty-five years old, reasonably successful, and poised on the precipice of the greatest deal of my life. I was about to make history, and I was all alone.

I held on to that thought as I returned the rental car and boarded my flight back to New York. I put Miles Davis's "Kind of Blue" on my Walkman and sipped a glass of undistinguished white wine as the great American Midwest gave way to the mad cacophony of buildings, roads and people that made up the northeastern part of the U.S. beneath us.

I thought about the love and caring and partnership that I saw Charmaine and Jerome Hardaway share and I felt the gnawing annoyance of envy looking for a grip on my soul. And as my thoughts and feelings wrestled with all of that, I found myself even believing, for a moment, that what Gordon and Kenitra Perkins had between them was a relationship worth having. As contorted and convoluted as their own reasons for being together may have been, so went my thinking, at least they had each other in their lives, and they were not alone.

As the plane cruised under the night stars, my feelings of grief and pain took full control. Tears welled up in my eyes. Miles knew my feelings and blew them through his horn into that special place where feelings really live.

And it was that point that the feeling that I had since driving back from Samantha's grave showed me the way to feeling bad all the time. I found the way to self-pity. I reveled in that awful feeling for a few minutes.

I thought of myself as all alone. Despite my many friends, my clients, colleagues, associates, the members of The Pride, my personal network of contacts . . . I thought of myself at that moment as being all alone. I could see no way out of this maze of bad feelings.

That made me realize once more that not only would I miss Samantha for the rest of my life, but that for the rest of my life I would always compare every moment that approached happiness to my times with her. And that would mean that not only would I be alone, I would also never be happy again. And I found myself starting to cry.

It was strange, crying like that. There have been times, like the funerals of my father and brother, when I did cry. But crying was not a part of my regular routine. But after Samantha's death, something changed.

Of course I cried in the hospital when the awful and final pronouncement was made by the doctors. And I felt more than a few tears coursing their way down my face during Reverend Wesley's eulogy.

But for some three or four months after Samantha died, I found myself crying in the morning. I simply cried at the beginning of each day.

I imagine that I cried because dawn was Samantha's favorite time of day. Whatever the reason might have been, for the next few months I was absolutely miserable in the morning. I found myself crying for no reason except that I felt the sadness and misery and desolation of missing a loved one who would never smile at me or be held in my arms again.

And then, one evening, after a few months of inexpressible misery every morning, I had an incredible and wonderful visitor. I was in my office, on the phone, looking at e-mail and leafing through my mail. I was multitasking and working late as usual. And then Samantha walked in.

"Hello, Paul. Trying to do too many things at once again, I see." Her smile was like a stage spotlight, lighting up the stage and my soul. And she looked wonderful.

"Samantha . . . ?" I simply could not find the words. All the things I had wanted to say to her were colliding with each other, looking to be the first to present themselves.

"Really Paul, I thought you might have a little bit more to say. Has it been that long?" The lilt of her voice, the tilt of her chin, the sparkle in her eyes. I thought I was dreaming at first, but it couldn't be. It was Samantha! Somehow Samantha was standing in my office!

"But Samantha . . . how? I thought that . . ." I felt like a puppy on ice . . . my mind had no balance. Nothing made sense. I was just starting to accept her being gone a little more every day. I was with her in the hospital that awful day. I flew with her casket to Gary. I placed a rose on her casket in the grave, for God's sake!

I knew that she was dead, but there she was, standing in front of me. She was smiling the smile that promised love and warmth for an eternity. I just could not comprehend the miracle that was before me. And I was so afraid to question my good fortune that all I could do was sit there, virtually speechless.

It was if she could read my mind. It had always seemed that she could do that. And she always knew what to say.

"Paul, you were the one to teach me not to believe everything that people say."

"But Samantha, the doctors . . . Reverend Wesley . . . ?"

"Paul, look at me. I'm fine. Just fine." She dismissed my doubts and questions like a fairy queen waving away the bad spirits with a magic wand.

"I have missed you so much, Samantha. So very much."

"Why are you missing me, darling? You can see I am right here with you. And I always will be with you. That is what you want, isn't it?"

"Yes, Samantha. You know that. You have always known that." I found myself starting to cry tears of joy and relief. I don't know what the feelings were, but they were real. Feelings as real as her standing in front of me.

"I have some things to do right now, Paul, but I'll see you soon. I love you, darling." And then she turned to walk out of my office.

"I love you too, darling. But Samantha! Wait a minute . . ." And she was gone.

And then I woke up.

I sat straight up in my bed as if I had been catapulted from my pillow. I have walked on beaches around the world and have known the true sensation of feeling the grains of sand beneath my feet. I have smelled the smells and seen the colors of life and I know reality when I encounter it. And I will swear for the rest of my life that I was really and truly speaking to Samantha and that in some dimension, in some different space and time, in the dream, we actually met and spoke for a few minutes.

Over time I have spoken to other people who have lost someone close to them. They all speak of that loved one returning in a dream a month later, four months later. There is no rule, of course.

But at some point that loved one has returned to let someone know that it is O.K. to move on, that life and death must take their turn. Some call it closure.

I just called it relief.

CHAPTER 69

Paul

Jagged jigsaw pieces

After that morning, I never felt alone. Many things have happened since then, including my getting married. Of course there is also the wonderful miracle of Paul Jr. But that visit with Samantha helped me to at least come to grips with the notion that life and death must indeed take their turn. From time to time, Samantha still visits, as do my brother and father.

And I am happier for their visits.

But as that plane landed at La Guardia that Saturday night, I did not know anything about closure or future visits from Samantha. I did know that there was work to be done.

I went straight to my office to continue to work on the merger. There were lawyers' documents with which I had been wrestling all summer. We were supposed to be meeting at Gordon's place in Sag Harbor in three weeks to finalize the deal. Even with an agreement in principle between Gordon, Jerome, and Diedre, there was a hell of a lot of work left to do.

As I walked into my office and spent my first Saturday night without Samantha in my life, I hoped that working on this deal of a lifetime might take my mind away from that cemetery in Gary.

The three weeks before that all-important meeting on Long Island moved like absolute lightning during the day. And time moved like some kind of macabre prehistoric glacier during the night. Thankfully, during the day there was a veritable avalanche of paperwork, phone calls, and negotiations.

It was a great idea not to have Jerome, Gordon, and Diedre negotiate with each other. But, as the clearinghouse for all comments, concerns, issues and criticisms, I felt like I was carrying the weight of the whole deal.

Given the circumstances, that was probably a good thing as it kept my mind off the pain I felt upon Samantha's death. It was impossible to just sit and grieve when there were interminable faxes, conference calls from hell and a general state of pandemonium which converted my office into some kind of firehouse on permanent four-alarm call.

And, there was other business to which I had to attend, of course. During those few weeks there were at least four round trips to Los Angeles, each trip for less than twenty-four hours, dealing with the sale of the dramatic rights of novels written by two different authors that I represented. Business was good and getting better. But those glacial evenings! And those doleful mornings!

At some point, the workday ended. At some point it was time to go home. And at some point, while I sat at home in the middle of the night, all the fine wines, fine cuisine and fine women could not make me forget that Samantha would never enter my doorway again. And then, with dawn would come the tears.

I remember taking on the task of packing up her apartment and shipping her personal effects to Mr. and Mrs. Gideon back in Gary. I tried to think of reasons to procrastinate. But it was my fate and responsibility to handle this task for her aggrieved parents.

In a strange, Catholic sort of way, I looked upon the whole experience as penance. Penance for the sins that I had committed and penance for the sins that I might commit in the future. As the great John Lee Hooker might have said, "It serves you right to suffer."

But somehow, someway, I was able to gently fold her clothes into the painfully plain and ordinary cardboard boxes that the moving company had provided. I took the framed posters announcing her performances in Gstaad and Nice and Compton off the walls and packed them carefully, as if Samantha might be looking at them again soon.

And by the time I finished on that hot August night, I had said goodbye to Samantha in a very special, painful way. Even so, a part of my heart would be saying goodbye to her forever.

And just like that, I was back at my desk, juggling phone calls and visiting clients. There were documents to be reviewed, deals to be completed, and deals to be chased. And then, there was that incredibly important meeting that was going to be held in Sag Harbor in just a little while.

I knew that if Samantha were alive she would want me to live my life to the fullest. And so I chased the deal of a lifetime with renewed vigor and energy. By the time the Thursday before Labor Day arrived, all the relevant documents had been faxed and hand-delivered to the principals. Hard copies of all signature documents had been sent to Gordon's Sag Harbor address via Federal Express.

As you can imagine, Gordon, Diedre, and Jerome commiserated as best they could after Samantha passed away. In an incredibly uncharacteristic moment of humanity, Gordon even suggested postponing the meeting if that would help me.

Of course I wouldn't hear of it. The truth was that my pain and mourning would not be assuaged by a postponement. And I knew what Samantha would have wanted me to do.

Diedre suggested a memorial service in New York for all of Samantha's friends and admirers. I have to admit that I was being more than a little self-indulgent and selfish when I asked Diedre to wait awhile. I just couldn't stand the public pain again so soon after Gary. Diedre understood and complied. And for that I was most grateful.

Jerome and Charmaine had me over for dinner about a week after I returned from Gary. I came by, even though I knew that their mission—to comfort me—was doomed from the start. But I appreciated their concern. And, as I looked at Jerome and Charmaine and their family, I think I started to understand what was missing in my own life.

CHAPTER 70

Paul

What a difference a day makes

I had a Porsche 911, which I kept garaged and rarely drove anywhere, except in the summertime. I decided to drive out to Sag Harbor early enough on that Thursday before the Labor Day weekend so that I could avoid some of the holiday traffic and be alone with my thoughts.

The 911 handled effortlessly on the cement ribbon that was the Long Island Expressway. I remember listening to the Modern Jazz Quartet play "Concierto de Aranjuez" with Laurindo Almeida from their "Collaboration" album. A true classic. It was the right music for the right time.

I had the top down. The sun was shining. I was on the verge of a true professional victory. And the warmth of the summer breezes dried my tears.

I also had some time to think. I could not forget that phone call with Sammy Groce back in January. I was still sure that it meant nothing. Nothing of note had surfaced since then that would back up any aspect of his story. But still . . . ?

And what about Ray Beard? Would he prove to be trouble, after all? He had been very quiet of late. And was this the right deal for Diedre, Jerome, and Gordon anyway?

And then I had to laugh. I laughed because I knew that I was guilty of taking myself too damn seriously. Samantha and Diedre were two people upon whom I could count to make sure that I didn't get too full of myself. But with neither of them around, I just had to laugh at myself. Whatever was going to happen was going to happen. I had a bright idea, and some very smart people thought that it was a good idea. We had all worked very hard to make it happen.

If it did turn out to be a disaster, none of us would have been smart enough to see it coming. So all I could do was laugh at myself and my worries and speed toward that pivotal, fateful meeting in Sag Harbor.

CHAPTER 71

Gordon

Hot fun in the summertime

The history of Sag Harbor is interesting. It is as interesting as the story of any number of vacation enclaves established and developed by black Americans over the years. Just under the radar screen of most of white America, Sag Harbor, Oak Bluffs, Virginia Beach, and Keyport were just some of the places that blacks decided would do just fine as vacation getaways. The primary attraction of these locations has always being an absence of discrimination and the willingness of white property owners to sell to blacks.

Over the years, Sag Harbor had become an exclusive refuge for many of the black elite in the New York City metropolitan area. You did not just win the numbers and move to Sag Harbor. Generations of families populated its environs, developing a class and caste system that would make the Cabots and Lodges pleased as punch.

And then The Pride arrived. Wall Street money in the hands of younger blacks changed Sag Harbor forever. In what seemed like an instant, it didn't matter whose mother knew whose grandmother. Fraternity and sorority and church memberships meant little or nothing.

All of a sudden, people like Jerome Hardaway and I would show up with a million dollars in hand, preferring to live in a predominantly black section of Eastern Long Island rather than someplace in the Hamptons or Quogue. And that's how The Pride moved into Sag Harbor, buying, building and changing that quaint little community in the blink of an eye.

When I decided to buy a place in Sag, my firm was already doing very well. I was personally clearing close to ten million dollars a year. So the idea of paying a half a million dollars for a house so that I could tear it down and build an eight-bedroom place with a three-bedroom guesthouse, complete with pool, tennis court, Jacuzzi and private dock for my yacht, made all the sense in the world to me. And I just did it.

Many other members of The Pride followed suit. Fabulous homes in Sag Harbor became one more badge of honor for charter members of The Pride to wear. And many wore it well.

I saw Paul's Porsche pull up the seventy-yard driveway that led to the house. He drove past my Benz limo and my idiot chauffeur who was polishing it. I still had not decided how to punish that mother-fucker for even thinking about fucking my Kenitra. But his time would come, of that I was sure.

I came down from the master bedroom into the foyer and hallway so that I could open the door to greet Paul myself. I always thought that, with the cathedral ceilings, multiple skylights and indirect lighting, the interior of my house resembled that of an alien spaceship newly arrived on the Planet Earth.

"Paul. Welcome to Casa Gordon." I embraced him and gave him a brotherly hug as he came in the door. "This is going to be a great weekend, brother. Just great. I remember what you said about history at the Water Club back in January. Paul, you've got me believing now."

"Glad to see you, Gordon. The weather's great. I had a wonderful drive out here. No complaints at all."

I didn't get to see Paul in too many casual settings, and I couldn't remember the last time I had seen him in a sport jacket and jeans. I remember him mentioning the custom-made tab collar shirts that he had made in Hong Kong, and I made a note to myself to remember to get the name of the tailor that he used there. I think his name was Tommy Lo.

"Did FedEx do its job and get all the paperwork to you?"

"Everything is fine. Everything seems to be in order. Just fine, just fine."

Paul was cordial and pleasant. I knew that he had been through a lot, what with his bitch Samantha dying and still having to keep this deal together. I know I would have handled things differently. But then, Paul and I have always been different people.

"Listen, man, I am sure that you want to get to your room, take a shower and change. Jerome and Diedre will be here soon enough and then we can have dinner and take care of business."

I showed Paul to his guest room which was actually a three-room suite on the side of the house opposite the master bedroom suite.

"Here you go, brother. Private bath, balcony overlooking the sea. If you have any needs, please let the management know. We are here to serve you, Mr. Taylor."

I said the last part with a falsetto voice, trying to get a little humor going. Paul laughed, but I knew better than to try to get too funny.

"Thanks, Gordon. Great house you have here, by the way. I am going to get settled and go for a run and then get ready for dinner."

"Make yourself at home. You should try running along the beach. It should be pretty good out there this time of day. When you get back you will find that there is a bar in your room. If you need anything, Hilda is in the kitchen and will fix you anything that you need. Kenitra is resting right now, but she will join us for drinks before dinner."

"Got it. Thanks again, Gordon."

CHAPTER 72

Paul

That's the way of the world

I could smell the salt air percolating off the surf as I ran on the hard-packed sand. Watching the seagulls and the petrels perform aerobatics in the azure sky helped me to forget just about everything for a little while. And I was more than grateful for that respite.

I finished my run by sprinting up Gordon's football field of a driveway and by then I was exhausted and spent. I was ready for a hot shower and a nap. I was not ready to eavesdrop on the loud, angry voices of a man and a woman in another wing of the house. It was damn sure none of my business, but I knew that it had to be Gordon and Kenitra illustrating one of the many facets of wedded bliss.

I was grateful for the long hot shower and the sound system that was in my suite of rooms. I had brought "Pieces of a Man" by Gil Scott-Heron, another classic that I always enjoyed . . . as did Samantha. I fixed myself a gin and tonic with a lime wedge, had a few sips and slept the sleep of the just and innocent.

Only the nagging feeling that I was missing something woke me up at some point. Otherwise I might have slept right through the evening and into the morning. The combination of the sun, the run, the salt air, the drive from the city and the total change of environment lifted the stress of the past few months and transported me to a land of deep, dreamless sleep.

But there was business to be done and now was the time. I sprang out of bed and dressed quickly and carefully. I entered the living room area of Gordon's sprawling manse just in time to see Jerome, Diedre, Kenitra, and Gordon sipping Henri de Cazenove champagne from exquisite crystal flutes while watching the setting sun cast its last light on the ocean. They were taking all of this in through the octagonal picture window that seemed to take up the entire side of the house.

CHAPTER 73

Jerome

When you wish upon a star . . .

"**C**ounselor! I see that you have gotten your sorely needed beauty rest."

Since Paul was the reason that we were all at Gordon's, it seemed fair to let loose a few jokes at his expense. And I knew that he wouldn't mind.

"Actually, Jerome, he was waiting for room service. With all of the gorgeous women coming to Gordon's party tomorrow night, he was hoping that he might get lucky and that one of the really early arrivals would get lost looking for her . . . bathing suit." Diedre had a way with words that could dazzle and dice at the same time.

"*Actually*, Diedre, since this is the first time that we are going to be sleeping under the same roof in almost twenty years, I was hoping that you might come tap-tap-tapping at my chamber door. But my hopes and dreams have died a sad and bitter death."

We all had to laugh at that last line. Paul could be genuinely funny at times. But I could swear that I saw Paul and Diedre exchange a look that I didn't quite understand at the time.

"Well, folks, it's time to eat and get down to business. Kenitra is going to have her dinner upstairs so that we can take care of business."

Gordon kissed her as one might kiss a mule or a favorite automobile. There was nothing resembling affection or emotion. But then, what was new?

Dinner was served by Gordon's almost invisible housekeeper and her assistant. There were incredible raw oysters, an excellent radicchio salad and grilled swordfish that Gordon confirmed was fresh caught—by him. Along with the Schlumberger Riesling, the meal was excellent.

And then, over espresso and port wine and Sambucca, we engaged in small talk. We talked about everything and nothing. And then it was time to get down to business. We had all read the documents that Paul had produced after countless conference calls with our lawyers. I had read my version at least a dozen times.

We all reviewed the documents one last time. By now it was close to eleven o'clock. It was late for me, but time was really not the issue that night. When Paul finished getting all the documents signed with executed copies circulated to all three of us, I could swear that a full two minutes of total silence went by. Something just told me that I had to say something or we might wind up just standing there all night.

"Paul, we all know that when we had lunch with you at the Water Club that day, we were friends and acquaintances. But partners? That was not part of the deal. We all were going our separate ways." I usually feel more comfortable pacing when I talk, and I did pace and talk that evening.

"I don't think that any of us were dead set against the idea of our being partners. Frankly, and I think I speak for my new partners, none of us had ever really thought of it."

"And then you came up with your bright idea and everything has changed for all of us. For better or worse we are all in the same boat now, and I keep thinking about what you said at the Water Club. We are making history and we are going to make even more history. This is one of those great moments that people are going to be talking about for a long time.

"Paul, you have been a friend to each of us over the years. And we all have thought of you as being a pretty good lawyer. Now you are our lawyer. And now you are a damn great lawyer!

"I can only imagine the grief and pure bullshit that you have had to put up with in trying to help us put this deal together. Getting the three of us on the same page could not possibly be an easy task." We all had to laugh at that last line. I continued to pace and talk. I really felt like this was something that I had to say.

"I know I am not a cuddly kitten when it comes to business and I can't imagine that Diedre is either. And then, of course, there is Gordon." We laughed again, but many times the truth is spoken in jest.

"Thank you, Paul. It has been great. And it's going to be great."

"Jerome, I am going to risk repeating what you have already said." There was no way that Gordon was not going to have something to say. But on a night like this, it was all right.

"Jerome and Diedre, I propose a toast to our new partnership, to our new firm, and to the best goddamned lawyer I have ever known." We touched glasses and began to drink.

"And Paul, you're not too bad yourself."

I had to hand it to Gordon. His timing with lines like that were just perfect. The moment collapsed into friendly laughter and relief. The deal was done! We were partners and our new firm was being born in front of our eyes.

As the day before the last weekend before Labor Day came to an end on the eastern tip of Long Island, it was as if a new reality, a new universe, was coming into being. That is certainly how I felt.

At that moment, everything, everything seemed possible. Our collective hopes and dreams were more than possible, they were going to come true. I just knew it.

"Paul, I just realized something." Diedre had something to say, and we all got a little quiet. She could carve a brother up with that tongue of hers.

"You aren't a lawyer at all! You must be a magician or a wizard, or something. To get me to join up with these two? I should have my head examined.

"But while I am waiting for an appointment with my psychiatrist, I know that we all owe you a debt of gratitude and thanks and . . . final payment of your bill." Diedre has a way of making the most serious of points with a smile on her face. And this was one of those times. And we all knew that she meant every word that she said.

I could tell that, for what had to be one of the few times in his life, Paul was without words. That should have been a memorable moment in and of itself. But that moment ended soon enough, and just at the right time.

"Thank you, all of you. A good idea doesn't mean a damn thing if there aren't good people with vision who know what to do with it. Diedre, Jerome, Gordon, you are certainly all different, incredibly different people. But, after all these months of being the middleman, I will let you in on a secret . . . you are also very much alike.

"You all like to win. All of you simply have to win to make it worthwhile. And I understand that and respect that." By now Paul really did have our undivided attention. It wasn't that often that I heard myself analyzed, and certainly not so correctly.

"And another thing. I don't care what you tell everyone else. You are all dreamers. All of you. You dreamed up the firms that you started. You dreamed the success that you achieved. And now, with this merger, you are dreaming again.

"I have never met a group of people with the drive and the talent and the ability that even comes close to the three of you." All you could hear was the surf in the distance. It was that quiet. There was no tinkling of glasses. There was no music in the background. There was just the group in silence. It was a very special moment for all of us.

"Thanks for letting me be a part of your dreams. And, congratulations!" Another toast followed and things started to wind down.

After we finished our last drinks, there was a palpable sense of anticlimax. There was not going to be any real work done until the following Wednesday. We decided that we would issue a press release announcing the merger and the formation of the new firm on Wednesday. But we also agreed to make a private announcement to the guests at Gordon's annual end-of-summer party on Saturday night.

I said my good nights and headed home to Charmaine. I left Gordon, Paul, and Diedre finishing their last drinks for the night. I had a feeling that a lot more was going to happen that weekend.

And it turned out that I was right.

CHAPTER 74

Diedre

Some enchanted evening . . .

Gordon, Paul, and I sat in the enormous lounging area for a few more minutes after Jerome left. And then Gordon said his farewells and went to the master bedroom suite, leaving Paul and me alone. For what seemed like the longest time, Paul stared at his glass saying nothing. I knew Paul long enough and well enough to leave him be. I sat silently sipping my drink.

I know Paul, probably better than just about anyone on this planet. I knew that the success of the evening probably seemed a little thin and watery to him. For the moment he seemed to not really care about the deal or The Pride.

"Want to talk?"

"Actually, I would rather take a walk." As he turned to look at me, all the celebration and gusto and bravado were gone. I saw emptiness and pain in his eyes. He was not tired. But he was certainly weary. His spirit was carrying many heavy burdens.

"Would you care for company? I'm really not that tired and I am certainly not ready to go to sleep." I found myself caring for this man who had been in my life, out of my life and now, a part of my life.

"Actually I would like that very much, Diedre. Yes I would. Thank you."

There was a sincere look of gratitude in his face and gratitude in his voice that I don't think I had ever noticed with Paul.

"Why don't you get a jacket or a sweater? It's starting to get a little cool on the beach. I'll freshen our drinks and meet you on the deck." You could almost see his spirit starting to revive. And I was truly glad to be there for him. And I found this to be amazing!

"I'll be right back. Try not to leave without me. I would hate to have to go looking for you in the dark." I could see him start to smile, and that was enough for the moment.

"Not a chance, my dear. You will have no trouble finding your escort for the evening." He was trying to keep a "stiff upper lip" I guess, and it was certainly better than him giving in to the clouds of despondency that were hovering over his head.

As I headed to the guest quarters, I could have sworn that I saw the dawn of the glimmer of the flickering of a smile on Paul's face. That was a good thing. I really didn't know what I wanted to find out about how Paul was feeling. But I was sure that I wanted to find out something that night.

After Paul and I broke up I had not retired to a convent. I had had a couple of grand and glorious affairs that could have resulted in marriage if I had been willing to fit my dreams into those of someone else.

At that moment, that day, that evening, there was no one special in my life. There was just the occasional social, and sometimes sexual, companion. I had gotten to the point that I was starting to wonder where all of this was leading.

To tell the truth, I wasn't even consciously thinking about all of that as I went to get my Peruvian shawl that I always preferred on cool summer evenings like this one. But to tell the truth I did skip up the stairs like an excited schoolgirl. I was very sure that I could not remember the last time I felt like that.

Gordon's house was designed so that there were two sleeping suites in each of the four wings of the house. I guess he called himself being diplomatic in putting Paul and me in separate wings so as to avoid any subtle implications in the sleeping arrangements.

The reality was that Paul and I had not been intimate during the past fifteen years. Not even close. We had become friends during the past five years. And that was all.

Nevertheless, I had to confess to myself that I had always found

Paul attractive in some eternal kind of way. He was the first true, the only life-altering love of my life. And as he matured and grew, he was a better man and in many ways more attractive than he ever was when we met and were together.

When I came back downstairs I found Paul standing outside on the deck with our drinks in his hands. He was staring at the stars.

CHAPTER 75

Diedre

Slipping into darkness

"Thinking about making a wish? Don't get too greedy, Paul Taylor. I have to believe that at least one of your dreams came true tonight."

Paul passed me my drink and then gave me a wan smile. And at that moment I knew his wish. And I knew that wish would never come true. There was nothing more that I could say or do at that point. I could swear that I could see an aura of pain around him at that moment.

"Let's walk, Paul. It's a lovely night. Come on." I placed my arm inside of his and headed toward the steps and the beach.

"Yes, it is lovely. You know, Diedre, a walk would be just about right just about now."

We walked along the beach sipping our Delamaine cognac and watching the surf relentlessly embrace and release the shore. We walked almost a mile in total silence. We had been quiet for so long that, when Paul finally spoke, it gave me a start. His voice was tissue whisper soft.

"Diedre, please tell me the truth. If I start talking about Samantha will it bother you? Because if it will bother you, I will just keep it to myself." He was staring out to sea as he spoke.

"It's fine, Paul. You know if it bothered me I would just tell you.

Just go on and talk about her, if you feel like it." He was in such pain and so vulnerable, I couldn't help but care.

We continued to walk in silence for awhile. He found a piece of driftwood and we sat down. We were facing the sea with the surf swirling to a stop a few yards away from our feet. Paul continued to speak in that whisper that sounded like gossamer to the ears. It was a voice I had never heard him use.

"You know, Diedre, after my father and brother died, I thought that I knew all that I needed to know about pain and loss. I thought I knew enough to last a lifetime, several lifetimes actually." He took a sip of his cognac and continued.

"I didn't think that I was immune to pain, I just figured that I had learned about how much I could hurt and how to handle it.

"And then, when I found out that Samantha was sick and was going to die, somehow the advance knowledge just did not prepare me for the reality of her actually dying. I guess I was in denial, you know, that river in Egypt. I simply could not believe that I was going to lose her. I couldn't believe that this star of a woman was going to . . . die."

He looked like he was about to cry right then and there. And then, just like that, he composed himself and continued.

"But Diedre, when I went to her funeral in Gary, I felt like the bottom had just fallen out of my world. And ever since then, every night I feel the pain, the real pain, of losing her. It hurts. It just hurts."

I sat in total silence listening to his every word. I did not look directly at Paul. I wanted him to speak freely. And I realized that during all of our time together he had never expressed his true feelings in such a sincere and real fashion.

I had heard him say all the words of love that a man is supposed to say to a woman. I had even heard him talk about his hopes and dreams a million years ago. But I had never heard him speak from the heart. Not like this. Not like tonight.

As he was speaking, I realized that Paul had changed in a very real way. Part of it had to do with time and the maturation process. As people mature, if they are lucky, they change for the better. I was sure, however, that Samantha's death had created a different Paul Hiawatha Taylor.

Pain can be like fire. It can consume a person, or it can temper a person like steel and make them stronger. Paul's willingness to open his heart to me was a clear sign, and a good sign. I could tell that I was sitting next to a different man. He was a different man that I was coming to like very much. I continued to listen to him.

"I know that every day millions of people all over the world lose mothers and brothers and fathers and sisters. My loss of Samantha is nothing special in the cosmic scheme of things. But it hurts me, Diedre. And to tell you the truth, I just don't know what to do about it."

It was starting to get cooler. We got up off the driftwood and started walking back to the house. The waves applauded our journey by gently slapping the sand. It took me just a moment to notice that we were walking more closely than we did on the way out to this spot on the beach.

"You know, Diedre, it's funny. During the day I am fine. I have my work, my appointments, my clients, my calls, my documents. All of that. But this feeling I have is like Dracula. It sleeps during the day. But at night, when the sun goes down, I get this feeling that tastes like iron filings in my mouth and it makes me want to cry for no reason. For no reason at all except, of course, that Samantha is gone forever." I could see his eyes misting and his voice starting to quiver. But he continued.

"I don't know why I am telling you all of this . . ."

"Paul, go on. You need to talk and I promise that I will keep listening. I promise. No conditions. No strings. Please, go on."

I placed my hand on his arm as we spoke and left it there. It certainly wasn't out of habit. It was something else entirely. Paul continued as we walked slowly on the sand. Only the stars and the waves were listening.

"And you want to know the strangest thing? I find myself looking at the night sky, almost every night, looking for the right star to wish upon. Is that weird or what?"

"I don't think so, Paul Taylor. What do you wish for when you see the right star? Inquiring minds want to know."

The lightness of my comment did not mean that I was not serious. And Paul knew it. I just thought that lightening the moment might help. I could have sworn that I saw the glimmering of the beginning of a smile on his face. And I could see that he had not truly smiled for a long time.

"One wish? My one wish would be that I could put this pain, this loss, this feeling, in some kind of place so that I could live my life. I know that Samantha would want me to live my life. She told me so several times in the weeks before she died. I just haven't been able to move on, at least not yet.

"I should be popping champagne bottles and cakewalking up and down this beach. You know how hard I worked on this deal.

"What you cannot know is how much I believe in what the three of you can accomplish. I have lived, slept and eaten this deal for the past six months. Even through Samantha's illness and death. I should be jumping for joy. But there's not much chance of that happening."

We could see the gleaming beacon of the lights of Gordon's mansion as we continued along the beach.

CHAPTER 76

Diedre

Once I had a secret love . . .

"Paul, listen to me. And listen well. You are just experiencing the phenomenon of being human. You are so used to thinking you are superman that you think you have to be superman all the time. And sometimes you have a hard time dealing with what is perfectly natural and perfectly human.

"Unfortunately, people we love die. Unfortunately, it hurts. That pain does not go away in a day or a week. And, if the truth be told, the pain never goes away completely. But most people find a way to move on.

"And you are more fortunate than most people in this situation."

"How is that?"

By now we were at the steps leading back to the deck. We paused to savor the sea, the night air, and each other.

"You are not alone." There, I said it. And I swear that I meant it. I just didn't mean to say it.

That was the last thing that I clearly remember about that evening. Neither of our recollections would be crystal clear. I do remember putting my cognac glass on the railing at about the same time that Paul did.

And then I pressed myself against him and kissed him like it was the end of the world and the beginning of the universe. At that moment I really felt that way. It was as if someone had ignited dynamite around both of our hearts and souls. The explosion was immense, and undeniable.

I could tell that he felt the passion and the warmth. And I could tell that he felt something else. And he also held on to me as if nothing else in the world mattered.

And for the next few hours, nothing did. I remember kisses and lips and fingers and thighs and breasts and shudders and groans and tongues and arms and legs and moans and a warm wetness that seemed eternal.

We awoke in each other's arms in Paul's suite of rooms. It was still before dawn. There was only the everlasting sound of the rolling sea. For a moment or two there was nothing to say.

"Diedre, did you make a mistake and wind up in the wrong room? Are you trying to get fresh with me?"

"Be quiet and pleasure me, you Mandingo warrior." It was a throwaway line from an old movie. But I meant it. And we both laughed as we embraced and made love again and again. And my world would never be the same again.

Afterward we giggled like teenagers in the backseat of Dad's car. And we tried to figure out the logistics of my getting back to my bedroom without drawing attention to the fact that I had been sleeping with Paul. And then we decided that we really didn't give a good goddamn what anyone thought. We were happy and comfortable with that. And that was enough for the moment. Tomorrow would always take care of itself anyway.

I kissed Paul one last time before going to my bedroom suite. We had already decided that it would not be for the last time. We would stay for the beginning of Gordon's party on Saturday and then go back to Manhattan for a quiet and romantic end to the holiday weekend.

And I couldn't wait. I don't know what miracle blessed us, but I was so happy that I could make Paul happy, happier than he had ever been with me before. And his response had been pure affection and passion. It was just what I needed. It was just what we needed.

CHAPTER 77

Paul

Now I shout it to the highest hills

Kenitra joined Gordon, Diedre, and me for breakfast. It was the first time that I really had gotten a really good look at her since Winner's memorial service. She didn't look like she had been suffering in her marriage to Gordon. Of course, the long sleeves and turtleneck in early September were clues to possible bruises and abrasions as well as evidence of the true nature of their relationship.

I had never known her to say much, so it didn't mean much to me that she was quiet throughout the meal. If I had been paying closer attention, as Diedre would later tell me, I would have seen the eyes of a caged and fearful creature, looking for an escape that just wasn't there.

After breakfast there were errands to be completed in Sag Harbor and the Hamptons. Flowers to be bought, incidentals, and who knows what. I gave Diedre the keys to my car and worked on the phone, tying up the loose ends of the merger and making sure that all the documentation was in place for the following Wednesday.

The plan that Diedre and I had was to have lunch on Gordon's yacht, a seventy-foot cruiser that would give us a glorious view of Long Island Sound. Unfortunately, there was a slim chance of a storm, so we decided to lunch on the yacht while docked in the harbor.

We had a casual lunch on the *Ike Turner*. Like most days, Gordon had an attitude the day he bought the yacht, so he came up with that name. And anyone who didn't like it could kiss his black ass.

The *Ike* was appointed like a top-of-the-line luxury home. Having lunch on the boat was like dining at the Water Club or Lutece. It was a floating masterpiece of style, taste and comfort, with just the right touch of excess.

I remember that we lunched on Blue Point oysters and rice and peas and cracked lobster. Gordon had found a wonderful Gavi di Gavi that was just perfect for the meal and the day. The lunch could be described as no less than exquisite, and we all took our time savoring the meal and the moment.

Through most of the meal we made small talk. We talked about the upcoming mayoral race in New York City, the New York Knicks, Bill Clinton, Nelson Mandela, Michael Jordan, and some truly scurrilous gossip which featured Naomi Campbell, among others. There was a lot of talk about everything and nothing of any real substance.

I couldn't help but notice that Gordon seemed different. After that near-fiasco at Diedre's, he had rarely been seen at any social event. And for a while, when he did show up, he was always jittery, nervous, and apologizing for his "cold." Lately he just didn't seem to be on top of his game.

But sometime in the late spring a different Gordon Perkins started to show up. First of all, he was on time. He didn't have a "cold" for which he had to apologize. And, he was not the consistently nasty son of a bitch that was his hallmark. He actually seemed to make an effort to be somewhat human at times.

By the time Labor Day came around, he really wasn't that bad. He was still the tough guy that you would rather have on your side. But he was definitely palatable, although still an acquired taste on his best days.

There was no telling what was going on between Kenitra and him, however. They were never expressive in public and no one knew what was really going on behind their closed doors. She just seemed to be more and more withdrawn as if she was always thinking about something else.

You could still count on Gordon to take the initiative though. As the third bottle of the Gavi di Gavi was served he took a big sip and got ready to take charge. The sunbeams seemed to dance over the waves that lapped and slapped against the *Ike*.

"Well folks, I hate to be the one to break the news, but the easy part is now out of the way. And now we are actually going to have to get to work." He took another sip and kept on talking. We all wanted to know where Gordon was headed this time.

"I think that it's a great idea that we have a quiet announcement at the party, maybe about eleven, before people get too carried away with the fun and frolic. But we have to have a more formal, first class announcement next week. What are we going to say then?"

"Well, for starters, the three of you have to make a final decision on the name for your firm." I just knew that my job wasn't finished when those documents had been signed the night before.

Diedre spoke first. I watched her through eyes made new by the night before and the morning after. I could see that she was still strictly about business when the occasion demanded. And I knew that it was one more thing about her that I could love again.

"Well, Paul. It seems pretty simple to me. Either we come up with some name like Blackstone or Argyle Tubman-Truth-Bethune Associates, or we use our names in alphabetical order."

"Diedre, as a literate member of our new firm I understand that the alphabetical route would put your name first." It was Jerome's turn now.

"I personally don't have a problem with that, but if we were to come up with a name, what could it be?"

For about twenty minutes all kinds of names were tossed around. Names like "Chaka Group" and "Ebony Ventures" and "Amistad Finance" are a few that I remember. And then it was time to make a decision—Morningstar Financial Services was the name chosen for the firm. I can't even begin to go into all of the reasons that were advanced in favor of this decision. I was just glad that a decision was made. Believe me.

"If all of you can live with Morningstar, I will have the final documents ready for your announcement next Wednesday." The dream now had a life of its own. And now the dream had a name. I knew that now I had better call Edwina McClure and let her know that the announcement was definitely on and give her the last minute changes like the name of the firm.

CHAPTER 78

Paul

A word with Edwina

Iexcused myself and found a phone in the salon. Edwina McClure was perhaps the preeminent black public relations professional in New York City, if not the United States. She was certainly one of the most successful, black or white.

She had handled matters for Quincy Jones, Michael Jackson, David Dinkins, along with the mayors of Washington, Newark, Los Angeles, and Houston. Her corporate portfolio included at least thirty of the Fortune 100 companies. She handled the sensitive cases and the outrageous ones. When a client wanted the best chance at widespread and favorable publicity, Edwina McClure was always on the short list of publicists to be chosen.

Edwina would never win the Miss Congeniality Award. But Edwina would always get the job done and she would skewer the stupid, foolish and clearly ignorant reporter who tried to do a hatchet job on one of her clients. In other words, it was a good idea to have Edwina on your side. And she was definitely on the side of Morningstar, thanks to the hefty retainer that had already been deposited into her account by the then-as-yet-unnamed firm.

I had known Edwina for years and we always maintained a good and pragmatic working relationship. We were never going to send each other valentines, but we also knew that we could play a role in our respective success. And so there was no reason for us not to get along, especially at times like this.

"Edwina darling, I know that your Labor Day weekend is about to start, but I have some good news for you. The merger is a done deal! Gordon Perkins, Diedre Douglas, and Jerome Hardaway are going to combine their firms. They want to do the announcement at noon on Wednesday in the Rainbow Room."

"Paul Taylor, you better thank your lucky stars that I am already on retainer. Calling me on the Friday of Labor Day weekend, you know you should be ashamed of yourself! Even with the retainer, I should tell you to kiss my ass!"

Edwina never, ever, never held her tongue. She could curse like a Macedonian sailor and reduce a Scythian bandit to tears. She just never seemed to give a damn as to what anyone thought. I just let her words roll by. I had a job to do, and so did she. After all, Emily Post had been dead for years.

"In that case Edwina, the name of the firm will be Morningstar Financial Services. There are a few major projects of the firm that will be announced at the press conference. One project is in corporate finance-biotech in nature, and the other is in the field of asset management. Diedre, Jerome, and Gordon feel that they are sufficiently sensitive that you don't need the details until Wednesday morning when I will provide you with the executive summaries.

"Okay?"

I knew that at the end of the day Edwina would never let her mouth lose her a dollar. She knew when she needed to just take care of business and this was one of those times.

"If that's how it has to be, Paul, my people and I can work with that. We were already working on the draft release and I will fax it to Sag Harbor tonight. I will call you at Gordon's tomorrow afternoon and we can go over it long before the partying begins."

"Sounds fine, Edwina. You are the best! You know that I love you madly."

"Paul, I forgot to wear my brown hip boots today. But thanks just the same . . . but Paul, one thing I need to ask."

I had already hung up mentally and I had to force myself to pay attention. After all, business was business and I knew Edwina did not like to just chat.

"Why are we having the announcement at the Rainbow Room instead of Hue & Me?"

I had to take a step back. It was a good question. It was a damn good question. Even though the Hue & Me restaurant was another of Edwina's clients, I knew that she was not speaking simply out of self-interest and double-dipping. There would be a lot of symbolism in having the announcement at this gathering spot of The Pride. Dorothy's By the Sea really was not set up for such an event, but Hue & Me was.

Hue & Me was owned and managed by Auburn Hue, a singer/model/actress who enjoyed more success in Europe and South America than she ever did in this country. Auburn, whose real name was Daphne Ann Murphy was from just outside of Birmingham, Alabama. She was as smart as she was beautiful and as shrewd as she was talented.

I remembered talking with Auburn when she was first kicking around the idea of a restaurant. This was long before I handled her corporate papers and liquor license and ancillary details.

I remember telling her how absolutely crazy I would get when I would go to a top restaurant in town and be treated in a shabby, half-ass fashion. There were just too many times that my reservation was lost, too many times that I was offered a table by the restroom. The list of slights and wrongs was endless and infernally creative.

I also remember telling Auburn that I wished that there was a place that I could go to without all of that hassle. This was around the time that the idea for Dorothy's By the Sea started becoming something more than an idea and turned into a plan.

Auburn listened. Hue & Me, located in Manhattan's theater district, was an instant and continuing success. Not only did the members of The Pride patronize her establishment all the time, its proximity to the Broadway shows made it a popular dining spot for all theatergoers, black and white.

Auburn was absolutely determined that her restaurant would be an elite spot and comfortable. So while it was possible to get fried chicken and macaroni and cheese at Hue & Me, *nouvelle cuisine* dishes prepared in spectacular fashion were also likely to appear on a menu which Auburn changed daily.

The wine list was regularly featured in *The Wine Spectator* and there was always a jazz combo providing a wonderful aural atmosphere.

As soon as I thought about it I realized that Edwina was right. She had excellent instincts. The Morningstar announcement should be made at Hue & Me. The announcement was important in terms of its impact on the world of finance. But there was additional significance in that a black-owned investment banking firm was signaling to the world that it intended to be a real player in the game as it was played on Wall Street. Having the announcement at one of the preeminent black-owned restaurants in New York City would put a sharper edge on the whole thing.

"Edwina, when you are right, you are right. Please set it up at Hue & Me. I am sure that Jerome, Gordon, and Diedre will be fine with it. I will tell them as soon as I get off the phone."

"Ciao, darling. I am glad that you recognize genius when it's right in front of you." Edwina and I both chuckled as she threw out that last line and we bid our farewells. There was lots of work to be done and not a moment to be wasted with small talk.

CHAPTER 79

Paul

Ain't no stopping us now

As I went through the salon and back to the deck, I had to admit to myself that Edwina McClure had her qualities and, that her place in my personal universe helped to make things a little more interesting. And, since I was not ready to retire and run a piano bar in Anguilla just yet, I could live with having to deal with Edwina and Gordon and Ray and all the other "interesting" members of The Pride.

But, I never let the thought of that piano bar get too far away. It was a dream that I continue to keep close to my heart, even to this very moment.

By the time I got back to the table, Gordon, Jerome, and Diedre had been busy. They had been outlining the details of the progress they had made for the Morningstar announcement that would be made the following Wednesday.

"We should absolutely NOT announce the New Orleans plan. It just won't help." Diedre's was the first voice that I heard as I walked in.

"Everyone on Wall Street knows that if you are going to make it in municipal finance, you have to pay to play." Jerome was referring to the common practice of contributing funds to various candidates in order to ultimately have access to deals.

"It really kills me how the white firms act like the inspector in

Casablanca pretending to be shocked that there was gambling going on in Rick's Café even as he was being handed his take for the night." Jerome had a very good point, of course.

"Black firms have come under a hell of a lot of scrutiny as far as this practice is concerned. And it's a bitch and a goddamned shame. None of us want to be in the spotlight as far as this issue is concerned, so I agree with Diedre, there's no point in bringing New Orleans up on Wednesday." Gordon was agreeing with Diedre, the moon and stars were clearly in a peculiar alignment.

"I do agree that we should announce that Morningstar will be handling the initial public offering for Herzog Technologies." Gordon was already moving on. No surprise there.

Herzog now held the patent rights for what was touted to be the successor drug to AZT in the battle against AIDS. The offering was expected to be at least $10 billion and would be handled by Jerome on behalf of Morningstar. It would be the firm's first foray into the deep waters of corporate finance and would clearly identify the firm as a real player.

"Well, I am prepared to announce that Morningstar will be managing significant parts of the pension funds of the municipal employees unions in Chicago, Detroit, Oakland, Philadelphia, New Orleans, and New York City. On day one, Morningstar will have over $30 billion in assets under management. This will, without a doubt, attract even more business to the firm." Diedre was clearly committed. This was starting to be truly wonderful.

I briefed them on my conversation with Edwina. Everyone immediately understood the significance of having the announcement at Hue & Me. The Rainbow Room was simply no longer an issue.

Morningstar would be formally introduced to the world at Hue & Me. Then it was back to the business of the day.

"Listen, I am more than sure that New Orleans is under control. Are you fucking kidding me? With all the money that we have spent supporting Prince Lodrig, you're goddamned right that the son of a bitch is leading Percy Broussard by at least twenty points in the latest polls right this very minute." Gordon had a way of putting things that was always hard to ignore.

"New Orleans is going to be a fucking stronghold for Morningstar!"

"Well Gordon, considering that so far we have raised and contributed about $250,000 for the esteemed Mayor Lodrig, I would certainly hope that he remembers our name." Diedre subtly let Gordon know that his ass was on the line with this one.

"And so far, it seems like money well spent." She took the edge off her last comment.

"Of course, the election is a few months away." And then put the edge back on again.

"Well, we should all remember that Morningstar will now be hosting a fund-raiser for Mayor Lodrig in D.C. in early October. That should raise another hundred grand. And that should do the job." Gordon smiled a smile that I just couldn't read. So I didn't even try.

I had already briefed the three of them on campaign finance laws and they were definitely within the law with all that they had done and planned to do. And, as far as New Orleans was concerned, Gordon was certainly saying all the right things. There just seemed no need for concern.

Except that there was. I was concerned. Worried would be a better word. I like to think of myself as a rational man. I believe in facts, real information, and real knowledge. Feelings, intuition, hunches— they are way in the backseat as far as I am concerned.

As we sat on Gordon's boat, something was telling me that I needed to think about Sammy Groce again. Sammy had mentioned something about a "surprise" in this campaign. There had been absolutely no signs of anything like a "surprise" to date. Everything was going just like Gordon said it would.

But that did not allay my fears. After all, that's why surprises were called surprises. You simply did not expect them. And I couldn't shake the feeling that Gordon had something to do with the "surprise" to which Sammy had referred to months ago.

As I thought about it though, it was hard to deny that Gordon had been exceedingly generous and forthcoming with his contacts and his business network was clearly at the disposal of the new firm. No question about it.

But I still had my doubts. I had nothing that I could rationally articulate, even to myself. So I kept quiet. And I paid close attention.

As the business of the day concluded, it was agreed that we would get together at Gordon's party on Saturday night and make a private announcement around ten o'clock. Between now and then, it was time to just relax for a moment or two. "That's fine with me. I have barely seen Charmaine and the kids between the Herzog deal and Morningstar." Jerome was smiling as he spoke with a satisfied look on his face.

"I know that you all won't miss me too much between now and tomorrow night while I reintroduce myself to my family. Hell, I may need photo ID."

"Sounds like a plan, Brother Jerome. Kenitra and I have already made plans for a private dinner. Seems that she thinks I have been neglecting her. Can you imagine?" The new Gordon was fascinating in his solicitousness.

"Diedre and Paul? I hope that you don't mind that I am cutting you loose for the evening. You do have a key to the house, after all."

We all laughed. Diedre and I had already decided on dining at a lovely, secluded seafood restaurant east of Sag Harbor in Montauk. And we had already talked about having an unmentionable dessert back at Gordon's guest quarters. At least for the moment, Morningstar and The Pride could wait.

As we disembarked from the *Ike*, I already found myself thinking about dessert.

CHAPTER 80

Gordon

*Smiling faces . . . sometimes . . .
they don't tell the truth*

As Jerome drove off and I watched Diedre and Paul head toward the guest quarters, I just had to smile to myself. I was pretty sure that they had started fucking again. In fact I was positive. And, frankly, I didn't give a shit. Whatever the two of them were doing was just fine with me. It all fit in perfectly into my plan. From the bottom of my heart I wished those two unsuspecting lovebirds well.

I know the old saying about not being able to fool all of the people all of the time. But I have never really thought that too many of those old-ass sayings applied to me. And, this time, I didn't care who was fooled as long as they didn't get in the way of my plan. And it was a plan that had very little to do with fucking Morningstar—or Paul or Diedre or Jerome.

The fact is that I knew that I had been slipping up earlier in the year and had to clean up my act. But I never gave up my partnership with the Dark Lord. I still continued to beat the shit out of that bitch Kenitra. I made sure to keep her in her place. And that place was somewhere beneath my heel.

The truth is that the more that I worked with Jerome and Diedre, the more I really came to despise those motherfuckers. And that's why my plan was so great. It would exact the greatest possible pain and damage from all of them. And, as far as I was concerned, they absolutely deserved it.

It was all about timing. I found that I could endure anything for a given period of time. Even working with those motherfuckers. From the time we sat in the Water Club for lunch after Winner's memorial, I knew that there would be an end, and I knew what that end would be.

As a result, I could easily endure the cordiality, the friendly meals and all of the appurtenances of friendship that I had to fake to keep the whole thing going. I could even provide real, substantive business resources to advance the cause, because I knew my cause was different from and superior to theirs.

Someday, these assholes would know that Gordon Perkins was beyond partnership, beyond affiliation and beyond their mortal asses. I knew that the day would come when I would stand astride Wall Street like some kind of goddamned colossus, invincible, implacable and unconquerable. And then it would be just me and the Dark Lord. It was just a matter of time.

In the meantime I just had to be patient. Just like the lion can sit in the brush by a watering hole for uncounted hours, waiting for the fat, lazy, unsuspecting wildebeest to wander a little too close. In the case of Diedre, Jerome, and Paul, it would take time. So the Dark Lord and I just waited in the brush. After all, we had a plan.

As I ascended the stairs that led to the private quarters and the master bedroom suite I stopped in one of the bathrooms along the way. I rarely traveled with less than a quarter of an ounce of cocaine, and I always kept a plentiful supply in Sag Harbor. I wouldn't want the Dark Lord to feel unwelcome.

As I helped myself to several heaping teaspoons of Colombian powder, I felt that all my problems were being solved and that my very life was being saved. And the Dark Lord and I reflected on the fact that I was close, very close, to becoming the most powerful black person on Wall Street. And then, the next step would be to be one of the most powerful people on Wall Street, period.

The fact that Diedre, Jerome, and Paul played minor roles in my personal master plan really was not my problem. It was their problem as far as I was concerned, and they would have to deal with it as best they could. I understand concepts like loyalty, trust and friendship. They just have no place in the World of Gordon Perkins and the

Dark Lord. And if I had to collapse their dreams while making mine come true that's just the way it was going to be.

So I filled my nose with some more of that wonderful white powder. It was the best Colombian product that money could buy. The presence of the Dark Lord confirmed that fact. I looked into the mirror and confirmed that I was indeed God's gift to the world and headed out of the bathroom and toward the master bedroom suite.

It was a suite that was palatial in its design and expanse, complete with a gorgeous fucking bitch who was going to do anything that I wanted her to do, whether she wanted to or not. In fact, I was hoping that she wouldn't want to do a few of the things that I had in mind. Making her do it would be just that much more fun for me.

The thing is that I had come to truly despise that bitch. Not because I figured that she was fucking my driver and God knows who else. Shit, I could give less than a fuck what she did when I wasn't around.

It was just that, at the end of the day, she was a trophy, after all, she had been a world famous supermodel. But after a while, any trophy gets boring. And I guess I hated Kenitra because she bored me.

I had to hand it to the bitch. Her survival skills were remarkable. Early on she figured out that she was going to have to find a way to survive in my world. She learned not to argue. She learned not to take visible offense to my insults and curses. She learned because I taught her. And she learned all of her lessons the hard way.

She learned to comply with any sexual demand that I might make, or that the Dark Lord might suggest. No matter how bizarre, no matter how kinky, no matter how degrading—she learned to do what I wanted. And she learned to do it over and over and over again.

I know that after a while she began drinking with me and when I was not around. And she took the pills that her doctor prescribed. Lots of them. And the cocaine . . . well, she would take as much as I would give her. And I gave her a lot.

With her survival skills working overtime, she endured the beatings and the cursing and there was no perversion that was beneath her. She intended to live even though that bitch knew that many times I was this close to killing her ass.

"Good afternoon, Kenitra. Are you ready for me?"

CHAPTER 81

Gordon

If there's a hell below . . .

There was only silence. And for good reason. Before I had gone to lunch on the *Ike* earlier in the day, I had Kenitra put on a leather studded bikini and watched her consume four barbiturate pills, half a bottle of tequila and two grams of coke.

She simply had to do it since I promised her I would beat the living shit out of her if she didn't. Then I blindfolded and gagged her and handcuffed her to the bed, spread-eagled. Just the way I liked to see her.

I saw her awake as I came into the room. I could see her try to scream through her eyes as I started on her with the cigarette lighter. And then she passed out.

I didn't really care. When I finally got tired of doing anything and everything to her, I unfastened her and went to sleep. I had a busy day ahead of me and my plan was better than anything she could offer me anyway.

I guess if I paid attention, I would have heard Kenitra crying. She was weeping, actually. But, like I said, I really didn't care. I slept well that night.

CHAPTER 82

Diedre

Have I told you that I love you?

Paul and I spent the rest of the evening like lovesick teenagers away from their parents for the evening. We rode Paul's Porsche all over the eastern tip of Long Island. We drove out to the very end, at Montauk, and we actually held hands while watching the ocean flow by on its dark path to Europe, Africa, South America, and everywhere.

I know that most everyone I know would figure that we just had to talk about the resolution of the prior fifteen years, or at least the past twenty-four hours. But the truth is, logic just didn't apply. There was just something about the flood of emotions that had been set free. It simply made the world different for both of us. And it set us free in the process.

We had both gotten to a point in life where we knew that we needed to appreciate the good things in life when they came along. We were both all too familiar with the sordid alternatives that time and circumstance could offer.

Frankly, there wasn't a lot of conversation about "where this relationship was going" or what kind of "commitment" who was going to make to whom. Instead, it was like we were savoring a fine wine that we had heard about and were finally getting a chance to drink. And it was absolutely wonderful.

The restaurant that we went to was just outside of Montauk.

Trastevere was its name. Trastevere was named after the oldest residential section of Rome, an area famed for fine family dining. On Fridays Trastevere featured cioppino, an Italian version of bouillabaisse, a fine, hearty, fish stew that had to be tasted to be believed. We entered the restaurant and I know that dessert at Gordon's was already on my mind. And Trastevere did not have what I wanted on its menu.

Paul ordered a Pinot Grigio that turned out to be somewhat spectacular and we made small talk as we ordered dinner and dined in unaccustomed peace and quiet. I remember thinking about all kinds of things as dinner continued.

We watched the moon and stars tango on the waters of the Atlantic as we dined. For those few moments the tranquility of the moment was as pleasurable as the passion of the night before and that morning. We both ordered espressos and decided against dessert in the restaurant.

Paul had purchased a bottle of his favorite champagne, Don Cazenove, which we were going to sample when we returned to the guest quarters. As we waited to be served our personal jolts of caffeine other thoughts came to mind.

"Paul, do you really think that Gordon has changed? I know he seems different, but what do you think?" I had been trying to figure this out for myself for months. It wasn't romantic to bring up the subject, but it was on my mind and I truly wanted to hear what Paul had to say.

"It's a little late to be wondering about your new partner, don't you think?"

It was exactly the kind of answer that I was hoping I would not hear. I knew Paul well enough to know that he was simply volleying the question back to me. He didn't know either.

"It's never too late, but a straight answer might not be such a bad idea right now." I looked Paul straight in the eyes as I said this. There was something about his answer that made me think that there was something he wanted to say.

"The way I look at it, Diedre, Gordon is never going to change. Not ever. He is what he is, and probably always will be that, and only that. He can change around the edges, maybe be a little less of an asshole. He might even be able to act like something of a human being around Kenitra.

"He seems to have his cocaine situation under control, although I wouldn't suggest making drug tests a standard policy for the principals of Morningstar just yet." Paul was good for giving a straight answer when needed. And this was a time that he clearly knew a straight answer was needed.

"The advantage that you and Jerome have is that you know Gordon for what he is. He should never be able to surprise either of you, or me, for that matter. And the partnership agreement that you signed protects you from him doing anything too bizarre or outrageous."

We both thought about what Paul had just said while sipping our espressos. The piano player was going through the motions of "As Time Goes By." As I recall, he wasn't half bad, as they say in Texas.

"Are you saying that I am going to have to watch Gordon for as long as we are in business together?" I couldn't just let this subject pass. It was too important.

"Give that girl a kewpie doll! Diedre, you better believe that as long as Morningstar has Gordon Perkins as a featured player, you are going to have to watch him. Not every now and then. You will have to watch him every day and all the time. That's who he is. You know it and Jerome knows it too."

"Sweetheart, Gordon is like a snake or a scorpion or a shark. You can't really get angry at a shark if it bites you. That's what sharks do. You survive by never giving a shark an opportunity to bite you in the first place."

Paul was calm and collected as he gave me his analysis. I knew that he was absolutely serious and I meant to pay absolute attention to what he was saying.

"With Gordon, you know that he doesn't give a shit about any of us at the end of the day. If he could find a deal that would result in him screwing the two of you, he would do it in a mosquito's heartbeat. And he would get rid of me in less than that heartbeat if it suited his purposes."

"If he has a heart." I just felt like adding something like gallows humor to the conversation.

"But, as you know, Diedre, all of Gordon's assets are tied up in Morningstar and he would have to be a fool to walk away from all that he has built up to date. I just don't see him doing that. Not because he is a good guy, but because he is nobody's fool."

"Your greatest protection from Gordon is that he is your partner. You know the old expression about holding your friends close and your enemies closer? That's the way it will always be for you and Gordon. And please, don't ever forget it!"

"Oh, great. I have a scorpion for a partner and a lawyer for a lover. How lucky can a girl get?" I was halfway joking. And Paul knew which half.

"I am not sure that I heard a compliment there, Diedre. I guess I will have to rely on my own self-esteem to find the punch line." Paul smiled as he said this, and I smiled as well. He knew exactly what was my concern, and it was certainly not him.

There was a very long pause. And then it seemed that our eyes danced together. Not with the starlight and the moon, but from feelings that came from within. We both knew that we were writing a new chapter in our lives. And I knew that it would be wonderful. It just had to be this time.

Paul settled the bill, over my objections. We settled the matter by agreeing that the next tab would be mine. Whenever that might be, and we both knew that it would be soon.

We rode in Paul's car and headed back to Gordon's compound. As we headed west from the easternmost part of the United States we listened to an old jazz standard, Herbie Mann's "Impression of the Middle East," a true classic.

We sat in Gordon's driveway and enjoyed the stars and the moon and the music. Then, almost suddenly, Paul turned down the volume and turned toward me. I thought he was going to kiss me. He spoke instead.

"Did I ever tell you the story about the scorpion and the frog?" I was all too familiar with the fact that Paul would tell a story at the drop of a hat. Indeed, if there were no hats around, Paul would tell a story anyway.

"I can't say that I do know that story, Paul. But you are going to tell me, aren't you?"

"Actually, for a change this is a story that might interest you. You see, once upon a time, a scorpion and a frog met at the bank of a river. The scorpion asked the frog to let him ride on his back so that he could get to the other side too.

" 'I can't do that, Mr. Scorpion, as soon as you get on my back, you will sting me and I will die.' The scorpion replied, 'But Mr. Frog, if I sting you when I get on your back, I will never get to the other side if I sting you in the middle of the river. You would die and I would drown and die too. When we get to the other side, you can get away from me before I can sting you.'

"The frog considered the logic of the scorpion's proposition, accepted his unassailable logic and agreed to give the scorpion a ride across the river on his back. The scorpion got on the frog's back and the frog began to swim across the river. Halfway across, the scorpion began to violently and viciously sting the frog, over and over, until the frog was full of the lethal poison. As the frog started to die, sinking into the river and taking the scorpion with him, he had one last, gasping, dying question.

" 'Mr. Scorpion. Why would you sting me? Now we are both going to die. Why would you? How could you?'

"The scorpion replied, 'Mr. Frog, I am a scorpion. This is what I do.' And with that they both sank beneath the water and died."

At this point Herbie Mann's flute solo, evocative of jasmine incense floating through the air of the most exquisite *hareem* just outside of Port Said, drifted through the speakers of Paul's car. I contemplated his little parable and knew what he was telling me. We all knew the obvious benefits of the Morningstar partnership. Paul was telling me the downside.

"Diedre, I really don't know how relevant this story is to Morningstar or our conversation about Gordon. But it occurred to me that, while we know that Gordon must always be watched, he may be working from a script that defies normal logic and reason. After all, he is not normally logical or normally reasonable. We will all need to watch Gordon, day in and day out."

"Paul, when you are right, you are right. And I am sure that this is something that we should discuss in the morning. By the way, would you mind holding these until we get back to the guest quarters? They simply won't fit in my purse."

The expression on Paul's face was priceless. When he realized that I had handed him my panties I saw pleasure, surprise and desire compete for first place. He had never even noticed me taking them off while telling me the story about the goddamned scorpion and that goddamned frog.

In what seemed like nanoseconds we were back in the guest quarters. All of the romantic good intentions about sipping champagne in some demure, sophisticated fashion went out the window. Buttons were unbuttoned, zippers were unzipped, snaps were unsnapped and clothing was thrown and strewn without care or concern. Love and passion was in the air. We were able to combine lust and caring into another wonderful night that I know that we will both remember forever.

And there was another reason that we would remember that night. Everything that happened afterward made our prior lives simple and uncomplicated by comparison.

CHAPTER 83

Sture

Don't tell me I'm dreamin'

As the manager of Dorothy's By the Sea, I had been attending Gordon Perkins's Labor Day parties for the past few years. I always came out late Friday night since the restaurant was closed for the weekend. I stayed at a guest house in South Hampton and watched dawn glide over the sand dunes of Long Island. I knew without knowing that various members of The Pride had various agendas. That was always the case. And that is what would bring them to Gordon's party that night.

Over the past six years, Gordon's party had become the party to attend. People were known to rearrange vacation schedules and international travel plans in order to be there. Part of the attraction was the sheer spectacle of the party itself. Gordon spared no expense—at least two live bands. Veuve Cliquot and Pommery and Cristal were the only brands of champagne that were served—and they were served by the case—at least one hundred by my casual count. The food was catered by Butterbean, of course, and Gordon would supplement that with truffles flown in from France and fresh oysters expressed in from the Nysna coast of South Africa.

There were always several multicolored tents pitched over the grounds of Gordon's estate with candles floating in the pool and fountains like luminescent lilies. He usually spent about $20,000 on floral arrangements alone. His landscaping contractor had annual instructions to make sure that the lawns, shrubbery, trees and all living plant life were prepared for a perfect presentation for the last Saturday in August.

Over the years it was clear to me that Gordon had worked very hard to make sure that this party was more than a social success. I have observed that social events can have tremendous business ramifications if handled properly. Every year Gordon made sure that anyone who he thought could help him or he thought he could use was invited.

Not all of the members of The Pride could help him or be used, but many were invited anyway. After all, his status within The Pride was important to his overall status—that of being one of the most successful black investment bankers of all time.

Gordon made sure that many of his white colleagues were invited. For those that came, it might be their only truly integrated social event of the year that was not a fund-raiser for some "worthy" cause.

Interestingly, I have learned that many of the white attendees never failed to have a good time—actually a surprise to first time guests. I guess, given their limited social experience with blacks by reason of their living in New York City, they just did not know what to expect—perhaps lawyers and bankers break-dancing around a cauldron, flames licking its sides while mumbo jumbo bubbled noisily into the night? One never knew about these things.

And, I have to hand it to Gordon. He left nothing to chance. He made sure that his wife, Kenitra, used her contacts in the modeling business so that at least fifty of the most gorgeous and successful models in New York City were in attendance in full battle regalia. This, of course, led to an equal number of equally gorgeous wannabees showing up. The result was an unscheduled beauty contest that was amazing to behold.

I don't mean to give the impression that the women of The Pride were mere bystanders in this festival of the senses. They had long ago put to rest the hoary notion that brains and beauty could not work together.

While Kenitra's associates had to be gorgeous to earn a living, more than a few members of The Pride could match them black minidress for minidress, stiletto heel for stiletto heel, hip for hip, thigh for thigh . . . well, you get the idea. For these extremely well-educated and talented and accomplished black women who had to carefully manage their sensuality and sexuality while on the job, events like Gordon's party, the Black Ski Summit, the Sun Splash Festival in Jamaica or the Congressional Black Caucus Dinner were opportunities for them to display and flaunt their other side of midnight. Romance was sought but fun was mandatory.

In addition, there were any number of young and not so young men of The Pride who knew the reputation of Gordon's parties, and they were determined to experience and enjoy the beauty and the wonder of it all. The combustible combination of gorgeous women and successful men was always a recipe for a successful party.

My experience was that Gordon's parties always started out as fun events that would get wilder and wilder as the evening wore on. In the years that I have been going, at least a dozen women and that many men would wind up nude in the Jacuzzi or the pool. In the morning after, Gordon's maintenance people would find underwear, pants, bras and other articles of clothing on the beach. I have heard that they also find condoms, remnants of marijuana joints and pieces of foil and twenty-dollar bills that had been used to hold cocaine.

Just like the policy that we have at Dorothy's, drug usage was something that was never mentioned. No one who attended ever asked about it. There is an unspoken code that those who indulge seem to understand. Since I don't indulge, I haven't quite cracked the code yet.

It was seemingly understood that Gordon would not object to the not so discreet use of marijuana and cocaine. And, although no one could ever remember seeing Gordon holding anything stronger than a glass of merlot or champagne, his assent was somehow assumed.

The use of so-called controlled substances produced some very interesting behavioral twists and turns. Many of the members of The Pride came of age in the late sixties and seventies when marijuana, acid, hashish, mescaline and cocaine were just party favors and refreshments of the day.

While not all of them may have inhaled, they all accommodated the presence of recreational drugs and really didn't seem to have a problem with it. But, in the aftermath of the Age of Reagan and the constant drumbeat of the campaign to "just say no"—combined with the very real wreckage of the lives of some who could never say "no"—there was a perceptible change in behavior.

It was no longer "cool" to publicly and obviously consume so-called "controlled" substances. I am told that there was a time when people would smoke joints and snort lines in plain view. That was clearly before I came to America.

By the time I came to the U.S. there seemed to be an unspoken code used by those who did indulge, and they enjoyed their illicit prizes in private and in secret. For some, it was the only way that they could still enjoy the pleasures of their youth.

I found it truly fascinating during my years of being around The Pride, at a big party like Gordon's, the secret society would somehow signal each other and they would find a place . . . a bathroom, an extra bedroom, someplace where they could smoke and sniff until they were where they needed to be. And then they would slip back into the crowd with that secret, guilty feeling, and try and blend in. The only difference was in their mind and it was a big difference at that.

CHAPTER 84

Kenitra

What's the deal—what's happenin'?

Meanwhile, as that day began, I moaned to myself, my body and soul and very spirit bruised and beaten and sore beyond any realistic hope of full and permanent recovery. As I saw the streaks of dawn ease through the bathroom window, I cursed the realization that the drugs and the beatings and the alcohol and the degradation and abuse visited upon me by Gordon had not killed me . . . again. That meant that there would be more nights like last night. It might even be tonight.

I looked over to the other side of the bed that had been my entire universe of humiliation and agony only a few hours ago, and had to smile to myself. It was only six o'clock in the morning, and Gordon, ever the manic control freak, determined to be the perfect host, was already awake, showered, shaved, dressed, and downstairs harrying and hurrying the household staff. I was very glad of this development.

It meant that there would be no more beatings or degrading descents into hell during this day. The night would be another matter. At least for now there would be no forced ingestion of drugs and alcohol and there would be no bondage and scarring and scaring. And this was enough for me to be thankful.

As I tried to ease out of bed without aggravating the bruises and lumps that now proliferated about my body, I had to struggle to remember that it was only a few years ago that men begged to be with me. Even Gordon. There was a time, not that long ago, when I believed myself to be beautiful, inside and out. And there was a time in my life when I believed in me.

Of course, Gordon had tried to take all of that from me. He had given me wealth and status and prestige and furs and diamonds and a front row seat in hell. And now, as I tried not to stagger to the bathroom, I knew that all I really had in life were drugs and a will to live.

I took a couple of those little yellow pills and summoned my will once more. The warm feeling I felt on my way back to bed let me know that it was going to be a good day.

I knew from experience that Gordon would send a maid to wake me around noon. That way I would be recovered and presentable by the time guests started to arrive and that was important for the moment.

CHAPTER 85

Diedre

As we stroll along together . . .

In another part of the mansion I worked on persuading Paul that there were other ways that he could keep his commitment to regular aerobic workouts in the morning without putting on sneakers and running all over Long Island.

I can't remember exactly what it was that I did that changed his mind, but eventually he did come to see things my way. This was one time that I was the one who was right when I was right.

CHAPTER 86

Jerome

Keep your eyes on the prize

At the other end of Sag Harbor, Charmaine and I rose for the morning. Neither of us ever slept late. First, our sons were human alarm clocks, and the first lights of dawn seemed to hurl them from their beds. But I have to admit, Charmaine and I have always been driven—driven to succeed, driven to accomplish, driven to make the world different.

So this Saturday was no different in that regard. We both stirred in our bedroom, getting ready to greet the day. We went over our plans for the rest of the day.

"Okay. I'll take the boys horseback riding while you get your hair done this morning."

"Fine. You know we're going to have lunch early in the afternoon, I've fixed something special for us." After all this time, her smile could captivate me like that first night at Yale.

"That will leave us plenty of time to get ready for the evening. Anything else we have to do?"

"No, Jerome. I think we have the evening covered. Consuelo is staying through the weekend so the boys will have company until they go to sleep."

"Not much longer for that. By next year they will want to start running the streets."

"Don't remind me. But Jerome, before I forget . . ."

"Yes?"

"I know that you have told me every detail about this merger that you are doing with Diedre and Gordon."

"And . . . ?" For the moment I had no idea what was on her mind. Then I knew. It was the same thing that had been on my mind for months.

"There is something about this that gives me a . . . well, a funny feeling. I know that this is a fantastic, historic, wonderful, once in a lifetime event for you, and for us . . . but there is something about Gordon . . . the only way I can describe it is as 'a funny feeling.'"

In reality, she didn't have to say another word. Gordon was beyond being a wild card. He was heaven as an asset and hell as a partner.

"It's not something that I can really express or put into words. There is just something about all of this that gives me pause. And every road leads to Gordon."

And then the doorbell rang. Everything should have been as clear as glass. But that was when things were starting to get interesting. I found that out as I answered the door and greeted the Federal Express messenger.

I guess I must have had a slightly dazed expression on my face when I came back into the kitchen. I know that it took me more than a moment to absorb and understand the letter that was in the delivery package. Frankly, I may never understand it.

The stationery on which the letter was written was some of the most expensive vellum bond that I had ever seen. It was typed in a curious script.

> *Jerome:*
>
> *By the time you read this letter, the* Wall Street Journal *will have received a press release announcing my resignation from your firm, effective yesterday. I really would have preferred to tell you this in person, but time and circumstances simply did not permit it to take place that way. I did not, however, think that it would be right for you to hear this from anyone else. Not after all that we have been through.*

An opportunity has arisen, and just as you have taught me, and would have done yourself, I had to take that opportunity. The release to which I referred will announce the formation of R.R. Beard & Company, a venture capital and asset management firm. My partner for domestic work will be Merrill Lynch. Merrill is providing me with much of my start-up capital as well as the initial infrastructure resources. I will be the majority shareholder.

You should also know that five members of your asset management group and three members of your firm's financial advisory group will be joining me along with five secretaries. I have attached a list of their names.

I truly wish that things could have turned out differently. I have learned so much in working with you. The most important lesson that I have learned is that business is business, and every opportunity must be seized at the right time. I think that is exactly what I am doing right now.

I truly hope that we can maintain our friendship although I know that you might not feel that is appropriate right now. But I am sure that you would have done the same thing . . . indeed, your new venture with Gordon and Diedre is proof of just that. In your new partnership I just don't see a place or a future for me. As we have worked together I always expected that my future would involve our continuing to work together. Obviously you have chosen another alternative. And just as I have had to understand, I hope that you will understand too.

Just for the record, I did not seek out this opportunity. I was initially approached by Merrill, and initially I turned them down. And then I thought about what you would do, and I called them back. There was no way I could tell you about any of this and there was no way that I could turn down the opportunity when our negotiations were finalized.

I could go on, but it is probably best that I close for

now. My new office manager (you will recall my secretary Lucretia) will call Berta on Wednesday to work out an orderly transfer of papers, belongings, etc., of all the people that are leaving and joining me.

Please give my love to Charmaine and the boys.

Ray

P.S. The New York Times *will be publishing an announcement that Monique and I will be getting married in June of next year. I want to extend the first invitation to the wedding to you and Charmaine. The two of you will always be like family to me.*

RRB

CHAPTER 87

Jerome

Circle the wagons

"Fellas, your mother and I have a few things to discuss. Why don't you finish up your cereal in the TV? room?" I felt a tremor in my hands that recalled my days of doing battle on the streets of Philadelphia, or was it New Haven?

I tried to maintain some semblance of control while asking the boys to leave the room. I could only begin to imagine Charmaine's reaction. I felt myself about to be blinded by rage and did not like the feeling at all.

The boys were cool. They could always tell when something was up, and this was one time when they instinctively knew that my request did not require discussion. They quickly and quietly left the room with their bowls of Cheerios in hand.

"Jerome, what on earth . . . ?" I simply handed her the letter and sat down heavily. I mindlessly watched the surf play with the sand while waiting for Charmaine to finish reading the news of the day.

"That son of a bitch! That motherfucking son of a bitch!"

In the almost twenty years that I had known Charmaine, I had heard her curse on only two other occasions, and both of those were during childbirth. But her choice of words this time was right on point.

"I just cannot believe it, Jerome. This is impossible. It's got to be a joke . . . Jerome, everything that Ray is, is because of you! You, Jerome! How could he? How?"

Charmaine got so upset that she started to cry. The hot tears that coursed down her cheeks were not from weakness or defeat. It was anger this time. It was rage, pure, distilled and unadulterated by anything resembling mercy or understanding. For long moments, all I could do was continue to stare at the letter that Charmaine was holding in her hands.

I remember going into another zone of consciousness. Listening to the surf, I could hear the undercurrent of the boys laughing and horsing around in the TV room. I remember thinking about how very fine Ray's stationery appeared. How very tasteful in his choice of the dagger with which he stabbed me in the back.

"Jerome? You haven't said a word. What are you going to do about this? You cannot possibly let him get away with it!" Charmaine's voice started to bring me back to the planet, but I still just sat there.

Rage and anger were rocketing and careening inside my skull and all I could think about for the moment was maintaining control. It was being able to maintain control that had gotten me this far. I was not going to let Ray Beard take that from me.

For another minute there were only the sounds of Grover Washington on the house sound system as Charmaine and I looked at the letter and each other. And then I stopped staring into space and took the letter from Charmaine, placed it on the counter. I held her hands as I spoke to her.

"You know that I have spent my whole professional life trying to build this firm so that it would be something more than a business—I have always wanted it to be an institution. I have wanted something that was not only going to be there for us and the boys, but something that would survive us all and be a part of history.

"As I have tried to build this firm I have looked at a lot of businesses, especially black-owned companies. One of the things that I have seen is that too many of these firms start as family operations and stay that way.

"Rather than trying to find the best people available they try and rely solely on family ties and familial loyalty. Then sons and daughters inherit control and management whether or not they are the most qualified to do so. I have never thought that this was the formula for long-term success.

"From the very beginning, Charmaine, you know that I have not wanted to make that mistake. I have always looked for the smartest, most ambitious, sharpest people out there who would work for me . . ."

"Jerome, I know what you are saying but . . ." Charmaine always had a knack for getting to the point, and she pointedly interrupted my little sermon.

"But what? You have just been stabbed in the back by your closest business colleague. I love you darling, but you sound like you are getting started on a lecture instead of getting ready to get a gun or a baseball bat and go looking for that goddamned Ray Beard."

We both had to smile in spite of what was in that letter with the fancy stationery. She knew me too well. And she knew that the Jerome Hardaway that she had met twenty-something years ago would not be in control. But times do change and so do people.

"Charmaine, you know that this betrayal is not something that I can neither ignore nor accept. I have to deal with it. I have always looked for people like Ray because he is smart, competitive and ambitious. When I found Ray I thought he was just the kind of person who I could mentor, groom and train to run the whole firm some day.

"Right now it sounds ridiculous, but one of the biggest sticking points in the merger discussions had been my insisting on putting Ray on the Executive Committee of Morningstar. Diedre, Gordon, and Paul wanted only principals, but I would not move on that point and they finally agreed. I had planned to tell Ray about it tonight."

"Talk about irony dipped in horseshit. I am sure that Gordon and Diedre are going to get a real kick out of this news." Charmaine always had a way with words.

"Tell me about it. But you know, when you work with smart, ambitious and competitive people, things like this are going to happen. Sure, I think that Ray is a disloyal son of a bitch, but in the real world of business, I just cannot take it personally."

"Well Jerome, it's clear from the letter that Ray did not trust you to look out for his interests in this merger and so he felt he had to look out for himself."

"Precisely. And if that is the way he felt, then his leaving is best for both of us, and for Diedre and Gordon too. And I am glad that I found out who he really is now instead of relying on him for something even more important in the future."

"So, what are you going to do now?"

CHAPTER 88

Jerome

Mine eyes have seen the glory . . .

"You know what, Charmaine? I am going to let Paul know and after that, I am going to do absolutely nothing. I am going to wish Ray the best of luck.

"I don't imagine that we will be very close or do much business together, but at the end of the day, business is business. It was my mistake to think that we were closer. But now I know and I have to move on."

"Well, it's a little early to be calling Paul. You might wind up disturbing Diedre."

We both laughed at her reference. I had been keeping her posted on the all too transparent reunion of Paul and Diedre. We were surprised and happy for the two of them.

"Without talking to Paul, I can tell you right now that there is very little that I can do legally. On Wall Street people come and go all the time. Sometimes they take key personnel with them, sometimes key documents and information . . ."

As I was speaking I was suddenly reminded of the need to anticipate the worst in people in these situations. I dialed Berta's number and was thankful that she had not gone away for the weekend.

I told her about Ray's letter and the imminent departure of several employees. She knew about the merger, of course, so there was not a lot of news there.

I then gave her explicit instructions to call a very special security company that I had had on retainer just for times like this. They were to be at my offices within the hour to secure the physical premises and to make sure that absolutely no one had access to any computers without my personal consent until I returned to the office on Wednesday.

The firm's local area network would be temporarily disabled denying all remote access. If Ray or any of his departing colleagues tried to access the firm's computers, a virus would be transmitted that would permanently scramble and disable the hard drives of their computers.

Standard instructions for canceling of credit cards and other privileges were also given. I also asked the security company to get a record of Ray's phone calls and internet communications. There was probably some very interesting information to be found there.

"Well, Charmaine, now I feel better." I turned to her as I concluded my call with Berta.

"At least I feel like I have taken some action. And now, we should just enjoy the rest of the day. I think that we have given Raymond Russell Beard III all the time he deserves. I am not going to spend any more time on him today, that's for sure."

"Well, as far as I am concerned, Ray deserves anything that happens to him."

"You are probably right, Charmaine. But we will just have to wait and see what happens to him."

CHAPTER 89

Diedre

Who knows what evil lurks...

By one o'clock on Saturday we were back at Gordon's dining room table for a light lunch and some further discussion. Jerome gave us the news regarding Ray Beard. For a few moments we were all silent, registering and digesting and analyzing this bit of news.

In the background you could hear the sounds of workers setting up tables, chairs, sound systems, lighting—all the appurtenances of a first class *soiree*. This luncheon was certainly not planned but Gordon, ever the proper host, had arranged for sandwiches and a light Chilean Sauvignon Blanc. The wine was just perfect for a sunny afternoon that provided just a hint that autumn was sitting in the waiting room.

Jerome had told Paul, Gordon and me about his correspondence from Ray Beard by phone, hence the luncheon. No one had a real agenda, but Jerome felt that this was a Morningstar issue and none of us argued with the notion that it would not hurt for the four of us to at least consider the import of this latest development.

As usual, Gordon was the first to speak. He had a sandwich in one hand and a glass of wine in the other. For a moment the image of a mythic black Falstaffian character crossed my mind. But it was time to focus on more important things.

"Frankly, Jerome, I don't even know why we are sitting here. The merger does not take place until Wednesday. So, technically and actually, Ray Beard is leaving your firm, and it's your business as to how you want to deal with it."

"Jerome, although there might be other ways to say it, I'm afraid that Gordon is right. I'm not too crazy about this news involving Ray. I am sure that he would have been an asset to Morningstar, and we all know how much you think of him." I took a sip of wine and continued, trying to stay calm even though my thoughts were all over the place at that moment.

"But it's your call as to how to deal with it. I am sure that we will support whatever you want to do." I couldn't believe that I was agreeing with Gordon so easily! But he was right.

"Look, we are partners now. Damn the legal dates. I just felt that as my partners you had to know about this right away."

"Jerome, you were right to do so. And I am sure we both appreciate your being up-front about this Ray Beard business.

"But you know I never liked the little son of a bitch anyway, and he was only going to be on Morningstar's Executive Committee because of you. So you won't see me crying any tiny tears over his departure."

Gordon had a way of putting things that would get under the skin of a rhinoceros. But this was one time when he was absolutely correct and I continued to find myself supporting his position.

"Jerome, let's think about this a little further. Ray may have been your protégé, but he wasn't Gordon's or mine. Key employees come and go all the time, and in the final analysis that's all Ray was, an employee. You paid him. He worked. He got a better offer. He left. That should be the end of the story as far as Morningstar is concerned.

"I know that Ray leaving like this must be a personal blow to you, but in the long run it won't make a difference to what the three of us are trying to do. I really don't know that there is a lot more that you need to say."

And, having already explained the situation over the phone, including the security precautions that he had immediately put into place, there really wasn't a lot more for Jerome to say.

"Well, I'm still glad that we met. Talking with the three of you has helped me to focus upon what was important. I didn't want to let my emotions get in the way, and obviously we just have to move on."

As Jerome was speaking I realized that I needed to stop thinking about being in bed with Paul. I just didn't remember him being so . . . adventuresome or insatiable. I tried to concentrate on the issues at hand as Paul spoke again.

"Well, since the three of you want to make the first announcement about Morningstar tonight, I would suggest that you do it around ten so that you will have a critical mass of guests here, but the party won't be in full swing. Just try not to get into too many details."

In trying not to think about the night before with Paul, and that morning and the night to come, I tried to focus on what he was saying and the plan of announcement and pre-announcement that we were considering. It wasn't easy. My mind was on the meeting, but my body wanted to be someplace else. Someplace close to Paul. My only hope was to keep talking.

"You know, we might want to consider that we are paying Edwina McClure a whole lot of money to hype this merger of ours at the announcement at Hue & Me on Wednesday. So why are we trying to upstage ourselves with this 'pre-announcement'?"

"Diedre, when you put it way, I see your point. We have been looking at this all wrong." It was amazing. Gordon and I were agreeing. Again.

"I see what you mean, Diedre. Perhaps we should just let a few selected friends know this evening—not too many. That will certainly get the buzz going, even if we tell them 'in confidence.'"

Jerome got a laugh from all of us with that one. We had all had experience with the fact that anything told "in confidence" was usually up and down the street within twenty-four hours.

"But you know, the more I think about it, Jerome, even the 'selected friends' distribution has its built-in problem. If we don't want Wednesday's announcement to be absolutely anticlimactic we should just keep the news to ourselves and family and let Edwina do what she is being paid to do."

I wanted to be sure that Jerome didn't think that I was being critical of him. I needn't have worried.

"Diedre's right. If we start talking tonight, by the time we get to Hue & Me, Morningstar will be old news, if it is news at all. Let's just keep a lid on it until Wednesday."

"That's fine with me. It will mean fewer headaches for us all. Can we plan to meet at my offices on Tuesday afternoon so that we can get the final details in place for the announcement. Let's say three?"

We all agreed with Paul's suggestion and then there was really nothing further to discuss. Jerome went back to his place to play with his boys. Gordon went back to his party preparations and I took the keys to Paul's Porsche to go into Sag Harbor to get my hair done, leaving Paul with the afternoon to himself. I wanted him to enjoy anticipating our next night together.

CHAPTER 90

Paul

The natives are restless

Having some actual quiet time, leisure time, on a sunny Saturday afternoon, was just fine with me. I decided to use the time re-reading one of my favorite books, *Mumbo Jumbo*, by Ishmael Reed, who happened to be one of my favorite writers. I always have found the experience of distancing myself from those things that I had to do by entering the world of things that I wanted to do was a perfect form of relaxation and liberation.

I slipped on my headphones and played Horace Silver's "Song for My Father" and went into my other world, sipping an excellent Belvedere vodka martini with a twist of lime on the deck of Gordon's summer home. For a moment I thought about the fact that I was a long way from Harlem. And then I realized that, in many ways, I was not that far from Harlem at all.

If Harlem was a state of mind, then I was not far at all. The Pride was changing the very concept of where black people were sup-posed to be and what we were supposed to be doing there. I thought about it for a moment and thought that this was a very good thing.

Reading the curious genius prose of Ishmael Reed while the piano virtuosity of Horace Silver coursed through the headphones, there was another channel of my mind that could not forget this Ray Beard business.

I always felt that Ray was a punk, but even I was surprised that Ray had the nerve to strike at Jerome this way. Business is business, and the reality is that, emotions aside, Ray got a hell of a good deal from Merrill and took it. That should have been the end of the story. But I had a strange feeling that there was more to the story.

Diedre was right about this Ray Beard issue being of no real import to Morningstar. Ray's leaving was just a bump in the road. And we were all correct in deciding that any pre-announcement would just be counterproductive.

And then I found myself wondering if she wanted me right now as much as I wanted her. And I thought about the serendipity of canceling the pre-announcement, allowing us to get back into Manhattan earlier in the evening. We could be away from the party and away from the world for a few days. And I wondered if her suggestion might have obscured that particular agenda.

I took another sip of the martini and savored it. I took in the view from the deck and tried to absorb the entire panorama of the ocean and the shore and the sailboats and yachts and the sky and the clouds. It was wonderful. It was relaxing as the lightest of breezes tiptoed across my face.

And then I thought some more. Gordon and Diedre said basically the same thing when it came to this Ray Beard matter. But when Gordon said it, somehow it elicited a different feeling. It was hard to describe but it was a very real feeling nonetheless. It was almost as if, on some level, Gordon saw Ray's decision as an act of betrayal, and it was an act that he appreciated, understood, and admired. Perhaps it was just my imagination running away with me, as the song goes.

I didn't know what it was. I sure as hell wasn't sure that I should make more of it than it was. And what was it, anyway? But I had learned to put a certain amount of trust in my intuition. I just could not figure out what it was telling me.

I already knew that Gordon was an asshole, someone not to be trusted. He was a scorpion and a snake rolled into one, but he could be a formidable asset if he was on your side. But was he on Morningstar's side?

He certainly seemed to be. He said all the right things and more important, he did all the right things. Just the contacts that he had provided for Jerome and Diedre promised to make Morningstar a ton of money.

His New Orleans strategy had all the earmarks of a masterstroke. If Mayor Lodrig was reelected, Morningstar would be one of the leading investment firms in the area of municipal finance within the year. Still there *was* something else that just wouldn't go away. There was the glimmering of an idea that was playing hide and seek with my imagination.

CHAPTER 91

Paul

Way down yonder in New Orleans

I have never been big on guessing games so something made me go inside Gordon's house and call Sammy Groce in New Orleans. Amazingly, I was able to reach Sammy at the third number that I had for him.

I usually had to call at least six numbers with a couple of callbacks thrown in for extra aggravation. I started to feel lucky until I started actually talking to Sammy.

"Paul, how's life in the big city?"

"I'm out on Long Island right now, Sammy. But New York was there the last time that I checked."

"Paul Taylor, you have got to be the funniest lawyer in America. But that's not saying much."

"Thanks for the compliment, Sammy, but you know damn well I didn't call to tell you jokes. What's going on with the mayor's race? Anything new?"

"Well Paul, as a matter of fact there is some news. I was planning to call you right after the holiday. You see I met this redbone gal in the Broussard campaign. She's as fine as fine can be. And I'm telling you Paul, I swear, the things that girl can do with her . . ."

"Sammy, Sammy, when we have time to run the bars in the French Quarter, you can tell me all about her. Right now, I need to know what you know." I knew that if I didn't cut Sammy off right away, I would end up hearing about all of his female acquaintances of the last six months, and that call could take hours.

"Okay, okay . . . I'm getting to it. The word is that on Wednesday, the Broussard campaign is going to announce a real blockbuster of a story about Mayor Lodrig."

I felt my blood run ice cold. It was still warm on that afternoon in Long Island, but icy chills were gathering to stampede across my skull and down my spine. I put down my Belvedere martini and listened intently as Sammy continued.

"I don't know all the details, but there is supposed to be something about the mayor and his taxes and illegal immigrants working in his father's chocolate factory up in Baton Rouge. At least that's what I hear."

I took a deep breath. This was turning out to be Surprise Saturday after all. And I have always hated surprises.

"Sammy, don't leave me hanging. How bad is this going to be? Is this going to be a real problem for Mayor Lodrig?"

"I don't have no goddamn crystal ball and I'm no smart lawyer from New York City. But I tell you what. This can't be a good thing. This may be the "September Surprise" I was telling you about months ago.

"And I'll tell you something else. If this story has any, what do you call it . . . corroboration? The U.S. Attorney down here is going to get a grand jury together faster than you can spit. And that can't be a good thing, even if you are running for dogcatcher."

As much of a fool as Sammy could be, he was deadbang right this time, even if his story was only partially true. If the story had any credibility it could kill the mayor's reelection campaign. It would be almost impossible to rehabilitate his campaign before the election in November. Hell, the primary was in three weeks.

"Sammy, check for a FedEx envelope coming next week. It will be a token of my appreciation. And I don't mean the kind that you use on the Storyville trolley. You have been a big, big help. You enjoy the rest of the weekend and I will call you on Wednesday."

"Thanks so very much for the 'token' counselor, and I will look for your call."

"Don't mention it. You really have been very, very helpful, Sammy.

Just keep your eyes and ears open and be careful. You may be swimming in some deep water."

"This old crawdaddy ain't going nowhere."

I was so engrossed in my conversation with Sammy that I never realized that Gordon was standing behind me for most of the time that I was on the phone. Actually, I did not realize that until much later on. Just like I didn't realize that I had just spoken to Sammy Groce for the last time.

On the following Monday morning Sammy was found dead of smoke inhalation caused by a fire in his bedroom. The New Orleans Fire Department determined that the fire had been caused by a cigarette that Sammy had been smoking in bed. That was real interesting news because I knew that Sammy had stopped smoking three years earlier.

CHAPTER 92

Gordon

Crosstown traffic

Listening to Paul's side of the conversation with Sammy Groce, I knew that it was only a matter of time before he put two and two together and got five. But time was on my side and there was really no need to worry. I could continue to be gracious and hospitable. I was enjoying playing this role.

"Do you want another Belvedere martini while I'm up?" Paul was more than a little startled when he turned and saw me. And I could tell that he wondered if I had been listening to his conversation. He would never know from my expression or behavior. I made sure of that.

"No thanks, Gordon. I am going to take it easy for now. Your parties have always been hell on my liver." We both had to laugh at the half joke, half truth.

"I have never noticed you having a problem before. Getting old, brother?" I decided to keep the banter light.

"I probably am getting old. Just like you and everyone else who is alive. But, to tell the truth, Diedre and I are going to drive back to Manhattan tonight, so I don't want to have too much to drink right now."

"Tonight? You are not going to stay for the whole party?"

"What can I tell you, Gordon? She wants to have brunch in SoHo on Sunday at Felix. What can you do?"

We both knew Felix. It was a lovely bistro on West Broadway near Grand Street. It had unpretentious French cuisine and could also regale you with reggae or samba music on any given day. I had to admire Diedre's choice of a place for brunch.

"Listen, Paul, it's none of my business—but are you and Diedre . . . , how can I say it?"

"An item? Back together? Getting down?" We both had to laugh. The Dark Lord and I noticed the wonderful weather and we both hoped that it would continue through the evening so that the party would be a success.

"Something like that. But all I really wanted to say is that I am happy for you guys. Not that it's any of my business, as I said, but you both deserve to be happy."

I could tell that for a moment or two, Paul absolutely did not know what to say. This was not the Gordon Perkins that he knew speaking to him. It was great to see him trying to figure out what to say next.

"I knew what people have said about me. That I could double sell the mortgage on my best friend's mother's house and then have dinner with him that evening. That butter would not melt in my mouth but that gold would melt in my hand." That made Paul's reaction all the more delicious to watch.

"Well Gordon, I have to thank you very much. I guess you would have to know that we both have felt a little awkward, kind of like teenagers trying to keep all of this a secret, particularly with Morningstar coming to a head. I guess we owe our new relationship to your lodging arrangements."

I could tell that Paul was trying to inject some humor in all of this and we both laughed. By now his wondering what I had heard of his conversation with Sammy Groce had to be receding into his mind. He would think about it later, and later would be just fine.

"Seriously, thanks for the sentiment. I really appreciate it. And you know something Gordon? I really hope it works for the both of us this time."

I am sure that later, Paul would hardly believe that he had had this kind of conversation with me. But sometimes some people just have to let their feelings out to another person, even if that person would happen to be me.

A bubble of quiet seemed to surround us as the workmen and staff hustled to get all of the party preparations completed. It was going on three. Six was when all preparations were to be finished and everybody working knew that disappointing me was simply the worst thing that they could ever choose to do.

For a few minutes neither of us spoke. We both looked out over the water. It was a lovely day. I could tell that Paul was trying to sort through all that was happening. He was no dummy and I could tell that he felt that there were pieces of some kind of puzzle and he just could not figure it out. the Dark Lord and I took some pleasure in watching him try.

And then it seemed to me that there was a moment of realization dawning on Paul. There was no reason for me to think that. It was actually something that the Dark Lord detected. It was time to change the subject and move Paul's attention elsewhere.

"You know, Paul. I have always wanted to be the boss. That's why I started my own firm in the first place. And that's why I have always pushed so hard to get to the top. And that's why I am at the top now.

"I never even thought about partnering with anyone. Until you introduced the idea of this merger, I would just as soon have run Diedre and Jerome into the ground if it would have advanced my cause. I hope you don't mind me being so frank and honest. But it's the truth."

"No, Gordon. Go on. I think I am past the point of my bubble being burst. Please continue."

"Paul, I want to be sure that we are clear on this. Your idea was absolutely right from the very first day. And I saw it. I have learned that working with other talented people can be something special.

"What I am trying to say is that I thank you for bringing the three of us together and for considering me in the mix when I could not have seemed an obvious choice for anybody as a partner."

"No thanks needed, Gordon. Like I said that afternoon at the Water Club, I really believe that the three of you are going to make history. And I am just glad to be a part of it. It's going to be fun seeing

Morningstar make its mark on Wall Street. Hell, it's going to be a lot of fun."

"I tell you what. A lot of our white brothers and sisters on Wall Street are going to fall out of their executive chairs when the news hits on Wednesday. I have heard more than a few of them say that they never see successful blacks in any field put aside their egos and self-interests to form bigger firms, companies, whatever. Won't they be surprised?"

"They will be surprised all right. And I'll tell you something else, Gordon. There will be more than a few black brothers and sisters who will be surprised too!" We both had to laugh at the truth that was not so well hidden in that statement.

"Amen, Reverend Taylor. Amen, I say!" I tried to smile as broadly as possible as I said that to make sure that Paul knew that I was joking. It was time to relax for a few minutes. There would be time for Morningstar and Ray Beard and Sammy Groce in just a little while.

"Well, Gordon, I am going to take advantage of your great deck and this wonderful view. That is, unless you need me to help out with something?"

"Man, I pay all these people you see and more that you don't see just to make sure that you don't have to do a thing but relax and enjoy. Thanks though. Just take it easy and I'll see you when folks start showing up. I have a few calls to make anyway."

"Thanks, Gordon. I think I can follow those instructions perfectly."

We both laughed again and I went back inside the house where the smile disappeared from my face immediately. I did have a few calls to make, starting with a very important one to some people that I knew in Louisiana. The Dark Lord knew just who to call. In Byzantine situations like this, I just followed his instructions. He never led me wrong.

But first he led me to one of the bathrooms in my private master bedroom suite. I had gone long enough without enjoying some cocaine. It had been at least an hour. It was time to reward myself with a reload.

CHAPTER 93

Diedre

When the hunter gets captured by the game . . .

When I returned from getting my hair done, Paul had this funny look on his face that he was reluctant to explain. I didn't think that it was about my hair.

"Paul, if you have something to say about my hair, after all the trouble I have gone through, you better say it now." I was smiling and trying to lighten the moment. His answer told me that I had at least partially succeeded.

"Actually, I was wondering how upset you would be if we just messed your hair up for the next hour or two before the party started."

"Paul Taylor, don't you even dare to think about it. But I will make you a deal."

"What kind of deal?" he asked as he moved closer, closing the guest suite door behind us as he caressed my back and hips. My hairdo was in real jeopardy.

"How about we postpone messing up my hair for now, and on the ride back you can tell me all the ways that you would like to re-arrange my hairdo. I will grant you *carte blanche,* Mr. Taylor."

"As the saying goes, that's an offer I cannot refuse. And you better know that I am going to hold you to it."

"You had better."

CHAPTER 94

Sture

Hot fun in the summertime

Because I manage Dorothy's By the Sea, I could have recited the guest list for Gordon's party by heart. It was basically a carbon copy of the guest list for the Winner Tomlinson memorial service. The difference, of course, is that the mood was much lighter.

People were still coming for business networking purposes and, one thing that I have noticed about The Pride, people always noted who was there and who wasn't. Who was with whom, and who wasn't, carried great importance. And I also noticed that many, if not most, of the conversations were liberally sprinkled with self-promotion and subtle searches for any kind of inside information.

Of course I did not know about Morningstar until everyone else learned about it the following Wednesday. Still, it was no big deal to see Jerome and Gordon and Diedre together at a function, certainly at Gordon's annual summer party. No one even thought about the business connection.

Actually, the big news was the obvious resumption of a relationship between Paul and Diedre. That was enough to set tongues wagging and eliminating even the least bit of consideration of anything else of importance being planned. As it turned out, Diedre, Gordon, Jerome, and Paul couldn't have planned a better diversion if they had tried.

And so, The Pride partied just as they did every year at Gordon's.

The champagne flowed and so did the conversation. People danced to the seemingly endless beat of the live bands and the d.j.'s. Some of the veneer of Wall Street and Corporate America started to fade as the evening wore on. As the saying goes, at least for that Saturday night, many members of The Pride threw their hands up in the air as if they just didn't care. And I am sure that, at least for that night, they really didn't care.

In many ways the party that night followed a most predictable path. Kenitra Perkins's model friends were gorgeous enough to almost break the necks of more than a few men trying to get an extra look as they would walk by, seeming sashaying on clouds of absolute sensuality and unbelievable promise. The other single, unattached women who showed up, some called them "wannabees," were as gorgeous, lacking only the aura that comes with the practiced expectation of adoration.

The single, and not so single, male members of The Pride made all of these young ladies feel absolutely adored. Gordon also had invited several professional athletes (given the season, the football players were in training camps, but baseball and basketball were amply represented)—good looking, engaging and wealthy young men only too happy to meet some of the female members of The Pride. For some of these athletes, these women were a welcome change from the models and aspiring actresses and team cheerleaders that they usually met.

Couples like Jerome and Charmaine, Paul and Diedre, even Gordon and Kenitra mingled and made small talk. I had been to enough of these types of events that I had no trouble enjoying myself. When I was growing up in Bergen, I never could have dreamed about being part of such a spectacular spectacle.

CHAPTER 95

Sture

If these walls could talk...

Iknew that those who desired the less conventional refreshments always found out that there was a place for them too. One of the many sitting rooms in Gordon's house led to a lounge with a balcony that was on the other side of the main party. A visitor to that room could not simply wander in, and anyone who was unknown would simply never find it.

When I went into the room I first noticed the sweet fragrance of frankincense combining with marijuana and hashish. I could also barely make out the nearly imperceptible sound of cocaine being sniffed from a silver plate with a silver straw that was being passed around.

Appropriately enough, Stan Getz was playing in the background and the room was as subdued as possible. No one really recognized or acknowledged anyone and no one would ever talk about the room when they left. It wasn't even clear how the refreshments got there. They just did and that was good enough for everyone.

As would be expected in any community, the gay contingent of The Pride, both male and female, was also in attendance in full force. Being members of The Pride meant having to compete and succeed in a professional environment that did not always think highly of gay black men and women. As a result, in order to succeed, they were required to keep that aspect of their lives even deeper in the closet than their white counterparts.

A party like Gordon's permitted a certain level of welcome relaxation and freedom. Not knowing and trusting everyone, most of the gay members of The Pride made a point of making an appearance at Gordon's party and then going to Fire Island where the atmosphere was a lot more conducive to their lifestyle. That was where they could let themselves go. And they usually did.

All in all, just about everybody who came to Gordon's party went home happy.

CHAPTER 96

Paul

Stolen moments

It was a little past midnight and we were still in my car heading back to Manhattan. We were still about an hour outside of the city and this was a lot later than we had planned.

But there were people to see, things to talk about and timing suffered. Now I was just trying to stay within the speed limit, wishing that Diedre and I were already in the Jacuzzi back at my house, exploring all the territories that we already knew but needed to explore again. We passed the time chatting up the postmortem of Gordon's party.

"You know, Jerome had to know that Ray Beard was going to show up, so I am not surprised that he was able to greet Ray and Monique in a civil fashion. He actually came across as somewhat friendly, don't you think?"

"That might be true, Paul. But did you see how Charmaine cut Ray dead in his tracks. I don't think I have ever seen that side of her. And I tell you what, I don't ever want to be on the receiving end of whatever she was thinking about Ray tonight."

We both had to laugh, even though we both knew that what Diedre said was absolutely true. If looks could kill, Ray Beard's family would have been shopping for a suitable casket by now.

"Did you check out the buzz that went around the party when Ray showed up with Monique? And then, when word started to get around that he had left Jerome and was starting his own firm? You would have thought that the brother had discovered electricity, sliced bread, *and* peanut butter."

"I will bet you another *carte blanche* that by the time the Morningstar announcement is made on Wednesday, any number of wagging tongues will put two and two together and come to the conclusion that Ray and Jerome had a falling out and the two new companies are the result. There will be a virtual hurricane of gossip."

" 'Hurricane of gossip'? That's an interesting choice of words. I think that you would win that bet, sweetheart. But I am still interested in that *carte blanche*."

The ease with which we had converted our relationship from business to friendly accommodation to passionate romance continued to amaze me as I negotiated the Porsche through the notorious traffic of the Long Island Expressway.

"But you know something, Paul? Ray Beard has been considered to be quite the eligible bachelor for quite awhile. But I can't think of a single woman to whom he has ever been linked, romantically, or even for a fling. So his announcement that he is marrying Monique Jefferson, quite a catch in her own right, has a lot of people talking. Combined with his new firm, this is like something out of a Hollywood script."

"What are you saying? His marriage to Monique is out of character?"

"Let's look at it this way. He is a healthy, wealthy, handsome single black man in Manhattan and is never seen in the social company of another woman. I know more than one sister who has speculated as to whether Ray has been gender bending or, that he just might be gay.

"Then, all of a sudden, not only is he dating one of the most gorgeous single black women in town, he is marrying her! I just don't think that this is the end of the story."

We rode in silence for awhile, listening to Antonio Carlos Jobim and taking in the necklace of lights that was the Triborough Bridge as it approached in the distance. I was thinking about all that Diedre was saying when I noticed that there was a rustle of clothing.

I chanced a quick look over at her and realized that she was starting to undress, in a very private striptease that threatened to send us careening into the East River. I am so glad that I had exact change that night so that the tollbooth attendant did not get his thrill of a lifetime. Mercifully, Diedre relented in her disrobing and we started to talk again. We could not get to my place soon enough as far as I was concerned.

"But you know something, Diedre? There was something very interesting that I noticed when Ray and Monique bumped into Gordon and Kenitra. It was real clear to me that they were not meeting for the first time."

"That's not surprising, Paul. It's a big city, there are lots of places that people might meet."

"That's not what I mean. There was an interaction between the *couples* that got my attention. Not the interaction between Gordon and Ray. It was the way that Kenitra and Monique chatted and laughed and embraced."

"Like they were close friends, certainly more than acquaintances . . ."

"Exactly. They were close and we both know that Gordon rarely socializes with Kenitra in tow unless it advances his immediate business interests. She is beautiful, charming and all of that, but we both know that Gordon has no love or respect for that woman, and he would only introduce her to other people for business purposes."

"You have a point there, Paul. So what is his business with Ray?"

"I have no goddamned idea. Gordon is inextricably bound to Morningstar and you and Jerome, there could not possibly be any benefit for him having some kind of side arrangement with Ray. But . . ."

"But, this is Gordon Perkins we are talking about." The conversation suddenly got very serious and we both put our passion on hold as we tried to figure out what the hell we were talking about.

"Paul, the four of them really didn't spend that much time together. Maybe you are reading more into it than is really there."

I wanted to believe that Diedre was right. Any other possibility was the beginning of a nightmare from which we all might never awake. I really wanted to believe that night.

"You are probably right, Diedre. I am just a little on edge. I am sure that on Tuesday afternoon when we meet, this will all be just a memory."

"You want to change the subject?"

I glanced over to Diedre while trying to negotiate the last half mile to my town house. She had begun to undress again. And then, there was something else . . . I looked to see what she was doing. She was caressing and touching herself and making herself moan, and I was glad that I was only blocks away from home.

Moments upon our entering the house we found a way to disrobe each other while going up the stairs. The Jacuzzi had to wait that evening as we went right to the bed, naked and ready to go to heaven. The Pride, Morningstar and next week would just have to wait.

Later, we would realize how fortunate we were to have this brief visit to paradise. We were about to enter the maelstrom.

CHAPTER 97

Diedre

Storm clouds are gathering

Political reality in New Orleans was not much different from that in many major U.S. cities in the 1990s. The Democratic Party primary usually determined the winner of the general election. Sometimes there would be a surprise Republican or Independent. But you could always bet your money on the Democrats.

Three weeks after the Morningstar announcement at Hue & Me, Paul and I lay on his bed at his home, watching the New Orleans primary returns on a Wednesday night. We were absentmindedly sipping port wine, a thirty-year-old Fonseca. As it turned out, it was the only pleasant memory that I have of that evening.

"I can't believe the job that Edwina did in getting Morningstar off the ground. She might be hell on wheels, but she sure as hell got the job done!" Paul was reflecting on the Morningstar launch, and I had to agree with him.

"Bitch and Edwina might be on the same page of the dictionary. But she is good at what she does. Goooood! Do you remember, Diedre? The guest list at Hue & Me read like the first ten rows of Winner's memorial service."

"Hell, Paul. Edwina had the chairmen of the New York Stock Exchange, the American Stock Exchange, and NASDAQ in attendance. You can't ask for more than that. It's almost an unheard of alignment of the planets and stars.

"And don't forget CNN, CBS, NBC, FOX, ABC, the *New York Times*, the *Wall Street Journal* and countless other media representatives were there. We were all on *The Today Show, Good Morning America, Larry King,* it was just awesome."

And it *was* awesome. For the next several days after the announcement it seemed as if we all had the Midas touch. Jerome put together the final pieces of the public offering for his biotech client and was able to raise one billion dollars. Not bad for Morningstar's first effort.

I was able to get the pension fund asset management assignment from the unions that I had been working on all year. The billions of dollars that came from that assignment meant that Morningstar had over thirty billion dollars under management within its first ten days of operation. That was another major Morningstar coup.

The only problem was a "problem" to those who knew the Morningstar strategy. Paul told me about his last conversation with Sammy Groce, and the "September Surprise" was not a surprise to me. And what a surprise it turned out to be.

The day after the Morningstar announcement, the Broussard campaign produced several "witnesses" and "authentic" documents which "proved" that Mayor Lodrig's father had been involved in a conspiracy to import Cuban refugees and to hold them in virtual bondage as laborers in his Baton Rouge candy factory. Since the factory had burned to the ground due to a "mysterious" fire one month earlier, there were no records that *Pere* Lodrig could produce to immediately refute the charges. The only records that survived showed that Prince Lodrig was a 25 percent shareholder in the corporation that owned the factory.

Not surprisingly, the very next day federal prosecutors announced that they had no choice but to convene a grand jury to investigate the matter. To make matters worse, Mayor Lodrig at a tearful press conference proclaimed his innocence and offered to resign. He then decided that he would try and retain Johnnie Cochran to represent him in this matter. As of the primary election it was not clear that Mr. Cochran would be acting in Mayor Lodrig's defense.

It was no surprise to any of us at Morningstar that the Lodrig campaign went into pure and absolute freefall. His poll numbers went from a lead of almost 25 percent to him trailing by 5–10 percent on primary day. Campaign money virtually dried up and Broussard went from being a sure loser to an underdog with a puncher's chance to be the winner.

CHAPTER 98

Diedre

Picking up the pieces

"You know, Diedre, what I find absolutely amazing is that all Gordon has had to say through all of this is, 'everything will be fine.' That is, when we are able to get a straight answer out of him at all.

"It's really curious how he has had to be out of the Morningstar offices on this matter and that. I know that his business is absolutely national, but I can't help but feel as if there is something strange about all of this."

"What are you trying to say, Paul?"

"Well, I have not been able to speak with Gordon since last Thursday. I am assuming that neither you nor Jerome has had any contact either?"

"True, Paul. Now what are you talking about?"

"I have just come across some real bullshit. I didn't want to say anything to you or Jerome until I had confirmation. I just got confirmation on my fax machine downstairs about fifteen minutes ago."

"Confirmation of what? What are you talking about, Paul?"

"You remember the story about the scorpion and the frog . . ."

"Goddamit, Paul! I absolutely do not want to hear about any fucking frogs or any motherfucking scorpions!" I was beyond crazed at this point. And the CNN announcers continued to drone in the background.

"Okay, okay. Do you remember how I mentioned how close Ray and Monique seemed to be with Gordon and Kenitra?"

"I do remember, Paul. Please, please get to the point." CNN continued unabated and undeterred by my distress.

"Well, I sometimes use the services of a private security firm that specializes in forensic audits. Really deep background research about the financial dealings of individuals. You probably would not be surprised at how much information is available with just a little effort."

"This has to do with Gordon, doesn't it?" I actually started to see the room take on a red tinge as rage struggled to take over total control of my total self.

"Yes it does, Diedre. It turns out that exactly one week before the Sag Harbor party, Gordon transferred $10 million to an account in his name in London. That Monday, the $10 million was transferred to an account in the Bahamas in the name of Kenitra Perkins. The next day that account transferred the funds to a Citibank account in New York, also in the name of Kenitra Perkins."

"I don't see the problem, Paul. The partnership agreement is quite clear in allowing all of us to do whatever we want with our personal assets. Gordon can move money all around the world every day of the week. What's your point?"

"The point, Diedre, is that on the Thursday after the announcement at Hue & Me, Kenitra Perkins deposited exactly $10 million into the account of Raymond Russell Beard and Company."

"What?" I simply could not believe what I had heard. I was in another dimension. Another planet. A brand new universe.

"The deposit went into the RRB venture capital fund and the fax that I just received downstairs confirms what I just told you."

My eyes were glued to the television set. My ears were trying to process what they heard and convey that to my brain. I wanted to curse and cry and scream. But I couldn't say a word.

"Diedre, I can tell you right now that Gordon will say that this is an independent venture by Kenitra and that he wanted her to have her own business interests. He will say it is her money and that he has nothing to do with this RRB investment.

"She is probably on the board of directors or something like that.

And you can be sure that Gordon's name is not on a single piece of paper."

"I am sure that Gordon's fucking name is not on any piece of paper, Paul. Just look at the television!" I could not believe my eyes and as I glanced at the shocked look on Paul's face, I knew that he couldn't believe it either.

CHAPTER 99

Diedre

Imitation of madness

The results of the New Orleans primary had just been announced. Under the circumstances, there was no surprise that Paul Broussard was the winner. The live remote broadcast showed the victorious candidate surrounded by his cheering supporters.

And there on the stage, as bold as life, a little to the right of the candidate, was Gordon Perkins. Cheering! Applauding! He was actually beaming with pride and elation. And standing next to Gordon—Raymond Russell Beard III!

"Diedre, I thought I knew how low Gordon could go, but . . ."

"Paul, he is not human," I heard myself saying. "He is not fucking human. I will personally kill this son of a bitch!"

The rage and the shock made me cry, and shake uncontrollably. And that just made me angrier. I could not believe that all of my hard work could just be taken away like this. It was beyond conception. It was beyond belief.

I was not crying as much as trying to somehow control the cauldron of raging emotions that whirlpooled my insides into Gordian knots. I did not want comfort just then. Not from Paul. Not from anyone. All I wanted was revenge. Deep, primal, basic, atavistic revenge. I could hear Paul speaking from somewhere in outer space.

"Diedre, if there was ever a time to step back and think, this is the time. I am sure of one thing. Gordon is counting on an emotional reaction. He is expecting it even as he is strutting around on that stage in New Orleans with Ray. That is why we have to step back and think!"

That is when the phone rang. It was Jerome. Paul put him on the speakerphone so that the three of us could speak freely. Jerome's voice was eerily still and quiet. I remember thinking about the blade of a knife for some reason. There was not a lot of time for formalities.

"I assume that you two are watching CNN."

"We are, Jerome. Paul and I are trying to figure out . . ."

"Diedre, with all due respect, there is nothing to figure out. Gordon has played us. He has played us for pure and simple fools. We just have to work out an exit strategy. Right now! It's that plain and that simple."

"What kind of exit strategy did you have in mind, Jerome?" Paul was trying to pull together the pieces while I was trying to pull myself together. Vengeance was still the overwhelming thought in my mind; an anger flowed over every aspect of my being like lava launched from some volcano deep in my soul.

"Exit. As in we need to get out of this deal with Gordon. Not soon. Now! I am willing to continue with Morningstar with you, Diedre, but Gordon has got to go, and right now.

"I don't need anyone to tell me that he has a hand in Ray Beard's play. And I am sure that Gordon is getting serious kickback fees for my biotech deal and your pension fund deals, Diedre."

"Well, Jerome, now that you mention it. Gordon is probably going to call you and Diedre tomorrow morning and inform you that he is exercising his right to leave Morningstar. And he will probably threaten to collapse both of your deals unless you waive your non-compete clauses." Paul always did have a way of getting to the point in crisis situations.

As counsel to Morningstar, I would advise the two of you to waive the non-compete clause. You have no idea what other time bombs he may have planted. It is best to get him out of Morningstar and to do it right now."

There was silence on the line. The three of us looked at CNN as it continued with news about other elections, guerrilla uprisings on the other side of the world and various sordid celebrity love affairs.

We knew that we would be seeing electronic images of Gordon and Ray on television every twenty minutes, mocking us for the rest of the night.

"Jerome, Paul was suggesting that we need to think before we act. And I am sure that he is right. Let's meet at his offices at eight tomorrow morning and see how we can sort this out."

"Let's hope there will be no more news between now and then." Jerome's wan smile limped its way over the speakerphone.

We wished each other a good night and Paul turned off the television. I remember that he put Billie Holiday on his sound system. She was singing "God Bless the Child That's Got His Own."

We held each other in the dark and were glad to have each other. We waited for morning, when we knew that we would do battle. In our heart of hearts we had to know that this battle was going to come some day.

CHAPTER 100

Paul

Excuse me while I kiss the sky

I have to admit that there was something about the events in New Orleans that night that relaxed me. Now there was no more speculation or guessing or fear or worry. There was going to be a battle. And I did not see myself as being on the losing side.

While my role was as outside counsel for Morningstar, I harbored no illusions. Gordon Perkins meant to destroy me as well as Diedre and Jerome. It was almost as if he had planned it from the very beginning, using my idea as the launching pad for his assault.

Now there was no need for guessing. No forensic audits. No investigators. It was now time to go to war with Gordon. And that was fine with me.

After shaving and showering the morning after, I fixed a shake made of bananas, orange juice and yogurt. I made a cup of green tea and turned on the coffeemaker for Diedre who would be rising soon. I needed to make some calls.

I reached my secretary and one of my associates and directed them to assemble certain information on Gordon and to review some key passages in the Morningstar partnership agreement. I also called the security firm that had done the forensic check on Gordon and made sure that they had copies of their report for Jerome and Diedre ready for our eight o'clock meeting.

I also tried to reach my man, Sammy Groce, but without success.

None of the eight numbers for my renegade contact worked that morning. It would be another week before I found out about Sammy's demise in the "accidental" fire. I never got to the bottom of the story, but I am sure that Gordon was somewhere near the bottom.

By the time I had finished my calls, Diedre had showered, had some coffee, and was starting to get dressed. She had a composed air about her, like an Amazon about to engage the enemy. I was glad that I was on her side. We purposely avoided talking about the night before and all of its permutations. There would be time enough for that.

"Have I mentioned that I love you today?"

"Paul! This is a hell of a time to get romantic."

"Well, if not now, when? I will be damned if I am going to let Gordon Perkins get in the way of me and you . . . no matter what."

"Sometimes I just don't believe you."

Like a splash of cold water, I was reminded of the days and months and weeks and years that we had spent together . . . before. But Diedre was always "the practical one" and I was "the romantic." This had been the source of more than a few of our differences, and was one more thing that ultimately frayed the bonds of our relationship to the breaking point.

As we stood in my kitchen that day, I was determined that this would not happen again. All I could do was shrug my shoulders and get some more green tea. We both had to get dressed to take the subway to the Morningstar offices near Columbus Circle.

This was one more thing that made New York City special to me. The subway system in New York was so efficient that millionaires and schoolchildren and homeless wanderers and investment bankers and welfare clients and teachers all rode the subway. It was the ultimate urban mixing bowl, if not melting pot. I have always been glad that it has been a part of my life.

As I finished my last cup of green tea I half listened to *The Today Show*. As the national news was being read, Diedre and I were rocked again for the second time in less than twelve hours.

CHAPTER 101

Gordon

The circle of life

Of all of the contingencies for which I had planned, being in the intensive care unit in a New Orleans hospital with tubes stuck up my nose was not in the script. I had never read a lot about what people experience in a comatose state, but there I was.

I could hear everything. I could see everything. But I could not communicate anything. It was worse than being dead. And then I had to listen to *The Today Show* broadcast the news. The ICU nurses gathered around the monitor and I could have died ten times before they had noticed. But, to be fair, it was some pretty big news in New Orleans.

> "In a shocking development in the New Orleans mayoral race, local police announced the discovery early this morning of the body of the victorious mayoral primary contender, Percy Broussard. The candidate was discovered with two of his financial supporters, Gordon Perkins and Raymond Beard of New York, both of whom are in intensive care in local hospitals in New Orleans. The three men were found in the suite of a local hotel where a victory celebration had been held a few hours earlier. All three men were found naked and the door was locked from the inside.

The cause of Mr. Broussard's death is unknown at this time, but a reliable source has told NBC News that a kilogram of cocaine and several bottles of vodka were found in the suite. Mr. Broussard appears to have died from cardiac arrest and Perkins and Beard are suffering from severe drug overdoses. This report will have to be confirmed after an autopsy is performed on Mr. Broussard and further toxicological tests that will be performed on Perkins and Beard.

NBC News has also learned that police responding to an anonymous call discovered documents which clearly implicate the Broussard campaign in a plot to forge documents and falsify testimony related to recent charges against Mayor Percy Lodrig and his father.

The Lodrig campaign is almost certainly going to demand a new primary election and it would seem, even at this early point, that Prince Lodrig will be reelected mayor of New Orleans."

It was unbelievable that I couldn't move a muscle, couldn't smile, frown or spit. All I could do is watch my absolutely foolproof plan unfold just because the Dark Lord got a special batch of cocaine for Broussard and my new best friend Ray Beard.

I will never forget the look on Broussard's face when his heart stopped. And I sure as hell will not forget those four bitches who stripped us naked and left us to die when the three of us started having seizures from the pure Colombian flake cocaine that had come from who knows where. One of these days they are going to have to have a talk with the Dark Lord and me.

But now I have these tubes up my nose. I guess I was in a coma. I had no idea where Ray Beard was and I couldn't give a shit. I just had to stay alive. I know that Paul and Jerome and Diedre were probably plotting right then and there. But as long as I was alive they would have to deal with me. And I planned to live.

CHAPTER 102

Diedre

Sunflower

"We better hurry to the office, Paul. This is getting too deep."

"You are probably right. But don't you think that we should at least give Kenitra Perkins a call?"

"A call, hell, she is probably out celebrating her liberation as we speak."

We had to laugh to keep from crying, as the song goes, and soon we were on the subway heading to the Morningstar offices. As we sped under the granite skies I tried to engage Paul in idle speculation.

"What do you think happened?"

"It's plain as the nose on your face. Gordon, Ray, and Broussard obviously got carried away with some local girlfriends. When they started to have seizures or whatever, the ladies left, and obviously one of the three locked the door thinking that they could get out of their dire straits on their own. That's why the door was locked from the inside."

"When the girls left, the three of them probably didn't even bother to get dressed, and in polishing off some vodka or rum or champagne, the three of them just passed out and Broussard passed along."

By the time we arrived at Morningstar's offices, Jerome was already there. He had heard the latest news and he shared the same cheated feeling that I had. He was really looking forward to doing battle with Gordon. After all, the battle lines were clearly drawn.

We went into a conference room. We sat in silence for a few minutes, and then Jerome spoke.

"If we are going to continue with Morningstar, Diedre and Paul, we have to be honest, now more than ever. I am not going to shed any tears for Gordon or Ray and we have to have a plan, right now."

"If we are going to have a plan, Jerome, it has to be something that people won't expect. They will expect us to run and hide and try and make up excuses. That won't work." There was something about Jerome being so focused which helped me stick to the issue of the day and save the emotions for another, more convenient time.

"The Japanese ideograph for 'disaster' also means 'opportunity.' I think that we should call Edwina and have her handle all the media contacts." Jerome clearly had some ideas and that helped immensely.

"We should also call Kenitra Perkins right now and offer to purchase her interest in RRB, which I would bet is a controlling interest. We can pay her with a note and the proceeds of the key man insurance that we'll receive after having Gordon Perkins declared incompetent to continue with Morningstar." It was clear that some kind of strategy was starting to take shape.

"One last thing. If Gordon is truly comatose, we will have to negotiate with his counsel or Kenitra to get his ass out of Morningstar. Our leverage will be that we won't sue him if he gets out now." Paul was getting into the spirit.

We talked about other details and then it was time to go. We had a plan and we could make it work and we would make Morningstar work. Paul and I left the office later that afternoon for other meetings while Jerome handled operations at the office. We stood waiting for the elevator.

"Paul, there is one last thing."

"What is that, Diedre?"

"Have I told you that I loved you today?"

CHAPTER 103

Paul

Somewhere beyond the sea

Despite the decidedly rocky start for Morningstar, it more than survived the "Battle of New Orleans" as it was later called. The plan that Jerome, Diedre, and I articulated in the aftermath turned out to work perfectly. It was a blueprint for success.

Mayor Lodrig's campaign did force a new primary election and he was re-elected in a landslide. And Morningstar was remembered in the best way possible. It became the main financial advisor and investment banker for the city of New Orleans. The death of Broussard and the demise of Perkins and Beard were not subject to official explanation.

Kenitra Perkins went along with the offer from Morningstar, and all the personnel from Jerome's firm returned to Morningstar and a new deal was negotiated with Merrill Lynch. RRB was simply no more. Just like that. Kenitra took the proceeds of her deal with Morningstar and moved to Arizona. She did not even try to pretend to take care of the entirely incapacitated Gordon Perkins.

Jerome's biotech deal and Diedre's pension fund assignment presaged even greater success. The success of those deals gave rise to a flood of business and the news of all accomplishments that was handled by Edwina McClure.

By the time New Year's Eve arrived, Jerome, Charmaine, Diedre, and I dined at my town house, for a quiet dinner after a hell of a year. That was when Diedre and I announced our intention to get married again in the New Year.

And that is why I have to end this story and go look after my son in the other room.

THE PRIDE

WALLACE FORD

ABOUT THIS GUIDE

The suggested questions are intended to enhance your group's
reading of *The Pride*. We hope you have enjoyed
reading this novel.

DISCUSSION QUESTIONS

1. What do you think was Kenitra Perkins's motivation in marrying Gordon Perkins in the first place? What was her thinking in staying with Gordon despite the abuse and the misery?

2. What kind of relationship did Monique Jefferson and Ray Beard actually have? Passionate? Strictly for appearances? A professional move by either or both of them?

3. Who would have been a better mate for Paul Taylor in the end—Samantha Gideon, Lisette Bailey or Diedre Douglas?

4. Gordon Perkins never believed that he had a problem with cocaine or the Dark Lord. Do you agree or disagree?

5. Jerome Hardaway prides himself on always being in control of himself. What would it take for him to truly lose his temper?

6. Would Diedre Douglas and Paul Taylor have ever gotten back together if Diedre had not made the first move?

7. When Gordon Perkins and Ray Beard pulled their "September Surprise" on the Morningstar Group, Diedre, Paul, and Jerome were stunned. Should they have seen this move coming?

8. Do you think that the relationship between Berta Colon and Jerome Hardaway was strictly business?

9. If Gordon Perkins survives his stay in the New Orleans hospital, what do you think he will do in the future?

10. What will Kenitra Perkins do now that she is financially independent and free of Gordon Perkins?